D1742547

Trad Japan,
Mod Nippon

Trad Japan, Mod Nippon

Copyright © 2011 Stuart Varnam-Atkin
ISBN 978-4-14-035098-0 C0082
All rights reserved.
Printed in Japan.

NHK Publishing Inc. (NHK Shuppan)
http://www.nhk-book.co.jp

No part of this book may be used or reproduced
in any manner whatsoever without written permission,
except in the case of brief quotations embodied in
critical articles and reviews.
For information: NHK Publishing (NHK Shuppan),
41-1 Udagawa-cho, Shibuya, Tokyo,
150-8081, Japan.

Japanese translation by Yoko Toyozaki
Notes by Yoko Toyozaki and Yoshika Suzuki
Editorial assistance by Yoshika Suzuki
Book design by Yuji Kimura and Nobuko Usami
Proofreading by Yoko Otsuka
Cover illustration by Kuniko Nagasaki
Photographs by Stuart Varnam-Atkin

Trad Japan, Mod Nippon

Stuart Varnam-Atkin

Preface

People sometimes ask me why on earth an Englishman like me would want to spend well over half his life in Japan. I have to admit it's a difficult question to answer; I can't easily pinpoint the reasons. I often come up with the Japanese expression *hada ni au*; somehow or other, I've always felt at home in Japan. My interest in Japanese culture gradually grew from reading old travellers' books, watching movies and viewing ukiyo-e prints at school and university. When the chance came up to live and work in Japan, it seemed only natural to give it a try. I've never regretted that decision.

Photography has been a passion since I was very young. As soon as I arrived in Japan—expecting to stay for only eighteen months—I started recording just about anything that appealed to my eyes, both as a kind of visual diary and to create images to show my family and friends. Up to then, I had been photographing with the restrictions of a fixed-lens rangefinder camera. Now I could branch out—with such a huge variety of second-hand cameras available, Japan was like paradise!

First, I acquired a wonderful half-frame Olympus Pen SLR, so good for portraits. Then I got my first Nikon, an F, which was made in 1964 and is still going strong today. Later, I tried all kinds of other makes and formats. Eager to preserve all the fantastic images of Japanese life around me, I would sometimes carry several cameras—one for black-and-white, one for colour prints, one for slides, and a Nikonos underwater camera for bad weather. Most of the negatives I have never had printed properly; rediscovering them now, I realize they have already achieved a certain historical feel—so fast do cars, buildings, lifestyles and fashions change. On the other hand, of course, there is a timeless quality about the more traditional images of performing arts, temples, shrines and kimonos. All the photos in this book were taken in the 1970s, many of them with that trusty Nikon F.

A major attraction of the country for me has always been the extraordinary mixture of the traditional and the modern. I was delighted to be asked to be a presenter on the NHK Educational TV series Trad Japan from April 2009. The programme explains many aspects of Japanese culture in English. This book is based on the mini-essays titled *Stuart's Titbits* which I have written ever since for the textbook of the series. They include many of my personal experiences over the years and are truly 'titbits'—trivial little comments on Japan as I see it. I hope you find the book interesting and entertaining.

I would like to dedicate this book to the memory of my friend and mentor Edward Putzar (1930-2009), translator, historian of Japanese photography, outstanding photographer, and true Japanophile.

Stuart Varnam-Atkin
Tokyo, November 2011

まえがき

　いったいどうして私のような英国人が、その人生の半分をはるかに超える時間を日本で暮らすことになったのか、と聞かれることがあります。答えに窮する質問です。その理由を特定するのは簡単ではありません。いつも「肌に合う」という日本語の表現で答えることにしています。どういうものか、日本にいるとくつろぐのです。私の日本文化への関心は、学生時代に、昔の旅行者たちの著書を読んだり、映画を観たり、浮世絵を鑑賞したことがきっかけで、徐々に広がっていきました。日本に暮らして仕事をするというチャンスが巡ってきた時は、そうするのがきわめて自然に思えたほどです。以来、その時の決心を後悔したことは一度もありません。

　写真には幼い頃から興味がありました。当初は1年半だけの滞在予定でしたが、日本に到着した途端、目に飛び込んできたものは、おおよそなんでも撮り始めました。それは一種の絵日記であり、同時に英国にいる家族や友人に見せる目的でもあったのです。それまでは固定レンズ式のレンジファインダー・カメラで撮っていましたが、日本ではさまざまな中古カメラが販売されていて、関心の幅を広げることができました。日本は私にとってパラダイスでした。

　まずは、ポートレート写真に非常にふさわしい、すばらしいハーフサイズのオリンパスペンSLRを買いました。次に、初めてのニコンF。1964年に製造されたものですが、頑丈そのもので今でも現役です。後に、他のあらゆる型や形式も使いました。自分を取り巻く暮らしのすてきな1コマ1コマをすべて永遠にしておきたくて、時に何台かのカメラを持ち歩くこともありました。モノクロ用の1台、カラー用の1台、スライド用の1台、そして悪天候のための水中カメラのニコノスを1台。きちんと現像していないネガが大半です。今、その写真の数々を再発見しながら、私は、車や建物やライフスタイルや

ファッションの変化の速さに、時の経過を実感しています。その一方で、舞台芸術、寺社、着物といったより伝統的な画像には時間に影響されない要素があるのは言うまでもありません。本書に収めた写真はすべて1970年代に、多くはその頼りになるニコンFで撮ったものです。

　この国の大きな魅力は、伝統的なものと新しいものが入り混じった印象的な姿にあります。私は、光栄にも、2009年からNHK教育テレビ（Eテレ）のシリーズ番組「トラッドジャパン」のコメンテーターを担当させていただいております。日本文化のさまざまな側面を英語で説明する番組です。本書は、そのシリーズのテキストに連載しているミニエッセイ、Stuart's Titbits から抜粋したものをベースにまとめたものです。テキストに収められているのは長年の個人的な経験の数々で、まさに titbits、つまり私の目で見た日本に関するちょっとしたコメントです。本書が皆さんの興味をそそり、読んで楽しい一冊になればうれしく思います。

　本書を、私の友人であり師であった、翻訳家で日本写真史の研究家、また自身がすぐれた写真家で真の親日家であった Edward Putzar（1930–2009）氏に捧げます。

　2011年11月吉日

ステュウット　ヴァーナム・アットキン

9

Contents

Cultural
Impressions

日本文化の印象

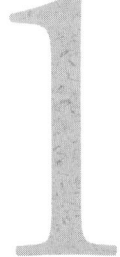

Images of Japan

One of my earliest images of Japan was a picture in my children's encyclopedia of a geisha standing under some cherry blossom with 'Fujiyama' in the background. These days, many foreigners say that those three images of Japan are long out-of-date. To me, however, it seems that they remain potent symbols which still mean a great amount to the Japanese, even though their country is now strongly associated with cars, anime and manga. After watching many TV documentaries and reading lots of old travel books about Japan, I had a variety of images in my head before I first came here in the early 1970s. But one thing I particularly remember is how I imagined Kyoto would be: atmospheric old temples and shrines, pagodas amongst the pine trees, dusty tracks leading through rows of stone lanterns, priests chanting, temples bells tolling, etc. So when I first visited the real Kyoto, in the days when there were still streetcars, I was shocked—it was such a huge modern city. Of course, Kyoto still had more than its fair share of temples, shrines, pagodas, lanterns, priests and bells, and many charming remnants of the past, but it took so long to get to them. So it was with some relief that I eventually found a place that truly matched my image of Kyoto—it was Nara!

⟨**Notes**⟩

encyclopedia：百科事典
out-of-date：時代遅れの
potent：強力な
associate with ~：〜を連想する
atmospheric：趣のある
pagoda：仏塔
amongst = among

pine tree：松の木
stone lantern：石灯籠
chant：(経などを)詠唱する
more than one's fair share of ~：ふつう以上の〜
remnant：名残
relief：安堵

＊Kyoto's streetcars lasted until 1978.　京都の路面電車は1978年まで走っていた。

日本のイメージ

私が日本に抱いた初期のイメージの1つは、子どもの百科事典に出てくる写真そのもので、「フジヤマ」を背景に桜の花の下に立つ芸者の姿だった。近頃は、その3つのイメージが過去のものとなって久しいと言う外国人が多い。今や日本といえば車やアニメ、漫画である。だが私には、「フジヤマ、芸者、桜」は日本人にとっていまだに大きな意味を持つ強力なシンボルであるような気がする。日本については数々のドキュメンタリー番組を見たり古い旅行記をたくさん読んだりしていたので、1970年代前半に初めて来日するまでに、私の頭の中にはさまざまなイメージがあった。特に記憶に残っているのは京都に対するイメージだ。趣のある古い寺や神社、松の木々の間にそびえる仏塔、灯籠の並ぶ土ぼこりのする道、経を唱える僧たち、ゆるやかに鳴る梵鐘など。だから、まだ路面電車が走っていた頃、初めて現実の京都を訪れた時の衝撃は大きかった。というのも京都は巨大な近代都市だったからだ。もちろん、京都はまだ寺や神社、五重塔、灯籠、僧、梵鐘ほか魅力的な歴史の名残をふつう以上にとどめていたが、その多くの場所にたどりつくまでにかなりの時間がかかった。

そんなわけで、やがて京都のイメージにぴたりと合う場所を見つけた時はいくぶんかホッとした。それは奈良であった！

完璧な高さ、グッドタイミング、ぴたりとはまった僧侶

Trivial memories

I was amused to note that after the APEC 2010 meeting in Yokohama, President Obama was eager to re-visit the Kamakura Daibutsu because of his most vivid memory of a childhood visit there— eating green tea ice cream! I suppose most of us remember many trivial moments like that from the past. In 2010, when Haneda once again became a genuine international airport, memories of my first arrival in Japan came flooding back. I landed there on a very hot, humid day at the end of July. My first striking impression was the hi-tech bus to the terminal: it was the first time for me to hear recorded announcements and see an electric display board on a bus! But actually getting into hi-tech Japan wasn't so easy. I had received my visa the previous year but delayed my departure for nine months, and they didn't have a record of it at the Immigration Desk. While they hunted for it, I sat on a sofa in a small side room, gazing out across the shining floor of the Immigration area as all the other passengers disappeared. I looked up at the huge clock on the wall, made by a famous Japanese company. It was out of order!

〈**Notes**〉

trivial：ささいな
vivid：鮮明な
genuine：本物の
flood：どっと押し寄せる
striking：際立った

get into ~：〜の中へ入る
hunt for ~：〜を探す
gaze：じっと見つめる
out of order：故障して

ちょっとした思い出

オバマ大統領が、2010年に横浜で開催されたAPECの会議の後、子どもの頃、鎌倉の大仏を訪れて抹茶アイスクリームを食べたことがいちばん鮮やかな思い出なので再訪を熱望している、と知って面白いなと思った。たいていの人たちが、そのような過去のちょっとした時間のことをたくさん覚えているだろう。2010年の秋に羽田空港が再び本格的な国際空港に生まれ変わった時、初めて来日した当時の思い出がどっとよみがえってきた。降り立った日は7月の終わりで非常に蒸し暑かった。まずはターミナルまでのハイテクバスが強烈な印象だった。というのも、バスの中で録音された車内放送を聞くのも電子表示板を見るのも初めてだったからだ。でも、そんなハイテク日本に正式に入国するのは簡単なことではなかった。私はその前年にビザを取得したのだが、出発が9か月間遅れて、入国管理所にその記録がなかったのである。係官が探している間、私は小さな別室のソファに座って、入国審査あたりのぴかぴかの床の向こうで他の乗客たちが消えていくのを眺めていた。壁にかかったかの有名な日本のメーカー製の大きな時計を見上げたら、故障中だった。

好奇心いっぱい、日本に到着したばかりの著者

32日って？

Is it a compliment?

Back in the 1970s, I worked in Osaka, and at that time foreigners were rather thin on the ground. I was tall, big-boned, and obviously non-Oriental, so I was somewhat conspicuous. Every day without fail, I would receive a chorus of *Gaijin!*, particularly from children, and *Okii!*, mostly from adults, some of whom would also pat my stomach as if I were a sumo wrestler. I found that slightly annoying at first, as I'm sure you can imagine. But once I realized that that kind of behaviour was good-humoured, I refused to let it upset me. Nowadays, there are foreigners everywhere as well as many tall Japanese, so I rarely hear *Gaijin!* or *Okii!* However, I do still get complimented on my skill at using chopsticks: *O-hashi jozu desu ne!* This conversation opener has always stuck me as more of a conversation stopper, akin to Japanese visitors to the UK being complimented on their ability to use teacups with handles. I say that because holding and using chopsticks has never struck me as particularly difficult once you get the hang of it, and in some ways it's easier than coordinating a knife and fork. I personally learned how to use them at Chinese restaurants in England as a student—and shiny round Chinese versions are much more difficult to handle. However, I have discovered that many Japanese suffer from rather poor chopstick handling skills. Anyway, I have a word of advice for you: if you're ever tempted to compliment a foreigner on their chopstick handling ability, try asking two questions first: 1. How long have you been in Asia?; 2. Do you often use chopsticks in your home country? If the answers are "Not long" and "No, I don't", then by all means praise them!

〈**Notes**〉

thin on the ground :
数が少ない
conspicuous : 人目をひく
without fail : 必ず
pat ~ : ～を軽くたたく
annoying : いらいらさせる
good-humoured : 愛想のよい
compliment on ~ : ～を褒める

conversation opener :
会話などの口火を切るもの
stopper : はばむもの
akin to ~ : ～と同類の
get the hang of ~ :
～のこつをつかむ
handle ~ : ～を扱う
be tempted to ~ : ～したくなる

それって褒め言葉？

1970年代、私は大阪で働いていた。当時はまだ外国人が珍しかった時代である。私は背が高くて、骨格ががっしりしており、東洋人でないことは明らかだったため、やや目立った。毎日必ず、特に子どもたちからは「ガイジン！」、そして大人からは「大きい！」という大合唱にさらされていた。中には、相撲力士であるかのように私の腹をポンポンとたたく輩もいた。これは、おわかりいただけると思うが、最初のうちはちょっと気に障った。しかしそういったことが愛想のよさからくる行為だとわかってからは、腹を立てるのをやめた。最近は、外国人はどこにでもいるし背の高い日本人もたくさんいるので、「ガイジン！」や「大きい！」という言葉はめったに聞かない。だが、箸を使う時はいまだに褒められることがある。すなわち、「お箸、上手ですね！」というやつ。私はこの会話の口火を切るものが、むしろ会話をはばむものだと常々思っている。英国を訪れた日本人旅行者が、持ち手のついたティーカップを使えることを褒められるのと同じようなものだ。そう言うのも、箸を持って使うことは、いったんこつさえつかめば特に難しいものではない、と思うからだ。ある意味、ナイフとフォークをコー

ディネートして使うよりも簡単である。私自身は、学生時代に英国の中国料理店で箸の使い方を会得したが、つるつるした丸型の中国版は日本の箸よりはるかに扱いにくい。それにしても、箸の使い方が比較的下手な日本人は多い。ともあれ、1つアドバイスを差し上げよう。いつか外国人の箸を使う能力を褒めてあげたくなった時は、最初に2つの質問をしてみてください。まず、「アジア圏にはどれぐらい住んでいますか？」。次に、「母国で箸はよく使いますか？」。答えがそれぞれ「長くない」と「いいえ」ならば、その時はぜひとも褒めてあげてください。

箸、驚くほどに便利な道具

Where's the exit?

Why did Sen no Rikyu invent the *nijiri-guchi*? Why did samurai have to enter a tea room without their swords? Why doesn't the host use the same entrance? Most foreigners come up with questions like these when they first encounter cultural phenomena such as the tea ceremony. "You see, guests have to become humble and naked," a Japanese tea aficionado once explained to me over a glass of sake. "The tea room is a place of peace and equality, and in fact nobody has ever been assassinated in one!" Well, I can understand the idea of everyone being humble and equal, but I'm not a samurai, and I have to say I have problems with those tiny entrances. First, they're almost impossible to enter elegantly and can even cause embarrassment, especially if you're large, tall, or have leg or lower back trouble. Is that really a polite way to treat guests? Second, they make the room rather claustrophobic: if the thatch caught fire, would everyone try to get through that hole head first? Or would the host kindly allow us all to exit elegantly via his or her exclusive entrance? I was reminded of that recently when I visited a basement *izakaya* in Tokyo. The food was excellent, the service was friendly, and the prices were reasonable, but I will never go back, for one simple reason: it was following the current trend of having a door only as high as my navel, just like a *nijiri-guchi*. And I'm not a limbo dancer!

⟨**Notes**⟩

phenomenon：現象
humble：謙虚な
naked：ありのままの
aficionado：愛好家
assassinate ~：～を暗殺する
tiny：ごく小さい
embarrassment：きまり悪さ

lower back：腰
claustrophobic：
閉所恐怖症を引き起こす
thatch：屋根葺き材料
exclusive：専用の
remind of ~：～を思い出させる
navel：臍

出口はどこ？

なぜ千利休はにじり口を創案したか？ なぜ侍は剣を外して茶室に入らなければならなかったか？ なぜ主人は同じ入り口を使わないのか？ 茶の湯などの文化的現象に初めて出合う外国人は、たいていがこのような質問をする。「つまりだな、誰もが謙虚で素にならなければならない。茶室っていうのは平和と平等の場であって、事実そこで暗殺されたものは誰もいないんだ」と、茶の愛好家が酒を一杯やりながら、かつて私に説明した。誰もが謙虚で平等という考え方は理解できるが、私は侍ではないし、正直なところあの小さな入り口は問題だ。まず、とりわけ、体が大きかったり、背丈があったり、あるいは足腰が不自由だったりすると、上品に入ることはほとんど不可能であり、きまり悪い思いをすることさえある。あれは本当に丁寧な客人のもてなし方なのだろうか？ 次に、いくぶんか閉所恐怖症を引き起こす部屋になっている。もし、わらに火が燃え移ったら、みんな頭から先にあの穴から出ようとするだろうか、それとも主人が親切に客人を主人専用の出口から優雅に退出させてくれるのだろうか？ そんなことを先日、地下にある居酒屋で思い出した。料理はすばらしく、スタッフも感

じがよく、料金もリーズナブルだった。が、二度と訪れることはないだろう。理由はたった1つ。まるでにじり口のように、入り口のドアが私の臍の高さしかないという最近の流行を追った店だったからだ。なにしろ私はリンボーダンスなんてできないからね！

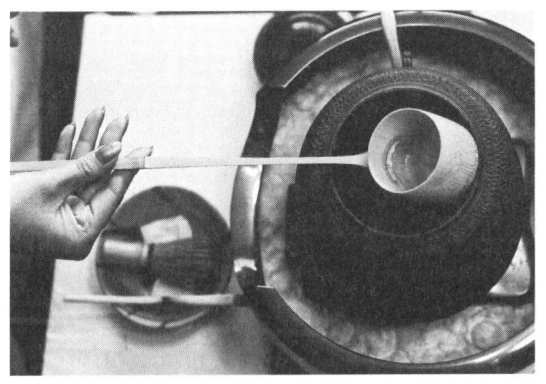

手も御点前の一部なり

The weeping cat

I've often wondered exactly what people in the good old Edo days did with their woodblock prints. Did they stick them on the wall? Did they write shopping lists or draw doodles on the back? I know some of them stuck them in albums for pleasure. And it's well known that pottery dealers used them to wrap china for export to Europe, much to the delight of the likes of the Impressionists, and Vincent van Gogh in particular. I also wonder who bought them and why. When Kabuki pin-up boy Ichikawa Danjuro VIII (1823-54) committed suicide, publishers smelled a good business chance and many *shini-e* prints were churned out. The one I have is rather surprising because the tragic subject matter is depicted in a tongue-in-cheek way. It's rather reminiscent of the 18th and early 19th century satirical 'cartoons' by British artists such as William Hogarth and

Thomas Rowlandson. The print shows a framed portrait of the actor in a pale blue kimono—to indicate he killed himself—surrounded by 29 mostly middle-aged female fans, a bald nun, an *oiran*, two children, and a baby, all weeping uncontrollably. Right at the bottom, there's also a cat with her paw to her face. The text says, "Even the female cats wept." Now who would have purchased that?

〈**Notes**〉

weep：涙を流す
woodblock print：木版画
stick ~：〜を貼り付ける
doodle：いたずら書き
china：陶磁器
the likes of ~：〜といった
the Impressionists：印象派
pin-up：
ピンナップ(壁に貼る写真)向きの
commit suicide：自殺する

churn out ~：
〜(作品など)をぞくぞくと作る
depict ~：〜を描く
tongue-in-cheek：皮肉な
reminiscent of ~：
〜を思い出させる
satirical：風刺の
bald：剃髪した
nun：尼僧
paw：(犬や猫の)足

＊ *Shini-e* were often published anonymously, but it's thought this one was painted by Utagawa Kuniyoshi (1797–1861). Danjuro was incredibly popular with female Kabuki fans. It's said that the water from a barrel he jumped into on stage was sold to fans for a great profit. Around 200 different *shini-e* were produced after his untimely death.

死絵は匿名で出版されることが多かったが、この死絵は歌川国芳(1797-1861)によって描かれたものとされている。団十郎は女性の歌舞伎ファンに大人気だった。舞台で飛び込んだ樽(たる)からあふれた水が非常に高く売れたそうだ。彼の早すぎる死の後、およそ200種類の死絵が出版された。

涙に暮れる猫

古きよき江戸時代の人々は木版画をいったいどう扱っていたのだ
ろう、と疑問に思うことが多い。壁に貼り付けただろうか？ 裏に
買い物リストをメモするとか落書きをしたのだろうか？ 楽しみで
アルバムに貼った人がいることはわかっている。また陶器取り扱
い業者がヨーロッパへの輸出時に、陶磁器を包装するのに使用
したことはよく知られている事実である。それはとりわけ印象派
の画家やヴァン・ゴッホといった人たちをいたく喜ばせることに
なった。それに、どんな人がどうして買ったのだろうとも思う。イ
ケメンの歌舞伎役者、八代目市川団十郎（1823-54）が自殺した
時、出版社は商売のにおいをかぎつけて死絵を大量に作った。
私が所有しているものは面白い。悲劇がテーマなのに、驚くほど
に皮肉っぽく描かれているのだ。ウィリアム・ホウガースやトーマ
ス・ローランドソンなどの英国のアーティストによる18世紀から
19世紀初期の風刺漫画を想起させるようである。その浮世絵は、
自殺を暗示する水色の着物を着た団十郎の黒枠の肖像を取り囲
んで、29人の主に中年の女性ファンたちが抑えきれずに泣いて
いる様子を表している。中には剃髪した尼僧や花魁、2人の子ど

もや赤ん坊もいる。いちばん下には前足で顔を隠す猫までいて、「メスの猫さえ泣いた」との一文もある。さていったいどんな人がこんな浮世絵を買ったのだろう？

浮世絵の巨匠のブラックユーモア

Japan
in the Raw

ありのままの日本

2

Red as a rockfish

The one and only time I've ever tried sea fishing was both a memorable and an embarrassing experience. Some students of mine invited me to spend a weekend with them at Shiono-misaki at the end of the Kii Peninsula. We headed out to sea early on a chartered fishing boat. My companions had all brought along their latest hi-tech rods; all I had was a long handline with lots of hooks on it. It was a fine day, and, as a typical Englishman, I took off my shirt the moment the sun came out. After several hours, my students had hauled in a few fish, but—much to their chagrin—I had pulled in far more, including some startlingly red rockfish with popping eyes. The real fishermen on board then demonstrated their expertise at catching a beautiful dorado. Following a dramatic, bloody fight with the fish after it had been hauled on to the boat, we immediately enjoyed some superb sashimi. That night we visited the local public bathhouse. The great treat for the local men was the sight of a large naked foreigner as red as the rockfish with popping eyes, unable to sit in the incredibly hot water and doing his best to hide his pain and embarrassment. Oh dear, how they laughed!

〈Notes〉

rockfish：カサゴ
one and only：ただ一つの
memorable：忘れられない
Kii Peninsula：紀伊半島
chartered：貸切りの
bring along ~：～を持ってくる
handline：手釣り糸
haul in ~：～を捕える
much to ~：ことに～

chagrin：くやしさ
startlingly：驚くべき
pop：飛び出る
expertise：専門的技術
dorado：シイラ
superb：すばらしい
public bathhouse：銭湯
treat：楽しみ

＊In a famous comic song by the playwright Noel Coward, there is the line "Mad dogs and Englishmen go out in the midday sun!"
脚本家ノエル・カワードの作った有名なコミックソングに「真昼の太陽の下で外出するのは狂犬と英国人」という一節がある。

真っ赤っか

これまでに一度だけやったことがある海釣りは、きまり悪さを伴う忘れられない思い出だ。英語を教えていた生徒たち数人に誘われて、ある週末を紀伊半島の先端にある潮岬で過ごした。私たちは早朝に貸切りの釣り船で海へ出た。仲間はみな最新式のハイテク釣り竿を持って来ていたが、私が持っていたのは釣り針がたくさんついた長い手釣り糸だけである。お天気のよい日で、典型的な英国人の私は、太陽が昇るやいなやシャツを脱いだ。数時間後、生徒たちは数匹の魚を捕まえた。が、彼らはさぞやくやしかっただろう、先生ははるかに多くを釣り上げたのである。中には、目が飛び出た驚くほどに真っ赤なカサゴもいた。その後、一緒に乗っていた本物の漁師たちが、腕前を披露して見事なシイラを捕まえた。船上での血が飛び交う魚との劇的な闘いの後、私たちは直ちにとびきりの刺身を味わった。その夜、近くの銭湯に行った。目が飛び出たカサゴのように真っ赤になった大きな裸の外国人が、途方もなく熱いお湯につかれず、日焼けの痛みをこらえ気恥ずかしさを隠そうと全力を尽くす姿は、地元の男たちにとって絶好のエンターテインメントになってしまった。いやはや、

どれほど笑われたことか！

紀伊半島沖の深海から引き上げられたカサゴ

A story of special spa service

      I sing the praises of those who go beyond
the call of duty to provide excellent service. Once
upon a time, four young foreigners spent their first
Golden Week in Japan driving around Kyushu—an
Englishman, an American man, and two American
ladies. On the ferry, they happened to see a poster
advertising Kirishima: it featured two young girls
sitting in a hot spring pool. When they reached
Kirishima, the four travellers went straight to the
Visitors' Information Office. And there was the
very same poster on the wall! "We'd like to go
somewhere like that," they explained in their very
poor Japanese. The friendly clerk nodded. "Follow
me!" he said. He led them outside and jumped into
his car. The two cars drove up on to the plateau.
After a while, the clerk stopped his car and got out.
"Follow me!" he said, heading off down a path
through the heavy mist. Where on earth was he

taking them? Suddenly he stopped and pointed down. They all stopped and looked down. There, in a steaming stream, was the very same pool they'd seen on the poster! The travellers thanked their guide profusely and he disappeared off into the mist. The bold ladies immediately stripped down to their birthday suits and jumped into the free bath. The shy gentlemen hesitated, but then followed suit. What a wonderful relaxing time they all had, communing with nature on that mysterious misty plateau! And they all loved *rotenburo* ever after.

〈**Notes**〉

praise：褒め言葉
the call of duty：
義務で要求されること
happen to see：偶然見かける
hot spring pool：露天風呂
the very same：まさしく同じ
nod：うなずく
plateau：高原
profusely：過度に
bold：大胆な

strip down：服を脱ぐ
birthday suit：裸
hesitate：ためらう
follow suit：先例にならう
commune：親しく交わる
ever after：それからずっと。
They all lived happily ever after.
（彼らは皆それからずっと幸せに暮らしましたとさ）で終わる定型文のもじり。

＊冒頭の I sing は、ホイットマンの詩集『草の葉』内の詩 *I Sing the Body Electric* （'the swimmer naked in the swimming-bath' という表現がある）を意識している。

温泉スペシャルサービス小話

私は、必要とされる以上の働きをして一流のサービスを提供する
人たちを称賛する。昔々、4人の若い外国人が日本で初めての
ゴールデンウィークに九州をドライブした。英国人男性1名、ア
メリカ人男性1名、アメリカ人女性2名である。フェリーの中で、
彼らはたまたま霧島を宣伝したポスターを見た。それは、若い女
性たちが露天風呂につかっているポスターだった。霧島に着い
た4人の旅人たちは、観光案内所に直行した。なんと壁にはまさ
しく同じポスターが貼ってあった。「あのような場所へ行きたいの
ですが」と、彼らは非常につたない日本語で説明した。親切な係
員はうなずき、「フォローミー!」と言った。そして彼らを外へ導き、
自分の車に飛び乗った。2台の車は高原まで走り、しばらくする
と、その人は車を止めて外へ出た。また「フォローミー!」と言って、
深い霧の中を、小道に沿って下って行った。いったい彼はその
旅人たちをどこへ連れて行こうとしているのか? 突然、係員が
立ち止まり下方を指さした。彼らも立ち止まり見下ろした。その
方向には、なんと、湯気を立てている細い流れの中に、ポスター
で見たまさにその露天風呂があるではないか! 旅人たちが何度

もお礼を言った後、その人は霧の中へ立ち去った。大胆な女性陣はすぐさま服を脱ぎ、生まれたままの姿で無料のお風呂に飛び込んだ。内気な男性陣はためらったものの、間もなく後に続いた。霧に包まれたその神秘的な高原で、自然と触れ合いながら、なんとすばらしいゆったりした時間を過ごしたことか！ それからずっと、4人は露天風呂が大好きだということだ。

その時、係員と温泉（霧島温泉郷）

The Case of the Missing Footwear

I'm rather fond of the garden of Ginkaku-ji in Kyoto, which is known as the Silver Pavilion in English. Especially charming is its two-metre-high cone of sand resembling Mt. Fuji. However, seeing it always brings back rather painful memories of my one and only trip up the real mountain. My friends and I started the climb in the late afternoon. I was wearing a comfortable new pair of British walking boots. All went well at first. However, we made the mistake of staying at one of the rest houses located at each 'station', where we had to pay through the nose for resting on half an old futon each and drinking a cup of green tea. When we got up a few hours later to continue the climb and see the sunrise, there was no sign of my boots in the *genkan*. In their place was a pair of very old soft rubber boots...my size. Yes, someone had stolen my boots on the sacred mountain! If you've ever been up that desolate peak, you know how hard its volcanic rocks are; it's no fun going up and coming down again in soft rubber boots. In retrospect, it's much better to go to Kyoto and quietly contemplate that miniature Mt. Fuji—without having to take your shoes off.

⟨**Notes**⟩

be fond of ~：〜が大好きである
cone：円錐形
station：合目
pay through the nose for ~：
〜のために法外な金を払う
rubber boots：ゴム長靴

sacred：聖なる
desolate：(土地などが)荒れた
volcanic rock：火山岩
in retrospect：今にして思えば
contemplate ~：〜を鑑賞する

履物紛失事件

私は、Silver Pavilion として知られる銀閣寺の庭が、かなり好き
なほうである。とりわけ、富士山に似たあの2メートルほどの高
さに砂を盛り上げた円錐形の山は、魅力的だ。だが見ていると必
ず、私の最初で最後の富士山登頂の、非常に悲痛な思い出がよみ
がえってくる。私は、快適な新しい英国製のハイキングブーツ
を履いて、友人たちと夕方に登山を開始。最初はすべて順調だっ
た。しかし、各合目に建つ休憩所に泊まったのが間違い。そこで
は、通常の半分ほどのサイズの古い布団と1杯の緑茶に法外な
代金を払わなければならなかった。登山を続けて日の出を見る
べく数時間後に起きた時、玄関に私のブーツは影も形もなく、代
わりにそこにあったのは柔らかくてひどく古いゴム長靴で、ふざけ
たことに私のサイズ。そう、聖なる山で、誰かが私のブーツを盗
んだのである！ あの荒涼たる頂上に登った経験がある方なら
きっとおわかりになるだろう。その火山岩がどれほど固いか！ 柔
らかいゴム長靴で上り下りするのは大変なことなのだ。今にして
思えば、京都へ行って、あのミニ富士山をじっと静かに鑑賞して
いたほうがずっとよかった。靴だって脱ぐ必要もないし。

静かなお寺の庭園

上るも大変、下るも大変

Can I eat it?

Being an English-speaking stranger in Japan is not easy if you can't speak or read Japanese very well. In European countries you can check unfamiliar words in your dictionary in a few seconds, but finding the meaning and pronunciation of an unknown kanji can take ten minutes. This is a potentially dangerous problem when it comes to food. For example, the first time I attempted to eat a self-heating *bento*, I misread the instructions and opened the bottom section; it contained a white substance I thought was some kind of rice. Wrong! It was the mineral responsible for the heating. The first mouthful made that very clear. Fortunately, I survived. One of my silliest experiences happened when I visited Nara with an American friend just after we had both arrived in Japan. A little old lady had a stall in the park selling various snacks; being a little peckish, we purchased some cheap brown biscuits. They had a rather rough texture and not very much flavour, but we consumed them anyway. Can you guess what happened next? Yes, when we entered the park we noticed that all the other visitors who had bought the same biscuits were feeding them to the deer. Oh, dear! Fortunately, we didn't grow antlers.

〈Notes〉

potentially：もしかすると
when it comes to ~：
〜のことになれば
attempt to ~：〜を試みる
self-heating *bento*：
自己発熱する弁当
misread ~：〜を読み間違える
substance：物質
mineral：鉱物

responsible for ~：
〜の原因である
mouthful：一口
silly：ばかばかしい
stall：売店
peckish：少し腹のすいた
feed ~：〜にえさを与える
antler：(雄鹿の)枝角

食べていいの？

英語圏の外国人の場合、日本語の読み書きがあまりできないと日本での暮らしは楽じゃない。ヨーロッパの国なら、なじみのない言葉も辞書で数秒のうちに調べられるが、知らない漢字の意味や発音を調べるとなると10分かかることもある。食べ物がらみだと、危ない目にだって遭いかねない。例えば、初めて発熱式弁当を食べようとした時、私は説明を読み違えて底の部分を開けてしまった。白いものが入っていたから、ある種のご飯だと思ったが、とんでもない！　それは発熱剤だった。最初の一口でわかった。幸い命に別状はなかったが。われながら特に間抜けだったできごとは、どちらも来日したばかりの頃、アメリカ人の友人と奈良を訪れた時のことだ。公園の売店で小柄なおばあさんがお菓子を売っていた。2人とも少し空腹だったので、安い茶色のビスケットを買った。かなりぱさぱさした食感で味もあまりなかったが、ともかく残さずに食べた。で、どうなったと思う？　そう、公園に入ってみると、他の観光客はみんなそのビスケットを鹿にやっていた。やれやれ！　角がはえてこなくて何よりだった。

疑うことを知らない外国人を待つ仕事熱心なせんべい売り

お持ち帰り用ビニール製の自分だけの鹿

片手で撞く鐘

The heads rolled!

I have to admit—with some sense of shame—that it's not advisable to leave items out on the street in Britain: even vending machines will probably be removed very quickly and taken away on a truck. However, in Japan, all kinds of things spill out on to the streets, such as shop products and plants, including bonsai. I used to have difficulty deciding what was *gomi* and what wasn't: "Has that bonsai in that nice hibachi really been thrown out or not?" However, like many other *gaijin*, I have on occasion recycled things that have definitely been discarded. That was mostly when I ran a low-budget theatre company: many of our most useful props cost us nothing, ranging from wooden stools and picture frames to a pink telephone. One night, on my way home rather drunk, I found a large plastic bag full of mannequin heads outside a hair salon. Oh, what a treasure! I picked it up and staggered along the road towards my house. But, as luck would have it, just as I arrived in front of the guard standing outside the Israeli Embassy, the bag broke, and I was caught in the headlights of an oncoming taxi. I still wonder what the guard and the taxi driver thought when they saw this large foreigner surrounded by rolling heads!

〈Notes〉

admit ~：～が事実であると認める
advisable：賢明な
spill out：あふれ出る
on occasion：時々
definitely：確実に
discard ~：～を捨てる
run ~：～を運営する
props：小道具

stagger along：千鳥足で歩く
as luck would have it：
運悪く（場合によっては「運よく」）
Israeli Embassy：
イスラエル大使館
oncoming：
（車などが）近づいてくる

頭ごろごろ！

恥ずかしながら、正直言うと、英国では通りに何かを出しておく
のはやめたほうがよい。自動販売機だって、たぶんあっという間
にその場から取り除かれ、トラックに載せて持っていかれるだろ
うから。ところが日本では、いろいろなものが通りにあふれ出てい
る。お店の商品やら植木鉢やら、中には盆栽も。以前はどれが
ゴミでどれがゴミでないのか見極めるのに苦労した。「あのすて
きな火鉢に入った盆栽は本当に捨てられたものか？　いや違う
か？」という具合に。とはいえ、他の多くのガイジン同様、私も他
の人たちが確実に捨てたものを時々リサイクルしたくちである。
特に低予算の演劇集団を主宰していた頃の話だ。木製のスツー
ルや絵画用額縁からピンクの電話機まで、最も役に立つ小道具
のほとんどはタダだったのである。ある日の夜、やや酔っ払って
帰宅中、美容院の外でマネキンの頭がたくさん入った大きなゴミ
袋を見つけた。わあ、これはすごい！　そのお宝袋を抱えて、私
は自宅への道をふらふらと歩いた。イスラエル大使館の守衛の
前にたどりついたちょうどその時、運悪く袋が裂けてしまった。し
かも接近してくるタクシーのヘッドライトに私の姿が照らし出され

てしまったのだ。あの時の守衛やタクシーの運転手は転がるマネキン頭に囲まれたこの大柄な外国人を見て何を思っただろう、と今でも思いを巡らすことがある。

大きな甕(かめ)のある静物写真

Topsy-turvydom

逆さまの世界

Topsy-turvydom

When working on TV scripts and translations, I often have long discussions on language points such as whether *go* stones are 'black and white' or 'white and black'? In English, 'black' generally comes before 'white'—as in 'black-and-white photos'—but 'white and black' seems to be more natural in Japanese. This is an example of a phenomenon that has long interested foreign visitors. In his book *Things Japanese* (first published in 1890), the great Japanologist Basil Chamberlain called it 'topsy-turvydom', meaning doing things in the opposite way to what Europeans think is natural and proper. The examples he mentioned included removing your shoes rather than your hat when you go indoors, and using a damp towel to dry your body. One language example he noted was saying 'east-north' instead of 'north-east'. I enjoy finding others: in sales, for example, Western shops put the lower number first, so prices are 'reduced 50-90%', but Japanese shops often say '90-50%'; and in motor racing, 'nose-to-tail' suggests the car behind pressuring the one in front, but for some reason it's 'tail-to-nose' in katakana, which to me suggests that the car in front is pushing backwards! However, not everything is topsy-turvy: when you want to say something is clearly right or wrong, good or bad, then it can come out just the same as in English—black and white!

⟨**Notes**⟩

topsy-turvydom：逆さまの世界
script：台本
go **stone**：碁石
phenomenon：事象
Japanologist：日本研究家
proper：適切な

damp：湿っている
instead of ~：～ではなく
sale：バーゲンセール
pressure ~：～をあおる
for some reason：どういうわけか

* In Britain, it has always been regarded as bad manners for men to keep their hat on indoors. People wash their body in the bath with a sponge or a small towel, and use only a bath towel to dry themselves. Many houses have a heated 'airing cupboard' where wet towels soon dry out.

英国では、男性が屋内で帽子を被っているのは昔から不作法であるとみなされる。浴槽で体を洗う時はスポンジや小さなタオルを使い、体を拭く時はバスタオルしか使わない。多くの家には「衣類乾燥棚」があって、濡れたタオルをすぐに乾かせるしくみになっている。

逆さまの世界

テレビの台本を作成したり翻訳したりする時、私は、碁石は「黒白」か、それとも「白黒」かなどと、言葉の使い方の点で長い議論をすることがよくある。英語では、black-and-white photos のように、黒が白より先に来るのが一般的だが、日本語ではどうやら「白黒」という順番がより自然であるらしい。これは、訪日外国人がずっと関心を持ってきた事象の一例である。1890年に初めて出版された Things Japanese という著書の中で、バジル・チェンバレンは、これを topsy-turvydom と呼んだ。それは、欧州人が自然で適切だと考えることの逆を行うことを意味している。例えば、屋内へ入る時、帽子の代わりに靴を脱ぐ、体を拭くのに水気を固く絞ったタオルを使う、などである。言葉で彼が書き留めた一例は、「北東」の代わりに「東北」を使う、だった。他にも例を探すのは楽しい。例えば、バーゲンセールの価格表示で、西洋の店は、小さな数字を先に置いて「50%～90%の値引き」とするが、日本の店は、「90%～50%」とすることが多い。また、nose-to-tail という表現は、カーレースで後ろの車が前の車に接近している様子を表すが、どういうわけか、そのカタカナ表示は

「テール・トゥ・ノーズ」である。私は、この表現だと、前の車が後ろの車を押しているような印象を受ける。だが、すべてが逆さまになるわけではない。物事の是非や善悪をはっきりと言おうとする時は、英語の語順と同じように「黒白」と言うこともある。

日本の屋根の造形美

Pushing and pulling

I have to confess that my university friends and I were fascinated by the exquisite movements displayed by the swordsmen in Kurosawa films. We used to surprise our neighbours by practising our crude katana techniques out in the street. I think it was the distinctive movements of the samurai that were a major part of the fascination, whether running, posing or striking. The rapid, fluid, low-centre-of-gravity actions were very different from those we used. Also different were the swords themselves, of course: they were handcrafted items of extraordinary strength and beauty specifically designed to 'slice', with a pull towards the swordsman. In feudal times in Europe, the heavy, clumsy swords of knights were designed to 'hack', with blows away from the swordsman; they would wound the opponent, but not necessarily produce a fatal blow. Ever since then, our saws and planes all cut with a pushing movement. When I arrived in Japan, I was intrigued to find that the equivalent Japanese blades are designed to be used with a pulling movement, just like katana. And it is always a delight to watch the skilled movements of Japanese chefs as they smoothly slice the sashimi with their razor-sharp blades—pull...pull...pull.... It would seem that pulling is in your DNA, whereas pushing is in ours!

⟨**Notes**⟩

confess ~ : 〜と白状する

exquisite : 鋭敏な

swordsman : 剣士

crude : 未熟な

strike : 打つ

fluid : 流れるような

low-centre-of-gravity : 重心の低い

feudal : 封建制の

clumsy : 扱いにくい

hack : (斧などで)たたき切る

opponent : 対戦相手

fatal : 致命的な

saw : ノコギリ

plane : カンナ

be intrigued to ~ : 〜して興味をもつ

equivalent : 同等の

razor-sharp blade : カミソリのように鋭い刃物

whereas ~ : 〜であるのに対して

押すこと引くこと

ここだけの話だが、大学時代、友人たちも私も、黒澤映画の侍た
ちが繰り広げる絶妙な動きに魅了されていた。通りで下手な刀
の技を実践しては、隣人たちを驚かせたものだ。走る、ポーズを
とる、打つ、いずれの動作にせよ、その侍の独特の動きが、夢中
になった大きな理由だったと思う。すばやくて、しなやかで、重
心が低いアクションは、われわれ西洋のものとは非常に異なるも
のだった。もちろん、刀そのものも違った。きわめて強度のある
美しい手作り品で、明らかに剣士のほうに引きながら「斬る」作り
である。封建時代のヨーロッパでは、騎士の刀は重くて扱いにく
く、剣士から遠いほうに振り払うようにして「めった打ちにする」作
りであった。つまり相手に傷は負わせるが、必ずしも致命的打撃
を与えるものではなかった。以来ずっと、西洋のノコギリやカンナ
はすべて、押す動きを伴って切る。来日して、同等の日本の刃物
が、刀の要領で、引く動きを伴いながら使用されるのを知って興
味をそそられた。それに、日本人のシェフが、カミソリのように鋭
い包丁を引いて、引いて、引いて、刺身をやすやすとスライスす
る。その巧みな動きを見るのはいつだって楽しい。どうやら引くこ

とは日本人の DNA であり、押すことは西洋人の DNA のようだ。

巨大な魚、狭いスペース、大きな包丁、素手

Isn't it strange?

I've lived in Japan for much more than half my life, and yet certain trivial aspects of life here still strike me as strange. One example is the plastic bags provided by many supermarkets. "What's strange about them?" you are probably thinking. Well, they have handles at the ends, rather than on the sides like regular bags. I find this very frustrating when I buy a large rectangular *bento*. If I try to carry the bag in the normal way, with palms facing my body, the bag sticks out and bangs against my leg. It's even worse if I'm carrying another bag as well. Searching for a reason for this design, I realized it may be connected to a distinct cultural difference: many Japanese women carry bags in the crook of their arm, with their arm facing forwards. That's a very awkward position for Westerners, but the supermarket bag fits it perfectly. I don't think I've ever seen a British woman carrying a bag like that, apart from a handbag at a cocktail party. However, one good thing which has resulted from the inconvenience of those bags is that I've started carrying my own eco-bag at all times in order to avoid them. I'm even considering advancing to that ultimate type of environment-friendly bag—the *furoshiki*!

⟨**Notes**⟩

trivial：ささいな
aspect：面
frustrating：いらだたしい
rectangular：長方形の
stick out：突き出る
bang against ~：～にぶつかる
crook：(腕などの)屈曲部
awkward：ぎこちない

apart from ~：～はさておき
result from ~：
～から結果として生ずる
inconvenience：不便
advance：進歩する
ultimate：究極の
environment-friendly：
環境にやさしい

不思議じゃないですか？

人生の優に半分以上を日本で暮らしてきたが、生活のいろいろな面で不思議だと思うささいなことはまだまだある。多くのスーパーマーケットでくれるレジ袋がその一例だ。「何が不思議？」って読者の皆さんは思っているだろう。あのビニール袋は、取っ手が通常のバッグのように横ではなくて端についている。大きめの横長の弁当を買うたびに、私はこれが非常にいらだたしくなる。手のひらが体に向く普通のやり方でこれを持とうとすると、袋が突き出て脚にあたる。袋がもう1つある場合はなおさらひどい。このデザインの理由を調べていて、それが明白な文化の違いに関連しているかもしれないと気づいた。日本人女性は、ひじを曲げて腕を前に向けた状態でバッグを持ち歩く人が多い。これは西洋人にとっては非常にやりにくいが、スーパーマーケットのレジ袋はそのやり方にちょうどよい。私は、カクテルパーティーの時のハンドバッグは別として、そのようにバッグを持ち歩いている英国人女性をこれまでに見かけたことがない。だが、その不便なビニール袋からよい結果が生まれた。つまり、そのいらだたしさを避けるために、私は常に自分のエコバッグを持ち歩くように

なったのだ。そのうち究極の環境にやさしいバッグ、風呂敷にレベルアップすることも検討中である。

バッグを持つテクニック

パラソルとプリーツスカートと
ハイソックスの参拝者

蒸し暑い夏の京都、ひんやりした床板は昼寝に最適
（東本願寺堂内）

Taxi Through the Looking-Glass

When I first saw IXAT printed on a Japanese taxi door, it took me a few moments to realize what it meant—of course it was TAXI. I wrongly assumed that someone had used a stencil the wrong way round and created 'mirror writing', in the same way that AMBULANCE is often written in the West so that drivers in front can read it correctly in their rear-view mirror. I only learned later about the odd Japanese tradition of painting company names, etc, on both sides of vehicles starting at the front. It's an example of the wonderful directional flexibility of Japan's writing systems. Now in the case of IXAT, it wasn't actually mirror writing at all, just the word written backwards. It just so happens that the letters A, I, T and X are all symmetrical—they look the same in the mirror...and come out as IXAT! Have you ever tried mirror writing? It was a skill much favoured by several offbeat geniuses, including Leonardo da Vinci and Lewis Carroll. It's difficult to write joined handwriting in reverse and from right to left, but it's easier to write and read mirror capital letters because some of them are symmetrical. Time for a quiz question: How many letters of the English alphabet look the same in reverse?

〈**Notes**〉

assume ~：〜であると想定する   **backwards**：逆方向に

stencil：ステンシル(型紙を使っ   **it just so happens**：
て刷る印刷技法)   たまたまちょうど

mirror writing：鏡文字   **offbeat**：風変わりな

the West：西洋   **symmetrical**：左右対称の

rear-view mirror：バックミラー   **in reverse**：逆に

* I am sure that Lewis Carroll (Charles Lutwidge Dodgson, 1832–98) would have loved sending text messages using a mobile phone. He often wrote letters using symbols just as we do today: for example, 'R' for 'are', 'U' for 'you', a picture of an eye for 'I' and a deer for 'dear'. Nothing is new!

ルイス・キャロル(チャールズ・ラトウィッジ・ドジソン、1832-98)は、間違いなく携帯でメールを送ることが大好きになっただろうと思う。彼は、今日私たちが使うのと全く同じように記号を使って手紙を書くことがよくあった。例えば、are を R、you を U、I を目の絵、dear を鹿で表した。何事も今に始まったことではない！

* クイズの答えは79ページに掲載しています。

鏡の国のタクシー

日本でタクシーのドアにIXATと書いてあるのを初めて見た時、それが何のことかわかるまでにしばらくかかった。もちろんそれはTAXIだった。前方を走る車の運転者がバックミラーで正しく読めるようにAMBULANCEという文字を書く時に西洋ではよくあるやり方で、誰かがステンシルを反転させて「鏡文字」を書いたとばかり思い込んでいたのだ。社名などを車の両側に前から後に向けて表記する変わった習わしが日本にあることを知ったのは後になってからのことである。これは日本語がすばらしく柔軟で書く方向を選ばないという実例だ。ちなみにIXATについては、実のところ鏡文字などではなく逆方向に書いただけのことだったのだ。A、I、T、Xなどは左右対称の文字だから、鏡では同じように見えて、たまたまちょうどIXATという結果になっただけなのである。ちなみに鏡文字を書いたことはありますか？ レオナルド・ダ・ヴィンチやルイス・キャロルといったちょっと風変わりな天才たちが好んだ技法である。手書きの続け字を逆に、しかも右から左へ書くのは難しい。しかし中には左右対称の文字があるので、鏡文字が大文字の場合は書くのも読むのも易しい。こ

こでクイズ。左右逆に書いても同じ形に見えるアルファベットは
いくつありますか？

実は右利き

Tastes from childhood

As I was growing up in Birmingham,
England, I consumed sandwiches rather than
onigiri, potatoes rather than rice, and sauces based
on malt vinegar rather than soy sauce. I still love
the same things. Thinking about it, various types
of sauce played a big part in my family's dietary life.
One of them was the famous Worcestershire sauce,
which is incidentally very different from Japanese
'Worcester sauce', even though many British people
also use the shortened term 'Worcester sauce'.
Invented in the 1830s in the ancient city of
Worcester, located on the River Severn north of
Gloucester, it goes especially well with Welsh rarebit
(cheese on toast) and is an essential ingredient of
the cocktail called Bloody Mary. There were also
the two types of thicker brown spicy sauce that
perfectly complement English breakfasts, shepherd's
pie, and other typical British dishes. One brand,

with a picture of the Houses of Parliament on the bottle, was made in Birmingham, and there was actually a pipeline running across a main road from the vinegar plant. I recently discovered two interesting things: those thick sauces, along with a familiar Japanese brand of soy sauce, are now mostly manufactured in the Netherlands, the country through which the spices they include originally flowed to England; and, in fact, *I did* grow up with soy sauce, because it's apparently one of the ingredients of Worcestershire sauce!

⟨**Notes**⟩

dietary life：食生活
incidentally：ちなみに
Worcester：
ウスター（イングランド西部の都市）
shortened term：短縮語
ingredient：食材
complement ~：
～を補って完全にする

shepherd's pie：
シェパードパイ（ひき肉をマッシュポ
テトで包んで焼いたパイ）
the Houses of Parliament：
英国の国会議事堂
manufacture ~：～を製造する
flow to ~：～へ流れる
apparently ~：どうやら～らしい

＊Welsh rarebit. The original name was 'Welsh rabbit' and it most likely has nothing to do with Wales. 'Welsh' used to mean something used as a substitute for the real thing, so 'Welsh rabbit' was probably a dish made when no meat (e.g. rabbit) was available.

Welsh rarebit のもともとの名前は Welsh rabbit だが、ウェールズとはたぶん関係ないだろう。Welsh は、かつて本物の代用として使用されるものを意味したので、Welsh rabbit は、十中八九、ウサギなどの肉を入手できなかった頃の料理だろう。

幼い頃からの味覚

私はイギリスのバーミンガムで、おにぎりではなくサンドイッチ、米ではなくジャガイモ、そして醤油ではなくモルトビネガーが基本のソースを食して育った。今でもその同じものが大好きだ。思えば、さまざまな種類のソースは家族の食生活に大きな役割を果たした。そのうちの1つが有名なウスターシャーソースであった。ちなみに、これをウスターソースと短縮して言うイギリス人も多いことは確かだが、日本のウスターソースとは似て非なるものである。グロスターの北を流れるセヴァーン川沿いの古都、ウスターの町で1830年代に発明されたこのソースは、とりわけウェールズ風トースト（チーズトースト）と相性がよく、ブラディーメアリーというカクテルには欠かせない材料である。他にも香辛料がきいた濃厚な2種類のブラウンソースがあり、どちらもイギリスの朝食や、シェパードパイ、その他の典型的なイギリス料理にぴたりと合う。ボトルに国会議事堂の絵がついた銘柄はバーミンガムで製造されていて、酢の醸造工場からの輸送管路が幹線道路を横切っていた。ところで、つい先日面白い発見が2つあった。1つは、その2種類の濃厚なソースが、よく見かけるある日本ブラ

ンドの醤油とともに、現在は主にオランダで製造されているという
こと。もともと香辛料はこの国を経由してイギリスに流れ込んだ
のである。もう1つは、厳密には私も醤油を食して育ったということ
と。というのも、醤油はどうやらウスターシャーソースの材料の1
つだったらしいのだ。

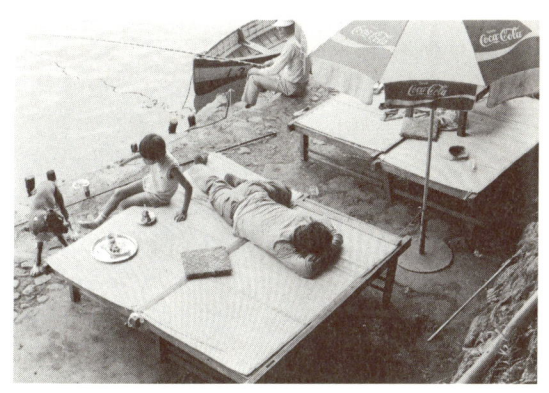

桂川のほとりでまったりと

Adventures with Language

言葉をめぐる冒険

What does it really mean?

In Chapter VI of Lewis Carroll's *Through the Looking-Glass*, Humpty Dumpty said that words only meant what he wanted them to mean. He clearly didn't believe in dictionaries. In fact, we can never be sure whether other people are thinking of the same meaning of any particular word, especially if they don't know much about the cultural background. Take the word 'wood', for example. Partly because of the Japanese title of Haruki Murakami's novel, many Japanese seem to think that The Beatles' song *Norwegian Wood* refers to a forest in Norway. Actually, 'Norwegian wood' refers to the plain wooden furniture from Scandinavia which was in vogue around the time the song was written. When it comes to the meaning of Japanese words, there's the basic problem that most foreigners can't read many kanji, so they may have no idea of the original meaning or nuance. *Maiko,* for example, is often translated literally as 'dancing girl', a term which suggests a pole dancer or stripper. And thanks to the American troops who associated with Japanese women calling themselves 'geisha girls' after the War, many people still think *geisha* is the word for a prostitute. As for *kagai*, it's rather difficult to translate into English these days. Many dictionaries still use 'red-light district' or the old-fashioned term 'pleasure quarters', which both mean 'brothel areas'. The moral of all this is: be careful about definitions of foreign words given in dictionaries!

⟨**Notes**⟩

Humpty Dumpty：ハンプティ・ダンプティ（童謡「マザーグース」に出てくる擬人化された卵）
partly：ある程度は
refer to ~：～を指す
plain：簡素な
in vogue：流行して
nuance：ニュアンス

troops：軍隊
associate with ~：～と交際する
prostitute：娼婦
red-light district：赤線地帯
pleasure quarters：花柳界
brothel：売春宿
moral：教訓

本当はどういう意味ですか？

ルイス・キャロル著『鏡の国のアリス』の第6章で、ハンプティ・ダンプティは言った。言葉というのは自分が意味したい意味を意味するだけなんだ。明らかに彼は辞書を信用していない。確かに、ある言葉の意味について他の人たちも同じことを考えているかといえば、私たちは確信がもてなくなる。その人たちが文化的な背景にあまり詳しくない場合はなおさらだ。例えば、woodという言葉。村上春樹の小説の日本語タイトルのせいもあってか、ビートルズの *Norwegian Wood* という曲はノルウェイの森のことを歌ったものと考える日本人が多いようだ。実のところ、Norwegian woodとは、曲が書かれた当時流行していたスカンジナビア産のシンプルな木製家具のことを意味している。日本語の意味はというと、そもそもたいていの外国人はあまり漢字を読めないので、その言葉の本来の意味やニュアンスがわからないかもしれない。例えば、「舞妓」は文字通り dancing girl と訳されることがしばしばだが、これはポールダンサーやストリッパーを示唆する言葉だ。また、戦後自らを geisha girls と名乗る日本人の女性たちと交流のあった米軍のおかげで、「芸者」は娼婦を意

味する言葉と考える外国人がいまだに多い。「花街」は、昨今、英訳が難しい言葉だ。依然として red-light district や古風な pleasure quarters といった表現を使う辞書が多いが、どちらも「売春街」や「遊郭」を意味する。このすべてから汲みとれるのは、辞書にある外国語の定義については、注意したほうがよいという教訓だ。

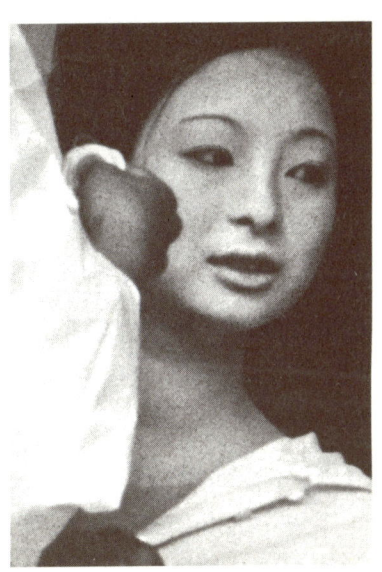

まずは白塗り化粧から……

Are you a posh traveller?

There are two types of Tokaido Shinkansen travellers who like to sit watching the scenery flashing by at the speed of a bullet rather than going to sleep or reading a book: those who choose to sit on the sunnier left side heading for Osaka, for views of Atami Castle, the ocean, etc; and those who prefer the shaded right side, for views of tea bushes, Mt. Fuji, etc. If you are the latter type, I think you have the right to call yourself 'posh'. Why do I say that? Well, although the origin of the term 'posh' is uncertain, the most attractive explanation comes from the days of the British Empire. Before planes and air-conditioning, most people travelled eastwards to India by ship, via the Mediterranean, the Suez Canal and the Red Sea. On the outward journey, the north-facing cabins on the left side of the ship, known as 'port', were shaded and much cooler than the south-facing cabins on the right side, known as 'starboard'. The opposite was true on the return journey, of course. Not surprisingly, the most favoured and expensive cabins were those that were 'Port Out, Starboard Home' (=POSH). However, if you want to be a *really* posh Shinkansen traveller today, you will have to be one of the 18 VIP passengers in the Hayabusa's Gran Class carriage!

⟨**Notes**⟩

sunny：日当たりのよい
shaded：日陰の
tea bush：茶畑
latter：後者の
British Empire：大英帝国
eastwards：東方へ
Mediterranean：地中海

Suez Canal：スエズ運河
outward journey：往路
favour ~：～を好む
Gran Class：
グランクラス(東北新幹線「はやぶ
さ」の特別車両)
carriage：車両

* The Tohoku Shinkansen Line's Hayabusa (=peregrine falcon) service, with a maximum speed of 300 kph, began on March 5, 2011. It had to be temporarily suspended following the Great East Japan Earthquake just six days later. The Gran Class service is likened to First Class on planes.

最高時速300キロの東北新幹線はやぶさは、2011年3月5日に開業した。そのわずか6日後に起きた東日本大震災のため、一時は運転を停止しなければならなかった。グランクラスのサービスは、飛行機のファーストクラスにたとえられる。

posh な旅行者?

東海道新幹線に乗って、寝てしまうか本を読むかということより
も、弾丸の速さで過ぎゆく景色を眺めたいという乗客には2つの
タイプがある。大阪に向かって左側の陽のあたる座席で熱海城
や太平洋などの景色を楽しむタイプと、右側の日陰の座席で茶
畑や富士山などの景色を好むタイプ。後者のタイプなら、皆さん
はご自分を posh と呼んでもよいと私は思う。なぜって? posh
の起源は定かでないが、大英帝国の時代が出所だというのが最
も興味をそそる説明である。飛行機やエアコンがなかった時代、
たいていのイギリス人は、東に向かって地中海、スエズ運河、そ
して紅海を経由してインドまで、船で旅をした。往きの旅では、
北に面する port という左側の船室が日陰になり、starboard とい
う南向きの右側の船室よりも涼しかった。言うまでもないが、帰
りの旅はこの逆だった。当然のことながら、最も好まれた高価な
船室は Port Out, Starboard Home、頭文字をとって POSH
だったというわけだ。けれども今は、「はやぶさ」の特別車両、グ
ランクラスに用意された18席の VIP 乗客の1人でなければ、本
当に posh な新幹線旅行者とは言えない。

正確な運行

東京から45分後の下りの0系にて撮影

Living, dying and dyeing

You may be surprised to hear that some foreigners find the term Living National Treasure—the official translation of *Ningen Kokuho*—somewhat amusing. The reason is that we tend to think about the opposite of words; the opposite of 'living' is 'dying' or 'dead', so in this case 'living' seems to be emphasizing that *Ningen Kokuho* are not dying or dead, even though many of them are very old. So how was the translation determined? In 1955, Japan introduced the term *Juyo Mukei Bunkazai Hojisha* (Bearer of Important Intangible Cultural Assets). The public soon started using the shorter *Ningen Kokuho* to distinguish them from tangible objects such as lacquer boxes or bronze statues. But how could *ningen* be translated into English? 'Human'? That wouldn't do because the opposite of that is 'non-human' or 'animal'. Instead, someone chose 'living'. In the case of a dyeing craft, such as *yuzen*, the situation is more complicated, since 'dying' and 'dyeing' have the same pronunciation. That means it can be very confusing to say, "This dyeing craftsman is a Living National Treasure" or "This form of dyeing is a dying art." All you can do to avoid misunderstandings is be careful which words you stress and say, "This form of DYEING is a dying ART." A dying CRAFTSMAN is a craftsman about to die, but a DYEING craftsman is a craftsman who dyes. Confused? I bet you're dying to move on to the next page!

〈**Notes**〉

somewhat：なんとなく
amusing：面白い
tend to ~：～しがちである
emphasize ~：～であると強調する
bearer：保持者
intangible：無形の
asset：財産
tangible：有形の

lacquer：漆塗り
bronze statue：銅像
wouldn't do (won't do)：
適切ではない
stress ~：～を強調する
be dying to ~：
～したくてたまらない

生きてる？ 死んでる？
染めている？

聞いて驚くかもしれないが、「人間国宝」の正式な翻訳である
Living National Treasure がなんとなく笑いを誘う言葉だと感
じる外国人が、中にはいる。それは私たちが、例えば、living（生
きている）の反対は dying（死にかけている、消えかけている）ま
たは dead（死んだ、滅びた）などと、単語の反対の意味を考えて
しまうからかもしれない。この場合、living という単語が、多くは
かなりの高齢者であるにもかかわらず、「人間国宝」はまだ生きて
いるということを強調しているように思われるのである。では、そ
の翻訳がどのようにして決まったのか？　日本は 1955 年から重要
無形文化財保持者という言葉を使いはじめた。世間一般ではじ
きに、より短い「人間国宝」という言葉を使って、漆塗りの箱や銅
像など有形文化財と区別するようになった。ただし、問題は「人
間」をどう英訳するか。human？　それではよくない。なぜなら、
反対語は non-human（人間でない）か animal（動物）だから。そ
こで選ばれたのが、living。友禅のような染織（dyeing）工芸の
場合は話がさらにややこしくなる。dying と dyeing は発音が同
じだからだ。すなわち、This dyeing craftsman is a Living

96

National Treasure.(この染織家は人間国宝だ)とか This form of dyeing is a dying art.(この染織法は失われつつある技だ)などと、非常にまぎらわしくなる。誤解を避けるためには、どの単語を強く言うかで区別するしかない。後者の例なら、dyeing と art を強く言うといい。a dying CRAFTSMAN と言えば死にかけている職人のことだが、a DYEING craftsman と言うと染色家のことになる。混乱したかな？ きっと、早く先のページに進みたくてたまらない(dying to)のでは？

夕暮れの静寂

FANatic

The two main meanings of the word FAN have completely different roots. The FAN you use to keep yourself cool with comes from the Latin word *vannus* (=a device for winnowing grain). But FAN as in 'football fan' is simply a short form of the word FANATIC, which is derived from the Latin word *fanaticus* (=devotee). An American friend who has long been an avid Yomiuri Giants fan has a business card saying 'Giants FANatic since 1981'. He strongly believes that a true fan supports only one team, and he can't understand the idea that a *gaijin* should support *gaijin* players on any team. He thinks nationality is irrelevant. Similarly, I am always glad to hear true sumo aficionados say that they support wrestlers they particularly like, whatever nationality they may be—just like children do. A British female TV sumo commentator once told me that in the days of the great Hawaiian wrestlers, many people assumed she would support them simply because they were foreigners like her. "Why should I do that?" she would reply. "Hawaiians are much more foreign to me than the Japanese, and in fact I'm a fan of several Japanese wrestlers."

〈Notes〉

device：装置
winnow ~：～（穀物）をあおって（もみがらなどを）除く
derive from ~：～に由来する
devotee：熱愛者

avid：熱心な
irrelevant：無関係の
aficionado：愛好家
assume ~：～であると想定する

熱中人

FANという単語の2つの主な意味には、全く異なるルーツがある。涼むために使う「扇子」のFANは、穀物を風選する装置を意味するラテン語の *vannus* に由来する。一方、「サッカーファン」のFANは単にFANATICの略だが、このFANATICは、何かに熱中している人を意味するラテン語の *fanaticus* を語源とする。アメリカ人で長く読売ジャイアンツの熱心なファンである友人は、Giants FANatic since 1981（1981年からジャイアンツ熱中人）という名刺を使っている。真のファンは1チームだけを応援するものだと強く信じる彼は、ガイジンならチームにかかわらず外国人選手を応援して当然、という発想が理解できない。国籍は関係ないと彼は考えている。同様に、ちょうど子どもがそうであるように、力士の生まれがどこであれ、自分が特に好きな力士を応援するという真の相撲愛好家の発言に、私はいつもうれしくなる。あるイギリス人女性でテレビの相撲解説者が以前に話してくれたことだが、ハワイ出身の偉大な力士たちが活躍していた頃、同じ外国人だからという理由だけで、彼女がその力士たちを応援しているものと決め込んでいた人たちが多かったらしい。「ど

うして私が？　私にとってハワイの人は日本人よりもはるかに外国人ですよ。それどころか私にはお気に入りの日本人力士が何人かいましてね」というのが、彼女の返答だったそうだ。

体の曲線、扇子の曲線

The 'M' factor

You may have noticed there's little consistency about the spelling, hyphenization and use of capital letters when Japanese names are romanized: some people write *Shimo-Kitazawa* because Kitazawa exists in its own right, while others, especially train companies, prefer *Shimo-kitazawa* or even *Shimokitazawa*. One problem is how to write the Japanese 'n' sound when followed by a 'b', 'm' or 'p'. Those claiming there's no Japanese 'm' sound without a vowel use *Gunma*, *Nihonbashi* and *Shinbashi*. On the other hand, those who say the sound is midway between 'm' and 'n' prefer *Gumma*, *Nihombashi* and *Shimbashi*, just like the English words '*summer*' and '*number*'. I've noticed that JR East is particularly fond of using 'm's and capital letters: e.g. *Shimbashi*, *Gumma-Soja*, and the rather strange *Kaihimmakuhari* and *Shim-Maebashi*. So how about *tempura*? Well, it's usually spelled like that—with an 'm'— because so are the Portuguese words that it's probably derived from, and also because there are many English examples of 'mp', such as '*camp*', '*pump*', and '*temple*'. Purists, however, claim that it's a Japanese term and should therefore be spelled *tenpura*. Well, however it's spelled in English, it's still incomparably tempting and scrumptious!

⟨Notes⟩

consistency：一貫性
hyphenization：
ハイフンで語をつなぐこと
capital letter：大文字
romanize ~：
~をローマ字表記にする
claim ~：~と主張する

vowel：母音
midway：中間に
derive from ~：~に由来する
purist：潔癖な人
incomparably：飛びぬけて
tempting：食欲をそそる
scrumptious：とてもおいしい

「M」のこと

日本語の名称のローマ字表記にあたって、綴り、ハイフン、大文字の使用などは、ほとんど一貫性がないことに皆さんもお気づきだろう。例えば、北沢という地名そのものがあるから *Shimo-Kitazawa* と書く人もいれば、とりわけ鉄道会社はそうだが、*Shimo-kitazawa* や *Shimokitazawa* とする人もいる。日本語の「n」の音が b や m や p の前に来る時にどう書くかということも問題だ。母音を伴わない m の音は日本語には存在しないという人たちは、*Nihonbashi* や *Shinbashi* を使う。一方、その音がm と n の中間だという人たちは、ちょうど英単語の *summer* や *number* のように、*Gumma* や *Nihombashi* や *Shimbashi* をよしとする。JR 東日本は特に m や大文字をお好みのようで、*Shimbashi* や *Gumma-Soja*、そしてちょっと不思議だが *Kaihimmakuhari* や *Shim-Maebashi* を使っている。「天ぷら」はどうだろうか？ 通常は m を使って書くが、たぶんポルトガル語に由来することと、*camp* や *pump* や *temple* のように mp が付く英単語の例がたくさんあるからだろう。しかし、潔癖症の人たちは「天ぷら」は日本語だから *tenpura* と書くべきだと言う。と

にかく、英語でどう書かれたとしても、「天ぷら」が最高にうまい

ことに変わりはない！

見苦しいローマ字

Eating
&
Drinking

食楽・飲楽

5

Sushi Life

I have never had any problem eating raw fish and I've been extremely fond of sushi ever since I first tried it. I also fell in love at first sight with both the appearance and the distinctive smell of sushi shops. However, like many foreigners, it took me a while to get used to certain elements of 'sushi life'. One feature is being able to watch the chefs at work; in Britain, the chefs are usually out of sight and you have no idea what they are doing or what the kitchen is like. Being able to observe them in Japan is not only interesting but also rather reassuring. However, sushi is prepared with bare hands, so you have to hope that the chefs' fingers really are clean! As for eating *nigiri-zushi*, it's not so easy, either with your hands or with chopsticks. Will I dip the rice into the soy sauce by mistake and create a horrible mess? How can I stuff this huge piece into my mouth? And there is also the danger presented by the miniature Mt. Fuji of wasabi served with sashimi. I once saw an innocent British visitor look admiringly at the beautiful little green mountain and then, before anyone could stop him, he swallowed it whole.... His face went a bright shade of *murasaki*!

⟨**Notes**⟩

raw：生の
be fond of ~：～が大好きである
at first sight：ただちに
get used to ~：～に慣れる
reassure ~：～を安心させる
bare ~：裸の～

mess：こぼしたもの
stuff ~：～を詰め込む
present ~：～を示す
innocent：無邪気な
admiringly：うっとりして
swallow ~：～を飲み込む

すしライフ

生魚を食べて体に支障を起こしたことはこれまで一度もないし、初めて食べて以来、すしは私の大のお気に入りだ。すし屋の様子も独特のにおいも一瞬にして私をとりこにした。しかし、私も多くの外国人と同様、「すしライフ」の構成要素に慣れるまでには時間がかかった。その1つは、作っているところが見られること。英国ではシェフの姿は見えないのが普通で、彼らが何をやっているのか、調理場はどんなふうなのか、客にはいっさいわからない。それが日本では職人の姿を見られるわけで、興味深いと同時にいくらか安心でもある。ただし、すしは素手で握るものだから、職人の指が清潔であるよう祈るしかない! 握りずしを食べるとなると、手でつかむにしろ、箸を使うにしろ、なかなか大変だ。うっかりすし飯のほうを醬油につけて、ばらばらにしてしまったら、どうしよう? こんなに大きな塊をどうやって口に入れろというのだ? さらに刺身に添えられた、あのミニチュアの富士山のごときワサビも危険だ。私は見たことがある。何も知らない英国人があの見事な緑の小山をほれぼれと眺め、誰かが止める間もなく、まるごと飲み込むのを……。その顔は、鮮やかな色合いのムラサキに変わったのだった!

下駄履きの打ち水（京都）

Economical eating

I hadn't been in Japan very long before I discovered the pleasures of eating *yoshoku*. The dishes looked and tasted kind of familiar, but were interestingly different. For example, spaghetti *napolitan* reminded me of a dish we used to eat in England when I was young that horrifies both the Japanese and the Italians—tinned spaghetti on toast! Of course, that was before there were many Italian restaurants in Britain and eating real spaghetti was not so common. However, *kare-raisu* proved to be rather disappointing because in those days it was so sweet and not very spicy. I lived in Kobe, and one dish I fell in love with at first bite was *okonomiyaki*, often translated as 'savoury pancake'. Even though it bears a strong resemblance to various Western dishes, everyone tells me it's not *yoshoku* at all, because it's generally eaten with chopsticks. But that's not strictly true: whenever possible, I eat it with a knife and fork—which I find much easier and more elegant. Well, it's fun to make (I prefer mine square, not round, by the way) and very easy to eat, but the six-syllable name was difficult for we 'new faces' in Japan to remember. An American friend solved that problem at once: it was a reasonably priced dish, so he dubbed it 'economy-yaki'.

〈Notes〉

interestingly：面白いことに
horrify ~：〜をぞっとさせる
tinned：缶詰の
prove to ~：〜であると判明する
love at first bite (love at first sight)：最初の一口で好きになること（一目ぼれ）

savoury：塩味の
bear ~：〜を持つ
resemblance：類似点
six-syllable：6音節の
dub ~：〜にあだ名をつける

＊ Tinned (canned) spaghetti is short pieces of spaghetti in tomato sauce usually heated in a saucepan and served on toast, like baked beans.
缶詰のスパゲッティは、短く切ったスパゲッティをトマトソースで和(あ)えたもので、通常は鍋で温め、ベークトビーンズのようにトーストに載せて食べる。

エコノミカル・イーティング

日本に来てほどなく、私は洋食を食べるのが楽しみになった。洋食は見かけも味もどことなくなじみがあるけれど、面白いことに、何かが違った。例えば、スパゲッティ・ナポリタンは、幼少の頃の英国でトーストに載せて食べていた缶詰のスパゲッティを思い出させた。と言うと、日本人やイタリア人をぞっとさせるが、言うまでもなく、その頃の英国にはイタリア料理の店は数少なく、本場のスパゲッティを食べることが一般的ではなかったのだ。しかし、カレーライスにはかなりがっかりした。非常に甘くてピリッとした辛さがなかったのだ。当時の私は神戸に住んでいて、最初の一口ではまったのが savoury pancake と英訳されることが多いお好み焼きだった。さまざまな西洋料理によく似ているにもかかわらず、お好み焼きは箸で食べるのが一般的だから決して洋食ではない、と誰もが言う。だが、厳密にはそうとも言えない。なぜなら私は、可能ならいつでもナイフとフォークを使う。そのほうがずっと食べやすいし上品に思うからだ。とにかく、作るのも楽しいし（ちなみに私は丸型ではなく四角に焼くのが好み）、食べるのも簡単。ただ、その6音節の名前を覚えるのは来日したての

新顔たちには難しかった。この問題を即座に解決したのが米国人の友人だ。値段の手頃な料理だったので、彼はこれを「エコノミ焼き」と名付けたのである。

スペルにはくれぐれもご注意を

トラッドジャパンの中の現代日本人

紙提灯、石灯籠、そして湯気

What would you like for pudding?

I have to admit I cannot resist that delicious Japanese treat called *purin*. Japanese dictionaries say the name is derived from 'custard pudding', although in Britain we know it as 'crème caramel'—as in French—or 'caramel custard'. Unfortunately, whenever I talk about various types of 'pudding', such as rice pudding or Christmas pudding, many Japanese seem to imagine some sort of exotic new version of *purin*. The word 'pudding' actually has a wide variety of meanings. It's probably derived from the Latin word for sausage (*botellus*) via Old French (*boudin*), and it's still used for savoury dishes such as black pudding (a sausage made from pig's blood, cereal, spices, etc, that is generally eaten for breakfast). The meaning later expanded to cover any dish boiled or steamed in a bag or cloth, sweet or savoury, and in many parts of Britain 'pudding' means any kind of dessert. So

where did the term 'custard pudding' come from?
Well, there's a strong possibility that it was used for
a popular dessert at a Yokohama hotel in the
1860s...by an Englishman! Anyway, please don't be
confused next time a Brit asks you, "What would
you like for pudding?"—they will certainly be
asking you what you want for dessert.

〈**Notes**〉

admit ~：～ということを認める
can't resist ~：～に勝てない
treat：おやつ
derive from ~：～に由来する
rice pudding：
ライスプディング（米を牛乳で甘く
煮込んだ英国の伝統的なデザート）

Christmas pudding：
クリスマスプディング（ドライフルー
ツ、ナッツ、香辛料などを入れた生
地を蒸して熟成させた英国の伝統
的なクリスマスケーキ）
exotic：風変わりな
savoury：塩味の
cereal：穀物
Brit：「英国人」の略

プディングは何がいいですか？

何を隠そう、私はあのおいしい日本のおやつ、プリンの誘惑に勝てない。日本の辞書には、プリンという名前はカスタードプディングに由来するとある。だが英国では、フランス語と同様にcrème caramel、あるいはcaramel custardと言う。残念なことに、私が、ライスプディングやクリスマスプディングなど、さまざまな種類のプディングの話をするといつも、多くの日本人は一風変わったプリンの新商品か何かを想像するようだ。実は、プディングという言葉にはいろいろな意味がある。おそらく、ソーセージを意味するラテン語の*botellus*が古代フランス語の*boudin*を経て、英語になったのだろう。今でも、ブラックプディングといった塩味の料理があるが、豚の血と穀物、そしてスパイスなどで作られるソーセージで、普通は朝食に食べる。プディングの意味は後に拡大して、袋や布に入れて煮たり蒸したりする料理なら、甘かろうと塩味であろうと、どんなものでも指すようになった。また英国の大部分の地域では、プディングはあらゆるデザートを意味する。では、カスタードプディングという言葉はどこで生まれたのか？ 1860年代に、横浜のあるホテルで評判だっ

たデザートを指して使われたという可能性が高い。それも、使ったのは英国人だとか。ともあれ、今度英国人に「プディングは何がいいですか？」と聞かれた時、混乱しないようにしてください。間違いなく、デザートには何が食べたいかと尋ねているのですから。

エレガントなデザート

How about a nice cuppa?

When speaking English, many Japanese have trouble with the all-important element of distinguishing clearly between strong and weak syllables. Let me introduce something which might help you improve your pronunciation. Try saying this popular advertising catchphrase introduced by the UK Dairy Council in 1958 exactly as it's written: DRINKA PINTA MILKA DAY. Now that's exactly how 'Drink a pint of milk a day' should be said. However, at the time the advertisement appeared there were many complaints that it was wrong to teach children incorrect spelling! In a similar vein, here's a colloquial way to offer a cup of tea: "How about a nice cuppa?" The term 'cuppa' (=a cup of black tea with milk) goes back around 100 years, and probably started in Australia. When tea first arrived in Britain in the mid-17th century, some people tried adding butter and salt, while others spread the brewed tea leaves on bread. But the general opinion was that tea with milk and sugar tasted the best. Writing about 'tea ceremonies' (sic) in 1890, Basil Hall Chamberlain noted that *matcha* 'resembles pea-soup in colour and consistency; foreign gourmets resident in Japan have discovered that a delicious ice-cream can be made out of it.' So there's nothing new about *matcha* ice cream! As for black tea, well, I wouldn't stop drinking cuppas and a pinta milka day for all the tea in China!

⟨**Notes**⟩

all-important：最も重要な
strong：強勢のある
weak：強勢のない
syllable：音節
catchphrase：キャッチフレーズ
UK Dairy Council：
英国酪農会議
complaint：苦情
colloquial：日常会話の

in a similar vein：
同じような傾向で
brewed tea leaves：茶殻
sic：ラテン語で「原文のまま」
pea-soup：エンドウ豆のスープ
consistency：濃度
not ~ for all the tea in China：
どんなことがあっても~しない

* The term 'milk tea' is only used in Japan. To anyone British, 'tea' automatically includes milk, so you have to ask for 'tea without milk' or 'tea with lemon' if that's what you want. 'Milk tea' suggests tea made in a saucepan with milk rather than water, like Indian chai.

「ミルクティ」という言葉は日本でしか使わない。どんなイギリス人にも、「ティ」にはミルクが入るのが当たり前。「ミルク抜きの紅茶」や「レモン入りの紅茶」を欲しい場合は、そのように頼まなければならない。「ミルクティ」はインドのチャイのように、水ではなくミルクを使い鍋で煮出した紅茶を連想させる。

おいしい紅茶はいかが?

英語を話す際、音節の強弱を明確に区別するというきわめて重要な要素に手こずる日本人が多い。ここで皆さんの発音の向上に役立つかもしれないことをご紹介しよう。英国酪農会議が1958年に普及させたこの広告用のキャッチフレーズを、書いてあるとおり声に出して言ってみるといい。DRINKA PINTA MILKA DAY. これぞまさしく Drink a pint of milk a day.(牛乳を毎日 1 パイント飲もう)の正確な発音だが、当時は、子どもに間違った綴りを教えるなんて間違ってる、という苦情が多かった! それと似たようなもので、お茶でも一杯と勧める時のくだけた言い回しが How about a nice cuppa? だ。cuppa.(一杯のミルクティのこと)の歴史はおよそ100年前、おそらくオーストラリアで始まった。17世紀半ばに紅茶が英国に伝わった当初は、バターと塩を入れてみる人もいれば、茶殻をパンに塗る人もいた。とはいえ大方の意見は、ミルクと砂糖を入れるのがいちばんおいしい、だった。1890年に tea ceremonies(原文のまま)について書いたバジル・ホール・チェンバレンは、抹茶についてこんなふうに述べている。「色といい濃さといい、エンドウ豆のスープに似て

いる。日本で暮らす美食家の外国人は、抹茶を使うと美味なる
アイスクリームができることを発見した」。というわけで、抹茶ア
イスクリームについて目新しいことは何もない。紅茶に関しては、
うーん、たとえどんなにすばらしいご褒美をあげると言われても、
私は cuppas と a pinta milka day をやめたりはしないだろう!

均質(homogenized)牛乳がホモ(homo)になる時

Oodles of noodles

The Japanese obsession with eating noodles has always interested me. When I used to travel to Europe via Anchorage, it was amusing to see many Japanese passengers rush to the overpriced noodle stall near the stuffed polar bear in the airport transit lounge because they couldn't bear to go for more than eight hours without stuffing noodles into their mouth. And then there is that overwhelming desire people seem to get to eat ramen late at night. I don't have any great passion for ramen: the idea of queuing for it for a couple of hours around midnight leaves me cold. I once lived near the Kan-7 ring road in Tokyo, where a central barrier had to be put along one stretch of the road because ramen-lovers were regularly knocked down trying to get across to a famous ramen shop! However, like many Brits, I do sometimes get a strong desire to eat a midnight snack of a bowl of cornflakes or a bacon sandwich. I suppose that suggests that the Japanese and the British are both cereal-oriented nations. The difference is that British supermarkets have many shelves dedicated to bread and breakfast cereals, whereas Japanese supermarkets have oodles of instant noodles.

〈**Notes**〉

oodles：多量
obsession：執念
overpriced：値段の高すぎる
stall：売店
stuffed：剝製にした
bear ~：~するのを我慢する
stuff ~：~を詰め込む
overwhelming：圧倒的な
queue：列に並ぶ

leave ~ cold：
~（人）に興味を与えない
Kan-7 ring road：環状7号線
stretch：区間
Brit：「英国人」の略
cereal-oriented：穀物志向の
dedicated to ~：~専用の
whereas：だが一方

麺どっさり

麺類を食べることへの日本人の執着に、私は以前からずっと関心をもってきた。欧州への旅がアンカレジ経由だった頃、空港のトランジット・エリアの北極グマの剝製の近くに麺類の立食い店があったが、値段の高すぎる麺類を出すその店にこぞって駆けつける日本人の乗客たちを見るのは、なんとも楽しかった。その人たちは、8時間以上も麺類を口にしないでいることに我慢できなかったのである。そして今、ラーメンを夜中に食べたくなる衝動に駆られる人たちもいるようだ。私は、ラーメンに対しては情熱のかけらもない。深夜に食べたくなって、そのために2時間並んで順番を待つなんて気にはとうていなれない。かつて東京の環状7号線の近くに住んだことがあるが、道路のある一部分の中央に柵が設えられた。なぜならそこは、人気のラーメン店へ行くために道路を横切ろうとするラーメン愛好者が、絶えず車にはねられる場所だったからだ。しかしながら、多くの英国人同様、私も時々、コーンフレークやベーコンサンドイッチの夜食を無性に食べたくなる時はある。ということは、日本人も英国人も穀物志向の国民であると言えるかもしれない。違いはと言うと、英国の

スーパーマーケットには、パンや朝食用のシリアルを並べた棚が
たくさんあるが、日本のスーパーマーケットにはインスタント麺が
どっさりという点だ。

麺を放り上げる瞬間

Dear Japan

親愛なる日本へ

Mt. Fuji, then and now

A Japanese friend told me recently that it's a good idea to strap *waraji* straw sandals on to your footwear when you climb Mt. Fuji; they provide a better grip and save wear on your soles. That comment brought back fond memories. Shortly after I went up to Oxford, there was a book sale in my college hall. I found a copy of *In Lotus-Land Japan* (1910), a beautiful book written by Herbert Ponting, the photographer on Sir Robert Falcon Scott's South Pole expedition (1910-12). The book contains many of his own photographs taken on a large-format camera, including some of the finest images of Mt. Fuji I've ever seen. In 1904, stuck for two days during a storm in a lodge near the summit of what he called 'Fuji-san', Ponting read *Kwaidan* by Lafcadio Hearn, which had just been published. In another of his books, Hearn described long yellowish lines of discarded *waraji* straw sandals all the way up what he called 'Fuji-no-yama'. Ponting also recommended strapping on *waraji*—two pairs for ascending, four for descending—and described the climbers as 'white ants' creeping up the black ash. When I went up Fuji myself, I was amazed to be halted several times by human traffic jams! I still treasure Ponting's book. When I first read it, I had no inkling that around ten years later I would be standing on the summit myself...without my own footwear.*

⟨**Notes**⟩

strap ~：～をひもでしばる
footwear：履物
grip：しっかりつかむこと
wear：すり切れ
sole：靴底
fond：懐かしい
go up to ~：～大学に進む（特にオックスフォード大学とケンブリッジ大学に進学する時に使う）

Sir Robert Falcon Scott's South Pole expedition：ロバート・ファルコン・スコットの南極探検
yellowish：黄色っぽい
discard ~：～を捨てる
ascend：登る
descend：降りる
creep up：よじ登る
halt ~：～を中断させる
treasure ~：～を大切にする
inkling：うすうす感づくこと

＊ The Case of the Missing Footwear （46ページ）参照

富士山の昔と今

先だって、日本人の友人が、富士山に登る時は履物にわらじを縛りつけるとよいと言った。そうすると、地面をよりしっかりととらえることができ、履物の底を損なわないからだそうだ。それで懐かしい記憶がよみがえった。オックスフォード大学に入学して間もなく、カレッジの食堂で古本のセールがあり、1910年に出版された *In Lotus-Land Japan* という美しい1冊を見つけた。1910年から1912年に行われたロバート・ファルコン・スコットの南極探検に同行した写真家、ハーバート・ポンティングの著書だ。その中には大判カメラで撮影した写真がたくさん収められているが、私が今まで見た中で最もすばらしい富士山の姿もある。1904年、嵐の中、富士山の頂上に近い山小屋に2日間閉じ込められたポンティングは、ラフカディオ・ハーンの新著である『怪談』を読んだ。ハーンは、別の著書に、捨てられたわらじの長くて黄色がかった線が富士山の頂上までいくつも続いていた、と書いている。富士山を、ポンティングは「ふじさん」、ハーンは「ふじのやま」と呼んだ。ポンティングも、上りは2足、下りは4足と言って、わらじを縛りつけることを勧めている。そして、登山者を、黒い

灰の中をよじ登る「白い蟻」と表現した。私自身が登った時は、人の渋滞で何度か足を止めなければならなかったことが驚きだった。ポンティングの本は今でも私の宝だ。初めてそれを読んだ時、まさか10年ほど後に自分がその山頂に立つとは思いもよらなかった。それも自分の履物を履かずに……。

＊履物紛失事件(48ページ)参照

「白い蟻」禿げ山の黒灰を下る

Tinkle, tinkle, little bell

It's always fun to learn some new trivia about Japanese culture, especially when it clears up some wrong impression I've had for many years. For example, I've always liked wind-bells and the idea that hearing them tinkle in the breeze makes you feel cooler. But until recently I thought that the rough bottoms of wind-bells made of glass simply indicated shoddy workmanship. And then I discovered that glass artisans create them that way in order to improve the sound. My apologies to all glass-makers! Actually, a few years ago I had an interesting experience related to wind-bells. Not long after I had moved into a new neighbourhood, my next-door neighbour came round to ask if it was me who had sent him an anonymous postcard complaining about his tinkling wind-bell. He had wrongly assumed that the new foreigner on the block might not like the sound. I assured him that

I loved wind-bells and would never do anything sneaky like sending an anonymous card but would present any complaints face-to-face instead. He accepted that and we have got on well ever since, but it does go to prove that one person's refreshment is another person's noise pollution. And he still doesn't know who wrote the postcard.

〈**Notes**〉

tinkle：チリンチリンと鳴る
trivia：雑学的知識
wind-bell：風鈴
rough：ざらざらした
indicate ~：〜を示す
shoddy：粗雑な
artisan：職人
anonymous：匿名の

assume ~：〜だと推測する
block：街区。new kid on the block（新顔）のもじり
sneaky：こそこそする
get on well：仲よくやっていく
refreshment：清涼剤
noise pollution：騒音公害

りんりん鈴

日本文化について新たな雑学的知識を習得するのはいつだって楽しい。特に、長年抱いていた間違った印象が明らかになった時は、なおさらのことである。例えば、私は風鈴好きで、そよ風に鳴るその音を聞くと気分的に涼しくなるという発想も気に入っているが、つい最近まで、ガラス製の風鈴の底のギザギザは、ただただ粗雑な作り方のせいだとばかり考えていた。ガラス職人たちが音色をよくするためにそうするのだということを知ったのはその後のことだ。ガラス職人の皆さん、すみませんでした！ 実は、数年前のことになるが、風鈴に関係のある面白い経験をした。新しい土地に引っ越して間もなく、隣の住人がやってきて、その方のお宅の風鈴のことで苦情の葉書を匿名で送ったのは私か、と聞くのだ。その隣人は、新顔の外国人は風鈴の音色が嫌いなのだろうと、誤った推測をしたのである。私は彼に対し、自分は風鈴が大好きで、匿名の葉書を送るようなこそこそしたことは絶対しないし、文句があれば代わりに面と向かって伝えると、きっぱりと言った。彼はその言葉を受け入れて、私たちはそれ以来仲よくやっている。それにしても、これは、誰かの清涼剤が他の誰かの

騒音公害になるということの証明である。ちなみに、その隣人は依然として葉書を書いた人を知らない。

携帯電話がなかった時代。街角の公衆電話

Paper recycling

Some years ago, there were predictions that in the 21st century we would enter the 'paperless society'. This certainly hasn't happened. And the endless flood of advertising flyers in Japan looks unlikely ever to cease. The number of flyers that arrive with Japanese Sunday newspapers, for example, is extraordinary, not to mention the piles of stuff that get deposited in my postbox. However, I have developed my own little style of paper recycling that never fails to please people who don't live in Japan, although it would probably seem very strange to most Japanese. Can you guess what it is? Well, I pick out the most colourful flyers, particularly those ones sent out by supermarkets that are full of pictures of Japanese food bargains, and I use them for wrapping birthday or Christmas presents. The paper is so interesting that my friends and family actually unwrap their presents carefully!

Sometimes they even keep the flyer because of its unusual Oriental interest. In fact, a supermarket flyer can be just as attractive as a piece of expensive *washi* paper, which only goes to prove again that one person's rubbish can be another person's treasure.

〈**Notes**〉

prediction：予言
flood of ~：
あふれるほど大量の〜
flyer：チラシ
cease：途絶える
not to mention：言うまでもなく

pile：(書類などの)山
deposit ~：〜を入れる
send out ~：〜を発送する
unwrap ~：〜(包みなど)を開ける
rubbish：がらくた

紙のリサイクル

数年前、21世紀はペーパーレス社会になるだろうと言われていた。今のところ全然そうはなっていない。膨大な数の広告チラシは、日本では一向にやみそうにはない。例えば、郵便受けに入ってくる山のようなチラシは言うまでもなく、日曜日の日本語の新聞とともに届くチラシの数はものすごい。だが、私は、自分なりのちょっとした紙のリサイクル方法を編み出した。これは、たいていの日本人にはたぶんとても不思議に思われるかもしれないが、日本に住んでいない人たちには必ず喜んでもらえるものだ。何かわかりますか？ いちばん派手なチラシを、特に日本のバーゲン食品の写真がたくさん載っているスーパーのチラシを選び、それを誕生日やクリスマスのプレゼントの包装に使うのである。チラシは明らかに興味を引くようで、友人や家族は丁寧にプレゼントを開ける。時には、珍しい東洋的な面白さのせいで、チラシをとっておくことさえある。実際、スーパーのチラシが、1枚の高価な和紙とまさに同じくらいの興味をそそるのである。つまりこれは、またしても、ある人のゴミが別の人の宝物になり得るということを証明する。

おとなしく電車を待つ（京都）

天神祭りの行列を待つ人たち（大阪）

Thanks for the miso!

Tea, hamburgers, *natto*, blowfish, *katsuobushi*, miso.... It's sometimes fun to stop and think about those moments back in the mists of time when certain processes or food items were invented. In some cases, we can clearly picture the decisive moment: leaves blowing from a tea tree into a Chinese emperor's bowl of hot water; Germans from Hamburg taking a fancy to the minced mutton which Tartars kept under their saddles, mixing it with beef and frying it; and the retainers of Minamoto no Yoshiie hastily wrapping their freshly boiled soybeans in straw before jumping on their horses—thinking it was 'mottainai' to leave them behind—and then, some time later, their master tasting the sticky, smelly result and crying out, *"Nanto biminaru mame kana!"* But how about blowfish? How many people died before someone discovered which bits were poisonous? Who on earth first managed to produce blocks of *katsuobushi*? And who had the idea of producing the first ever bowl of *miso shiru* from miso paste? Whoever it was, I thank them every time I sip my soup to get rid of a hangover!

〈**Notes**〉

blowfish：河豚
decisive：決定的な
take a fancy to ~：～が気に入る
minced：
(肉などを)細かく刻んだ
mutton：羊肉
Tartar：
タタール族(モンゴル系の一部族)
fry ~：～を油で調理する
retainer：家来

hastily：あわてて
sticky：ねばねばする
result：できたもの
bit：一部分
poisonous：有毒な
who on earth：いったい誰が
sip ~：～を少しずつ飲む
get rid of ~：～を乗り越える
hangover：二日酔い

みそに感謝！

紅茶、ハンバーガー、納豆、河豚、鰹節、みそ……。時には、ある工程や食べ物が発明されたはるか遠い昔の、その発見の瞬間にしばし思いを馳せてみるのも楽しいものだ。その決定的瞬間がありありと思い浮かぶこともある。例えば、中国の皇帝の白湯を入れた碗の中に、茶の木から茶葉が風に吹かれて落ちた時のこと、ハンブルクのドイツ人たちが、タタール族が鞍の下にしまった羊のひき肉を気に入り、それを牛肉と混ぜて油で焼いた時のこと、源義家の家来たちが（戦場に向かうべく）馬に飛び乗る前に、置いていくには「もったいない」とゆでたての大豆をあわただしく藁に包み、しばらく後に主君が強烈なにおいのするそのねばねばしたものを食して「なんと美味なる豆かな！」と大声を上げた時のこと。しかし「河豚」はどうだろう？ 河豚のどの部分が有毒かを誰かが発見するまでに何人の人たちが死に至っただろうか。「鰹節」の加工に初めて成功したのはいったい誰なのか？ そしてペースト状のみそからみそ汁を作ることを初めて思いついたのは誰か？ それがどんな人であれ、「みそ汁」を飲むたびに二日酔いを治してくれてありがとうと感謝する私である。

健全な憩いの広場
洋酒喫茶 ワインリバー

Flow with   ビール (Beer) ············· ¥200
the Fun   カクテル (Cocktail) ······· ¥200
the Food   フィズ (Fizz) ············· ¥200
the Fine Drinks 寿 司 (Sushi) ············· ¥300
the Friendly Feeling グリル (Grills) ····· ¥200
Kyoto's Unique
WINE RIVER
BAR & GRILL   PM6:00～AM2:00
lowest prices in town
G&G ニッカウ井スキー

古き良き昭和の憩いの広場（京都）

穏やかに万物の起源について黙想する

The Japanese in Spring

Restrained, refined and rather quiet,
Living on a simple rice-based diet,
Smiling in an inscrutable way,
Dedicated workers, not much time to play,
Simple wooden houses free of mess,
Conservative in manner, conservative in dress...
Or so they seemed before I knew
That not all stereotypes are really true.
To generalize is a dangerous way to think,
And yet it's true they love to drink
And eat and sing and dance and shout
In April when the flowers come out:
Happy corporate warriors, *hachimaki* ties,
Sausage, sushi, cold French fries,
Blue plastic sheets to mark the space,
And smiles on every drunken face.
Above their heads, the flowers blush,
Below the flowers, the humans crush...

Transience of life, for better or for worse,

A delicate thought to put in verse;

Not the beginning of the end,

Because it's spring, my friend;

Just the end of the beginning,

No time for losing but for winning!

As the petals flutter to the ground

And fade away without a sound.

⟨**Notes**⟩

restrained : 節度がある
refined : 上品な
diet : 食事
inscrutable : なぞめいた
dedicated : ひたむきな
conservative : 控えめな
generalize : 一般化する

corporate warrior : 企業戦士
blush : 恥ずかしさで顔を赤らめる
transience : はかなさ
verse : 詩
petal : 花びら
flutter : ひらひら舞う

春の日本人

節度があり　上品で　ややおとなしい

米中心の質素な食事で暮らし

なぞめいた笑みを浮かべる

ひたむきな働き蜂　遊ぶ暇はあまりない

きちんとした簡素な木造家屋

控えめな物腰　地味な服

などと思われたが　気づいてみれば

既成概念がすべて正しいわけではない

一般化は危険な発想である

とはいえ　桜が開花する４月

確かに　よく飲み

食べ　歌い　踊り　大声を上げる日本人

浮かれた企業戦士　ネクタイを鉢巻きに

ソーセージ　すし　冷たくなったフライドポテト

青いビニールシートでスペース確保

酔っぱらった顔はいずれも笑顔

頭上には　きまり悪くてほのかにピンクの桜の花

花の下には　押し合い圧し合いの花見客

善かれ悪しかれ　命のはかなさを思う

その繊細な概念は一篇の詩にふさわしい

終章の幕開けではない

なぜなら時は春　わが友よ

単なる序章の終わりなのだ

弱気にならず　前向きになる時だ

花びらがハラハラと地に舞い落ちて

ひっそり消え去る今この時は

静かに楽しむ花見

Stuart Varnam-Atkin

Stuart was born in Birmingham, UK, and graduated from Oxford University. He first came to Japan in 1972 and has been working as a writer, actor, narrator and teacher. He co-founded Birmingham Brains Trust in 1991. He is a presenter on *Trad Japan* (NHK Educational TV) and *Jissen Eigo* (Hoso Daigaku, where he is a Guest Professor), the narrator for *Begin Japanology* (NHK World) and *Japan Video Topics* (Foreign Ministry), and a guest sumo commentator (NHK). He also teaches drama at Meiji University and is the voice coach for Japanese actors in many TV dramas (including *Ryoma-den* and *Saka no ue no kumo*). His books include *Who Invented Natto?* (IBC Publishing), *Ordinary Japanese Life* (DHC) and *Asaki-yumemishi* (Kodansha Bilingual Comics).

ステュウット ヴァーナム・アットキン

英国バーミンガム出身。
オックスフォード大学卒業。1972年に来日。
執筆家、役者、ナレーター、講師として活躍。
1991年にバーミンガム・ブレーンズ・トラスト
(BBT)を設立。NHK教育テレビ(Eテレ)の
「トラッドジャパン」のコメンテーター、
客員教授を務める放送大学の番組
「実践英語」のプレゼンター、NHKワールドの
「ビギンジャパノロジー」や外務省ビデオ情報誌
「ジャパン・ビデオ・トピックス」のナレーター
などに携わるほか、大相撲英語放送では
ゲスト解説を務める。また明治大学で演劇を
教え、「龍馬伝」や「坂の上の雲」など多くの
テレビドラマの英語指導も行う。著書に
『日本の衣食住まるごと事典』(共著、
IBCパブリッシング)や『英語で伝えたい
ふつうの日本』(共著、DHC出版)、
『あさきゆめみし』(共訳、講談社
バイリンガルコミックス)など。

Acknowledgements

My sincere thanks go to Naohide Kambayashi and Yoshika Suzuki for their wholehearted editorial support, Yuji Kimura and Nobuko Usami for their fine design, Kuniko Nagasaki for her charming illustration, Shiori Saeki and Yuko Okamoto for their editorial work on the original essays, Yoko Otsuka for her proofreading, Yukako Tanaka for her DTP work, and Yoko Toyozaki for taking such great care to translate my nuances into Japanese. Finally, a big thank you to all the members of Team TJ, without whom this book would never have been born, and all those who, unwittingly, have become characters in my visual record.

Stuart Varnam-Atkin

謝辞

誠心誠意の編集作業を進めてくださった神林尚秀さんと鈴木由香さんに、素晴らしいデザインを提供してくださった木村裕治さんと宇佐美暢子さんに、チャーミングなイラストを描いてくださった長崎訓子さんに、テキスト連載時に編集を担当してくださった佐伯史織さんと岡本祐子さんに、校正をしてくださった大塚葉子さん、DTP を担当してくださった田中佑加子さんに、そして私が言わんとすることを丁寧に翻訳してくださった豊崎洋子さんに、心より感謝します。最後に、Team TJ のみなさん、ありがとうございました。みなさんの存在なくして本書の誕生はありませんでした。またはからずも写真に登場することになったすべての方々にも謝意を表したいと思います。

ステュウット ヴァーナム・アットキン

Trad Japan, Mod Nippon

2011(平成23)年11月20日　第1刷発行

著者
Stuart Varnam-Atkin
(ステュウット ヴァーナム・アットキン)
©2011 Stuart Varnam-Atkin

発行者
溝口明秀

発行所
NHK出版
〒150-8081　東京都渋谷区宇田川町 41-1
電話
03-3780-3308(編集)
0570-000-321(営業)
ホームページ
https://www.nhk-book.co.jp
携帯電話サイト
https://www.nhk-book-k.jp

振替
00110-1-49701

印刷・製本
共同印刷

乱丁・落丁本はお取り替えいたします。
定価はカバーに表示してあります。
Ⓡ＜日本複写権センター委託出版物＞
本書の無断複写(コピー)は、著作権法上の
例外を除き、著作権侵害となります。
Printed in Japan
ISBN978-4-14-035098-0 C0082

＊本書は、「NHKテレビテキスト トラッドジャパン」
(2009年度および2011年4月号〜7月号)の連載エッセイ
Stuart's Titbits から30編を選び、加筆修正の上まとめたものです。

Printed by Amazon Italia Logistica S.r.l.
Torrazza Piemonte (TO), Italy

62472875R00197

D1741153

TOOTH, INJUSTICE, AND THE BANYON WAY

When the Tooth Fairy goes MIA, his insurance agency hires Crag Banyon to find the dental delinquent. Madison Insurance Equities has never paid out a claim in its hundred year history, and it's not about to start now. Not to mention that a class action lawsuit from a world full of crying kids with bupkis under their pillows could put the venerable company out of business.

It turns out Mr. Fairy has run afoul of a mysterious "queen," whose threatening notes have sent the simply fabulous sprite with the million-dollar smile into hiding. But who is this queen, and why does it seem like someone is making good on Shakespeare's most sensible suggestion to bump off every ambulance chaser in the tri-city area?

Banyon doesn't have to drill too deep to find out the rot goes all the way to the root. And in a city already filled with decay, the authorities would be happy just to brush this one aside.

Four out of five dentists agree that in this case the biggest cavity could wind up being a lead-filled one in the middle of a certain luckless P.I.'s chest.

SWISH, SPIT, REPEAT

HABEAS A NICE CORPUS

A Crag Banyon Mystery

JAMES MULLANEY

James Mullaney Books

Cover art: Scotty Phillips

Cover design/layout: Micah Birchfield

Interior design/layout: Rich Harvey

Editor: Donna Courtois

Copyright © 2014 by James Mullaney

All rights reserved.

These stories are works of fiction. Names, characters, places, and incidents are either products of the author's imagination or used fictitiously. Any resemblance to actual events, locales, or persons, living or dead, is entirely coincidental.

No part of this publication can be reproduced or transmitted in any form or by any means, electronic or mechanical, without permission in writing from the author.

For Joan and Roger

HABEAS A NICE CORPUS

1

If the Gallup people were commissioned to take a poll on America's least favorite morning of the week, Monday would beat both Dewey and Truman hands down.

The nation as a whole would be much happier if Monday morning were shifted to later in the week; preferably after midnight on Friday when the bars have been in full swing for a few hours and everybody was too happily gassed to recognize how goddamn miserable they are. However, shuffling the deck on a scale great enough to get Monday morning the hell away from its current hated position would take an act of God or Congress, and these days neither entity was very much interested in the mundane misery of mere mortals. We — and, most tragically that day, I — were stuck with Monday morning smack-dab in its usual spot at the front of the week, shoving that smug M in all our faces, admonishing us for the previous weekend's intemperance, and already disapproving of everything we intended to do to ruin the brand-new week that lay before us.

I was reasonably certain when I awoke that particular Monday morning that I was lying in my own bed. I came to this conclusion with eyes closed, since to open them would confer reality on a morning whose existence I had

not yet decided to acknowledge.

I was pretty sure I was home sweet goddamn home, since it was unlikely that anyone who didn't have scoliosis with more twists than a bag of Snyder's pretzels would own a mattress equally shitty to my own. Were I to throw my appalling Posturepedic out by the curb, bums desperate for a good night's unconsciousness would be discerning enough even in the midst of alcohol poisoning to forego dragging it to their corrugated bedrooms under the nearest overpass to piss and pass out on it, in whichever order was determined by the coin toss between brain and bladder.

There were lumps as if someone had torn the mattress open and scattered a peck of apples inside before stitching it back up. I was currently being gouged by a familiar McIntosh pattern up and down my back. It was definitely my mattress. Which meant I was in my apartment. Which was reason enough to continue to keep my eyes closed. This Monday, however, I had an ulterior motive to feign sleep beyond a deep and abiding hatred of life. There was a horrifying possibility that I was not alone.

I had a vague memory from the previous evening — like the boozy view through a fish tank filled with cheap gin — of a lovely young dame who, after finding herself the lucky recipient of my considerable charms, had smacked me across the kisser with a right cross that would have laid out Joe Frazier.

"That, madam, is not the cascade of romantic ice water you imagine it to be," I believe I'd charmingly informed her, although my precise memory of the night, like most nights, was fuzzier than the newly reforested pate of a Hair Club for Men client. "My former wife was famous for pitching far more vicious woo than a single slap across the mush, and I managed to remain sentenced to marriage to her for ten years."

The drunken fish tank of my memory got murkier after that. I'm not sure what my next amorous advances entailed, but the denouement was me getting a drink splashed in my face and the dame foolishly storming away from the luckiest break of her life.

She had revealed herself in that one act not to be the girl of my dirty dreams. If you're going to fling a half-filled glass of booze in my face, give me a chance to open my yap so I at least have a fighting chance to be a hero and save its goddamn life.

My night had gone downhill from there. Most of it had been diligently wiped from memory with a generous application of cheap amnesia juice. I didn't think I'd made up with the dame later on. If I had, she might at that very moment be a foot away, balanced like a fakir on Granny Smith spikes, and waiting for me to wake up so she could hit me with that accusing morning-after glare that a night of ecstasy with yours truly violently engenders in the fairer sex.

I remained for the better part of an hour in a struggle of wills with what turned out to be an imaginary conquest before I finally cracked open my bleary eyes and gazed at the vacant space that had prevented me from acknowledging yet another rotten Monday morning for such a healthy chunk of it that, according to the clock on my nightstand, there was only an hour of it remaining.

I resolved to track down the dame who'd unwittingly saved me from the worst part of the week and, as a reward, give her a third, fourth, or fifth chance on paradise, depending on how many drinks she'd doused me with during last night's blackout.

When I swung my feet out of bed I hit the floor on the first attempt, a portent, I imagined, of a week perhaps slightly less shit-filled than most.

My big-mouthed optimistic brain had spoken too goddamn soon.

"*Open up in there! This is a legal notice of eviction!*"

Whoever was hollering in the hallway outside my apartment was using his fist to italicize, boldface, and underline each word. The door on which he was pounding was a tin can at the far end of a vibrating line of string. The nearer end was apparently the empty Campbell's tomato soup can that I never realized was lodged in my cerebellum.

It was true that my feet had miraculously found the floor on the first attempt, but they were damned if they knew what to do with it. My hands crushed a pair of Red Delicious mattress lumps into apple sauce before I finally managed to rock myself out of bed into what evolution considered a more or less upright position.

"*We know you're in there!*" the faceless bastard's voice hollered from the soup can inside my head.

From my bedroom it was unclear whose door the evictor was tenderizing. I'd planned to play it safe and assume it was mine. The ol' fire escape was a-calling. Besides, I didn't have time to play at home since I had a client meeting at…

I checked my watch, which disagreed with my bedside clock to the tune of one full hour. My meeting was anywhere from right now to an hour ago. In either case, I didn't have time at the moment to be thrown out on my ass.

When I stepped into the hallway outside my bedroom, I realized that a fire escape escape wouldn't be necessary that morning (or, if my Timex was right, afternoon). It was evident that the assault was taking place on a front door other than mine.

"The late Mr. Archibald Jessup, I am talking to you!" the screaming SOB out in the hallway screamed.

I determined that this wasn't some elaborate trick to evict me. It would have been far too clever for my building's superintendent, a troglodyte ex-Mobster with no thumbs, whose only exposure to smart was me, and I wasn't exactly the patient zero of brains.

Very rarely do I get to relish misery that isn't being inflicted on me, and so I stuck my head out my front door to enjoy a little schadenfreude, sans schaden.

Four men were crowded outside the apartment two doors down.

The massive shape of Harry "No Thumbs" Hooligan had dressed up for the occasion. He looked like somebody had wrapped a necktie around a John Deere tractor, assuming John Deere tractors are able to scowl and grimace and otherwise look like the "before" image in a laxative commercial. I'm from the city. For all I knew about farms, this was exactly what tractors did when they weren't plowing fields and planting the corn and barley that would eventually grow up and leave the bucolic fields of home to visit the faraway big city and my exotic liver therein.

Standing next to No Thumbs was a guy two feet shorter than the hulking superintendent, and whose necktie fit considerably less tractorly. His suit was impeccably tailored but decades out of date, since the cheap bastard refused to upgrade. This second SOB was my landlord, the employer of No Thumbs Hooligan, and the building super had elected to show his deep respect for his asshole boss by donning a suit jacket that looked like somebody had sewn a pair of sleeves onto a sofa slipcover.

I didn't know bastard number three, but I recognized his outfit. He wore pitch black coveralls with a zipper in the front that ran from his crotch all the way up to the Roman collar at his Adam's apple. When he shifted, I could clearly read the legend "Father O'Flynn's Exorcism

Van" painted between the shoulder blades of his coveralls. The blue collar priest wore a bored expression in his five o'clock shadow and carried a spray nozzle attached to a canister marked "Extra Strength Holy Water."

I didn't know to whom the final bastard in the quartet belonged.

His face was bright red, with a map of downtown Pittsburgh written in busted capillaries on his ruddy cheeks and bulbous nose. His suit was new, but inexorable weight gain was already straining freshly tailored seams. He clutched some papers in one hand, and was using his free hand to announce himself to whoever was hiding out inside.

I could smell both booze and smug from two apartments away, the latter coming off in waves so powerful I could have surfed them from here to Oahu and back. There was only one creature that drunk and arrogant so early in the week and morning.

"We know you're in there!" the goddamn lawyer self-righteously howled.

The attorney continued to pound an angry fist against the warped door, which caused me to wonder briefly if there was such a thing as a happy fist. I supposed that my ex-wife's fists had been deliriously so innumerable times during our twelve round marriage, which had ended in a bloody K.O. of both my will to live and future earnings.

"Banyon!" someone snarled in my direction.

I glanced up, then — since the talking head was a good foot higher than human heads ought to be — up some more to find the plug-ugly mug of No Thumbs Hooligan glaring at me from down the hallway.

"Whadda you want?" the building super growled.

"Bullets and an air-tight alibi," I replied.

I was robbed of his confused spluttering reply when

a fifth face abruptly appeared amongst the crowd of four that was standing in front of the neighboring apartment.

A glowing, luminescent blue head had poked straight through the door, presumably attracted by the sudden lack of pounding that had resulted when the attention of the quartet had briefly shifted in my direction.

I very vaguely recognized the features, although it wasn't so easy to spot an identifying scar or mole when you can look straight through somebody's head.

I'd passed him in the hallway and rode down in the elevator with him dozens of times over the years. Early on in our lack of a relationship, he had twice attempted to engage me in seasonally appropriate conversations about humidity and snow, and the stridently adversarial position he had staked out vis-à-vis both. I had informed him the first time that there were tax-supported park benches from which he could hurl unsolicited blather at passersby or bread at pigeons if there was a lull in traffic. The second time, I told him that his elevator observations about weather would find a more receptive audience up his goddamn ass, and I further assured him that I did not control the focus of his apparent fixation, the proof being the lack of a bolt of lightning to his goddamn dentures.

These brief conversations were back when he was alive, a condition from which he was apparently no longer deriving pleasure. My chatty, weather-obsessed neighbor whose name I'd never given a shit enough to learn when he was alive had become, at some point, the late Mr. Archibald Jessup.

The ghost offered me a translucent scowl.

"The TV's calling for light drizzle this *eeeeeevening*," the spirit moaned. "Not that you care, Banyon, you *aaaaasshole*."

All four sets of eyes immediately snapped back to the

door and the head that was jutting out of its center like a prize deer trophy.

The exterminator priest from Father O'Flynn's Exorcism Van wasn't quick enough with his holy water spray. The glowing blue head of dead Archibald Jessup quickly vanished back through the veneer of cracked and chipping paint. All the priest managed to do was soak a circle on the outside of the door where the noggin had been.

The lawyer resumed pounding on the door. "You can't stay here!" he yelled.

"It's rent controlled. *Reeeeeeent* controlled," came Jessup's ghostly reply.

The blubbery lawyer flashed a "now I've got him" look to his companions. He attempted to hitch up his belt with pudgy hands in that supercilious way assholes enjoy, but his distended belly was pending litigation against Twinkies for not being celery.

"You obviously don't understand the law," he smarmed. "Mr. Archibald Jessup ceased to be a resident of this building the moment his dentures were struck by lightning when he was sitting in the park feeding pigeons three weeks ago. As the ghost of the deceased Mr. Archibald Jessup, you are legally considered an entity separate from the aforementioned living Mr. Archibald Jessup, the term 'living' having been defined by the Supreme Court in The Haunted Outhouse versus the Ghost of Robert Byrd."

God, how I hate lawyers. The legal bastard's condescension oozed from every pore, along with a considerable quantity of greasy sweat.

I left him to party-of-the-first-part a door into legal submission while his three eager companions looked on, and I ducked back into my own shithole apartment.

As I got ready for a brand-new week on a miserable Monday morning (or possibly afternoon), I wondered if

I might actually control the weather after all, since old man Jessup had apparently met an ugly end identical to the one I'd wished on him on one of our shared elevator rides. I concluded that it was a shit gift even if I could control it, since I'd told the old buzzard he should get zapped in the mouth at least five years ago. I can get a box of lightning delivered from Amazon via the USPS faster than that.

When I exited my apartment twenty minutes later, I was looking quite the dapper rogue in my trench coat and fedora.

I noted that a couple of new arrivals had joined the crowd at the late Mr. Archibald Jessup's door.

A pair of paramedics in white were working on the sprawled fat form of the greasy lawyer, who was lying flat on his back on my ghost neighbor's welcome mat. The attorney's belly quivered as the pair of EMTs pounded on his chest in a manner not dissimilar from that which the legal eagle had earlier been employing against Jessup's door. The lawyer's eyes were wide open and glassy, and his pasty tongue was protruding from between a pair of lips too pale to ever again pour three times the legal limit of Seagram's between them.

There was a silver hip flask lying on the floor near the lawyer's hand, spilling its golden contents onto the threadbare carpet. I absently frisked my own coat, with a futile longing that the lightness it had been experiencing in certain key areas had been magically addressed during the night. With no surprise but with deep regret, my searching hands turned up nothing but empty trench coat.

My SOB landlord was standing on the far side of the paramedics, along with the priest from the exorcism van. No Thumbs Hooligan had been separated from the others, and was standing just outside my door. The building super

was chewing on an index fingernail as he anxiously observed the fruitless labors of the EMTs.

When he heard my door shut behind him, No Thumbs jumped, startled.

"He's dead," No Thumbs informed me. He nodded in wide-eyed shock at the lawyer's unresponsive body — Deceased, Esq. — on the floor. "He was in the middle of hollerin' at dat ghost in there, and he just up and keeled over."

I nodded vigorous approval. "One down, all the rest of them to go."

I checked to see if my door was locked. It wasn't. Good. Maybe somebody would wander in and burn the dump to the ground while I was at work.

This was turning out to be the best Monday morning (or afternoon) in recent memory. Cheered by the bloated corpse of a lawyer, I headed for an elevator on which the city's population of old bastards who accost you for opinions on meteorological phenomenon you don't give two shits about had been gloriously reduced by one.

2

It was nearly two in the afternoon when I reached my office twenty minutes later. (I need to throw out all my clocks and invest in a goddamn sundial.)

My temporary ebullient mood engendered by the unrevivable attorney in my apartment building hallway had evaporated by the time I pushed open the door to Banyon Investigations, Inc., the firm to which I'd given half my name and little of my enthusiasm.

I can't say that I have a complete lack of interest in either the success or failure of my business. I am, in fact, keenly interested in the latter, and had at one point purchased streamers, balloons, and a celebratory bottle of cheap champagne for my last day in business. I'd even bought a festive "Congratulations, Failure!" hat from a party supply store, which itself had gone out of business ages ago due to the inability of its clinically depressed owner to grasp what or why the hell normal people celebrate.

My complete lack of interest in the success of Banyon Investigations was overcompensated for by the unbridled enthusiasm of the deliriously happy figure that greeted me upon my arrival in said rat-hole.

"Good afternoon, Mr. Crag!" cried Mannix, a former

North Pole elf who had ditched a long and boring life of hammering wheels on wooden wagons to take up residence as my office assistant. "Miss Doris called to say she wouldn't be in today. The outlet mall is having its annual sale on wedding dresses."

Miss Doris was my secretary, Doris Staurburton. At least I thought she was. The dame managed to find her way in to work so infrequently that she might have quit months ago, and Mannix might have been talking about an entirely different Miss Doris who had been hired to replace her namesake but who was equally shit at showing up at the office.

I glanced at Doris' empty desk. The cobwebs and six inches of dust that should have been engulfing it weren't, thanks entirely to Mannix's fastidiousness. What was there was a computer monitor, every square inch of which was loaded with goddamn cat stickers. If my Doris had quit, she'd have peeled every one of them off and restuck them to an inappropriate surface at her new place of employment. If she'd been hired to secretary at the Vatican, the Pope wouldn't be able to do his job since the altar at St. Peter's Basilica would be clogged with stickers of mangy felines batting balls of yarn.

"Is Doris finally buying a wedding dress to get married?" I asked.

Mannix pulled a sincere sympathetic frown. "Sincere" was all he was capable of, even when it came to his tragically comical coworker.

"No, Mr. Crag," the elf said, shaking his head sadly.

I didn't think so. There had already been a dead lawyer on my doorstep that morning. I doubted I'd get so lucky twice in the same day.

Doris and I had dated on occasion. She had put a stake through any girlish hope she might have had of a blissful

future with me when she dragged me dress shopping to an outlet mall. I'd only gone along because I didn't know what exactly she was shopping for. Also, due to the presence there of the state's biggest discount liquor store, since my liver is a shrewd shopper always in search of a bargain.

When I found out that Doris' destination was Miss Havisham's Irregular Bridal Gear (slogan: *Cheap Rags, for Cheap Slags*) I hastily loaded enough bargain hooch in my car to flatten the rear tires and burned clanking rubber the hell out of there.

Once she'd taken the three buses back home, screamed at me for a week, and quit her job a few dozen times, I found out that I was not necessarily the reason Doris had made her pilgrimage to the bargain dress store, a fact I might have learned earlier had I not chivalrously abandoned her ass in a runaway groom-shaped cloud of dust a hundred miles away from home.

Apparently, her trip to Havisham's was a regular event. It was a sad spinster Hajj for Doris. She'd been going there annually ever since the first time she'd turned twenty-five, as well as each subsequent time she'd set the odometer back to the increasingly ludicrous quarter century mark. Each visit, she'd bought a new dress in the latest style and in her latest size so that she'd be ready to leap into matrimonial costume when her knight in shining armor finally came along to sweep her off her hooves.

In a hilariously counterproductive attempt to land her daughter a husband, Doris' battleaxe mother had attempted to get her on the NBC news division's summer series on pathetic old maids, "Groomless and Gormless: Women Unattached from Reality." But apparently dressing a dozen mannequins in rotting wedding gowns on the front porch every Valentine's Day alongside a heart-shaped "SUITERS INQUIRE WITHIN" sign wasn't batshit crazy enough for

the producers of *Dateline*.

The office was always pleasantly noise free when Doris wasn't around. The steel marble inside the hairspray can she was constantly rattling was a lead maraca to the side of the head, and there were complaints from NASA that the continuous suction from the never-ending removal of lipstick caps was altering the orbit of satellites.

I tugged off my coat, feeling its unaccustomed lightness, and asked my assistant the same question I'd asked every day for the past week.

"Any word on my flasks?"

Mannix had, unbeknownst to me, stripped my coat of every hip flask I had secreted in the garment and had sent them out to be polished and relined. Apparently overuse wreaks more havoc on the things than the manufacturers would lead one to believe, and the corrosive internal damage to the metal was a stark contrast to the total lack of harm caused by the contents when dumped down a biological organism.

There was a tear in the lining of one of my coat pockets which acted as a walking safe, and down which I stuffed my most valuable items. Mannix, in his infinite efficiency, had even managed to ferret out the doomsday emergency flask I'd squirreled away in my coat's hidden depths. I could have bought another dozen of the things, but the elf had very wisely placed me on an allowance, and with a tavern on every corner my limited cash was better spent elsewhere. There was no sense purchasing replacement flasks if I then had no funds remaining to load them up.

When Mannix's little face scrunched up into a frown, I knew I was shit out of luck.

"They're not ready yet, Mr. Crag," my assistant informed me. "I spoke to Mr. Buck at Buck's Flasks 'n' Casks this morning, and he said they're having a problem

with the threading on the lids. It's very worn. Some of the caps might have to be replaced. He said you're very lucky that they weren't spilling all over your clothes."

"I suppose the last thing I need is winos sucking on my coat while I'm waiting for the bus," I conceded, as I hung my coat and hat on the corner rack. "And speaking of things I don't need, I hope, Mannix, that my predictable tardiness means that you directed my morning clients to a competing investigative agency that will give a shit about whatever the hell they wanted."

"Oh, Mr. Robert called this morning and asked me to reschedule the meeting for this afternoon. He said he thought it would be a better time to catch you, especially on a Monday." The elf glanced at the clock on the wall which, since it was under Mannix's supervision and not mine, kept more accurate time than Switzerland. "They'll be here any minute," he added helpfully.

I forgot that the client I was dealing with was a goddamn chess grandmaster.

I had my hat on backwards and only one arm desperately half-dressed in a flapping trench coat sleeve that wouldn't unknot over my hand when the office door suddenly sprang open. The victorious moon face and well-fed torso of Robert Sherman Planck glided into the antechamber of Banyon Investigations like a triumphant aircraft carrier returned from a five-martini lunch on the Navy's dime.

"Ah, Banyon," Planck announced when he spotted me sexually assaulting my trench coat sleeve in the corner of the room. "So glad I caught you in."

I gave up the fight with my coat.

"Check and goddamn mate, Planck, you bastard," I conceded with a grunt.

I took off the half of my traitorous trench coat that I'd

managed to don and grudgingly replaced it, along with my fedora, to the coat rack.

Planck was most definitely a bastard of the highest order, and because of this overriding personality trait he was infinitely qualified to work in the insurance field

Robert Sherman Planck was a vice president for Madison Insurance Equities, a tax-dodging limited liability Delaware corporation which, like every other insurance company, specialized in cashing premium checks from customers for their entire lives, then hanging out a "do not disturb" sign on every policy that gets cancelled the minute some poor sucker gets hits by a train and tries to make a claim.

Planck threw occasional work my way, mostly to uncover scammers who'd successfully navigated his Byzantine claims department and were on the terrifying precipice of successfully receiving a settlement. Madison Insurance Equities had been a major, NYSE-traded company for over a hundred years, during which time they had managed to not pay out a single penny for a single claim, and they weren't about to change course and experiment in honorable business practices now.

The insurance VP SOB held my door open wide and presumptuously ushered three more unwelcome guests into my offices.

One haughty dame, one whipped bastard, one kid. For all parties involved, it was hate at first sight.

"Are you *sure* this is necessary, Mr. Planck?" the dame asked as soon as she'd cast her disdainful peepers around my tidy, squalid digs.

"This is the man I was telling you about, Mrs. Thompson," Planck replied. "He's the best P.I. in the business."

"If that's true," I offered, "it speaks less of my skills and more to the utter stupidity and all-around uselessness

of my fellow private investigators. I'm not being humble, they really are that shit at their jobs."

The woman gasped. I was pretty sure it was due to my use of the perfectly accurate application of the word shit in describing the shit skills demonstrated by my fellow P.I.'s who were, to a man or dame, shit. I tried a lexical experiment.

"Shit," I said.

Her hands were already clapped over her kid's ears, so all she could do to block a repeat entry by the offending word was press them in harder. For a moment I thought that the vise-like pressure would shoot junior's brain out the top of his cannon head, and I worried about liability if it blasted through to the actuary's office upstairs, since my insurance company only paid out claims in the form of top hats, monocles, and wheelbarrows full of cash for the crooked executives of said criminal insurance company.

"*Mr. Planck*," she haughtily Margaret Dumont-ed at the insurance bastard.

Planck assured her, in sotto voce loud enough for me and half the building to hear, that while I was arguably the worst human being on the planet, every other P.I. was even worse.

God, I hate clients. I resigned myself to the fact that there would be no avoiding the reality of a day's work — or at least a few minutes — this Monday afternoon.

Mannix was already fussing around the office, delightedly preparing a contract. The brat would be safe in the boring company of my terrific assistant while I dealt with his horrible parents.

"Step into my office," I said. "You can leave the kid out here with Mannix."

The dame sniffed offense so hard I thought she'd suck up half the overdue bills in the room.

"He doesn't even know what this is about," she snapped at Planck.

"We're fine. It's all fine, Mrs. Thompson," the insurance fraud informed her. To me, he said, "Little Timmy here is the reason we're here today."

He attempted to jovially pat the kid on the head, but the horrified mother latched onto his wrist before hand brushed hairdo.

I looked at little Timmy. He was wearing pressed short pants, a suit jacket and tie, and a pair of gleaming Buster Browns. The blond-haired kid had a cowlick that looked like it had been lifted off the label of a bottle of Ocean Spray.

I guessed the smarmy punk was about six years old, and if he didn't get the shit royally kicked out of him every day after school I was going to send a stern letter to the principal to let her know that her bullies were dodging their responsibilities.

I herded the lot of them into my inner sanctum, resisting the urge to attempt to usher them straight out through to the fire escape and locking the window and drawing the blinds behind them, since I didn't think anybody but milquetoast Pater Thompson would fall for it.

Mother and son took the wooden seats before my desk. The kid's old man and Planck stood behind them.

I slid into my chair behind my desk which, thanks to Mannix, was tidier than I'd left it Friday afternoon. The crumpled racing forms and empty bottles were presumably vacationing at the local landfill, and the time sensitive half-eaten pastrami on rye in my outbox had doubtless been mailed to the deli for re-mustarding. Mannix had set a coffee mug next to my desk blotter and had stocked it with pencils and pens, all of which I would no doubt lose by the end of the business day. In fact, there already seemed to be fewer than when I rounded

my desk a half-second before.

"We haven't had a formal introduction, have we?" Planck said once we were all settled in. "Banyon, this is Wilda and Reg Thompson. And, of course, this is their son, little Timmy."

Old man Thompson attempted to lean between his wife and offspring with an extended hand. The wife slapped it away, and the poor whipped bastard retreated back behind her chair.

Timmy Thompson appeared to take more after his arrogant mother than his dominated old man, who had yet to open his yap, and who looked so browbeaten by the other two-thirds of the Thompson clan that I assumed the equipment that had been an ugly necessity for the conception of his ingrate brat had been detached on completion of the act and stored on a high shelf where it was impossible to reach due to the Thompson patriarch's visible lack of a goddamn spine.

"The Thompsons are clients of Madison Insurance Equities," Planck said. "They, along with many of our other clients, are seeking restitution through us for the alleged actions — or, more accurately, alleged *in*action — of one of our other clients."

"There's nothing alleged about it," old lady Thompson snarled. "He failed to do his job, and as a result my little Timmy suffered severe emotional and physical trauma, in addition to a significant loss in revenue. If Madison Insurance doesn't pay up, we're going to join that class action lawsuit along with all the other parents."

"That's right, mommy," Timmy interjected.

"*Mommy is talking now!*" the dame screeched at the snot-nose so fiercely I checked to make sure the glass in the window behind me hadn't cracked from the terrifying vibrato.

The kid fell sullenly silent and began swinging his dangling legs angrily. When his father attempted to rest a comforting hand on his shoulder, he smacked it away. Apparently "like father, like son" did not apply in the Thompson household, but, rather, "like mother, like Satan's monstrous, evil devil spawn."

"If I can interject an observation into the proceedings," I ventured, "you people are appalling. Spectacularly so. I can't remember the last people I met who I despised so immediately and intensely as the three of you. But Planck delivered you here, and the business he's thrown my way in the past has paid for several of the finest blackouts I've ever owned, so I'll give you an overly generous twenty more seconds to get to the point, then somebody's getting thrown out of here. I'm betting it'll be me, since," I said to Mrs. Thompson, "I doubt I'd last one round with you, sister. Go."

I could only pretend to time them with my wristwatch, since it had apparently died immediately after I'd looked at it back at my apartment. Lucky bastard watch.

"It's the Tooth Fairy, Banyon," Robert Sherman Planck quickly blurted, with a hint of worry in his usually scrupulously unruffled voice. "There have been reports — not fully substantiated reports as of yet, mind you — that Mr. Fairy has possibly, *maybe* disappeared. Children who have placed lost teeth under their pillows are claiming the teeth were still there in the morning, and that Mr. Fairy left them no money. Many dental insurance policies these days cover Tooth Fairy-related claims. Mostly broken toys or lamps knocked over when Mr. Fairy gains entrance to the child's bedroom. That sort of thing. There's a clause about making good on payments for teeth if they're not removed from under pillows in a timely manner, but nobody has ever made a claim before. The Tooth Fairy has, until now,

maintained a hundred percent satisfaction rating. We are, of course, conducting our own in-house investigation into this matter. However, some of our clients such as the Thompsons are unhappy at the speed with which our investigation into the alleged behavior of the Tooth Fairy is proceeding—"

"He's a stupid dumb idiot, and I hate him!" little Timmy Thompson screamed at the top of his cowlick. His constantly swinging legs gave the underside of my desk a boot so vicious that it launched a couple of ICBM pencils from their coffee mug silo. "I want my money!" screeched the adorable moppet who I already wanted to send to a military boarding school; preferably in a country that hated spoiled American kids more than I did, if such an unlikely nirvana existed.

"If you don't mind my saying, you two are evidently horrible parents. You don't mind me saying that, do you? I find that most horrible parents like yourselves are very receptive to child-rearing criticism from childless strangers. But in this specific case, you've clearly not only exposed your nightmarish offspring to the transcripts of my divorce proceedings, you've forced him to memorize them verbatim."

The uncanny accuracy with which the brat had parroted the courtroom words of the former Mrs. Banyon sent a cold shiver up my bank account. I dumped out the remaining intercontinental ballistic Ticonderogas onto my desk's blotter and flooded the silo with the contents of a bottle I'd retrieved from my desk drawer.

"You aren't *drinking* in front of my son?" demanded a horrified Mrs. Horrible.

I looked from the bottle that now towered like the Washington Monument over the rest of the contents of my desk, across the killing field of displaced pencils and

pens that appeared to be slowly vanishing to some neth-
erworld to which all my writing implements inevitably
flee, and finally to the now half-empty mug from which
I'd just derived the fortitude to deal with Monday clients.

"If it makes you feel like a better mother than you
demonstrably are, no," I informed her. I polished off my
breakfast with a swig, then clinked bottle to mug a second
time for lunch. They were just those kinds of people.

Planck interposed himself between me and the streams
of cobra-like venom that Mrs. Wilda Thompson was spitting at me from both fanged eyes.

"The Thompsons simply want the money for their
son's six missing teeth," Planck hurriedly offered.

"Six?" I said.

Good, I thought. *At least somebody is punching the
little bastard in the mouth.*

When the dame gasped, I realized that I'd actually
spoken the words aloud which, in all honesty, I rather
suspected had been the case.

"They're five whole dollars each," Timmy Thompson
snarled.

I was tempted to reach into my wallet and fork over
the thirty bucks myself. It'd be worth every penny to
remove these cretins from my office before they slithered
into my case files with all the other misfits and miscreants
who darkened the door of Banyon Investigations, Inc.
However, I had a reasonable degree of certainty that my
wallet was filled only with IOUs I'd written to myself, for
which I'd most likely stiff myself. The terrific kick-in-the-
ass of the universe being that, were I successful with this
case, the little knobby-kneed bastard who was once more
kicking the underside of my desk would wind up more
flush with cash than yours truly.

"The Thompsons will be your clients, but Madison

Insurance Equities is underwriting your fee on this, Banyon," Planck said.

Insurance companies are famously generous. They'd hire a thousand tax write-offs like me if it meant they didn't have to pay a claim.

When Mannix brought in the contracts a moment later, a stampede of wild horses couldn't have kept old lady Thompson from giving them her Jane Hancock just to get the hell out of my charming presence. I was eager to assist, unfortunately all the pens on my desk had disappeared and taken all the pencils with them as hostages.

"Goddammit," I said.

Mannix, of course, came prepared. With the elf's pen, the contracts were put in order, and five minutes later I was ushering the quartet the hell out of my office.

The Thompson family hustled up the hallway while I hung back with Robert Sherman Planck.

"You have any leads where this fairy might be?" I asked.

The insurance thief shrugged. "You're the detective, Banyon, not me. Just make this one count. There's a million kids out there with a million mouths losing millions worth in teeth every day. A payout like this could ruin Madison."

"Yes, I can't imagine the financial chaos that would erupt if insurance companies were forced to start fulfilling their ends of contracts. It's too bad you can't do what you usually do, but I guess there were just too many of these Tooth Fairy claims for you to just happen to have cancelled all the claimants' policies yesterday."

In her desperation to remove her family from my presence, Mrs. Thompson had stabbed the elevator button repeatedly and viciously, as if it were Duncan and she was trying out for the lead in a gender-swapped version of Macbeth. When the doors at last rolled open, she practi-

cally shoved son and actually shoved husband aboard the car.

Robert Sherman Planck stepped on after the Thompson family, turning around to join the others facing me.

"Find that fairy, Banyon," Planck insisted, as the doors began to close.

"Unlike the rest of you, it was a genuine pleasure talking to you," I called to the mute husband in the back of the car, whose trapped expression as the elevator doors closed could not help but elicit a pang of sympathy from any man who'd ever had to gnaw off his own foot to escape the bear trap of wedded bliss.

Once the doors were shut, I picked up the scrap of paper Mr. Thompson had dropped from his cupped palm to the threadbare hallway carpet, and which had gone unseen by the rest of his companions.

I was hoping for the kind of enigmatic clue that sets off a series of exciting and increasingly improbable adventures that would have this goddamn case over within the hour, hopefully culminating with me hanging not from Mount Rushmore, but from the generous endowments of a barmaid in the thrilling denouement.

Thompson had scrawled three words on a torn-off flap of an old envelope, possibly with one of my missing pencils.

Divorce attorney! PLEASE!!!!

"Please" was underlined eight times.

Shit. I was going to have to do this the hard way.

It wasn't that I was unsympathetic to his cause, but the person he was looking for could be found with a combination of testosterone and the yellow pages, whereas the bastard I had been hired to find could be anywhere on the planet.

I dropped the cowed coward's note into the sand of a hallway ashtray.

Instead of heading back to my office, which was the last place on the planet I wanted to be, I headed down to the other end of the hallway to seek out the penultimate place I most desired not to be.

The suite at the far end of my hall was occupied by one Myron Wasserbaum, D.D.S., a dentist so lacking in basic competence that he could only locate a patient's mouth by giving them a sandwich and then watching from the corner of the room to see what hole it went into. Wasserbaum was to the science of dentistry what Socrates' final bartender was to the art of mixology. I would, in fact, happily down a gin and hemlock before I'd consider settling into the frayed reclining chair of Myron Wasserbaum, which was no doubt the preference of anybody who'd ever made the mistake of letting the criminally negligent tooth jockey chase them around his office with a drill in one hand a handful of hitherto attached incisors rattling around in the other.

Although I was normally inclined to avoid Wasserbaum's office as much as I do my own, the case which I had just taken on made a quick incursion to the dark end of the hallway an ugly necessity.

I entered Wasserbaum's empty waiting room to find a surprising lack of screams rolling down the open hallway next to the reception desk. At first I quite naturally assumed the exceptional silence was due to the fact that Wasserbaum was quietly formulating an excuse while waiting for the medical examiner to collect his latest patient.

My logical hypothesis was shot to hell when I caught a glimpse of my asshole dentist neighbor hovering over some poor slob in his exam room chair.

For some reason not immediately apparent, Wasserbaum was not alone in the small room as he attempted not to kill his latest patient.

Standing next to the terrible dentist, breathing down Wasserbaum's neck as the tooth mechanic attempted to change his patient's spark plugs, was an oily fat creep in a business suit. The stranger was using both hands to clutch the handle of his briefcase, the broad leather side of which was pressed tight against his crotch in the mistaken impression that somebody might be interested in whatever he was keeping fresh on the other side of it. He strained on the tiptoes of his dress shoes to better witness the oral atrocity Wasserbaum was committing against his temporarily still-breathing patient.

"I don't think you drilled that enough," said Wasserbaum's companion.

"You should let him spit," the fat stranger suggested.

"Are you aware of the ADA's guidelines for proper brushing?" the tubby asshole — whose occupation I was beginning to strongly surmise — asked.

"Here, do you want me to do that for you?" the know-it-all fatso volunteered.

He started to put his briefcase down, but Wasserbaum stopped him.

"Which one of us is the dentist here?" asked Wasserbaum, who was technically one, although barely, like Ellen DeGeneres is technically a comedienne.

I hated Myron Wasserbaum. Myron Wasserbaum hated me back. The two of us shared a mutual disrespect that went back many a pleasant year. The only thing on earth that could make me feel bad for Wasserbaum (and even worse for the poor bastard suffering in the chair) was the worst dentist on earth being distracted for some reason by the presence of a goddamn attorney second guessing every mistake Wasserbaum was making while he worked.

The new addition to the office was evidently a lawyer,

given the fact that he thought he was a better dentist than an actual dentist. Of course, in Wasserbaum's case it was probably true, but the attorney penchant for know-it-all-ism in all walks of life is unsurpassed. If they could find a tall enough ladder, lawyers would instruct the clouds how to rain.

"You're doing that wrong," the attorney insisted.

It was, perhaps, the one thing Wasserbaum had ever been doing right since he'd hung out his shingle, but the world would never know since he was unable to seal the deal. A second after the lawyer had interjected, the patient yelped in pain, and the dentist was suddenly scrambling for wads of cotton to mop up the blood. The lawyer didn't actually help, but he did point out everything Wasserbaum was doing wrong as the dentist tried to staunch the flow of blood geysering from his struggling patient's mouth.

I considered myself lucky that Wasserbaum hadn't seen me come in, and that he now had the fresh distraction of the erupting plasma on which he was currently slipping hilariously around his skating rink floor. I had enough nuisances to contend with in my life as it was, with a potential whopper in store as I approached the waiting room's reception desk. On top of everything else, I didn't need my dentist nemesis hollering at me to get out of the joint while flinging mini-tubes of airplane toothpaste at my head.

Wasserbaum's knockout receptionist — who was far too attractive to be banished to so shitty an oral gulag — wore a pink smock and an insincere smile. Had she removed the former at the sight of me, it would have been the best part of my day, while, granted, remaining a professionally questionable move in a workplace environment. Unfortunately, her smock stayed put, as did the casabas barely restrained therein, and it was her phony smile that she instantly removed when she raised her eyes from her

paperwork and saw that it was I who'd parked it in front of her reception counter.

"Banyon," the dame said, her voice as well as her eyes (but still definitely not her chests) utterly flat. "Whadda you want?"

"To begin with, for people to stop asking that in such an accusatory tone. It's possible I'm here on a perfectly pleasant social call—"

I left the sentence momentarily unfinished.

I went out with the dame once, but for the life of me I could not recall her name. I wanted to say Beatrice, Bonnie, Betty…something beginning with *B*, since I recalled cooking up the incredibly clever mnemonic device of linking her name to the first letter of her most spectacular assets. Although, as I stood drawing a blank before her counter, I realized in hindsight that the trick didn't quite work as it was equally possible that her name was Tammy, Tracy, or a hundred different *T* names.

I took a surreptitious glance at her nametag, and nearly tumbled headfirst into her cleavage. My eyes barely escaped her grand Tetons with their blinking lives.

"—*Beverly*," I completed.

"We went out and you don't even remember my name," the dame snarled. "You read that off my tag."

"I only glanced at your tag strictly out of concern for my fellow man," I assured her. "I'm worried that you might one day slip while pinning it on and the resulting blast could take out half the city."

For some reason beyond my ability to comprehend, Wasserbaum's stacked receptionist didn't succumb to my hitherto irresistible charm. Her beauty queen mug lost all expression and she rested an elbow on the cheap, shabby Formica counter. She aimed a pen like a stiletto at my necktie.

"Did you know you can decapitate somebody with a piece of dental floss? I looked up how-to after our date. I've got a lot of floss back here, Banyon, and I've been waiting for you to dare show your neck in here again. Now whaddaya want?"

"A new life where dames don't threaten to floss my head off would be a good start," I said. "In the meantime, do you have an address on the Tooth Fairy?"

She lowered her switchblade pen. "Why didn't you say so?" she asked. "No, asshole. He's a fairy. Fairies live in the fairy realm. Look there. Now do me a favor and get the hell out of here. Then do me an even bigger favor and drop dead."

I, of course, knew that fairies had their own exclusive realm, which was largely inaccessible to humans. It wasn't that we couldn't get in, it was that fairies tended to be so much smaller than humans that we had to walk around all hunched over. It was murder on our bad backs, and we were always bumping our heads on the clouds.

"I'm not interested in visiting the fairy realm," I said. "Have you ever been there? The sky is pink, the ground is like walking on marshmallows, and it stinks like the perfume counter at Macy's. I made the mistake of getting loaded before my one and only trip there, and wound up redecorating half the landscape with every meal I'd drunk in the previous month. The Tooth Fairy spends so much time in this world that he must have some kind of contact information on our side. You, like every dentist, have a ton of his shit merchandise here. It must ship from somewhere."

I waved a finger around the empty waiting room.

There was a plush Tooth Fairy doll on the counter, propped up against a wilted potted plant that apparently thought death was preferable to scrubbing the carbon

dioxide from the air asshole Myron Wasserbaum breathed. A little plastic display box bearing the Tooth Fairy's image offered pamphlets, the cover of which was a picture of the Tooth Fairy warning about the dangers of tooth decay. A poster of the Tooth Fairy covered most of the cracked plaster on the wall above some waiting room chairs that looked like they'd been salvaged from a wreck at the bottom of the Atlantic.

"Banyon, do you really think every dentist's office in town hasn't fielded a hundred calls from parents asking if they know where the Tooth Fairy has been the past couple of weeks? Even the kids are calling. You think I wouldn't let them know if I had a clue where the Tooth Fairy disappeared to, just to get them off my back?"

"I would make it my life's mission to find him if I thought it would help to get you on your back," I said.

Some guys say it with flowers, but why shell out two bucks for an expensive bouquet when I'm the undisputed king of the sweet talkers?

Fortunately, the dame's typewriter was too heavy to launch at my head, although I gave her an *A* for effort. While her arms were wrapped around the thing, I tried my best to avoid staring directly at her double D'stractions, as I was on the clock and I am nothing if not professional. She gave up on the typewriter and dropped it back to the counter, where it suffered what sounded like a fatal, internal comic *boing* of a dislodged spring.

"I'm billing you for that," she snarled.

"Look, you just said you're getting nuisance calls looking for him. I'm trying to track him down, you want him found. Instead of bench pressing antique office equipment — which runs the risk of expanding a chest that already obstructs the sunrise when you sleep on your back — maybe I can help you out."

I would have used her name but I'd forgotten it again, and I dared not cop another feel with my eyes since I needed something from her more than a Smith Corona to the temple. I flashed her a disarming rogue's smile.

This time the spark in her eyes suggested that she might just manage to pick the typewriter up over her head, like one of those mothers who under intense pressure lifts a car off a child to give better access to the department of social services to take them away, since parking on children is still frowned upon for some reason.

The bell by which I was saved was not the ding of a carriage return against my forehead, but of the telephone at the dame's elbow that suddenly squawked to life.

Before she could answer, I quickly pointed to the doll on her counter.

"May I?" I asked, ramping up the flame of my charm so high that the entire floor was at risk of sexy third-degree burns.

She exhaled surrender as she scooped up the phone.

"Whatever. Knock yourself out. I mean that, Banyon. Pick up something heavy and hit yourself on the head with it." Into the phone, she snapped, "Dr. Wasserbaum's office. If this is about a lawsuit, you have to call Dr. Wasserbaum's attorney."

As the dame dealt with the caller, I picked up the stuffed Tooth Fairy doll from the counter and gave it a quick once-over.

Like its real-life namesake, the thing had a big conk, curly blond hair, and a glittering smile you wanted to punch. It was decked out in pink tights, matching ballet slippers, and a sparkling vest over a bare chest. Unlike the real thing, the doll's wings were black wire frames covered in sheets of transparent plastic.

If anything ever came flying through my bedroom

window in the dead of night that looked like that and wasn't the product of my brain going through the hallucinatory stage of unwelcome sobriety, not to mention tried to stick its hand in my mouth, it'd get a .38 caliber welcome to its glittering diamond tiara.

There was a tag on the ass of the doll. I prayed to Buddha, Allah, Morgan Freeman, and anybody else up there who might be listening that I'd never get close enough to see if there was a corresponding tag on the real thing.

On the little scrap of nylon was printed a local address.

I checked the poster on the wall. This one was a PhotoShop image of the real McCoy. The Tooth Fairy was sitting on a barstool with his legs crossed like some silver screen ingénue from the 1940s. He was flanked by an array of six-foot tall toothbrushes. The legend at the bottom of the poster, for which an ad agency genius had no doubt reaped millions, read, "BRUSH, BRUSH, BRUSH, DARLINGS!"

There was some much smaller type in the lower right-hand corner of the poster which I assumed was an apology or, possibly, a suicide note from the repentant ad man responsible for the half-assed promotion.

Under the copyright was an address identical to the one on the doll.

I didn't have the Tooth Fairy himself, but at least my hazardous incursion across the hallway DMZ into Wasserbaum's office had yielded a lead.

As I wandered back to the counter to replace the stuffed doll, the voice of Wasserbaum's lawyer shadow was echoing down the hall next to the desk.

"You need to remove this bicuspid," the attorney insisted.

Through the open door, I could see that the lawyer had set his briefcase to the floor away from the puddle of

blood and was clutching a pair of X-rays above his head, one in each hand, the better to officiously examine them in the buzzing light.

"The patient came in for a filling," insisted Wasserbaum. "And that's not a bicuspid, those are his molars."

The asshole attorney offered a patented patronizing lawyer smile.

"I think, Dr. Wasserbaum, that you'll find it's a bicuspid."

Although I'd gotten the Tooth Fairy lead I was after and was ready to hightail it out of there, the most perverse kind of morbid curiosity — interest in the life of Myron Wasserbaum, D.D.S. — got the better of me.

The receptionist was hanging up the phone and blowing a frustrated lock of hair from her forehead. She shook her head in weary annoyance.

"I'm *so* sick of answering calls about the Tooth Fairy," she muttered.

She was talking to herself, not me. Most dames who've had the pleasure of my romantic company take a vow of silence — and very occasionally of revenge — when it comes to yours truly. She grew even more irritated when I chimed in.

"What's with the shyster?" I asked, nodding up the hall.

The latest Tooth Fairy call had worn her down. She didn't even attempt to pick up her typewriter She merely glanced over her shoulder, then shook her head.

"Dr. Wasserbaum's malpractice premiums are through the roof," she explained. "The only way he could continue to practice was with a court-appointed lawyer in the office during business hours. We've had a lawyer assigned from Shnoz, Fleming & Spitz here every day since last week."

The lawyer from the marginally humorously named

law firm was back to hovering over Wasserbaum as the dentist assailed what was left of his patient's choppers.

"You aren't doing that right," the lawyer said. "Here, give me that drill. I can show you how to do it properly. I went to law school."

All Wasserbaum could manage in response were a few emasculated bleats.

I very nearly felt sympathy for Myron Wasserbaum before I remembered that he was a horrible human being, an incompetent dentist, and that I hated him pretty much more than anybody else on the planet to whom I had not at one time been married.

"I can think of no more deserving a soul to have a lawyer burrowed termite-like into his miserable existence than Myron Wasserbaum, D.D.S.," I informed the receptionist. "At least Jack the Ripper had the decency to skulk along alleys and pounce on his victims from the shadows. Wasserbaum has the audacity to send them a bill after he's marauded through their innocent mouths. And he thinks a free toothbrush afterwards makes him even for the countless crimes he's committed in the name of dentistry."

The receptionist — whose name, my fatally faulty mnemonic device was insisting, rhymed with "knockers" — had reached her limit.

"Get the hell out of here, Banyon," she insisted, doubly pointing the way to the door hands-free, with only the aid of the office air conditioner.

I was on my way out when the dame called after me.

"Oh, and Banyon?"

"Yes?"

"Go to hell."

"Sister," I informed her as I closed the door, "my life is where hell comes to get a laugh."

3

The address I got from the criminally negligent dentist's office was in a rundown building on the corner of Stereotype Avenue and Hate Crime Boulevard.

I met a United Nations assortment of potential lawsuits in unrepeatable situations ranging from amusing to improbable to hilarious on my way up to the sixth floor.

A priest, a minister, and a rabbi were carrying a canoe with a monkey in it onto the elevator as I got out of the car, and I was sure the patrons of the bar they were no doubt on their way to were about to be treated to the funniest story of their lives that they could never tell another living soul without risk of receiving the electric chair.

Say Cheesy! Partnership, LLC was in need of a better lock, the proof being the ten seconds it took me to pick my way through the front door with a couple of paperclips I'd lifted from the bottom drawer of my absentee secretary's desk.

I doubted Doris would miss the paperclips, as the drawer contained roughly twenty-billion more of the things, which Doris had apparently been linking together in the free time she had when she wasn't doing her job. Since not doing her job occupied every minute Doris

was at work, she now had a paperclip chain that could reach from her desk to the sun. My hope was that she'd one day flee up it when I asked her to do some filing and burn up in the sun's corona, creating a massive, mascara-fueled solar flare that would wipe out her hag mother while she was watching *Divorce Court* reruns in her living room in that same goddamn blue housecoat she hadn't taken off since some asshole shot J.R.

There was a pile of mail just inside the Tooth Fairy's door. I was not incommoded by the USPS shit heap, since it had already been swept back against the wall by whoever had busted into the office before me.

Dust danced on streaks of sunlight that streamed through louvered blinds, slashing clawed shadows on the walls. Mixed in with the fine dust particles, sparkling airborne glitter saw to it that my last remaining undam-aged organs — my goddamn lungs — would now, at my autopsy, resemble a couple of deflated disco balls.

I took a moment to listen. I didn't hear anything but the scratching of my liver's fingernails on the inside of my abdomen; a reminder that it had been hours since it had been submerged in the alcohol bath on which it relied for its continued existence, and that if I didn't hurry up it would take matters into its own hands.

It was possible that whoever had busted into the place before me had done so three weeks or three minutes ago. If it was the latter, they might be hiding out somewhere in the office, ready to leap out and murder me on the spot. I only hoped I had time to thank them for their service before they killed the hell out of my grateful ass.

I got down on one creaking knee and took a couple of minutes to flip around the pile of unopened mail.

There were some postcard thank-you notes from kids who'd received payment for their lost choppers. The

postmarks on these ended nearly four weeks ago.

Some kids got only a quarter, others a buck, still others — like Timmy Thompson, the brat hellspawn of my repugnant clients — got five whole bucks and even more for their missing teeth. The amount paid out apparently varied according to the expectations of the parents. That probably explained why as a kid I only ever got bent Schlitz bottle caps and used chewing gum under my pillow.

Bills stamped **PAST DUE** had begun showing up in the past week. Gas and cable were demanding payment. Also a company called Whoosh, which was one of those magic portal outfits that bend time and space in order to help supernatural beings like the Tooth Fairy reach all the places they need to get to in a single night.

Wherever the Fairy had gone off to, he wasn't meeting the financial obligations that a polite and functioning society expected of him. I was already warming to the deadbeat bastard.

Near the top of the pile was a business envelope, addressed by hand, with no return address. According to the postmark it had been delivered a month ago. With that date, the envelope should have been at the bottom of the heap, not the top.

The block text on the front read simply, "**To: Fairy c/o Say Cheesy! Productions**," along with the address on the door of the joint I had just busted into.

The flap was ragged. Someone had torn it open, and I presumed that someone had not been the Tooth Fairy, as the letter had been haphazardly stuffed back into the pile of unread mail.

The P.I. code of conduct says it only counts as tampering with the U.S. mail if somebody else hasn't already tampered with it before you. Kind of like how pawn

shops stay in business not by stealing property, but by purchasing at bargain prices all the stolen shit real thieves bring in. So I was legally, morally, and ethically in the clear to read the mail of the missing bastard whose business I was illegally searching.

I shook a three-by-five card out of the envelope.

THE QUEEN IS NOT HAPPY.

I flipped the card over. Blank.

I shook the envelope. When nothing more fell out, I rooted around inside. Nothing else. Just a single cryptic phrase. Five words carefully printed on a lone card. The handwriting on the note matched the writing on the envelope.

I very carefully replaced the card inside the envelope, and then allowed my hand to do whatever it felt like with it. I honestly thought it would put it back in the mail pile, so imagine my surprise when it slipped it deep into the pocket of my trench coat.

Obviously I couldn't be held responsible for what my rogue hand does, a defense I'd used multiple times over the years with furious dames on crowded trains and buses. I abandoned the mail pile and ventured deeper into the office.

The gloomy main room was packed with cardboard boxes. I took a peek inside a few, and found them crammed full of plush Tooth Fairy dolls identical to the creepy one in the waiting room of Myron Wasserbaum, D.D.S. Other boxes contained Tooth Fairy jackets, Tooth Fairy mouse pads, Tooth Fairy mugs, Tooth Fairy T-shirts, and anything else the missing SOB could think of to plaster his mug on.

An answering machine hooked up to a phone on a broad desk beneath the shaded windows blinked a red digital 99. I stabbed the message button.

"Mithter Tooth Fairy? Thith ith little Bobby Mathon," an adorable little voice lisped from the answering machine's speaker.

Little Bobby Mason had either just lost a front tooth to the inevitable process of growing adorably up or to an adorable little meth habit.

"I left my tooth I jutht lothted under my pillow latht night, and you didn't leave me money like you were thuppothed to," said the aggressively endearing moppet on the tinny answering machine speaker. "My daddy hath lotth and lotth of money, an' he'th gonna get a lawyer an' thue your ath. Thcrew you."

The machine beeped, and an electronic voice announced that the message had been recorded three weeks ago. There was another beep, and the machine began playing the next message in the queue.

"Thith is little Thimon Baxthter," lisped little Simon Baxter, apparently another kid with a jack-o-lantern smile and a Ma Bell account on his goddamn Fisher Price phone. "I mithed you coming to my houthe latht night. It made me very thad to find my tooth under my pillow thith morning. You are a aththole, Mithter Tooth Fairy."

They grow up so fast, which is fine with me because legally you can beat the shit out of them when they turn eighteen.

I could only stand to listen to another half-dozen messages before I found my views on corporal punishment for lovable tykes morphing into wholehearted endorsement of capital punishment for the greedy little short pants set. Every one of them was some lisping little six-year-old ingrate who was pissed at a total stranger for not giving them a handout. I was listening to the graduating class of Berkeley, circa sixteen years from this very goddamn minute.

Assuming the Tooth Fairy ever returned to his office, I figured I'd do him a favor by not saving any of the messages I'd listened to, but it didn't matter that I wiped out eight of the little bastards. I was spooning out an ocean of avarice. The phone's ringer was turned off, but messages continued to roll in even as I listened to the oldest ones. The digital counter skipped up to 97, 98, then locked back in at the 99 maximum.

I was momentarily grateful for the largely silent phone back at my office (which I'd been known to unplug and stick out on the fire escape during peak business hours), and I felt a pang of guilt that I might somehow manage to do the job I'd been hired for and find the poor missing slob, returning him to what was revealing itself to be a miserable grind filled with teeth, blood, spit, and a limitless parade of greedy midgets.

My guilt trip lasted only until I pulled open one of the Tooth Fairy's desk drawers and it detonated like a landmine in my goddamn face.

The bastard had rigged it to explode like a paint packet in a bag of stolen bank loot. I was momentarily disoriented by the pop and the flash, like an anorexic actress on a red-carpet coke bender blinded by the screaming attention of a thousand paparazzi.

I noted several things at once.

First, I was reasonably certain my head was still attached. That was the best news I'd had all day, since that's where I kept the hole I pour alcohol down, an action I planned to undertake as soon as I got out of this goddamn office.

Second, I'd been hit not with a C4 blast, but by a goddamn glitter bomb.

Third, another drawer was partially open on the other side of the desk. It was smeared all around with glitter,

a fact that I had, of course, noted but which, not being a lunatic, I did not attribute to the prior detonation of an effeminate office IED.

Fourth, I hastily surmised that the glitter that was currently circulating amongst the dust in the air and which I'd spotted on my way in was not a regular feature of the joint but had been blown there in the relatively recent past by whoever had opened that other desk drawer.

Fifth, through the sparkling glitter cataracts that were probably permanently half-blinding me in the least heterosexual but most fabulous way possible, I was barely able to make out the perpetrator of my previous supposition flying out from where it had been hiding in the john. The small figure rocketed across the room for the front door.

My resourcefulness under pressure is legendary, largely because, like most legends, it's utter bullshit. Fortunately in this case, all that was required to inhibit the egress of the fleeing intruder was me picking up and heaving the nearest heavy box.

The corrugated cannonball caught the little running bastard square between the shoulder blades. The box burst open, dumping Tooth Fairy calendars out in every direction, and the running figure went sprawling face-first onto the pile of unopened mail.

I raced around the desk, tripped over a wastebasket I didn't see thanks to the pound of goddamn glitter I was still blinking madly out of my eyes, but managed to get back to my Florsheims and race to the door before little SOB could escape.

Due to the small stature of the trespasser, as well as my sudden inability to see anything through the kindergarten art project that was glued to my retinas, I thought I had already captured the guy I'd been hired to track

down. Less than an hour on the job and I'd already cracked this case wide open. I had already set aside a significant block of time for getting shit-faced that night, but I could now make my imminent inebriation more festive by calling it a celebration rather than the more customary "Monday night."

The figure was slipping on the mail and grabbing for the doorknob when I grabbed him by the shoulders. Only then did the kaleidoscopic clouds scraping across my eyeballs part enough that I could see the guy I'd nabbed didn't have a set of wings protruding from his back. He wasn't the goddamn Tooth Fairy after all.

Also, on closer inspection, he was, in point of fact, a dame. More specifically, he was a dame of Asian heritage, whom I got the impression was attractive, although I couldn't be entirely certain since I was viewing her through sparkling goddamn glitter smog.

"Let go of me!" the diminutive babe snapped, struggling out of my grip. "This is police brutality! I know my rights! You're in big, big trouble, detective!"

The furious dame shook like a dog that had just padded in from a downpour. A shower of glitter cascaded from her hair and clothes, onto the mail pile that she proceeded to kick at like a bastard, scattering it all around our feet and halfway to the desk.

"First off, the only victim of brutality is my eardrums. You scream like a goddamn air raid siren."

"I want your badge number!" she yelled so loud that I was pretty sure local civil defense was searching the horizon for low-flying Mitsubishis while scrambling to assemble barbed wire around every Japanese takeout joint.

"I've spent the past ten years targeting the brain cells that contained that information," I informed her. "I've

successfully scrubbed away everything but the number two. If you want the others, you'll have to check my badge. I left it for safekeeping in the main police station, fourth floor men's room, sixth stall. Wear your galoshes, because it caused a fairly spectacular flood, and I don't trust the union government custodial staff to have the place mopped up in only one piddling decade."

"Aren't you a cop?" she yelled.

"Lady, I'll be whatever you want if you'll show me where your volume knob is."

She was hollering so loud, half the neighbors had probably called the real cops.

It was time to get out of Dodge. The Tooth Fairy's office was a bust. Not that it mattered. Even if there were a hundred more clues to uncover, I wouldn't be able to find them from the backseat of a squad car. Besides, I had to get to the emergency room to deal with the pound of glitter that was clogging up the Mardi Gras celebration currently taking place in my mucus membranes.

I quickly tore a random month off one of the calendars that had fallen open nearby, and started to pocket it for later use.

This time it was I who attempted to flee the scene and the dame who tried to stop me. As I was shoving the calendar page into my pocket with one hand, she jumped in my path when, with my free hand, I reached for the doorknob.

"Where do you think you're going?" she demanded in the universal ex-wife tone.

I don't handle bellicosity well. This bellicose dame, on the other hand, proved remarkably easy to handle, which I demonstrated by taking her by the shoulders, lifting her away from the door, and setting her down behind me.

When I headed out into the hallway, I was thrilled as all goddamn hell to hear the pounding of furious little rhinoceros feet chasing after me.

"You just stop right there, mister," the dame commanded.

I obeyed her order, albeit at the far end of the hallway, and then only because it took the elevator I'd summoned a minute to arrive at our floor.

While I waited, she ran back inside the Say Cheesy! offices, reemerging a moment later, breathless and clutching a purse. She shut the door, tested it to make sure it was locked, then sprinted in my direction.

The elevator bell dinged and the doors parted behind me, and when I stepped onto the car I thought I'd make good my escape. I stabbed the ground floor button, and the doors began sliding shut once more. A look of angry determination descended on my pursuer's face faster than did the sluggish car in which I was a helpless observer.

The dame made it through the gap sideways, in last-moment Indiana Jones fashion. She glared up at me, triumphant.

"You won't be getting away from the law that easily," she insisted.

"You want to turn me over to the cops, sister, that's fine. While you're turning me over, I'll turn you over. If they put us on the same chain gang, we won't need sledgehammers. You can bust up the rocks by screaming at them."

"I don't know what you mean."

As lying dames went, she was one of the coolest customers I'd ever met.

Any time I'd caught the former Mrs. Banyon in a whopper of a lie — like, for instance, whenever I came

home unexpectedly to discover a gallon of cottage cheese under our bed and the milkman's trousers in the fridge — my ex-wife would attempt to sell an untruth by increasing volume and pitch. This little Asian number, on the other hand, immediately killed the histrionics she had been heretofore displaying in both voice and conduct. She was, in point of fact, suddenly inscrutable, an observation I kept to myself since I had enough to wash off in the shower what with all the glitter, and I didn't feel like having to soak in a bathtub full of paint thinner for a week in order to try to clean off the indelible tar of a goddamn hate crime accusation.

"What I mean," I informed her, "is these."

I plucked the couple of envelopes that were jutting from her purse. A sprinkle of glitter dust dropped to the floor of the elevator car.

They were business envelopes identical to the one I'd found opened in the stack of mail on the floor of the Tooth Fairy's office. Four letters in all, with date stamps going back over one month. They were addressed in the same manner, with identical handwriting.

The dame tried to grab them back, but she lacked sufficient reach. I shook the card out from one envelope, which she had helpfully tampered open.

THE QUEEN DEMANDS AN EXPLANATION

"Breaking and entering," I said as I replaced the card in the first envelope and moved on to the second. "Stealing mail. Resisting arrest. I don't know with certainty about that last one, but you seem like the type."

THE QUEEN IS CONFUSED
THE QUEEN REQUIRES YOUR PRESENCE

These were the next two letters in their respective entirety, each printed on note cards. The last one was the most ominous:

YOU HAVE INCURRED THE WRATH OF THE QUEEN

I wasn't their intended recipient, but reading these sinister, out of context notes, along with the one I'd stashed in my pocket back in the Say Cheesy! office, was nearly enough to make me lam out of town. I didn't blame the Tooth Fairy for disappearing. Given the creepy nature of the notes, it was possible that he didn't disappear of his own free will, but had been involuntarily disappeared by a secret admirer.

"Who's the queen?" I asked, as I stuffed the last note back in its envelope.

The dame had grown sullen and silent as I picked through the letters.

"I don't know," she said.

She appeared to be telling the truth. On the other hand, I'd bought my ex-wife's cottage cheese story the first few times I'd found strange pants in our Frigidaire, so what the hell do I know about the veracity of untrustworthy dames?

Her face brightened at a sudden genius thought.

"No, you don't work for the Tooth Fairy," I interjected before her lips could form the first syllable of the lie her brain had just cooked up. "You didn't turn on any lights, you didn't open the blinds to see better, you hid when I came in, you tried to run out the first chance you got, and most damaging of all to your credibility, you got blasted in the face just like I did. If you worked for him, you'd know the Tooth Fairy's drawers are full of glitter."

I handed over the four envelopes. I had one of my own already, and the only thing the other ones told me was the Fairy had pissed off some queen over the course of several weeks and that he appeared to not have replied to any of her letters.

I assumed this dame had been the one who opened the fifth note, and had only put it back in the pile so as not to appear greedy. An eighty-twenty split was fair to her, which just happened to be my ex-wife's attorney's idea of alimonial equity.

A sudden thought occurred to me.

The dame was in the process of doing a much better job hiding the stolen envelopes in her purse this time. While she was occupied, I peered down at her with narrowed eyes, hoping that the gesture would not be misinterpreted as mocking by some voyeur guard viewing us on a security camera, since I didn't feel like wasting the next eight weeks in the travesty of goddamn sensitivity training.

She was an Asian hot tamale with a side order of American spitfire. Five-foot-two, eyes of black, and a business jacket and skirt so smart they could have enhanced their college applications by tutoring stupid clothes. The purse was a top-of-the-line model: Versace, Christian Dior, or some other fancy-ass saddlebag peddler.

She was far too upscale to be a fellow P.I., and so the conclusion was obvious.

"Lawyer," I announced.

Her head snapped up. Her eyes were pulling a shocked Caucasian at what they deemed to be the surprise surmise of the century. Bing-goddamn-O.

"I won't hold it against you," I told her. "I personally couldn't do it on — unbelievably, if you knew me beyond the light burglary — moral grounds, but I guess somebody has to. It's like those bugs that eat shit. Nobody wants to be the thing that eats the shit, probably not even the shit-eating bugs themselves, but something out there has to do it. Although, having dealt with my share of lawyers, it's us non-lawyers who inevitably are the ones eating

the shit, so the metaphor is itself shit. But, hey, if you can be a lawyer without having to shower fifty times a day, it's no skin off my nose. Speaking of which."

I hauled out a crumpled Kleenex and blew a Tommy Tune Rorschach. Goddamn glitter.

The longest elevator ride in history ended with a gentle bump and the doors parting like a burgundy sea beneath a merrily illuminated lobby *L*.

The dame chased me out into the street.

"You're probably wondering what I was doing up there," she said, desperately and futilely pumping her short legs to keep pace with a thirsty inebriate's happy-hour stride.

"Not interested," I assured her. "The less I know about what lawyers do, the easier I sleep at night. It's like not wanting to know how sausages are made. Although I know enough to know that sausage-making is easier on the pig than lawyering is on society."

For once in my life the buses were running on time. I hailed a passing 55-seater. The public servant driver produced the most cheerful middle finger my taxes were paying for and continued the half-block drive to the nearest official stop.

Only one person was loitering at the stand. She was an old lady, but unfortunately seemed pretty spry for a multiple octogenarian. Years of experience had taught me that the bastard driver would happily leave me sucking on a cloud of dust the instant the old bag tripped and busted her hip on the WATCH YOUR STEP stair.

My body was already vowing revenge against me even before I started sprinting. I could hear the panting dame falling further behind with every step.

"Shit," I huffed.

The old bat was speedier than I'd imagined. The

driver didn't even give her a chance to get seated. She was desperately clutching onto a hanging strap and swinging like a chandelier in a gale-force breeze as the bus tore away from the curb.

Fortunately, a taxi had just pulled to the curb behind the departing bus, from which exited a white guy, a black guy, and a Mexican holding a genie's lamp. There was no way in hell I was getting involved in whatever that toxic assemblage was up to, but I took the opportunity of the open cab door to leap for my life.

I managed to slam the door shut, but my speedy Asian pursuer practically lunged through the half-open window, her face glistening with sweat (much of which I realized upon closer scrutiny was sparkling glitter).

"The circumstances certainly could have been better," she panted, "but it was nice meeting you, Mister—?"

She was more transparent than a pair of cellophane pasties. The crafty dame was fishing for a fall guy in case her adventure in breaking and entering blew up in her face like one of the Tooth Fairy's jerry-rigged strip-club desk drawers.

"Myron Wasserbaum, D.D.S.," I replied. "The Tooth Fairy and I have a long history together, since most of my patients wind up losing all their teeth. Stop by my office some time and I'll clean the shit out of that shit-eating grin you're suddenly sporting."

I instructed the hack to get me the hell out of there posthaste. It was nearly three in the afternoon, and at this late hour there was no doubt the city's liquor smugly assumed it would make it through the day without being introduced to my bladder.

The self-satisfied look on the mush of my fellow burglar surpassed any I'd imagined on the label of any liquor bottle as she withdrew from the taxicab window.

The cab pulled into traffic, leaving the sexy Asian lawyer dame panting on the sidewalk where she would hopefully remain rooted for all eternity and, notwithstanding feeble foreshadowing, stay the hell out of the rest of my goddamn life.

4

O'Hale's Bar was my own personal island in a tempest-tossed taxicab, and my heart — no doubt goaded on by my taste buds and at least one of my ne'er-do-well kidneys — longed to see once more her silvery shores that I might walk her sticky floors, breathe deep her fetid air, and squander precious pence in her busted pay toilets.

I, unfortunately, had one stop to make on the way to the dilapidated nirvana that was O'Hale's.

The Tooth Fairy's Say Cheesy! office was in a neighborhood significantly less shitty than either the wrong side of the tracks where was located the headquarters of Banyon Investigations, or the Beirut-like hellhole where I rented my crummy apartment.

It was the kind of neighborhood where the potted plants that bracketed the doors weren't smashed after one night, where even the muggers politely asked for your wallet and apologized for shooting you, and where doormen weren't rolled up in their own red carpets and unfurled over the nearest overpass just because the cable was out.

A good P.I. knows the location of every watering hole in town, since one never knows when or where a sobriety emergency will hit.

In the neighborhood in which the Tooth Fairy's aban-

doned office was located, Fairyland was the bar that catered to the fairy set, and as a hotspot for fairy activity was the next logical stop where I might pick up a lead on the missing SOB.

If O'Hale's Bar — my preferred rundown alehouse on the other side of town — was a rabid mutt of unknown lineage with mange in the walls and fleas in the booths, Fairyland was one of those puffball pedigree poodles with a diamond collar and an American Kennel Club stamp of approval inked onto its shaved ass.

A barely glowing, powder blue neon sign above the door was kept lit twenty-four hours a day. "Fairyland" was spelled out in impeccable script. There was nothing more out front to inform the passing public of the establishment's reason for being.

The door was black, but it glowed under the merciless assault of coat upon coat of high gloss paint. There wasn't a single nick or scratch in the surface, a claim that could not be made about the front door at O'Hale's Bar, which looked like a toboggan that had been lost in the woods for forty years then nailed to the front of my preferred dump tavern just high enough off the ground so as not to incommode the rats.

I passed through the simply fabulous black door and stepped into a joint that was not only crawling with fairies, but which clientele and description thereof likely would torpedo forever any chance I had of ever hosting the Academy Awards.

It looked like every variety of the race was represented, at least according to the definitive work on the subject *The World Handbook of Fairies*, by Sir Elton John who, like Jane Goodall with the chimps, had spent years immersed in fairy culture.

According to the handbook's introduction, which is

pretty much all I managed to slog through in the abandoned copy I found on the bus, fairies can be nearly the size of very small men or smaller than Barbie dolls. Many are hermaphroditic, but most are either male or female. The book was basically everything every sixth-grade school kid has learned about fairies if he's been paying any attention at all in biology class, but with a bonus "Don't Go Breaking My Heart" CD insert that's only useful if you want to torture Zombie Manuel Noriega or if you're worried about water stains on the coffee table.

There were special accommodations at a couple of tall metal tables just inside the door for several garden and woodland fairies, which as a species tend to max out at two feet. Plastic booster seats raised them high enough to reach their drinks, which they clutched tight in grubby hands. The filthy little bastards spent their nights digging in dirt, which wasn't a problem for them since their bodies emitted a creepy phosphorescence, like Kathie Lee Gifford but without their eyes pulled tight like a Marine's bed sheets.

A party of about a dozen fairy godmothers was whooping it up at a long table in the middle of the floor. The tallest of the lot was only about five feet, but the height of all of them was nearly doubled by those giant, brightly colored dunce caps that always make those dames look like they should be standing around a highway hazard. Every one of them could have used a Jenny Craig membership, and as they rolled around on their chairs like giggling bowling balls they were practically busting through the seams of their gowns. (Doubtless the wish of every man in the bar in the event of that happening — immediate blindness — would be instantly granted, no goddamn magic wand required.)

As I approached their table, one rowdy fairy godmother

was in the process of waving her wand. In a flash, the empty glasses of all her companions were magically refilled. Also, a bunch of mice and birds appeared from cracks and crevices around the room to clear off empty nacho trays and dirty napkins.

A nervous human waiter hustled up and began explaining that there was staff at Fairyland that would clear the table, and that the shit their rodent and avian friends were copiously producing was a violation of local health ordinances.

In a flash, the anxious waiter was transformed into a giant pumpkin.

The fairy godmothers howled with delight, while in the corner the bar's harried manager made a rapid erasure and hasty addition to the bill he had been furiously scribbling, presumably tacking on the cost of a spell reversal. I hoped for the sake of the pumpkin waiter that his boss wasn't crooked. I heard of a similar case when I was a cop that wound up cooling on a Thanksgiving Day windowsill.

I was picking my way past their table and doing my best to avoid catching the eye of one of the drunken fairy godmothers when one of those tiny little glowing, dive-bombing fairies appeared out of nowhere at my twelve o'clock and buzzed my right ear.

"Hey, handsome," a little squeak of a voice cooed.

The six-inch dame soared off and joined a giggling gaggle of girlfriends circling — and repeatedly bouncing off of — a ceiling light. As they zipped around the light, the swarm of sparkling little fairies kept looking my way and laughing, doing a near perfect miniature recreation of all the dames I knew in high school.

I made a vow to generously donate a bug zapper to Fairyland the next time I had a couple of extra bucks

burning a hole in my ego.

My first stop was the bar, where I demanded a perfectly ordinary drink. The weary human bartender returned momentarily with a sweating pink monstrosity that was festooned with paper parasols and garnished with goddamn fruit wedges.

"This isn't a drink," I informed the barkeep. "This is a Barbados beach cabana whose bright colors are clearly designed to abuse the eyes of those of us suffering from a bout of life-threatening temperance. Clearly you misunderstood me. I asked—" I added, because the bastard had clearly forgotten in the sixty seconds since I'd placed my order, "—for alcohol."

As I spoke, I pulled out several of the tiny umbrellas, which were apparently shoved into the mess to keep the fruit salad beneath them from getting a sunburn.

"Also," I said, since removing the umbrellas had given me a clear view of the contents of the sweating glass, "pink is the color of lemonade and sexy women's underwear."

The exhausted bartender shrugged.

"This is Fairyland, sir," he explained. "Our drinks are festive. You know, fun."

"I was married," I informed him as I rescued the last of the drowning produce department from my drink. "I'm unacquainted with that word."

The SOB had spoiled liquor for me. I couldn't take a swig now. What with all the umbrellas and various fruits gasping for air where I'd dumped them on the bar, I felt like God looking down after I'd just thrown a cleansing Sodom and Gomorrah tidal wave at Provincetown. Instead of drinking, I fished around in my trench coat.

"You know this guy?" I asked.

The exploding box of calendars I'd tossed at the lawyer

dame back at the Say Cheesy! offices had given me a
decent photo of the SOB I was looking for. I held out the
July picture of the Tooth Fairy, decked out in a skimpy
Uncle Sam outfit and holding a lit sparkler in each hand,
and let the bartender take a good long look.

"Of course," he announced. "Everybody knows the
Tooth Fairy." He squinted at me like I was some kind of
a dental Bolshevik. "Weren't you ever a kid, mister?"

"Technically, yes, but I wasn't very good at it. I don't
make a much better adult, considering my twin pillars of
massive failure: career and marriage Also, I lost my car
on a lake, and an elf pays my taxes. And, yes, I said 'on'
a lake, not 'in.'" I tapped a finger on the calendar photo.
"He come in here?"

"Yeah," the bartender said. "Good guy. He gave me a
buck for every tooth I lost when I was a kid. Course, little
Jimmy Wingard got *two* bucks apiece, that bootlicking
A-hole. I've mentioned it to Mr. Fairy a couple of times.
Told him how pissed I was at him when I was little. We
had some good laughs about it. No complaints out of me
now. Jimmy Wingard lost all his teeth playing for the
NHL, and Mr. Fairy's more than made up in tips for the
couple of bucks I got screwed out of as a kid."

"Call Netflix," I advised him. "They'll no doubt give
you a development deal and ten million for that thrilling
anecdote. Personally, I don't give a shit about your life
story, I just want to know the last time he was in here."

"Gee, mister," the bartender said, frowning thoughtfully, "now you come to mention it, I haven't seen him in
a few weeks."

"Nobody has," a voice to my right grunted. "Oh, no,
the world's coming to an end! The goddamn Tooth Fairy
is MIA!"

I glanced over to find a fairy sitting in what had previ-

ously been an unoccupied stool a couple down from my own. I hadn't even heard the slightest sound of the stealthy little bastard opening a portal and materializing next to me.

He was the same breed of fairy as the bastard I'd been hired to track down, but while the Tooth Fairy was polished to a dazzling shine, this fairy looked as if he'd been dragged through the mud, then dragged back through a second time just in case they missed a spot. He wore a rumpled plaid sports jacket with massively large lapels of such profound sartorial ugliness that it never even should have come into fashion, but which had been forced out of style at gunpoint in the early 1980s. He'd slipped his wings through twin slits that had been sliced up the back of the coat. The ragged flappers were folded over one another in prayer.

The four-foot tall fairy raised an empty glass he'd picked up off the bar and gave it a shake, the universal sign of a rummie stoolie who'd spill his guts for a belt.

"Oh, maybe this gentleman can help you," the bartender said, brightening. "He's the Tooth Fairy's brother."

The grubby fairy in the Oscar Madison sports jacket waved a backwards hand in an attempt to erase his famous brother from existence.

"Bully for me, having such a bigshot in the family," he said, rolling his eyes. "If that came off bitter, I don't give a shit." He gave a massive snort, sucking down a beak-full of mucus. "How you doin', pal? I'm the Snot Fairy."

He didn't offer me his hand, which was a lucky break for him since I would have shot it off.

I took over the empty stool between us, sliding down in front of the Snot Fairy the pink concoction the bartender had foisted on me.

"You have any idea where your brother is?"

"*Everybody's* asking where he is," the Snot Fairy said. "I'll tell you the same thing I told a dozen different cops. I ain't got no clue."

He raised the glass to his grimy lips and took an experimental sip. Deeming it not entirely objectionable, he took a larger slurp.

"You know if he had any enemies?"

"He's racking up more than his share right now," the Snot Fairy replied, taking another, more vicious and victorious slurp. "Every kid that bites an apple and comes out one tooth short is pissed as all hell at him these days. Serves him right. Always been the movie star of the family. Always 'Tooth Fairy this,' and 'Tooth Fairy that.'"

He was on a resentful roll, sucking quickly at his drink again, then flinging open his yap once more before I could slide a word in edgewise. He tried to affect a squeaky kid's voice, but came off sounding like a resentful, mud-smeared old drunk.

"'Dear Mr. Tooth Fairy, please take the molar that's under my pillow and leave me money,'" the Snot Fairy mocked. "It's easy to be a rock star when you *buy* their affection. And the parents. Oh, they go right along with it. But not when it comes to me. No parent wants a visit from the Snot Fairy. Or the Toenail Fairy. He's another brother of ours. Can't get any work fairying at all. Stuck working at a carwash in Anaheim. Our oldest brother, the Dingleberry Fairy, couldn't take it anymore, poor bastard. Flew straight into the windshield of a semi out on the interstate. They wore out three squeegees just to get him in the casket. I'm the only one of us left other than Mr. Perfect who even bothers keeping a Whoosh account. You know, the magic portal outfit? Although I suppose I should cancel it. It's great for appearing on barstools or popping into movie theaters without paying, but movies suck and

I can just drink at home."

I had to admit that it was a nice change of pace to encounter somebody who's had the shit kicked out of him by life more than me. The delightfully cynical Snot Fairy gave me pause to reflect on my own life, and to perhaps even consider the possibility that I might not have it so bad after all.

I determined after a nanosecond's introspection that my life was still, in every meaningful way, shit. Still, I did feel for the bastard.

"I'd offer to buy you another drink, but I'm already not paying for that one," I said. "You know anything about a queen your brother was mixed up with?"

The Snot Fairy's mud-encrusted eyelids narrowed.

"Are you hate criming? Because if you are, the yellow pages are filled with a million lawyers who'd stampede over one another to take me on as a client."

"While I would delight in the fatalities that would result in an actual stampede of attorneys, no, I'm not. At least not intentionally. He never mentioned a queen to you? Maybe somebody he crossed in business? He peddles a lot of merchandise. Could be someone he owes money to. Maybe even a ticked-off parent or a snot-nosed kid."

"'Snot-nosed' is a pejorative term and is deeply offensive," he bristled. "Mucus is a perfectly natural substance secreted by the body. You produce it your whole life. It's a hell of a lot more natural than having your goddamn teeth drop out of your head, and you wouldn't call somebody 'tooth-mouthed,' would you?"

"Mary Tyler Moore and most of the Kennedy family, maybe, but that's it," I admitted. "Wait, also character actor William Devane and that donkey-mouthed figure skater who got whacked in the kneecaps. They're both pretty tooth-mouthed, as well. And Gary Busey, obviously.

Now, if I pretend to feel bad for using the term 'snot-nosed,' which I'm not, will you answer the question?"

He scowled, but gave up trying to convert me to a booger cause than me.

"No," the Snot Fairy said. "No queen I know about."

I glanced at the bartender, who'd wandered off for a couple of minutes to tend to some other fairy patrons down the far end of the bar, but who had returned in time to hear me asking about the mysterious queen. The bartender shrugged and shook his head.

"Even if he was tied up with a—" The bartender stopped himself before using the word "queen," which might invite an avalanche of hate crime accusations in a bar crawling with fairies. "One of *those*, he wouldn't have said it in here. Our customers are very sensitive about the association words like that have with, you know, what they are."

The Snot Fairy shot the bartender a glare, and the barkeep — knowing he'd said something potentially career-threatening but, in keeping with the shifting standards for the unnavigable goddamn 21st century, not having a clue what — instinctively ran off to check on some customers who hadn't summoned him to the end of the bar.

"Your brother," I said to the Snot Fairy. "What happens if he stays missing?"

"Beats me. He doesn't turn up, maybe one of us has to take over." He raised his drink in salute to his vanished brother. "Thanks a bundle for that, jerk-ass. With my luck, it'll be me. I know everything there is to know about snot and next to nothing about teeth, other than people think for some reason that you can't see them using the latter on the former when they're behind the wheel of a car."

Upon reflection, it was actually more disconcerting

than it was the initial pleasant change of pace I'd thought it to be to look in a mirror and catch a reflection of yourself as a dirty little fairy.

When I was sure the bartender wasn't looking, I left the Snot Fairy to drown his misery in my stolen drink while I hightailed it for the exit.

I nearly made it when, halfway to the door, I was dive-bombed by another glowing miniature fairy. She wore a skintight green cocktail dress, and a stern expression. Her wings flapped like mad as she hovered in the air before me. Her friends who were still endlessly circling the warm yellow ceiling light were giggling and egging the tiny little fairy on.

"You're an asshole, Banyon," the six-inch dame squeaked in a tiny little voice. "I wanted to make sure you knew that before you snuck out of here."

Apparently I had crossed this fairy at some point, but I couldn't place her face, at least not without the sudden return of my much younger eyes or, failing miraculous, spontaneous ocular rejuvenation, a goddamn electron microscope.

"I'm not sure who told you that fact was in dispute," I said. "It manifestly is not. Now if you'll excuse me, on a completely unrelated note, I'm off to buy a can of Raid."

The furious little dame flew back up and was bouncing her head repeatedly off the ceiling light as I hustled out the door through which I'd ingressed.

5

O'Hale's Bar was conspicuous in the way it seemed to sink sullenly back from the rest of the businesses with which it shared a curb, averting its eyes from passersby in an attempt to remain unnoticed and unpatronized. If O'Hale's had been a person instead of a filthy saloon, it would be the moron in a police lineup who telegraphs his guilt to everybody on the other side of the one-way glass by trying way too hard to avoid notice.

The attempt to repel potential patrons with its seedy appearance worked only on the types of timid, abstemious souls who'd never consider venturing inside in the first place, and had no effect whatsoever on a robust and dehydrated bastard like me.

Inside, O'Hale's smelled like the funhouse at an abandoned amusement park. A delightful combination of moldy old wood and rodents pissing in the walls.

The air of the busy bar I'd recently departed flooded the nose with tantalizing smells of sizzling steaks, burgers, fries, and more. Patrons of Fairyland enjoyed their limited menu in an atmosphere of forced fun. If fun ever tried to sneak into O'Hale's, it'd be dragged into the alley out back and shot. As for a menu, that of O'Hale's was even more limited than the one at Fairyland, consisting of a

bowl of peanuts (sans peanuts) and some stale pretzels over which a local university had once conceded defeat, and could only best-guess a broad carbon date range from 1952 back to the Pleistocene Epoch.

The greatest appeal of O'Hale's Bar over a joint like Fairyland was a near total lack of customers. The stools of O'Hale's were the Sahara or the Alaskan tundra. Drop your ass down in the middle of one, and you were isolated from the rest of the world for as long as the booze and your brain cells held out.

At least that was usually the case.

As I fled the warm and unwelcome sunshine for the refreshing dank of my favorite decaying pub, the first thing I noticed was that some SOB was hogging my seat.

The fat slob's ass was devouring my stool by osmosis. His pudgy legs were in perpetual motion as the toes of his wingtips repeatedly kicked the oxidized brass bar that was meant to be a footrest but served merely as a reminder to get a tetanus booster.

"So, long story short, I got this guy who had been taking care of his parents for thirty years thrown out of his own house," the fat bastard was announcing to the only other set of ears in the joint. "Rest of the siblings never lifted a pinkie for 'em, but the one sucker who did it all — laundry, shopping, cooking meals, doctor appointments, hospitalizations, recoveries from surgeries — he had to go out and hire his own lawyer to keep from drowning. Lawyering, huh? What a racket."

He whacked the bar with a jubilant hand and threw back his head to either guffaw mightily or because he expected a mother bird to swoop in and throw up lunch down it.

Behind the bar, his lonely one-man audience attempted a smile.

"That's real funny stuff, Mister Attorney," said Ed Jaublowski, weakly.

Very little terrified Jaublowski as much as did lawyers. As proprietor of O'Hale's Bar, the barkeep was acutely aware that every corner of his dump was an unexploited lawsuit. The air was toxic even years after a citywide smoking ban. Every light switch was a code violation. The men's room floor was Disney on Ice to get to the urinals. And those were just the legitimate lawsuits. There were a million frivolous suits that could bankrupt the poor slob who owned O'Hale's, such as too-cold ice cubes, splinters from tables, and discrimination on the basis of looking at a lawyer the wrong way.

It was a liability minefield for Jaublowski whenever one of the legal bastards found their way into his establishment, which he invariably attempted to navigate with a revolting level of obsequiousness that would embarrass even a sycophantic asshole like Jimmy Fallon. That Jaublowski barely had strength enough for an exhausted smile indicated to me that the lawyer had been camped out in O'Hale's all afternoon.

"Oh, hey, Jinx," the barkeep announced, brightening somewhat when he saw me trudging toward him. "This is my new friend. He's an attorney. Mister Lawyer Attorney, sir, this is Crag Banyon, one of my best customers."

"Hey, there, friend," the lawyer said, raising his glass in greeting. "I'm a lawyer."

"I am not now nor will I ever be your friend. Being a lawyer, I expect you've heard that dozens of times today alone."

"*Not from me*," Jaublowski hastily inserted.

I had never seen the barkeep so quick on the draw. He had a drink poured and slid in front of me before I could

fully settle my weary ass on an alien barstool three down from where the ambulance pursuer's flabby stink cheeks were perpetrating a hotel Kevin Spacey on my heretofore chaste stool.

It was obvious Jaublowski's unusual speed in slinging me a drink was to keep me from engaging the lawyer. He need not have worried. I had as much interest in holding a conversation with a lawyer as I did in sticking my face in either end of an alligator.

The legal asshole abruptly had as little interest in me as had I in him, presumably because I was as unimpressed with his profession as everyone else who didn't desperately stab out the 800 number whenever one of those 'you or someone you love' ads slithered across our TV screens.

"Another libation, my good tavern keeper," the attorney announced. He raised his glass in a salute to getting pounded which, being a lawyer, he presumably excelled at.

Jaublowski was quick with a refill for him, as well as one for me, as I'd already murdered the contents of my glass and was in need of a second victim.

"I was accepted into Harvard, you know," the lying lawyer announced after he'd sucked down half his drink. "Of course, I found the Ivy League to be too unchallenging, which is why I didn't go there. I opted instead to skip the two hundred-odd law schools in between, and attended the seventh shittiest law school in the country. You don't truly appreciate a real challenge until you take four years of night and summer school to get a three-year degree. Of course, after graduation *every* big firm wanted me, so naturally I didn't take any of their offers and went to work in a shitty little office by myself."

And, just like that, I now hated O'Hale's Bar, the only miniscule corner of the entire planet that until now I'd hoped the asteroid would hit last.

I took a glance at the fat asshole, in the unlikely case that I'd wind up a witness rather than the prime suspect at his murder trial.

He had a big, bloated nose full of busted capillaries. His thinning hair was cut short and dyed a ludicrous shade of red, but for twin spots of gray at the temples that the middle-aged models in the L.L. Bean catalogue misinformed him was fashionable. The overfed gas-pot had ballooned beyond any hope of wearing a business suit, and so opted for a jersey that was straining to fit three hundred pounds of shit into a two hundred pound capacity Izod. The open neck of the shirt displayed layers of neck fat in the style of those colored, increasingly larger stackable rings kids used to have fun with but which were probably sued out of business this afternoon by somebody just like the asshole who was using my favorite stool as a suppository to flush out what I thought of his law degree.

His pompous circumference was every inch the reason the rest of us hated lawyers. Humility was something that happened to other people. There was nothing he didn't know, which was why he wasn't arguing before the Supreme Court and was stuck hanging out a shingle in this one-horse hick burg. The last thing the fat bastard had ever learned was on his last day of law school forty years before, which didn't prevent him from telling everybody else they were wrong about every topic he was ignorant of.

He was the perfect specimen of his species, and I was about to bum a quarter off of Jaublowski to call the zoo to tell them one of their raging assholes had escaped.

"Lemme get back to how I screwed over that guy who took care of his parents when none of their other kids would help," the lawyer was spouting at Jaublowski.

Ed Jaublowski, pinned in place behind his bar and unable to flee the unwanted attention of his asshole cus-

tomer, managed a weak, half-smile that exposed a terrifying string of teeth that would have had the Tooth Fairy, were he still in business, flinging his dollar bills into the air and flying screaming into the night.

Before the lawyer resumed boring Ed, the fat bastard took a mighty swig, draining his glass dry. He slammed the glass to the bar, wiped his mouth on his bare forearm, and opened wide his pompous pie-hole.

"—" he very nearly began.

And he promptly fell backwards off my favorite stool.

I'd seen more than my share of corpses in my career as a cop, which had extended straight into my current occupation as a P.I. However, never before had I seen a human being turn so utterly dead so quickly.

It was like someone up there had flipped a switch. Decades too late, since the bastard should have long ago been struck by lightning, like my dead ghost neighbor Archibald Jessup, preferably when the fat dead son of a bitch had crossed the stage to grab his law school diploma (after which, not being terminally zapped from on high, he likely sued the institution for a resulting paper cut). But better goddamn late than never.

Ed Jaublowski was in shock. One moment he was suffering through the tedium of listening to his mind-numbingly dull SOB customer, out of justifiable fear that a lack of interest could result in a lawsuit for being an inattentive bartender, the next instant he was watching the fat bastard who'd been boring the hell out of him all afternoon disappearing backwards and landing with a thunderous crash on the speakeasy floor.

Jaublowski had been mopping out a glass with the end of a dirty bar rag, and both glass and rag were still in hand as he leaned over the bar.

The bloated A-hole in the bulging jersey was lying

flat on his back, tongue lolling from his open mouth. His bloodshot eyes were open wide and staring glassily at the mildewed bar ceiling. His flabby man-boobs sagged to either side, no longer rising and falling with the rhythmic wheezing that had previously supplied oxygen to the organ in his chest that I imagined to be a bloated and clogged heart. Although, since he'd been a lawyer, I wouldn't bet junior's college fund on it.

"What the hell happened, Jinx?" the barkeep asked, wide-eyed.

"I'd say proof of the existence of the Almighty," I replied, raising my glass to cheer on a bearded sky king who rarely involved Himself in the affairs of mortals these days, and so needed all the positive reinforcement He could get when He did.

Unfortunately, I didn't knock back my drink fast enough.

The temperature in the bar suddenly plummeted. Crackling frost spread like fast-growing vines around the glass in my hand. The booze I had not had presence of mind to fling back before catastrophe struck abruptly froze solid, becoming a brown hockey puck

I heard a howl of wind to my right. Bar napkins that weren't permanently stuck to puddles of mysterious hazardous waste took flight. My cheap polyester necktie flapped a windsock sayonara as it attempted to flee over my left shoulder.

I put down my frozen glass before it could give me frostbite, and I glanced over my right shoulder.

A black, swirling vortex the size of a catcher's mitt had yawned open above the body of the lawyer. Mist seeped into O'Hale's through the otherworldly portal, accompanied by the sepulchral moans of thousands of eternally damned souls.

Behind his bar, Jaublowski's arms were suddenly paralyzed. The rag he'd stuffed in the glass was locked in place. Although his arms had failed him, his unseen legs were still sufficiently functioning to back him slowly away from the bar. He could only take a few steps before he backed into the shelf that ran along the rear wall.

Dancing bottles clanked a teetering samba. I held my breath for fear they might take the final plunge to the floor, but they held steady. That was a relief. The bottles were far enough away from the sinister whirlpool that their sloshing contents had not frozen. After avoiding going to the ER for aspirating a mouthful of glitter, I did not now want to have to explain to some nosy sawbones why my tongue was full of splinters.

In a flash, the vortex stretched wide, from floor to ceiling, and a figure emerged. The instant the creature had fully materialized, the portal snapped shut, blowing one final burst of dry-ice fog before collapsing to the size of a quarter, then vanishing altogether.

The new arrival wore a black hood and flowing, tattered black robes. He stood an imposing seven feet tall. Eight if you counted the scythe.

The wooden handle was old, having been carved from one of the original trees. The blade arced three feet to a merciless point. The metal was decayed and shedding rust along its length, but the business edge was gleaming and new, honed to razor sharpness.

The towering figure's back was to me, and I could see the outline of every vertebra up the back of his gossamer robes. The fog around his ankles swirled and dissipated across the barroom floor as he slowly turned to confront me.

If he'd ever had a face, it would have taken a forensic scientist to reconstruct it. As it stood now, it was nothing

but a pale skull crisscrossed with ancient fissures.

There were no eyes. Limitless black sockets that had peered down at all the ages of man fixed me with a stare beyond time.

I could see my breath forming irritated clouds as the Grim Reaper — for it was unmistakably he — unfurled a long, slender finger of pure white bone at my conk.

"Oh, hey, Banyon," the Eternal goddamn Footman said.

"Look, I don't want no trouble, buddy," warned Jaublowski, who apparently didn't deem having to sweep up a dead lawyer body at the end of the evening to be any trouble whatsoever.

Death did what everybody did with Ed Jaublowski. He completely ignored the moron barkeep. The hooded figure nodded to the frozen boozesicle in my glass.

"This isn't a social call, Banyon," the Grim Reaper said, as if I'd invited him to pull up a stool, which I was, thanks in part to him, in no way drunk enough to do. "Wish it was. They're running me ragged. You hear about that bus crash? The bridge? Took out that commuter ferry down below? Some of my best work, but, man, that took some planning. Run, run, run. Always hustling here, there and everywhere. This the stiff?"

Death nudged the body with the blunt handle of his scythe.

I got the distinct impression he was trying very hard to display displeasure, but that was just my best guess. Without eyebrows to form an angry *V* and no muscle or flesh to create a frown over his bone jaw, it was difficult to be sure. Death is easy as shit to beat at chess, but he'd make the best goddamn poker player on the Vegas Strip.

"Hold on one damn minute," he demanded, giving the corpse another deep jab with the butt end of his scythe.

"Was it a lawyer?"

"I don't think he mentioned it," I said.

Death leaned over the body. The empty socket where a nose should be sniffed suspiciously at the air about the esquire's stiffening corpus. The Reaper's skull nodded inside his cowl and he straightened back up.

"Oh, hah-hah," he snarled angrily. "Barbara at the home office thinks this is a real laugh riot. Everybody knows these goddamn things don't have souls."

With a pop, he was gone, leaving only a lingering sulfur smell, a soulless legal eagle decaying on the floor, and hanging me with the cost of a frozen booze disk that I'd have to wait all night long to thaw lest I risk freezer burning my uvula. Still, you can always find a silver lining if you're an ebullient bastard like me.

"Ed, this is the second dead lawyer I've encountered today," I informed Jaublowski. I held my frosted glass aloft. "A round of drinks for the house."

Since I was the only living person there besides Jaublowski himself, the barkeep took down a glass and started to pour himself a drink to help speed along recovery from the past ten shocking seconds. I, naturally, stopped him.

"Not for you, Ed," I said. "I'm not made of goddamn money."

6

The one drawback of having a dead lawyer on the floor of my favorite watering hole was the inevitable descent of a million cops with muddy shoes into my parlor. On the other hand was the big plus of having plenty of booze at hand with which to get drunk while the army of flatfoots badgered Jaublowski and me with endless questions.

As it turned out, interest in the fatly departed wasn't as high for the boys in blue as I'd anticipated.

Only one cop in a black-and-white answered the call that Jaublowski made after he'd liberated enough cash from the dead lawyer's wallet to cover the cost of the deceased's afternoon of drinking, a comically generous tip, and the price of the spare filthy apron the barkeep had spread over the attorney's gently grimacing rictus puss.

"You don't know if Mr. Shyster had any enemies?" asked the wet-behind-the-gills cop, who looked like he was nervously tardy for freshman band practice.

"We didn't even know that was his hilarious name until Ed started hoovering out his wallet," I said to the insanely young cop.

The law firm of Shyster, Pilfer & Fraud rented space downstairs from Banyon Investigations. The dead lawyer wasn't the same Shyster from that criminal outfit with the

improbable name, which was as common to lawyers as "Smith" was to the rest of us, although the former all seemed to drift into law, while nearly all of the latter would call the cops if you brought a horse into their accounting firm for re-shoeing.

Jaublowski was back behind the bar, having hidden inside the locked cash register the only tip he had ever received or, indeed, would ever receive, posthumously or otherwise. The barkeep's simultaneous lopsided grin, spastic shrug, violent head shaking, and panicky chuckle were more information than the kid cop was interested in collecting. He attributed Jaublowski's explosion of guilty mannerisms to the fact that the barkeep was a complete asshole and slapped his notebook shut.

"Thank you, gentlemen," the toddler cop said. "You've been very helpful."

He left, presumably to collect his clarinet from the trunk of his cruiser and wait on the corner for his mom to drive him back to police school.

Even the medical examiner wasn't interested enough in this one to send out anybody other than two interns with a stretcher and, by the time they were through hauling the lawyer's fat, dead ass to the entrance, a couple of massive hernias.

"Wait!" Jaublowski cried before they could fully cram the corpse out the door.

The barkeep collected his spare apron from the deceased bastard's mug before permitting the sweating and swearing M.E. kids to depart his establishment.

The existence of the second apron was startling. I'd always assumed that Jaublowski only had one, and that he'd be buried in it, just as several previous bartenders appeared to have been buried before him in the same filthy garment.

Ed returned with the apron clutched in his fist.

"Crazy night," the bartender said of what was still technically late afternoon. He shook his head as he resumed his post.

"Actually, it was suspiciously *not* crazy," I replied.

The casual disregard for the life of a lawyer was fine with me. My personal opinion is that they should all be lined up against a wall and forced to watch YouTube videos of stupid people injuring themselves by misusing brand-name products, then not allow them to bring a lawsuit against Weber because somebody asphyxiated from grilling in the crapper. The heads of half the lawyers in the country would explode in an hour.

However, my thoughts on society's cure of those in the legal profession had not been, as far as I knew, adopted as public policy, and so the near total lack of attention given to the late Mr. Albert Shyster — Funny Name, Esquire — was a curiosity.

The lack of interest by the authorities in one dead lawyer suddenly became less of a concern to me than the fact that Jaublowski was wadding up the spare apron and replacing the makeshift burial shroud on a shelf under the bar.

An unbridled disregard for hygiene at O'Hale's was part of its charm the very first time one walked through the door, but I had rarely witnessed the birth of a brand new reason why the health department should burn the place to the ground and salt the earth to prevent another saloon from ever again taking root there.

The only way I could cope with the loss of my new best friend, the dead asshole lawyer whose name I'd already forgotten, coupled with Jaublowski's cavalier disregard for cleanliness, was to get as thoroughly shit-faced as humanly possible, an undertaking that consumed

the better part of the next unknown number of hours.

I don't know how long I spent passed out on the sticky O'Hale's bar. It had to have been a lot longer than I'd have desired since I felt disturbingly sober when, sometime after midnight, Jaublowski nudged me awake and prodded me to the door, locking it firmly behind me after he'd deposited me on the sidewalk out front.

Night had taken firm grip on the city during the hours of my intoxicated confinement. The damp ground was evidence of the light drizzle foretold by my ghost neighbor, the late Archibald Jessup. But the rain had passed while I was passed out and the night was now clear. Somewhere up above my fedora were stars, or so I'd been reliably informed. I could only imagine their existence, as the ambient light from the slumbering city washed the black out of the sky, leaving only a depressing perpetual twilight haze in that languid gap between sunset and sunrise.

Closer to earth, the atmospheric scuff of my Florsheims on pavement echoed back at me from the crumbling brick facades of buildings that were piece-by-piece attempting to flee the neighborhood. So far, all they'd managed in their attempted exodus was a handful of bricks scattered here and there along my path, but it was a patient effort and I had no doubt that every building would eventually be relocated to the city dump, if not in my lifetime, a hundred years hence.

I was very nearly to the corner of the block when I realized I was not alone.

The first echoing scrape came from one lone shoe out of tune with my own footfalls. It was rapidly joined by so many more that I was reasonably sure I was being dogged by a Ziegfeld Follies chorus line.

I maintained an unhurried pace and glanced in the side-view mirror that was pretty much all that was left of

a car that had been unwisely parked in a neighborhood where the lowlifes will steal the bones from your legs if you stop running for five seconds, then sue if their mutts got sick from the marrow.

I only got a quick glance at the dark figures that were following me.

Five in all. The bastard objects were closer than they appeared, and so were nearly upon me when, a moment later, I reached the end of the block.

My options were limited. I am neither a lover nor a fighter, despite the fact that my aforementioned twelve-round disaster of a marriage combined the ugliest aspects of both amusements on most Saturday nights. My only real option available was to break to the right at the corner, then run like hell. It was possible that my pursuers would attribute my sudden and mysterious disappearance around the side of the last building on the block to the Rapture, and assume I'd ascended to P.I. heaven.

On the other hand, and more probably, they'd almost surely tackle and beat me to death before I'd gotten ten cowardly paces.

I was gearing up for the two-second sprint of my life when, before I'd even reached the corner, a car sped into view and slammed on its brakes, squealing to a stop curbside. The rear door sprang open and an asshole whose fat mouth couldn't quite manage to twist up in a smile stuck his face out over the sidewalk.

"Mr. Crag Banyon," the not-quite-grinning SOB said, in a voice so oily you could have mixed it with croutons and blue cheese and dumped it over a Caesar salad. "This is a dangerous neighborhood to be walking in all alone. Please let me offer you a ride."

He was older than the others. His thinning hair was dyed Bozo orange, with dashes of natural white permitted

to remain at the temples to vainly assume the entire weight of a copper-plated loss of hirsute dignity. There was something very familiar about the fat bastard's smug, full-moon mug, and not just that I wanted very much to punch him in its oleaginous center, which is my default autonomous response when dealing with lawyers, which the arrogant asshole with the Rust-Oleum head clearly was.

"That's obviously an appealing offer," I said, "coming from a creepy, oxidized stranger who somehow knows my name. However, I am not, in point of fact, alone."

My five tails had hustled forward, eating up the space between us. I could hear their labored breath, which flooded the street corner with the stink of stale booze.

"Oh, I think my friends can persuade you to join me," insisted the arrogant, orange-headed bastard hanging out of the car. "We need to discuss a certain Tooth Fairy."

I glanced over my shoulder at his persuasion squad.

The five mooks were big. Mostly in the overstuffed, all-you-can-eat buffet sense. They all wore off-the-rack business suits, as well as neckties ugly enough to run for Congress. In order that they might more effectively wring my neck, they had freed up their hands by placing their briefcases on the sidewalk.

They'd perfected their tough guy act through repeated viewings of *West Side Story*. One of them was cracking his knuckles. Another, who apparently questioned the effectiveness of the very first fist his hand had ever formed without a bottle's neck clutched in it, was testing it against the palm of the opposite hand in a manner that would have been more intimidating if he wasn't missing the mark thirty percent of the time.

That I had been set upon by an entire gang of lawyers became crystal clear when the tallest and fattest of the crowd raised his hand to make a motion.

"It's the opinion of this court that you're getting your ass in that car," he growled.

The rest laughed. God, I hate lawyers.

"Actually," I said, "I have a counterproposal that involves not only all of you, but also the horse you rode in on. I don't see the equine in question at the moment, so why don't you all get to work on yourselves for now, and we can subpoena him later."

None of them laughed. God, how I hate lawyers.

"Oh, yeah, smart mouth?" the biggest of them said. "Subpoena this."

The big bastard hauled back and flung a fist in my direction.

He really meant it, the poor asshole, and he put all he had into the effort. It was evident that, even if this was not his first time assaulting someone, he was still really, really shit at it. I had ample time to duck back from the wildly flung fist, and I enjoyed the gentle breeze as it soared straight past my chin.

The initial swing-and-a-miss was not entirely unproductive. It was only a question of how one measured success.

The fat bastard spun completely out of control on his heel and smashed his wildly flying fist straight into the jaw of one of his unsuspecting companions. There were simultaneous cracks of bone. Not only did the jawbone of the asshole lawyer victim crack in two, but several smaller snaps issued from within the assaulting SOB's fist.

The big goon with the busted fist (hereafter referred to as "Asshole One") howled in pain and crammed his busted hand up into his opposite armpit. The SOB with the busted jaw (hereafter referred to as "Stupid Bastard Two") went soaring backwards, landing in a crumpled pile of fifty-percent of his most recent Men's Warehouse

two-for-the-price-of-one purchase.

"For future reference," I instructed Asshole One, "when making a fist, you shouldn't wad your goddamn thumb up inside it. Although, frankly, you probably shouldn't ever do it again. You're really massively lousy at it."

Broken bones were forgotten. My final comment instantly raised the ire of all five of the bastards who'd trailed me from O'Hale's. Five heads on the pavement snapped hard in my direction, faces furious. Even the bastard whose head was jutting out of the back of the car looked angrily at me at the mere suggestion that his comrade with the busted thumb hadn't formed the most perfect fist in pugilistic history.

The one overriding rule when dealing with lawyers is to never tell a lawyer that they don't know absolutely everything about every subject in the history of the known and unknown universe. A nineteenth century porcelain doll dropped from the International Space Station is not as fragile when it hits the ground as an earthbound lawyer's ego. Overcooked butterscotch pudding has thicker skin.

Telling a lawyer they're bad at something is a leap into a lion's den populated by all the insecurity they've spent a lifetime denying with bravado, booze, broads, and — if my personal experience with their breed is any indication — copious amounts of cocaine.

A briefcase was suddenly firing like a cannonball at my head. I managed to dodge to one side in the nick of time. The case struck the brick wall behind me, busting its latch and launching an explosion of paperwork all around the area of combat.

Another briefcase was swinging hard at my head. I grabbed it on both sides, arresting the forward momentum, and shoved it back into my attacker's face. The lawyer went sprawling on his ass, the monogram "TJH" firmly

embedded in his forehead. The back of his head met cement, and he, along with the busted bone twosome, was down for the count. Only two were left standing.

Except I'd neglected to take one asshole into account.

I hadn't heard the older, orange-headed son of a bitch from the back of the car clamber out behind me. I only knew Orangehead had jumped into my blind spot when I felt his fat arms wrap around my chest, pinning my hands to my sides.

Movies are generally for shit when it comes to fight scenes. Most of the fisticuffs I've had the misfortune to be involved in are one punch and done, usually with me on the unconscious receiving end. However, for the first time in my life I was afforded a genuine silver screen opportunity, and I wasn't about to waste my one shot at perfect movie choreography.

The bastard from the car was holding me in place as his two remaining pals who weren't groaning on the sidewalk charged. With the unwitting aid of the SOB behind me, I raised both legs and slammed as hard as I could into the chests of the remaining pair.

Unfortunately, I'm not goddamn Baryshnikov. Years devoted to the relaxed lifestyle of a professional tippler had left me with nonexistent abdominal muscles, a markedly unfair trade-off, as I avoid the unhealthy option of the liquor store six-pack, so I damn well should have been rewarded with the alternative variety.

Still, I was not so slack-gutted that I did not manage to kick one of the charging bastards in the gut and the other in the family jewels, sending the pair of them gasping for breath on the cement with their comrades.

My brilliant move was carried out to cinematic perfection. However, when showcasing a similar stunt, the movies, as did I, fail to take physics into account.

By shoving off the pair of charging bastards with both legs, I successfully managed to launch backwards myself and the asshole whose arms still encircled me.

The pair of us crashed into the parked car. Orangehead's arms sprang loose and he fell into the rear seat of the sedan. I was a sitting duck, clinging halfway inside the open door of the car, my ass hanging over the seat. Only one agile bastard would be needed to tackle me inside, toss a bag over my head, and we'd be off to my funeral.

I felt the asshole in the car lunge in from behind, trying to grab onto me and drag me inside. We had a momentary prom night struggle in the back seat before I managed to break away and scramble to my feet.

None of the injured crowd came charging forward to slam me back through the open door. With a free field before me, I took a few hasty, breathless steps away to survey the bruised and broken scene.

Men and briefcases were scattered everywhere. Loose documents blew around prone bodies.

Behind me, the asshole with the bad dye-job refused to accept when to quit. Panting, he hauled himself from the rear seat. He aimed a pinkie-ringed finger at me.

"You're coming with us, Mr. Banyon, whether you like it or not!" he yelled.

"First off, I would not get into a car with anybody who wears a ring on his goddamn pinkie. Second, what kind of an asshole points with his pinkie finger? Use your index finger like everybody else, for Christ's sake. Third, no, I'm not. That's in answer to me getting in your car, in case you forgot. Fourth, here's why."

I calmly aimed my gat, which had fortunately not fallen from my shoulder holster and down a storm drain during the previous minute's exciting melee, at a spot

directly between the arrogant bastard's eyes.

Instead of running like hell, the only smart response when confronted with a semi-loaded SOB with a fully loaded .38, the captain of my assault flashed a haughty grin. He very slowly raised his arms, but not in sensible surrender. Instead, he struck up something akin to a martial arts pose.

"Hyah!" the fat, orange-haired bastard shouted, snapping his arms rigid.

It was late, I was now largely sober, and I was too tired to play any more hopscotch with a herd of rampaging barrister maniacs.

Kung fu stance notwithstanding, I socked the prettily posing pettifogger square in the kisser and sent him sailing back into the car's rear seat.

The ease with which his case fell apart on the stand was only shocking to anybody who hadn't dealt with know-it-all lawyers before.

"You don't actually know karate, do you?" I said.

"I'm an attorney," Orangehead groaned. "I assume I do." Despite the fact that he and his forces had evidently lost the day, he managed a lopsided smirk as he struggled back to a seated position. "And now you *will* be getting in the car. *Voluntarily*. We've got you over a legal barrel. You've assaulted six innocent men. We'll all witness for one another. You've got nobody. If you don't come with us, we'll all sue you, Mr. Banyon. We will tie you up in court for the rest of your life."

He oozed self-satisfaction, as well as a few dribbling streaks of blood. The latter was my doing. The former, however, could be credited entirely to a degree in juris-goddamn-prudence.

"So, the truth that you assholes jumped me doesn't matter," I said.

"Mr. Banyon, don't be naïve. Truth has no place in a court of law," the smarmy lawyer replied, flashing a victorious grin.

He'd delivered his trump card.

The threat of interminable legal inaction might have worked had not I, as it so happened, slipped an ace of my own up the sleeve of my trusty trench coat.

"Fortunately for me then, it won't just be my word against yours," I informed him.

At first, Orangehead didn't get what I was saying. We were clearly the only assholes loitering in the lonely, post-midnight street. He followed my finger — index, not goddamn pinkie — to the spot where I was pointing, above the door of the store in front of which the mob of lawyers had staged their attack.

The store was one of those joints with signs plastered in the windows informing passersby that inside could be purchased — for a reasonable price — gold, silver, samite, mithrill, cubic zirconia, and any other precious materials industrious thieves managed to steal from friends and relatives in order to support a dissolute skid row lifestyle. The store was called Gold, Gold, Gold, and although the owner was creatively bankrupt when it came to names, he did not skimp in other necessary areas.

Due to the nature of the clientele and the crummy neighborhood in which the store was located, a metal grate was lowered across the entrance at night in order to discourage after hours shopping by the same criminals who were welcomed with open arms during open hours.

Above the door, encased in a dull black orb, was secreted a camera that kept constant digital watch on everything that transpired on the sidewalk out front.

"Damn, we're screwed!" the wide-eyed bastard with the copper-stained follicles hollered at his pals. He wheeled

on me, practically foaming meringue out of his pie hole. "That's not an admission of guilt!" he added as he threw his suit jacket up around his Crayola-dyed head and dived back into the rear of his car.

The five attorneys on the sidewalk had followed my finger, as well. When they spotted the dome that housed the camera, the entire crowd simultaneously shit their legal briefs. Broken bones, bleeding skulls, and bruised junk were forgotten. The team scrambled to their feet, grabbing up their briefcases.

"Get the paperwork!" a muffled voice yelled from inside the rear of the car.

The papers that had spilled from the busted-open briefcase were still blowing around the street. The quintet snatched up as much as they could manage on their mad dash for the parked sedan, into the back of which they flung their asses one after another with Olympic diving team accuracy.

The counselor clown car tore away from the curb, leaving twin strips of burning rubber. The rear door was still hanging open as the vehicle flew off, and I could see Asshole One with the broken thumb nearly falling out as he repeatedly and amusingly attempted to yank the bouncing door shut as the car tore off down the street.

Not content to flee one measly felony, the law-mobile creamed two light poles, a parked car (which, from a distance, looked suspiciously like my own missing Pontiac), and clipped a fire hydrant in its haste to make a mockery of the oaths its occupants had sworn to uphold the law. It slung in whip-like fashion around the corner, and although it vanished out of sight, the subsequent fading cartoon crashes indicated that, come morning, city crews would have their work cut out for them sweeping up the Tornado Alley carnage it left in its wake.

The fleeing lawyers had done a remarkably thorough job snapping up the papers that had spilled out of the broken briefcase, a skill likely developed snatching up their secretary's discarded undergarments when their wives came unexpectedly home.

They hadn't collected all the loose paperwork, however, and I snatched up one errant scrap that had gotten caught under a busted police call box.

I was able to read the header in the light of one of the few working streetlamps my attackers hadn't demolished on their demolition-derby path out of the neighborhood.

The Law Offices of Swindle, Steele & Robb.

I'd seen their billboards around town for years. That a collection of improbably named individuals had found one another was remarkable in and of itself, but that they were all three of them lawyers who had then formed an oblivious partnership that combined their names to hilarious effect was utterly extraordinary.

What's more, I finally knew where I'd seen the fat son of a bitch with the ridiculously bad orange dye-job before. My blubbery chief assailant was none other than Montague Swindle, founding partner of Swindle, Steele & Robb, whose face had for years appeared on billboards, phonebooks, and TV commercials, alongside those of his two partners and a phalanx of malodorous SS&R partners and associates.

What interest the firm of Swindle, Steele & Robb had in the missing Tooth Fairy — to the point that they were willing to dispatch Senior Partner Montague Swindle to commit assault against my innocent ass, and attempt kidnapping of same posterior — was one mystery too many for my sleep-deprived brain.

My alcohol-deprived liver had much to speak on the

matter as well. Fortunately, there was a sofa in my office that could handle one of my problem organs and a bottle in my desk drawer that would drag me across the hepatological finish line.

I snatched up the handful of documents the gaggle of asshole lawyers had left behind, and shoved them far into the depths of my increasingly crowded coat pocket.

The car up the street that the attorneys had sideswiped still looked suspiciously like my misplaced Pontiac. If it was, in fact, my wayward internal combustion pain-in-the-ass, I had no desire to deal with its honking recriminations, its windshield wiper overflowing with parking tickets, or its registration that had expired circa the Crimean War. I struck off in the direction opposite my possible car in order to locate a bus stop, with only a thin hope that resident vandals hadn't stripped my city bus lifeboat to its chassis before it could whisk me the hell out of this benighted neighborhood.

7

The neighborhood that housed Banyon Investigations, Inc. was nearly equally benighted to the one that housed O'Hale's Bar, but with the aforementioned delightful difference that the tavern in my desk was open all night.

Although the block where my offices were located was shit by day or night, a marked improvement over the daylight hours was that the fish market that occupied the ground floor of the sandstone shit palace in which I kept my offices was closed at night.

This night, as always, Vincetti's For the Halibut Fish Bazaar was buttoned up tight, and as I approached its darkened façade I could nearly hear the collective moan issuing from the slack mouths of the hundreds of long-dead fish who for decades beyond their expiration dates had been making the dump their post mortem home.

The stink that flowed freely from the door of Vincetti's during the day was bottled up tight at night. The nightly build-up of toxic gas had thus far been safely released on a gasping neighborhood when the old fascist whose festering business it was hobbled up in the a.m. and sprang the front door. I feared that the day Vincetti did not show up on time to release the pressure would be the day the entire building was blown to Jupiter on a solid rocket booster

of fuel derived from ten-year-old rotting mackerel heads.

Beyond the bottled-up stink, the second significant difference between day and night was that Vincetti the fishmonger wasn't out on the sidewalk with a broom, screaming in Italian and chasing away everybody who tried to park in front of his store.

Vincetti made it his mission in life to harass anybody who made the mistake of pulling into a space out front. The demented old buzzard insisted that he was saving the spaces for paying customers, but since the rest of humanity insisted that we'd shop there over our dead bodies — an end that would be instantly achieved with one ounce of lethal salmon — the spaces by and large remained empty.

Tonight, while Vincetti was home recharging his bile, someone had possessed the temerity to park in the spot directly in front of the fish market's closed and barred door.

I was impressed by the reckless audacity of anybody who'd entrust their vehicle to the untrustworthy denizens of my neighborhood, who'd steal the lungs out of your chest and come back later for the air. I noted the license plate on my way to the entrance.

"LWSUET."

The only time of day that the building was tolerable was the dead of night, not only because Vincetti's stink zone was closed, but also as there were no screams emanating from Wasserbaum's darkened dental abattoir, as well as the fact that the students who regularly stampeded through Madame Carpathia's top floor dance studio were off somewhere soaking their maladroit hooves.

The only unwanted company that sometimes appeared after midnight was an old ghost janitor who had, when he'd been alive years ago, become entangled in a cord while cleaning the hallway floors and accidentally buffed

himself to death.

The janitor's ghost was rarely seen. Mostly because no one ventured down to the old unused boiler room where he had spent most of his living days dodging work and getting drunk and where now, dead, he hung out rattling chains and knocking over bottles of Mr. Clean that pissed him off.

When I entered the downstairs hallway, I found it perfectly in keeping with my latest round of rotten luck to see that the building's resident janitor ghost had abandoned his boiler room and floated up to the main floor directly in my path.

The dead bastard was floating around near the ceiling trying to change a light bulb, but evidently couldn't quite figure out why his incorporeal hand kept passing through the goddamn thing. I took note of several busted bulbs on the floor. Clearly, he'd managed to bring some spares up from the basement, but now was unable to swap out one forty-watt Sylvania for another. His inability to change the bulb wasn't a surprise, since the effort a spirit must exert in order to move a physical object is wearying. The dumb dead bastard had likely drained his battery when, for some goddamn reason known only to him, he'd schlepped a stepladder up from the basement.

The ladder was propped open five feet to his right, and he was floating five feet away from it, standing on his tiptoes on nothing but air.

I was on tiptoe as well, and had made an admirable effort to slip past the ghost, when the specter janitor's sunken eyes nabbed sight of me.

"*Heed my words, mortal!*" he intoned, in that overly dramatic way the biggest asshole ghosts think makes them sound like Hamlet's old man on Elsinore's roof, but actually sounds like the fattest slice of British ham to graduate

last in Sir Ian McKellan's Classy Acting Class. "*Insurance is a scam. A scaaaaaaaaaaam!*"

It was the same goddamn thing every time I ran into him. The old, dead bastard was like a cartoon lizard or that dame whose mush everybody wants to punch: always droning on about insurance. The only difference with his performance this time was that it was punctuated with an accidentally dropped light bulb.

"*Damn,*" he moaned down at the corpse of the latest busted bulb.

Since I was in close proximity of a ghost, I was actually able to see the floating spirit of the intact light bulb drift up from the shattered remnants and fade into oblivion. Even dead light bulbs didn't want to stick around this asshole.

The custodian ghost moaned a heavy sigh before floating down to the Sylvania box to retrieve another incandescent victim.

I can't stand ghosts. For one thing, they could put the rest of us chronic complainers out of business with their eternal ax-grinding. Normal humans can't wait to shuffle off this mortal coil, for a million different reasons. Who wants to stick around the joint where they made you learn the alphabet, get a job, pay taxes, and where they continuously wave a finger in your face if you don't eat all your goddamn vegetables? Then there's option B, where you could be hanging out on a cloud with Humphrey Bogart, General George S, Patton, and every junkie Playboy centerfold who ever croaked on the operating table during a botched knob job. Ghosts are so tied to something in the corporeal realm that the dumb bastards have checked "decline to attend" on the everlasting RSVP postcard. As a result, they were missing the biggest after-party in the universe. In the case of my building's dead janitor, he had

— unbelievably — stayed behind to harangue everybody he met on the evils of insurance companies.

I felt under no obligation to engage the living, and avoided people with heartbeats whenever possible. That went treble for ghosts. I left the glowing spectral janitor to play serial killer to the rest of the bulbs in his box and headed for the elevator.

I pressed the third floor button and the doors obediently closed, but before the car began to rise a bluish head jutted through the steel doors.

"*Insurance company still won't pay my daughter. They wooooon't paaaay!*"

"I've explained to you innumerable times my policy when it comes to ghosts," I told the wild-eyed transparent face. "Apparently you're in need of a reminder."

I blew hard in his face, as if it were a nonagenarian's bonfire birthday cake, and the ghost's head instantly dissipated in a swirling cloud.

The car jostled, then began to rise, sans ghost head.

"*You're a bastard, Banyon!*" the dead janitor's fading voice called up from the elevator shaft. "*A baaaaaaaaaaaaastard!*"

Thirty blessedly spirit-free seconds later, the elevator disgorged me into the darkened third floor hallway.

I had nearly reached my office door when I spotted the quick stab of a flashlight raking across the translucent glass.

I stopped dead.

My office was broken into so often that I'd been considering installing a tollbooth in the hallway and retiring to Tahiti in six months with a sack of quarters and the sexy attendant I'd hire to staff the thing.

There was no telling who was inside. The lawyer gang might be lying in wait for me. Dozens of irate clients and

disappointed dames always topped the list. Doris may have returned from her wedding dress pilgrimage with a justice of the peace in one hand and a blackjack in the other. In point of fact, it could be anyone inside, but whoever it was would almost certainly make my living hell of a life just that much more miserable.

I could make it easy on myself and just turn around and go home.

On the other hand, I was mere yards away from the bottle of liquid cowardice I'd crossed half the city to rescue.

As usual, life gave me no choice. The bastard.

For the second time that evening, I slipped my gat from its holster.

The door wasn't locked. I steeled myself for what I hoped would be, if I had any luck at all, my execution, and stole into my offices.

The outer room where Mannix worked during the day while Doris sometimes watched him was empty. Filing cabinet drawers hung open. Files were dumped all over the floor. Only one file was left at viewing height, lying open on Doris' desk. In the glow of a splotch of phosphorescent nail polish, made by a secretary so incompetent that she couldn't even goof off without making a mess of it, I read the client's name off the tab:

Little Timmy Thompson.

Whoever it was who'd busted into my office, they were there because of the Tooth Fairy. The joke was on whoever had liberated the file from its cabinet, since all that was contained therein was the contract Little Bastard Timmy's parents had signed on his little bastard behalf, and the few sparse notes Mannix had managed to jot down before I'd hustled the worst family on the planet from my office.

The lack of information had not dissuaded the burglar from venturing further into Banyon Investigations, Inc. The flashlight beam that I'd seen from the hallway was now slicing like a laser lightshow around my inner office.

The door was only partly open, and I approached it with as much panther-like stealth as the popping corn in my middle-aged joints allowed.

When I flung the door open and hit the light switch, the intruder was in the process of poking around the drawer wherein cowered the terrified bottle of booze I'd traversed the city to rescue. The figure jumped, but before the flashlight beam could swing in my direction I heard the crash of a bottle as it struck the floor.

The Asian lawyer dame whom I'd last caught skulking around inside the Tooth Fairy's bathroom nearly jumped out of her Prada pumps.

"Tell me, lady," I asked her, "why I shouldn't shoot you, since you have just destroyed my only reason for living?"

She looked down at the remains of the bottle I'd just seen her kill in the ugliest fashion imaginable, then through the door behind me where was partly visible the ruins of Mannix's impeccably ordered case files. She instantly fell back on her lawyer training.

"Everything was exactly like this when I got here, as far as you know, and the door was open, and I definitely didn't pick the lock, so somebody on your staff obviously neglected to lock it, which I took as an invitation to enter, and anyway this is a public business where you expect people to walk in, so it's not breaking and entering."

There was a considerable upside to shooting her. She would bring the total up to three dead lawyers in less than twenty-four hours, not to mention the six I'd just kicked the snot out of, who were now at home shoveling said

booted mucus under their pillows to await the arrival of the Tooth Fairy's less reputable sibling.

I was beginning to think I was responsible for all the wonderful ills befalling the local legal profession. However, shooting her would mean filling out miles of paperwork with the cops, and on top of that pain in the ass I didn't feel like traveling all the way to Washington for the medal that a grateful nation would doubtless demand be pinned to my chest for my role in reducing the nation's bloated legal ranks.

I reluctantly stuck my piece back in its holster.

The lawyer dame took the move as a victory for her Clarence Darrow-like rhetorical skills.

"Now, I am going to leave here, Mr. Banyon," she haughtily informed me. "And you won't be telling the police I was here. I have the advantage. "*I* know who *you* are, but *you* have no idea who I—"

"You're Attorney Sue Yu," I informed her, just in case she'd forgotten her own ridiculous name. "You work for the law firm of Crook, Shaft & Fleece, which is the second hilarious law firm name I've encountered tonight. You drive a red Volvo. In point of fact, the red Volvo that is parked out front, or at least which was parked out front a few minutes ago. It's likely that it's someone else's Volvo and is halfway to Peru by now. Your vanity plate is L-W-S-U-E-T. That actually spells 'law suet,' as in fat, rather than 'lawsuit,' as in your asshole profession's poisonous lifeblood, which is what I assume you were going for. You can either sue the motor vehicles department for that mistake, or the entire educational system — from kinder-garten to law school — for permitting you to pass ever higher up without informing you that you're a shit speller. I'm guessing by that sudden agitated look on your face that it's the latter. Since you apparently can't spell, that's

'L-A-T-T-E-R,' as in last, and not the one with two D's, which the ghost janitor in the lobby is currently not climbing in order to blitzkrieg the linoleum with a merciless light bulb barrage."

The dame shook her head. "How—"

I slapped onto my desk her business card, which gave her name and law firm, which I'd deftly lifted from her purse when I removed the letters that the mysterious queen had sent to the Tooth Fairy, and which Miss Sue Yu had stolen.

The dame seethed at my obviously genius-level resourcefulness.

"I suppose the only question now is how I found you," she began, smugly assured that she at least had one thing over me.

"Probably my fault for missing the bus," I volunteered. "Cab drivers are famous for being fundamentally dishonest, possibly nearly all terrorists, as well as reeking bastards who would only take a shower if they knew it belonged to somebody else. What they aren't known for is being paragons of discretion. You found out from the cabbie where I went after I left the Tooth Fairy's office. I was dead to the world at O'Hale's long enough tonight for you to sneak in and question Jaublowski. He's not smart enough not to blab. You could buy every last one of his brain cells with a nickel and still get enough change for the parking meter. Not to mention that I gave criminal dentist Myron Wasserbaum's name as my own. A hilarious joke at that moment, but which probably came back to bite me on the ass, since he's headquartered just down the hall."

As I spoke, the dame grew more and more angry at the fact that a mere mortal had been able to spring the back of the wristwatch and so easily figure out the complicated operation of the intricate gears and springs of her

fabulous lawyer mind.

"Get out from back there," I said, beckoning her out from behind my desk. "I have an elderly bottle of cheap champagne stuffed in the back of one of those drawers that I don't intend to open until the day I go out of business, and I don't need you christening the floor with my future hangover."

The dame looked like she was trying to figure out a way to sue me for squatter's rights to the space behind my desk as she reluctantly rounded over to my side.

"I probably won't call the cops and have you arrested," I said. "That's assuming you tell me exactly what you were looking for when you busted in here. Let me get you started. It has to do with this mysterious queen about whom you're about to tell me everything you know."

My superior smirk apparently made for an excellent target.

I had not taken into account (largely for fear of being carted away in manacles for Asian stereotyping) that this unassuming little Tokyo Rose with the dynamite body might conform to the hoariest type of stereo in the entire goddamn appliance store.

I suddenly saw a foot.

Now, of course, seeing feet was not in itself unusual. However, traditionally, one sees them where they belong, which is either on the floor or, more happily, dangling from a barstool. What was out of place about this particular dainty little clodhopper was that it was not on the floor, but was several feet in the air. What's more, it had gotten there in spectacularly blinding fashion. It was not sticking straight up in the air and harmless like Hanoi Jane's extended peg on the cover of a 1980s VHS exercise tape. No, this sinister, speeding appendage was rocketing at my sluggish, three a.m. melon like a hundred mile an hour fastball.

In the slow-motion moment before the stars exploded and night descended, I saw beyond the foot a calf so perfectly formed it would have won the blue ribbon at the county fair. I also saw the V slit in a black skirt, but just before I could spy anything really good, the dame's flying foot made martial arts mincemeat out of the side of my head.

The world snapped back into fast motion just long enough for me to feel the blast of excruciating pain in my temple, to watch a superlative Fourth of July fireworks finale, to see the shocked look on the face of the dame who apparently hadn't expected her assault against my head to be so enormously successful, and to realize that, all things considered, this still wasn't the worst goddamn day I'd ever had at work.

And then the lights flickered out and the floor wanted to have a word or two with me about concussions.

8

When I awoke the next day with a pounding in my head, there was a blissful moment in which I made the mistake of assuming I'd had a good time the previous evening. I did, after all, have a pounding in my head, and I distinctly remembered a smashed bottle, the emptying of which generally denoting great fun.

Then I remembered that the busted bottle had been nearly full at the time, which was beyond horrifying.

Then I recalled that it was a bottle I had paid for, which was a nightmare akin to being strapped to a Pompeii beach chair and forced to wait for Vesuvius to roll down a river of molten suntan lotion.

Finally, I remembered being mule kicked in the noggin by a little lawyer dame who mistook my forehead for a shoe tree for her size three pumps.

I released a slow groan that was entirely insufficient in expressing the extraordinary levels of unparalleled shit I felt.

"Are you all right, Mr. Crag?" a worried nearby voice asked.

I had not yet opened my eyes in the vain hope that if I kept them closed long enough someone would come along and shovel dirt over me.

I dragged up my eyelids to find Mannix sitting in a little chair next to the sofa on which somebody had dumped the body. My assistant's face was deeply concerned. He had the phone from my desk resting on his lap.

"I called Dr. Charlotte," the elf said. "Her office is going to call back."

I let loose another unintentional groan as I hauled my remains to a seated position.

"Tell her office that my office is fine," I said.

Mannix clearly didn't agree with my diagnosis.

"I wanted to call an ambulance very, *very* badly."

Mannix was under strict orders not to summon the paramedics unless parts of me that should be on the inside have somehow found their way outside, or vice versa.

"I'm fine, Mannix. I just had some little Mitsubishi pull an unexpected kamikaze on my forehead flight deck."

Something large slipped from my head and dropped to the couch beside me. I quite reasonably assumed it was a chunk of dislodged skull.

I hadn't even felt the ice pack my assistant had apparently settled on my head while I was passed out. The throbbing lump was large and painful enough that, were this Mount Olympus and not my shithole office, I'd expect it was at the end of its third trimester and was ready to give birth to a fully-formed adult goddess brat.

My office was in complete disarray. Mannix would ordinarily have set to work cleaning the mess — and have an extraordinarily and bizarrely enjoyable time doing so — but had evidently been more concerned about my well-being when he arrived at work that morning and found me dead on the floor.

My assistant noted my half-mast eyes surveying the damage.

"I *wanted* to call the police," the elf said.

Mannix was under even more strict orders to only call the police in the event that we were bored and needed a really good laugh.

"A million people have busted in here over the years, Mannix, and the only one who ever gets perp-walked out of here winds up being me. And this time it was a lawyer that did all this. Have you ever been one hundred percent right and gone up against a lawyer, Mannix? Being right is worth shit. Picture getting caught in their rigged system like getting the biggest, fattest, stickiest wad of Bazooka bubblegum stuck in your hair. Now picture having to pay a second wad of gum a small fortune to climb up in your hair to discuss for a decade what the goddamn weather is like up there. Shave my head, paint a bull's-eye on the back, and march me across the nearest shooting range if I'm ever stupid enough to think there's a chance in hell the system hasn't been designed with a crooked eye towards fattening the legal profession's bank account."

Mannix, the poor naïve bastard, seemed unconvinced of an assessment which, frankly, painted too rosy a picture of the corrupt mountain of congenital cowflaps that was the American legal system. I hoped for his Pollyanna sake that he never ran afoul of a two-bit lawyer with an ax to grind and time on his drunken hands. Decency was in short supply in the world — hell, it was virtually absent from my office — and I despised the thought of what the crooked system would do to an innocent elf like him.

Before Mannix could offer a futile counterargument from Planet Gullible, the phone in his lap rang with sufficient volume to detonate my brain.

I clutched a hand to my throbbing temple while Mannix, sussing the situation re the goddamn stroke the ringing phone was giving me, grabbed up the receiver and hustled back over to my desk. While my assistant spoke

in hushed tones to the office of my sexy doctor, I surveyed the surrounding damage.

Sue Yu's business card, which I'd slapped victoriously down on the corner of my desk, was gone, naturally. I supposed she didn't want to leave behind anything that linked her to my murder just in case my brain fell out while I was napping. Or maybe, like me, she was cheap and only carried around one business card.

Shit, I suddenly thought, my excremental attention immediately drawn closer to home.

After she'd kicked a field goal with my cranium, the dame had apparently moved on from searching my office to rummaging around me, apparently in the wholly mistaken belief that I wouldn't have permitted her to feel me up while I was awake.

The pockets of my trench coat were turned inside-out, and I saw that the few items she'd found inside, including my lone yellowed business card, were dumped out on the floor next to the couch. For the first time in days I was happy that Mannix had sent my collection of flasks to the cleaners, as lawyers are notorious alcoholics and Sue Yu could have completed her entire law firm's Christmas shopping with the customary contents of my wardrobe.

I reinserted my inside-out pockets and conducted a search through the one with the torn seam. Sue Yu, brilliant attorney-at-law and extraordinary high-kicker, hadn't discovered my top secret hiding place.

I dragged out the items I'd secreted deep in the lining of my coat and laid them out on the empty sofa cushion beside me. There was a total of eight pages of paperwork that I'd picked up from the sidewalk after my post-midnight legal assault, plus the envelope that contained the ominous note to the Tooth Fairy from the mysterious queen.

I picked up a random scrap of paper. Under the blazing

banner of the law offices of Swindle, Steele & Robb was page three of, according to the footer, forty-nine. The rest of the document had either remained in the busted-open briefcase or had been scooped up by the fleeing gaggle of lawyers, so I'd walked in while the movie was already in progress.

"…whereas, your clients have heretofore suggested wherein this aforementioned whatnot matter (see appendix XIIV) have howsoever failed to…"

It was, of course, utter gibberish written by and for individuals who were fluent in deliberately mystifying twaddle, and was crafted solely so that the eyes of non-bullshitters would glaze over in less than one nanosecond. My eyes were no exception, and were glazed over so quickly you could have served them for Easter dinner with mashed potatoes and corn. I put the paper down before it caused me to lapse back into a coma.

The boring legalese mumbo-jumbo had, paradoxically, seemingly jumpstarted one part of my brain, increasing the blood flow to my temple. The throbbing, softball-sized bump felt like the natives were using it as their ceremonial dinner drum.

"Dr. Charlotte wants to know if you know what the date is and who the governor is," Mannix called over from my desk.

"No," I replied. "The only thing I remember is that when you're caught out in a lightning storm you're supposed to lie down in a field. Most likely because you've been hit by lightning. Also, that trees excrete oxygen, so we're all basically breathing tree shit."

My physician had apparently heard my response, as Mannix's big eyes grew even wider, and he shook his head.

"I can't tell him *that*, Dr. Charlotte," Mannix said.

His little face blushed crimson, and he pressed the phone hard to his pointed ear in order that I might be spared the four-letter prescription being dictated by my physician. Mannix stretched the phone cord long, retreating to a corner.

I gathered up the papers from the couch and brought them over to my desk. Sue Yu had thoughtfully dumped most of the junk from the surface onto the floor, so I had plenty of room to spread out the eight pages, one beside the other.

I shook the three-by-five card from the envelope I'd liberated from the Tooth Fairy's office and set it down below the papers, close to the edge of the desk.

THE QUEEN IS NOT HAPPY

The note was less threatening than some of the ones Sue Yu had swiped from the Say Cheesy! headquarters, but that didn't make it any less creepy.

In the corner, Mannix was wrapping up his phone call.

"Thank you very much, Dr. Charlotte," the elf announced. "Yes, I'll tell him," he added reluctantly. "Thank you."

He brought the receiver back over to my desk to hang it up.

"Dr. Charlotte said if you're not going to the emergency room, you should at least take Tylenol for the pain," Mannix said.

"That's why God, in His infinite wisdom, made alcohol, Mannix," I replied, as I continued to peruse the lawyerly paperwork. "I can't question His divine plan."

The elf's voice grew deeply concerned.

"She also said that you shouldn't drink right now."

"I'll get a second opinion on that from Ed Jaublowski later on," I said. "For the time being, cruel fate has robbed

me of the option."

The crunch of busted glass beneath the soles of my Florsheims was a constant reminder that my office had suddenly become one of those appalling dry counties that still exist for some horrifying reason but have fallen so far off the radar that even the ghost of Burt Reynolds didn't speed through them any longer.

"Dr. Charlotte also said that if your head drops off, I should mail it to her," my assistant said, clearly reluctant to repeat my M.D.'s suggestion. "She made me swear I'd tell you that, even though I know she was being funny. She said some other things, but they were too naughty to repeat."

My head was throbbing, more now due to the fact that I was attempting to read through the papers that had dropped out of one of my lawyer attacker's briefcases. It was an effort to drag across each line. My eyeballs already wanted to commit suicide.

"Dr. Charlotte Cheese's remarkably filthy mouth is a credit to the medical profession," I said. "And she's right about one thing, Mannix. Run into the bathroom and grab me about a million Tylenols, assuming Doris hasn't emptied us out again."

It was clear from the look on his face that my faithful secretary had raided the office pharmacy in one of her brief incursions into work. She and that battleaxe mother of hers hadn't bought a single aspirin or Band-Aid in the past ten years. She'd have stolen the bathroom sink out of the wall if she could figure out how to hide a mile of dripping plumbing in her handbag.

Mannix volunteered to run to the corner store for my brain medication, and I settled into my chair to thoroughly read through every last word of the eight pages of legalistic crapola to see if there was any kind of connective tissue

between them, me, Sue Yu, the law firm of Swindle, Steele & Robb, said law firm's interest in the missing Tooth Fairy, and whether the papers might offer some clue as to his whereabouts.

It took a full twenty minutes to scrape my exhausted peepers across every last boring line. On several occasions I nearly needed to slam my hand in my desk drawer to keep from falling permanently asleep. In the end, there was nothing. No unifying thread between the papers themselves, nor anything that connected them to my current case. They looked to be normal legal documents. Written in Asshole, the language of lawyers, but not extraordinary in the slightest. There were a couple of contracts, four wills, some real estate claptrap, and a page of an incomprehensible estate settlement. That was it.

I picked up the note card that expressed the unhappiness of the unknown queen in bold print and tossed it across my desk, then leaned back in my chair.

As it stood right now, I had very little to go on.

Attorney Sue Yu of the firm Crook, Shaft & Fleece had an obvious interest in the Tooth Fairy, but what that interest was I had no clue, nor did I desire the kick in the head she might generously inflict on me were I to track her down to ask her.

Montague Swindle, Esquire, and the rest of the bastards from Swindle, Steele & Robb might know. That was a lead on which I could follow up if I became desperate. As it was, my philosophy of steering clear of lawyers if at all possible was still in effect. Despite the fact that their attack on me had been recorded by the camera outside Gold, Gold, Gold, there was still a chance that there were six personal injury lawsuits whizzing their frivolous way in my direction at that very moment. I'd avoid those SOBs unless absolutely necessary.

There was the Tooth Fairy's brother, the Snot Fairy. He had the animus, and even though he claimed he didn't want to take over his missing brother's job, I had dealt with enough jealous bastard siblings over the years to trust the strength of his word about as much I'd trust a wicker toilet at Melissa McCarthy's house.

I had done a great deal of thinking in a short period of time, and it had put a severe strain on my head lump.

I opened my eyes, girded my loins, steeled my pancreas, and sat up straight in order to more firmly give up on the legal papers on my desk and, quite possibly, this whole goddamn case. Let all of the Little Timmy Thompsons of the world stop sticking teeth under their pillows and start using said pillows to muffle their cries of despair like the rest of us.

My wandering P.I. eye fell across the paperwork on my desk.

I paused.

I blinked.

Whatever it was I saw was gone.

I blinked again.

It was very nearly there once more. Whatever it was, I couldn't quite see what it was, but I knew now that I had definitely seen something.

I played a few minutes of hide-and-seek, blinking, glancing, getting to my feet, walking around my desk, sneaking up and trying to catch by surprise whatever it was I thought I might have seen unhooking its brassiere in the upstairs window and flashing me a glimpse of paradise.

Q.

The letter jumped out at me once more, even though I wasn't aware that's what I'd seen the first time around. It was part of a word on one of the wills. The rest of the

word was blocked by the three-by-five card I'd tossed to my desk, which had landed at an angle across that particular legal document. The rest of the word looked like it might have been "equity." Why my eye was telling my throbbing brain that one letter in one word was so vitally important, I had no goddamn clue.

I was reaching for the card when my keen observer's eye noticed yet another something, purely by chance. I fully intended to get that lazy eye bloodshot and in drunken crossed conflict with its mate as soon as possible in order to punish it for not picking up on the second clue when I'd asked it to do its goddamn job a minute before.

My indolent eye had spotted the letter *U* on the line below the *Q*.

This second letter appeared at an angle underlined by the side of the card that I'd lifted from the Tooth Fairy's office.

E. Then another *E*.

The letters in the next two lines down, respectively, still at an angle.

Finally, on the fifth line down, an *N*.

It was buried in the body of the document. They appeared as random, angled letters on different lines. But together, they formed the word "queen." I was looking at a goddamn Sunday newspaper game page word search.

At the same angle, from upper left to lower right, the entire hidden phrase read:

"We love the queen."

Now that I knew what I was looking for, I checked the next sheet of paper.

This phrase was upside-down, and ran from lower left to upper right:

"We worship the queen."

I checked all six remaining papers. Some contained

repeats, but the remaining sheets all contained hidden phrases.

We love the queen.
We worship the queen.
We live to serve the queen.
We would die for the queen.

And, most ominous for my kid client's missing Tooth Fairy: *We will kill for the queen.*

None of these phrases had anything whatsoever to do with the documents in which they had been hidden. The white-hot pounding in my temple footrest had been reduced to a dull throb when I got to my feet and hustled into my outer office.

The place was still largely a mess, courtesy Attorney Sue Yu. Mannix had apparently not sat shiva next to me the entire morning, and had popped out to do a little tidying. I found the files I was looking for re-filed.

I'd dealt with the downstairs firm of Shyster, Pilfer & Fraud a dozen times throughout the years, as both client and victim. I hauled out one of the contracts I'd signed with the bastards from five years before.

I scanned down the first page until I found the first appearance of the letter Q, then followed it at whatever angle the nearest U on the next line took me.

We honor the queen.

Next page.

We live for the queen.

Following page.

We worship the queen.

A lawsuit the same asshole firm had brought against me on behalf of one of my ingrate clients three years ago contained the same hidden messages.

When Mannix popped the door open a few minutes later, I was sitting in a spare chair in his outer office con-

templating the great implications of my brilliant discovery.

"Please take care of yourself, Miss Beverly," Mannix was saying with deep concern as he backed into my offices.

While the door was briefly open, I could see from my unaccustomed vantage point that my assistant had been offering his sympathies to Wasserbaum the dentist's receptionist, who was standing in the hallway just outside my door. I spotted Madame Carpathia the dance instructor, and some other asshole in a business suit who rented space on the second floor loitering in my hallway, along with several uniformed cops. As Mannix shut the door, I spotted the same pair of interns from the office of the medical examiner who'd carted the bloated lawyer corpse from O'Hale's Bar the previous day. They were just making their way out of Wasserbaum's office at the far end of the hallway, hauling with them a sheet-draped gurney.

"I have the medicine, Mr. Crag," the elf said, offering me a rattling CVS bag.

The pounding in my skull had improved greatly since Mannix's departure, mainly due to the many troubling thoughts that were forcing the pain to find a home elsewhere.

"Hide the bottle somewhere Doris will never find it," I said. "If you can find a way to stash it under the esoteric concept of 'hard work,' she'll never locate it there." I aimed a chin at the closed door and the busy hallway beyond. "What's going on at Wasserbaum's?"

"It's very sad," Mannix said, shaking his head somberly. "A poor man died."

"Did Wasserbaum accidentally fill a patient's entire head with helium instead of nitrous oxide and float him out the window again?"

Mannix shook his head. "No, sir," the elf said. "Dr.

Myron has had a nice man helping him with his work the last few days. He was a very smart man. He told me so himself when I was riding up in the elevator with him the other day. Miss Beverly said he just died for no reason at all. It's very sad."

The court-appointed attorney who had been overseeing Wasserbaum's practice could be added to the list of lawyers that had keeled over in close proximity to me. That brought the total up to three dead lawyers in less than twenty-four hours.

"Is something wrong, Mr. Crag?" my worried elf assistant suddenly asked.

"Very much so, Mannix," I replied, nodding somberly. "Something or someone is killing off the lawyer population in town. They might, in fact, be out to murder them all. It has not, as far as I know, broken in the papers or on the TV news, and I am deeply, deeply concerned that the authorities will find out and stop whoever is behind it before they can succeed."

9

What do you call three dead lawyers? The fifty percent of the population that hasn't graduated law school would answer, naturally, "a good start," while the remaining fifty percent would run to court to file a defamation lawsuit against the first fifty percent, as well as the long-dead editors of *1001 Lawyer Jokes*, publication date June, 1952.

Until two days ago, that ancient lawyer gag was merely wishful thinking. However, I was suddenly up to my pretty little shoulder holster in room temperature attorneys. There was no denying that the good start was already history.

I had been willing to ignore the dead lawyer in the hall outside my apartment, and I was delighted to celebrate the death of the bloated bore at O'Hale's. But Dentist Myron Wasserbaum's court-appointed shadow was the third strike. Three was a big enough crowd that it was clear even to a skull as numb as mine that something big was going on.

Ordinarily I'd have sat back and let beautiful nature take its course. When the deer population gets too big, we wisely unleash an army of drunken fatsos in orange vests into our backyards to shoot things, some of which are deer. When forests become too attractive, we let them all burn down to teach pine trees to keep it in their pants.

Under different circumstances I'd have presumed Mother Nature was culling the lawyer herd, a long overdue restoration of balance between that flabby and overpopulated species and its prey: namely all the goddamn rest of us. However, given the fact that I'd been attacked by an, albeit comically ineffectual, band of lawyers the previous evening, and adding to that Attorney Sue Yu's persistent appearances that were becoming more numerous than Joey Bishop's guest spots on Carson's *Tonight Show*, and, finally, on top of everything else, the shocking discovery that perhaps every legal document in history contained a cryptic reference to an as yet unidentified "queen," I was inclined to think that lawyers somehow figured heavily in my current case.

What the legal profession had to do with the missing Tooth Fairy, I had no clue. Nor had I any interest in finding out, but for the fact that I would have to deal with recriminations from the truly horrible Thompson family and, worse, return the dough Robert Sherman Planck of Madison Insurance Equities had floated for them, if I didn't at least pretend to shag my ass around town in service to their case for a day or two.

The headquarters of the city's medical examiner were in the basement of Police Main Headquarters, Precinct #1.

If possible, I tried to make my visits to the M.E.'s office outside normal business hours. There is little (outside, that is, my own life) more depressing than the blasé bureaucratic nine-to-five hustle and bustle of a morgue in full swing. On one side of the front desk, families who've just had to identify the body of Aunt Bertha with the croquet hoop through her bowels are bawling their eyes out, while two feet away bored civil servants are grousing about stale Snickers in the vending machine. Human interaction is

ugly enough everywhere else it's thrust upon me, but a busy morgue comes closest to my wedding night for the discomfort, grief, and apathy, not to mention a bunch of sheet-draped strangers lying around on their backs patiently awaiting their turn.

However, I discovered when I stepped off the elevator that this day was markedly different from most normal weekdays. Although it was only eleven o'clock on a Tuesday morning, for some happy reason today the city morgue was like a morgue.

The lone dame at the front desk brightened at my approach, despite the fact that she knew me. A sign on her desk read "The Morgue the Merrier," suggesting that, for her, the constant presence of formaldehyde and death in the air supplied an insufficient quantity of bad taste.

"Banyon, how are you today?" she chirped, a reaction to my arrival so uncharacteristically pleasant that I glanced over my shoulder to make sure she wasn't the distraction while one of her pen-pusher pals in city government snuck up behind me and clobbered me over the head with a keyboard.

The hallway back to the elevators was devoid of human life.

I turned back to the dame at the desk.

"You're horrible and surly," I reminded her, concerned. "Did you forget?"

"Oh, you," she said, waving a playfully dismissive hand.

"Yes, me. You, however, not you. You, clearly someone else. Do you need me to call an ambulance? I won't, because I don't give a shit what happens to you, because you have been unremittingly awful to me at every encounter prior to this one, but I'd be delighted to know if you did need an ambulance and I didn't call one for you."

"You were a police officer before you became a private detective, weren't you?" she persisted, oblivious to my end of a conversation I had no interest in having, but which spider web I was apparently vacationing in as a fly nonetheless. "That's very interesting. I imagine there must be as many similarities as there are differences with those jobs."

I could see now the desperation in the smile she had plastered for too long across her straining cheeks. Her eyes were pleading for social interaction.

"There is one big similarity between being a cop and being a P.I. Both jobs are shit. Primarily due to the horrible people, such as your appalling self, you encounter. I'm here to see Doc Minto."

I'd called ahead. The city's chief medical examiner was expecting me.

As I passed the receptionist's desk, her hand lashed out cobra-like and latched onto my wrist.

"*Please, Banyon*," she said. "I've got nobody to talk to. I'm bored out of my gourd here. Everybody from the office they can round up is out on calls all over town. Normally, that'd be fine. With business so good, we'd have civilians lined up around the block to identify bodies. I could make them wait while I chatted on the phone with friends, pretended to file paperwork while I actually checked Facebook, disappeared for forty-five minutes when I told them I'd be back in one. You know, the fun stuff. But look—" She waved her hand to the empty waiting area and vacant hall beyond. "There's nobody coming in here these past couple of days. I'm going crazy out here all by myself."

"The last time I was in here you called me a two-bit gumshoe and said that I couldn't detect my ass in my pants if you kicked me a roadmap. I'm not saying that's inac-

curate, but think how you'd feel if I called you a callous clock-punching harridan whose only experience with hard work is furiously suckling on the public knocker?"

My own words sounded eerily familiar. With a snap of my fingers, I remembered where I'd heard them before.

"I mean if I said that to you again today," I P.S.'ed

Her tight smile had curled out to her earlobes, but as I spoke it slowly retracted back into her more customary scowl. She released my wrist.

"You're an asshole, Banyon."

"Welcome back," I said, warmly. "I'm sure your dumper and the chair it's been glued to for your past ten motionless years missed you."

Pleased that the dame had at last remembered the traditional nature of our relationship, I left her to glower in disquieting silence at her vacant waiting room as I headed up the hall at her back.

I got a sense that there was trouble when I noted the many occupied gurneys that lined the usually empty hall outside every closed door. The only time I figured I'd have a chance to rest my weary dogs was when I was dead, but with my luck today would be the day I bought it; while the city morgue was standing room only.

I pushed my way through the swinging door into the main exam room, and immediately bumped in the head somebody to whom I didn't need to apologize.

There were bodies, bodies everywhere. The exceptionally small number of cadavers that were thin enough were forced to share slabs with ex post facto roommates, back-to-back. The more corpulent corpses, of which there was no shortage, were piled high on slabs, counters, floor, and anywhere else they could be crammed in, on and, in the case of a pair of dangling bare feet in an ancient dumbwaiter, up.

Someone had raided every closet in the building and brought down every electric fan they could find. The appliances were plugged into outlets low and high, all around the room. The collective hum from the mismatched collection of running fans made the room sound like I was standing on the tarmac waving goodbye to Ingrid Bergman.

The only clear space in the room was a desk near the door, and it was at this work station, piled high with stacks of teetering paperwork, that I found Chief Medical Examiner Harry "Doc" Minto having a nervous breakdown.

Doc Minto was not just as old as the hills, he appeared to be substantially older than them. When the hills were still in first grade, Doc Minto had already graduated college and was reporting in person to Hippocrates for medical training.

The old codger wore a pair of flea-bitten wool pants with cuffs so frayed they could have deserted the French army. His vintage 1970s cardigan was an all-you-can-eat moth buffet, with so many holes it looked as if it had been lined up against a wall and shot. The few buttons that still clung to the sweater's front were as big as ashtrays, and dangled like spelunkers from threads thinner than a Milan runway model.

Doc Minto wore a pair of spectacularly thick glasses that made his hugely magnified eyes swimming around behind them look like a pair of startled Mafia fish hiding out from the Feds inside a couple of bulletproof aquariums.

The M.E. was dining on takeout. A Styrofoam tray from Pirate Pete's Fish 'n' Chips yawned open before him, and when I stepped into his parlor the old coot was shoveling coleslaw into his mayonnaise-smeared maw.

"No," the M.E. announced without looking up when I entered the room. He swirled slaw onto the white plastic

spork he was wielding like a surgeon's scalpel. "No more in here. Full up, full up. No more room. They're storing them up in the cafeteria now, in the fridge, between the stuffed peppers and the relish. If they're full now, try the delicatessen across the street. There. Off you go. Go, go."

He shoved the plastic silverware at his mouth hole and succeeded in flying nearly none of the coleslaw into the airplane hanger.

"Hi, doc," I said.

The aquariums looked up and the fish squinted hard at my mush. The light of recognition clicked on in his face, which was always an iffy proposition. A smile broke out in the Hellmann's goatee that he'd painted in Barbasol fashion around his wrinkled mouth.

"Crag, my boy," Doc Minto said. "Happy to see you. Happy to see anyone with a functioning pulmonary system these days. Sit. Here, sit down."

He generously motioned for me to have a seat beside him. The only available spot for me to rest my wary ass was the blubbery back of a face-down corpse, which Doc Minto patted warmly as if the deceased slob was a park bench.

"Thanks, doc, but the phrase 'over my dead body' leaps salmon-like to mind."

"No? Suit yourself. No other spot here for you to sit. I'm swamped these days, Crag. Absolutely swamped."

He whacked a teetering pile of paperwork with the back of his hand to illustrate just how busy he was. The leaning tower of papers promptly toppled over, splashing like a crashing wave across the stack of corpses lined up on the floor next to the desk.

Anybody else would have cursed an azure streak at accidentally dumping an entire day's work all over the floor. Doc Minto merely gave the fresh mess a look as if

he were passing somebody else's accident on the highway, shrugged, then turned back to me.

"Oh, Crag, my boy. Didn't see you come in," the senile old bastard said.

His brain was a dying bulb in an antique lamp, sparking intermittently and always on the verge of burning the whole house down.

"Doc, I wanted to ask you about three bodies that were brought in here since yesterday morning," I said.

"You'll have to be specific, Crag. I've had nearly a hundred since then."

To illustrate his point, he reached to pat the stack of papers he'd just launched to the floor, and when he discovered they were no longer on his desk for some reason unknown to him, he proved the statement by accidentally dumping another massive cascade of paperwork on a body that was propped up on the opposite side of his desk.

"Apologies, young fellow," he said down to the sheet-draped body, now further covered with dozens of 9x11 paper sheets.

"These three were lawyers, doc," I said.

The swimming fish eyeballs nearly burst from their twin tanks.

"They're *all* lawyers, Crag," he replied. "Every last man jack one of them."

He waved a shriveled hand to encompass the entire room, which was like the aftermath of some forgotten battlefield where the soldiers on both sides wore bed linen uniforms and attacked one another not with rifles or bayonets, but with cholesterol and eighteen martini lunches.

It now made sense why the dame out at the desk was not being overrun with loving family, despite the booming business going on behind the counter. The only people who'd expect a relative to give a shit about a dead lawyer

are people who've never had a live lawyer for a relative. All over the city were conga lines of delighted family members who would no longer have to listen to how they were mowing the lawn wrong, making the Thanksgiving gravy incorrectly, doing a lousy job in their chosen professions, and were otherwise terrible at absolutely every undertaking in their lives, and here's why.

"Exactly how many lawyers have you processed through here?" I asked.

"Ah. Oh. Let's see." The ancient M.E. consulted a computer printout that, by an amazing stroke of luck, he hadn't dumped on the floor. "In the past three weeks, we've rushed through three thousand, two hundred and seventy-eight dead lawyers. Including my own, that son of a bitch, may he rot in hell, etcetera." He ate a french fry.

In the previous three weeks I'd read the paper daily, caught a handful of local news broadcasts, and suffered nightly through Ed Jaublowski's grousing summary of the day's major news stories, which rundown always incentivized me to get drunk faster. At no point did any of my sources of information make known to me that this happiest of epidemics was sweeping like a unicorn rainbow buzz saw of murderous sunshiny pixie dust through the inebriated ranks of the city's most upstanding demimonde.

I was late to this party, but it was clear I wasn't the only one who didn't give a shit. If the authorities, the press, and the civilian population were even aware of the mass carnage, they were too busy hanging streamers, blowing up balloons, and renting bouncy houses to do anything about it.

"To what do we owe this great good fortune, doc?" I asked. "I need to know which god is responsible so I can

run right out and convert."

The old bastard's face in its normal state was already like a shriveled apple that had rolled to the back of the vegetable crisper and been lost for a decade. But at my question, Doc Minto's puss puckered so far in on itself that I thought I might have to continue my conversation with the back of his head.

"Come with me, Crag," he said.

He led me past piles of bodies and several slowly rotating fans, the purpose of which in an already freezing room I had yet to determine but which I had tentatively chalked up to the fact that my elderly friend was batshit crazy.

Doc Minto brought me over to one of the few areas in the room not piled as high as an elephant's scrotum with lawyer corpses. At the bottom of a sink at the back of the room was nestled a silver tray, on which sat a partially dissected brain.

"The lawyer brain is, for the most part, similar to the human brain," Doc Minto said, in suspiciously expository fashion. "With one major difference. Do you know what the right supramarginal gyrus is?"

I hadn't the inclination nor inspiration to crack wise, as my medical examiner pal had, for illustrative purposes, begun chasing remnants of the brain around the bottom of the sink with the mayonnaise-smeared spork he still clutched in his arthritic hand, and although I couldn't recall my last meal, I was reasonably certain I'd soon have a chance to identify its remains. Not to mention that I had caught the antediluvian M.E. in a reasonably lucid state, and every second of a delay brought us closer to the point where he'd put his shoes in the break room microwave and pull his sweater up over his head to take a nap.

"No, doc, I have no idea what the hell that thing you

just mentioned is," I replied.

The fish behind his aquarium lenses seemed disappointed.

"Oh. Oh, well. No harm. It's located here—" (He deployed his spork once more, joined this time by prying fingertips.) "—at the junction of the parietal, temporal, and frontal lobes. This, Crag, is the fountainhead of human empathy. Our ability to feel for our fellow man springs from this area of the brain. This is, in large part, what makes one a sociopath or not. It is an area, quite naturally, and with very rare exceptions, utterly dead in lawyers."

I was grateful that he dropped his spork in a trash can beneath the sink. He even scrubbed his hands with anti-bacterial soap. I wasn't sure if the brain's owner had a dirty mind in life but, if so, the dismembered gray matter in the sink below got a healthy shower of suds. The bath succeeded as well in washing at least some of that gray right out of the sink, as a few of the smaller chunks were swept off the tray and spiraled down the drain, where hopefully they'd succeed in giving the alligators who lived in the sewers a taste for lawyer brains, just in case any of the legal bastards survived this mysterious purge.

"All the bodies I've examined—" the M.E. began.

Here he was cut off by the sudden appearance of a head through the wall.

The bluish ghost who'd rudely interrupted our conversation ignored both me and the ancient medical examiner. He was craning his transparent neck to get a better look deeper into the room.

Doc Minto took the appearance of the ghost's head in stride. A revolving 1950s fan with a frayed cloth cord sat, naturally, in a puddle next to the sink. Doc picked up the electrocution hazard and aimed the caged blades square in the face of the unwanted ghost.

The ghost's eyes barely had time to shoot daggers at the M.E. before its head dissolved in the breeze. Doc Minto set the fan down in the same spot, but this time directed it at the area of the wall from which the ghost had appeared.

"Damn ghosts," Doc Minto complained. "Cropping up all over lately. Can hardly get a damn autopsy started without some damnable ghost popping up through a chest cavity."

I glanced back at the room. Suddenly, the thousand fans made sense. The incorporeal nature of ghosts makes many of them susceptible to a stiff breeze, especially the newer ones who haven't yet gotten the hang of their ethereal abilities. I could see now that Doc Minto had directed the fans in an ingenious fashion that covered virtually every square inch of wall, floor, and ceiling. In fact, as I watched, the same ghost from the sink emerged once again, this time down through the ceiling. He encountered an upwardly-aimed rotating fan and quickly broke apart.

"*Shiiiiiit,*" moaned the goddamn ghost from somewhere up beyond the humming florescent light.

"Are these their ghosts?" I asked, stabbing a thumb at the dead lawyers.

"Maybe," Doc Minto replied, peeved. "Doesn't happen as much as you'd think, but ghosts do show up at their own autopsies now and again. Very awkward when it happens. No one knows where to look. Anyway, I've got enough work to do identifying the corporeal, Crag, without worrying myself over what ghost goes with which body. Do you want to know what I've found out about these damn corpses, or not? Because I've got a…thing that I have to…lunch…over there…"

He evidently thought he was waving his spork in the direction of his coleslaw, and was surprised to find his

hand empty.

The clock in his brain was winding down.

"Empathy, Doc," I said, directing him back to the subject at hand that wasn't plastic fast food cutlery.

"Empathy?" He frowned. He turned said frown on its head. "Oh. Ah. Yes. Empathy. The lawyers. Well, they suddenly somehow got it. All at once. Something kicked the dormant right supramarginal gyrus into full power all at one time. Overinflated the tire and blew it out." He slapped his weathered palms together with a surprisingly powerful crack. "Just like that. An entire lifetime of empathy exploded in their brains at once. Being lawyers, they couldn't take the overload. Dropped dead."

It was astounding to imagine that a lawyer could not only have empathy, but that it could be present in sufficient quantity amongst all of their ranks that, scraped together, it could make a single one of them give a shit about anything beyond the tip of his own rum-blossomed conk. That the very thing they lacked most was the very thing slaughtering all of them was almost enough to make me feel bad for them. However, since they were lawyers, I still didn't give one shit beyond how it might relate to me.

"What would cause that to happen, doc?" I asked.

"Ah," he said, raising an index finger so crooked it could have run for public office. "That's the question. Damned if I know the answer."

He shrugged his bony shoulders and shuffled back over to his desk where, after battling past the piles of paperwork he'd pitched on the floor, he dropped back into his seat. He patted his pockets in search of the spork he'd tossed in the trash, but coming up empty he fished around in his trousers, producing a MasterCard from his wallet, the side of which he began using to hack apart his Pirate Pete's deep-fried fish.

As the old buzzard medical examiner resumed shoving his lunch between his wrinkled prune lips, I took a walking tour of the perimeter of the room.

Most of the faces of the dead I didn't recognize. However, I did note a couple that had been screaming at me from my TV for years to enlist their law firms for assistance if I or someone I loved ever had a doctor try to help me or a pill try to cure me, that I might sue the shit out of same. I was certain that they had already been replaced on-air by a fresh wave of ravenous law school graduates, stabbing their lawyer fingers into the eyes of viewers, repeatedly shouting "deserve" at the undeserving, flashing a rapid-fire scrolling list of easy-money frivolous lawsuits that covered every inch of human existence, and promising huge cash settlements, only the major amount of which would find its way into their law firm coffers. The dignity of the legal profession hadn't been reduced when its sleazy practitioners had finally been allowed to advertise on TV alongside Tampax and Lucky Charms, its nonexistence had merely been revealed.

I was momentarily surprised to see two of the bastards who'd assaulted me down the street from O'Hale's Bar the previous night. Asshole One with the busted thumb and Stupid Bastard Two with the cracked jaw were piled up near some supply cupboards.

I assumed their injuries sustained prior to death wouldn't be linked back to me, since the dumb bastards had busted their own bones, so at least I was off the hook there.

I noticed a strong odor coming from the SOB with the broken jaw. I leaned in close and took a careful whiff.

"Doc, something's making those supraorbital gyroscopes go nuts," I called over to the lunching M.E.

"What?" Doc Minto asked, withdrawing his credit

card from his vending machine mouth. "Oh, hello, Crag. Supramarginal gyrus? Well, yes. I haven't yet been able to determine what's causing it to overload."

I didn't need a medical degree to have a strong suspicion.

After he'd jumped into the careening clown car with the rest of the lawyer street gang, Stupid Bastard Two had apparently attempted to self-medicate away the pain. However, with a busted jaw it was difficult to ingest his medicine of choice. Much of it had spilled over his face and run down his chin and neck, there to begin deliciously embalming the undeserving son of a bitch.

I thought of the leaking flask next to the dead lawyer in the hallway outside my apartment the prior morning, as well as the last moments of the royal bore at O'Hale's Bar just before he'd pitched over backwards and put us all out of his misery.

"It's booze, doc," I announced.

"It's on my list," Doc Minto replied. He sucked some ketchup off the end of a french fry and brought the soggy tip back to the puddle of Heinz for a second dip. "It'll be a bear to confirm if that's the case."

I knew what he meant. The bar exam was the last bar most lawyers passed. But I'd seen firsthand one lawyer croak after tossing back a belt of Jaublowski's drain cleaner, and the sweating bastard pounding on the apartment of the ghost next door had dropped dead with a flask in his mitt. The stink of cheap hooch coming off the stiff with the busted jaw at least suggested a pattern.

One thing was certain. If there was something in the city's alcohol supply that was killing lawyers, the already long list of benefits of that most magnificent of liquids would have to make room for a new number one.

"Let me know if you find anything, doc," I said.

My old pal's massively thick glasses didn't turn my way, but he did salute me with a french fry, accidentally bisecting his forehead with a ketchup stripe.

I was heading for the door when a fresh blue head shoved its way through the wall over Doc Minto's desk. The transparent eyes were hopeful as the specter attempted to take rapid inventory of the bodies lying all over the autopsy room.

"Dammit, can't a man eat in peace?" the M.E. groused. He snatched up a manila folder and began maniacally fanning the ghost away.

The spirit's eyes were the last item to break apart into a vanishing soft blue cloud. They had continued to desperately scan the room, but when the ghostly eyes locked on my corporeal peepers, the spirit's swiveling head stopped deader. They barely had time to grow wide with shock when Doc Minto swept his folder angrily through them and they, along with the rest of the incorporeal head, disappeared.

The ghost was gone, but definitely not forgotten, for I heard a forlorn voice carry back through the wall, like air trying to force its way up through ancient, rusted pipes.

"*Oh, shit. Baaaanyon,*" the ghost of my late neighbor, Mr. Archibald Jessup, faintly groaned from the Great Beyond, which this day was the other side of the cheap plastic morgue walls that could be easily hosed down if an autopsy got too fun.

I hustled out into the hallway in time to see the late Archibald Jessup running the hell up the corridor, puffs of ghostly fog trailing in his wake. His legs were pumping like mad, even though he was a foot off the floor, and he was huffing so hard his invisible lungs were launching locomotive steam into the air.

"*Oh, dear. Oh, dear. Oh, dear,*" the pathetic and,

frankly, shit-of-a-ghost was moaning as he hightailed it up the gurney-lined corridor.

Clearly encountering me had startled him so much that the recently deceased dumbass had forgotten entirely that he was a ghost, with all the spectral benefits that come along with being dead. Like, for instance, walking through goddamn walls.

I actually had a chance of catching up with him, and I took off at a sprint, hoping to head him off before the moron realized his finger was sticking straight through the elevator buttons.

"Hey!" snapped the helpful receptionist dame as my ghost neighbor furiously floated past her desk. "I've told you a hundred times these past three weeks, you ghosts aren't supposed to be here. I'm warning you, I'm gonna call the exorcist van if you don't stop materializing down here."

And, just like that, reality sank in.

The old ghost gave one more glance over his shoulder, then banked right and disappeared straight through a solid concrete basement wall.

The dame glanced at me as I puffed my way to a stop next to her desk. She had a game of solitaire spread out before her, and was in the process of carefully scrutinizing every card in the deck in order to select which random one would come next.

"*You're* as welcome as *they* are down here, Banyon," she snarled.

I considered shooting her. I'd gotten my gat through the sieve-like security upstairs, and I was reasonably certain it was loaded. On the other hand, her murder was probably just the sort of action she so desperately craved down in what apparently was very nearly literally becoming a ghost town.

Instead of violence, I opted for a kind word.

Actually, two words.

Actually, two words which were not particularly kind, especially when placed side by side.

Also, I threw in an accompanying hand gesture, free of charge.

On my pensive journey back to the elevator, I dodged a coffee mug hurled at the back of my head, as well as a dozen charged epithets which, frankly, might have played a role in why the colicky receptionist dame was having such a hard time making friends with anybody other than ghosts lately.

10

The first place on earth I enjoy visiting the least is the headquarters of Banyon Investigations, Inc. A close second would be my apartment, which is nearly equally depressing but has the single benefit of having a bed I'm not likely to be thrown out of at the crack of dawn when daylight rings in an inevitable case of buyer's remorse. (Settling firmly in the antepenultimate spot was the entire rest of the world, but I was stuck with that until I could flag down a friendly passing comet of sufficient size and ruthlessness).

Fortunately I didn't have to return to my office at the moment. Unfortunately, I now had a reason to go home. However, the late Mr. Archibald Jessup was evidently one of the worst ghosts in recently deceased human history, and instead of accessing the ethereal plain to whisk him back to his apartment, he was likely standing on a street corner — virtually if not actually invisible in broad daylight — attempting to flag down a taxi that wouldn't have stopped even if the cabbie could see him. While more experienced ghosts can figure out how to manipulate objects, including cash for tips, most of them only carry around whatever was in their wallets when they punted the pail. And since ghostly dough dissolves on contact

and returns to the deceased's equally ghostly wallet, no hack in his right mind stops for a cheapskate ghost.

There is a ghost bus, but it only runs after midnight and it smells like ghost piss.

It was likely that idiot ghost Archibald Jessup would eventually decide to float all the way back to his apartment, which in the current light breeze could take hours. In the meantime, I was as goddamn lucky as Lou Gehrig that I had something else to keep me busy.

From a pay phone outside the police station, I stabbed out the first number on my emergency contact list.

"O'Hale's Bar," the deeply suspicious voice of Ed Jaublowski asked.

I didn't blame the barkeep for mistrusting the phone. In all the years I'd spent slumped over a dirty glass in his grimy dump, I couldn't recall the last time the phone at the end of the bar had rung. Even telemarketers found it too depressing to call O'Hale's, and had put the ratty watering hole on their reverse do-not-call list after several aluminum siding salesmen who'd spent ten minutes talking to Ed Jaublowski had climbed up to the roof and taken a parking lot swan dive.

Jaublowski probably came this close to having a heart attack when the phone rang, Ed having assumed that his busted fire alarm had somehow returned miraculously to life to warn his broken radon detector that the missing batteries from the smoke detector that had been relocated to the bar's TV remote control had gone dead.

"Ed, it's me. What brand of hooch were you pouring down that lawyer yesterday? The dead one with the mildly amusing name 'Albert Shyster.'"

Jaublowski's tone grew instantly cagey.

"The cops didn't care, why should you, Jinx?" the barkeep asked.

Obviously Jaublowski had given some overnight thought to the death of his only other customer from the previous day. Attorney Shyster had keeled over immediately after taking a hit from an O'Hale's Bar glass. Although it was likely that it was the same grubby glass that Jaublowski had filled with the same booze all afternoon, for liability purposes the barkeep wasn't taking any chances.

"Ed, tell me what it was or I'll remind the health department that your establishment does, in fact, still exist, and that you're still operating under the certificate they issued you fifteen years ago, before that clerical error erased you from their system."

"Geez, you know about that?" Jaublowski asked.

"Ed, I've watched you at least six times over the years down at the end of the bar furiously erasing the date from that thing and scribbling a new one in before you've hung it back up again. It's not even the original paper in that spot any longer. You wore it through so much that you've currently got the flap off a Heineken box jammed in there."

Jaublowski the master forger was clearly disappointed that his greatest triumph had been uncovered.

"It came from My Grain Distillery," he grunted.

I was more of an expert on Jaublowski's suppliers than the bartender himself, since over the years I had ordered several items without his knowledge and billed them to O'Hale's. Not once had I ever seen a product from that particular business cross the mildewed threshold of my favorite miserable establishment.

Before I could pose the question, Jaublowski's flapping tongue took flight.

"They sent a complimentary case about three weeks ago. I ain't had cause to bust it open till yesterday. That's why I thought maybe something might be wrong with the hooch, what with that lawyer goin' ass over teakettle after

drinkin' it. But youse is okay, Jinx, so it must not be the booze what done him in. I talked to Stan Linette. You know, over at Stan's Tavern? Stan says My Grain sent a case to him, too, only Stan says they also sent some to every other bar around town, too. Stan told me some of the others got more than one free case 'cause they do bigger business than him and me. My Grain got kinda lost once they got bought up by Bandito-Pharmaceutical. They must be tryin' to boost their profile or somethin'. Maybe that's why all the freebies. They's keepin' the promotion quiet, 'cause I ain't heard of it nowhere else but from Stan."

The worst thing one can ever do is engage Ed Jaublowski in conversation, since there was always the risk — as was the case now — that he might take you up on the offer. When he stopped long enough to suck in a breath, I charged unto the breach.

"Park your tongue, Ed," I said. "That breathless monologue was surprisingly salutary, considering how uninteresting and uninformative your blather generally is. Quit while you're ahead. Also, thanks very much for not telling me about any suspicions you had about that particular booze yesterday, after the lawyer croaked. If you were pouring from the same bottle for me, I certainly wouldn't have wanted to have time to run to the emergency room and get my stomach pumped or anything."

"Sorry, Jinx," Jaublowski said, sheepishly insincere.

"Forget it, Ed. It's not like you're not already poisoning me a little bit every time I sling my ass onto one of your stools. It just usually works more slowly than the toxin you dumped down that lawyer yesterday."

"Toxin? That's like poison, right? You really think that's what done him in?"

"It is my strong suspicion," I replied.

"Then why ain't you dead, too?"

"I demand the universe answer that same question every morning when I open my eyes. As yet, however, the universe's lips are sealed. In the meantime, package up a bottle from that crate and ship it over to Doctor Harry Minto at the city morgue."

I made him repeat the name back to me, and after guiding him through a half-dozen mispronunciations and misspellings, the moron bartender finally got it close enough to right that Larry Minstrel in Cincinnati was reasonably unlikely to be receiving a gift from an asshole bartender who couldn't take dictation if his goddamn miserable life depended on it. I told Jaublowski to include a note saying the hooch was from me, and that it was in relation to what Doc Minto and I had discussed that morning. With luck, the senile M.E. would remember enough about my visit to test the liquor.

"Get FedEx to pick it up and bring it over right away," I instructed. "Don't wait, Ed. If I find out you didn't do it, or that you cheaped out and brought it to the post office, I'll be on the blower with the health department faster than your indigenous rats can run. Remember that army of rats that chased that barfly out into traffic last month when she tried to use the ladies' room where they've apparently been plotting their takeover of O'Hale's? That's how fast I'll make the call, Ed. So no screwing around."

It was necessary with Ed Jaublowski to hammer the point home. Ideally this was done with an actual hammer, but he was there and I was here, and so I had to rely on a threat to do a job far more suited to a ball-peen.

"Who's paying for all this?" Jaublowski asked.

"If it makes you feel better, we can pretend I am."

Since I had been pretending for years that I was going to one day pay down my enormous bar tab, the lie satisfied

the guy most used to being lied to by me.

"I can't believe you was gonna blackmail me, Jinx," the barkeep said.

"I can't believe you don't realize I already did," I replied. "So when you think about it, Ed, we're both victims here. Get that bottle shipped to Doc Minto, stat."

I hung up in his hairy ear before he could talk at me again.

I would have preferred to take a bus, however, time, like everything else, was not my friend.

It already had not been lost on me that lawyers had started dying at pretty much exactly the same time as Little Timmy Thompson, my horrible junior client, stopped getting visits from the missing Tooth Fairy. And now that same three-week timeframe lined up perfectly with free cases of booze from My Grain Distillery suddenly being shipped to saloons all over town. Toss in my attempted kidnapping by a mob of lawyers, two of which were now resting in peace at Doc Minto's body shop. A to B to C, likely to me eventually in a box sawing an eternal parade of Zs if I didn't sort out the rest of this goddamn alphabet soup.

I waved my arm at the passing parade of cars, and a single yellow cab broke away from the herd, squealing to a stop at my toes. I hopped in the back.

"My Grain Distillery," I commanded from the cramped and dirty rear seat. "If you can keep your lip buttoned the entire trip, there might be a tip in it for you. Although, frankly, I wouldn't hold my breath. You, on the other hand, are welcome to hold yours as long as humanly possible, since I can smell your skunk's ass breath from here. If you can hold it all the way to our destination without passing out, I'll double the tip I'm not going to give you."

I got the distinct impression by the flash of greed in

the rearview mirror that the only words his selective hearing zeroed in on were "tip," "double," and "tip" again.

The cab screeched away from the curb, plastering me to the back seat with the force of a space shuttle launch. The taxi somehow avoided a half-dozen certain collisions before merging once more with the flow of traffic.

I was not sure if this would lead me to the Tooth Fairy. I thought once more of my lawyer attackers, who seemed to think I might have information on tracking him down. It was unlikely they were working for whoever was wiping out lawyers, especially since two of them had bought it since my attempted abduction, which left as their possible boss another player not yet visible on the field. All of those roads seemed to lead to the mysterious queen.

I at least needed to find who was behind whatever the hell was going on before they snuck up behind me and planted a bullet in the back of my head. I quite possibly wanted to shake their hand before they murdered me since they were, after all, killing lawyers, which remained a proposition I was finding it difficult to be entirely against.

Up in the front seat of my hurtling cab, my driver had kept his mouth screwed shut for nearly twenty whole seconds. It was quite possibly the world record for his profession, and the lid could be kept on Old Faithful no longer.

"Ghosts!" the hack exploded, shaking his head. Freshly dislodged clumps of amazingly enormous dandruff thudded to his shoulders. "You ever gotta deal with ghosts, mister? My advice? Don't. Me, I get stuck in traffic two blocks back. While I's parked there, this ghost floats straight through the door and sits down right where you is sitting. Wouldn't leave when I told him get out. I hadda turn this on him." On the other side of the cage that separated us, he presented a hair dryer, which he had ingenuously

plugged into the cigarette lighter port. "Only way to deal with them ghosts," he said, holstering his Conair sidearm. "Shitty tippers, every last one of 'em."

For some reason he was under the mistaken impression that I would be more generous with a gratuity than the dead. He couldn't have been more wrong, particularly considering it had taken him less than half-a-minute to open his fat trap.

I gave him my dump apartment building's address and asked if that was where the ghost had been heading.

"Yeah," he said, surprised. "You know him?"

"Will you be terribly offended if I ask you to mind your own business and shut the hell up?" I asked. "Because it's very likely that I'll be saying something along those lines quite soon, and if you're the kind of loquacious, bad-breathed asshole who's easily offended, you might want to pull over and plug your fingers in your ears."

At least I knew that the late Mr. Archibald Jessup was heading home. If I wasn't dead myself in a few hours — quite possibly at the furry-knuckled hands of the hack in the cab's front seat, who was, for some reason, suddenly shooting me a murderous glare in the rearview mirror instead of watching the road — I could question my late next door neighbor when I got back to my apartment.

I allowed the massive G-forces to gently settle me back amongst the viciously jagged springs of the taxi's rear seat and wondered what the hell I was going to do once I got to the other side of town.

11

For an unapologetic inebriate, a trip to a distillery should have been as thrilling as a creepy nerd freak being invited over to Mr. Spock's house for high goddamn space tea. However, far from being a twenty-four hour drunken fraternity soiree, with vomit in every pot and urine in every driveway, the modern distillery that My Grain Distillery operated was a godless, sanitary affair of bleak Kubrickian design. Everything delightful that might have escaped into the neighborhood air was evidently filtered and corked into oblivion, and I noted when I climbed out of my cab that what should have been a deliciously debauched breeze instead stunk unwholesomely of fresh air and lilacs.

My driver hadn't gotten the message, and had, after only ten seconds of wanting to kill me, yapped nonstop on the trip across town. I, therefore, felt entirely justified not paying him the tip I'd already promised to withhold, and he, consequently, felt justified nearly driving over my foot when he peeled away from the curb in front of the distillery.

The billboard attached to the fence out front read:

My Grain Distillery
A Division of Bandito-Pharmaceutical

Before it had acquired its pharmaceutical division, Bandito had already been a powerhouse in the shit food industry. Their corn chips offered an inedible alternative to both chips and corn, and was a product so enjoyed by children that the wives of some politicians had banded together to get them banned from school cafeterias, since the mission of political wives is to fart in the elevator of everybody else's good time.

Pasted at the bottom of the billboard were the logos of a half-dozen famous companies, mostly chain restaurants, that were part of the Bandito-Pharma conglomerate, including the skull-and-crossbones pirate hat of Pirate Pete's Fish 'n' Chips, the burrito-shitting burro of Tuco's Tacos, the grinning child cowboy of Some-Kind-of-Meat-in-a-Bun, and the two brawling Irishmen, Mickey & Mikey, of O'Drunkegan's Pubs.

The pharmaceutical division of Bandito-Pharmaceutical specialized mainly in palliative pills that pretended to address all the lucrative ailments the other branches of their corporation inflicted on the drunken, corpulent, impotent, arrhythmic patrons of their many fine dining establishments.

My Grain offered hourly tours of their facility, and as luck would have it a group of old bats from a local senility center was being power-loaded to the pavement from a private bus just outside the gate. The youngest member of the group had a good three hundred million years on me, so it was more than a slight kick to my ego's crotch that I went so easily unobserved when I fell in amongst the walkers and canes.

Our group shuffled through the gleaming glass front doors of the distillery, and we were directed to a table behind which sat a grinning dame with teeth so bleached you could have dried your hands on them. Her phony

tour-guide cheerfulness was exhausting, and my opinion of the Greatest Generation diminished considerably when it became clear that nobody was going to beat her to death with a cane.

The dame took names, then issued stickers for the old coots to tape to their sweaters. When it was my turn, I offered the first name that came to mind.

"Attorney Albert Shyster, Esquire."

The dame's phosphorescent smile wavered ever-so-slightly.

"Oh, you're a lawyer?" she said. "What kind of law do you practice?"

"The kind that scrupulously and immorally looks for opportunities to abuse the spirit of the law in order to profit off a bloated, sclerotic, and fundamentally corrupt system. So just the regular kind of law."

She took special care in filling out my name tag, and I could feel cataracts forming when she offered me a supernova smile.

"Here you are, Attorney Shyster. Enjoy the tour."

I don't want to know anything about what alcohol allegedly was before it finds its way into a bottle. For one thing, I don't subscribe to the ludicrous idea that booze was once amber waves of grain poking up through a pile of cow shit that some stump-toothed farmer dumped out in a field. I much prefer to imagine that the sterilized bottles are placed empty on Heaven's windowsill by liquor angels, and that the eventual contents are the miraculous combination of morning dew, sunshine, and holy Christian magic.

In order to maintain my purity, I paid little attention to the squat, fat tour guide who met the group I had ingeniously infiltrated. He wore a dark blue shirt with the sleeves rolled up, and matching dark blue trousers. If he

didn't know he resembled a mailbox with a Caesar's laurel fringe of absurdly uncombed white hair, I intended to let him know in the satisfaction survey at the end of the tour.

Due to the advanced decrepitude of my slowly shuffling tour group, I suspected that before we broke for lunch we were going to witness firsthand the growth to maturity and harvest of the dirty little seeds that would eventually become magnificent alcohol.

The slow motion shambling eventually became too much for my restless legs to stand. I was grateful when an overly curious old bag lost her dentures, glasses, a dozen prescription bottles, and some cheap TV jewelry from the Joan Rivers collection in a vat of mash. The entire production facility squealed on the brakes, and while our mailbox tour guide's attention was diverted, I ducked up an empty corridor.

It happened the hallway I found myself in was labeled "Research & Development.." It seemed as logical a place as any to find out with what My Grain was spiking its hooch, not to mention that my curious liver could discover the alcoholic innovations that future me would one day pour over it to get it to dissolve once and for all.

My Grain still tested their products on animals, a practice I found to be monstrously unfair to those of us humans who would have eagerly signed every waiver under the sun to switch places with their blotto rodents. No sooner had I thought of the word "waiver" than I remembered that every page of such a document would doubtless contain some hidden sign of the preparer's loyalty to his or her mysterious queen.

I set off no alarms that I could hear as I wandered past windowed laboratories in which monkeys and pigs were having a far better time than me.

Men and women in white lab coats didn't care how

racist their lab coats were.

A set of double doors at the end of the hall made an attempt to halt intruders with a "TOP SECRET RESEARCH" sign.

I decided that if they truly wanted their secrets to remain so, they would have made it more difficult for somebody impersonating a dead lawyer who had infiltrated an old folks' home tour group to wander through those doors. The ease with which the doors swung open with a light shove demonstrated to my satisfaction that they clearly wanted me to see what the hell they were up to on the other side.

The cheery light of the previous stretch of corridor was replaced by a more ominous gloom, which murkiness was always an admission of something sinister. It was, I noted as I continued up the hall, the preferred bedroom lighting of my ex-wife, but I doubted in this case that the distillery was using their reduced electricity output to hide a naked Portuguese army squadron in strategic locations around the room.

As in the section of hallway back beyond the double doors, there were large windows open onto each lab I passed. However, in this case the blinds were drawn tight on whatever activities were taking place inside. Only in the very last window at the far end of the hall had someone not made sure all the slats on the blinds were shut tight.

I jammed my eye up to the gap in the blinds in Norman Bates fashion, hoping like hell that I wasn't pulling a peeping asshole number on a couple of lab swine in the middle of reenacting Roseanne Barr and Tom Arnold's wedding night.

I got a good look at a sixty-something scientist wearing a white lab coat over a brown tweed jacket. He had an overly kind face of the sort that always makes anybody

in their right mind assume ax murderer. He had pudgy, rosy cheeks, a mouth that always seemed on the verge of breaking into a grin, warm and happy eyes, and a button nose so adorable it looked like he'd mugged it off a snowman. His protruding belly was so jolly I could have built a holiday poem around it, or at the very least poked at it until he giggled like a girl and ran off to bake some crescent rolls.

Less visible than the cheerful little scientist was the glowing blue ghost he was talking to.

My first thought was of my dead neighbor, the late Mr. Archibald Jessup, last scene running like hell from the city morgue. Indeed, given the possibly unreliable report from my angry cab driver, I didn't dismiss the deceased old codger as the suspected ghost. I couldn't see the specter very well at all, since it was standing behind a column, not to mention my bloodshot eyeball glued sideways to an Anderson picture window wasn't exactly in the best position to offer a positive identification.

The cherubic scientist was nodding and biting his lip nervously as he listened to whatever it was the ghost was moaning.

All I could make out through the window was what might have been a voice, but which could have been a piece of malfunctioning lab equipment. It was a sort of protracted "yaaaaargh," and I made the great mistake of straining so hard to try to hear it and everything else that I had no chance of properly hearing on the other side of the glass that I didn't pick up on the scuff of a shoe two inches behind me until it was too late.

Because I was apparently dealing with a scientist assailant, my attacker didn't have the decency to club me on the head or jam a chloroform-soaked rag over my mouth. Simultaneous with the scuffing foot, I felt a needle

jab like a vicious wasp in the back of my neck. My head instinctively snapped forward and my forehead rapped a cheery hello on the windowpane hard enough to rattle the glass in its frame, and loud enough to alert the bastards inside the room to my presence.

The chubby scientist's benign face snapped in my direction.

Of the tubby bastard's companion, I momentarily caught slightly more than just that vague blue, neon-sign nimbus that ghosts project. From behind the column appeared a single glowing arm with what appeared to be a poofy, dangling sleeve adorned with a monstrous, pale white buckle.

Whatever the SOBs of My Grain were up to in their labs was suddenly of secondary concern, after my primary concern for my ass, the immediate rescue of which had jumped the line to become the most pressing item on the morning's agenda.

The needle was in and out of my neck in a second, and in the precise moment my forehead was slamming against the glass, I sent an elbow back, hard.

I might have missed my assailant entirely. As a general rule I'm lucky to hit the floor after a particularly productive session at O'Hale's Bar, and I only manage that on most nights thanks to gravity. If it were solely up to me, I'd likely wake up most mornings with my back pressed firmly against the ceiling, a satellite, a star, or the underside of a 747 bound for Pittsburgh. Lucky for me, I didn't dislocate my shoulder, since instead of striking empty air I felt a satisfying crunch of bone, and heard the even more satisfying howl of pain from the bastard who'd jabbed me.

Something fell at my feet. I recognized it as a syringe, but it looked very far away, as if I were viewing it through

the wrong end of a telescope.

I jumped on the needle.

A hand was already there.

I took inventory of my own hands. Both were accounted for at the ends of my wrists. For the hell of it, I made a fist with one of them.

I sent a roundhouse into the jaw of the bastard whose hand was fighting my own for possession of the syringe.

The goddamn nerd in the red-streaked white lab coat who'd pulled a Pearl Harbor on the back of my neck flew back onto his ass on the floor. Blood poured from the nose I'd busted, and I hoped that Miss Sally Ginerva with the enormously distracting rack would stick a gold star on his forehead as a reward for a job well done.

I suddenly realized that Miss Ginerva had been my second-grade teacher, that her knobs were probably a hundred years old and migrating to the South Pole by now, and that whatever the bastard on the floor had dosed me with was having a crocodile laser light show in Marilyn Monroe's diet chamber.

I realized that didn't make a lick of goddamn sense, and rather than attempt to figure out my own rambling, psychedelic hippie thoughts, I jabbed the bastard in the gut with the needle I'd retrieved from the floor, emptied what was left in the syringe that the son of a bitch hadn't unloaded in my neck, took a moment to revel in the look of horror and pain on his snotty red puss, and then passed out with a final hope that I wouldn't awaken until my flight landed in Pennsylvania.

12

Waking up is, for me, generally an iffy proposition, but for the past few days it was proving to be a greater minefield of exploding excrement Claymores than usual.

When I awoke after being stabbed in the neck by some maniac nerd armed with a syringe and a jihadi bloodlust for anybody who didn't have to inflate their prom date, I was as careful to keep my eyes shut as tight as I had been the previous day at home. In the earlier case I was afraid a troublesome, non-inflatable date might ask me to cook an egg or, worse, marry. In this case, I was just plain scared shitless.

I heard no voices. In point of fact, I heard nothing other than the sound of my own heart pounding a red alert on the inside of my loosening ribcage.

My face was pressed against something cool and flat. I opened one eye a sliver and found that I was lying on what appeared to be a glass floor.

There wasn't enough room for me to be stretched fully out. In fact, I'd been crammed pretty thoughtlessly into a tight fetal position, which I imagine was hard enough on me as a flexible in utero infant, but which was a level of gymnastics nearly impossible to achieve — certainly impossible to maintain — now that my aching corpse was stuffed

full of creaking middle-aged joints and stale bar nuts.

Eventually the main benefit to keeping my eyes closed — not being immediately murdered — was outweighed by the long-term costs, such as numb legs, sore shoulders, aching back, bed sores, prolapsed organs, and natural death. Besides, I reasoned, if they'd wanted to kill me, they wouldn't have encased me in—

I opened my eyes wide.

—in an upright glass tube that resembled a giant beaker. There was even a convenient height chart written in red up the outside that measured the contents in liters. I presumed it wouldn't be me they'd be measuring, since I was currently still largely a solid, and the scales usually didn't tip toward liquid for me until well after midnight.

I amended my previous reasoning. They might, in fact, still very much want to murder me — murder, in fact, the goddamn hell out of me — they just wanted to play with their food a little first.

I had no idea how long I'd been out, but I gathered it was more than a refreshing catnap as my legs were virtually useless as I attempted to haul myself to my feet as quietly as clumsiness and terror permitted. The pins and needles in my extremities only helped to remind me of the needle that had been jabbed into my neck.

Check that.

Shit.

Shit, shit, shit.

No, the pins and needles only reminded me of themselves, and the intense pain they were inflicting on me as my ancient goddamn legs began to thaw out.

I tried to analyze my environment to take my mind off the fact that fire ants were gnawing through every square liter of my legs from the inside out.

At the center of the glass floor on which my rubbery

legs were about to give out was a plastic plug the size of a manhole cover. What appeared to be a half-dozen drains were arranged in a circle around the plastic disc. Six inches off the floor, six nozzles were set around the wall of my beaker prison. On the outside, hoses that attached to the nozzles snaked into holes in the metal floor.

Just beyond the reach of the nozzles was another wall of pure white that entirely encircled the platform on which my beaker stood. The solid white partition prevented me from seeing anything in the room beyond it, which was a definite selling point as I suspected that it was likely that nothing wholesome — such as a gallon of whole milk or a tooth-mouthed Osmond — was hanging out on the other side.

When I shifted, something unexpected bumped the side of my chest just under my armpit, and I reached under my coat to take surprise inventory.

Whoever was being paid to frisk prisoners needed to have a chat with HR about their job satisfaction, if they were truly serious about making the best effort possible as a My Grain Distillery henchman, and whether or not they should take time to evaluate if the Bandito-Pharmaceutical family was a good fit for them, because the slipshod asshole had generously left my gat firmly nestled in my shoulder holster.

I rapped the glass with my knuckle. I had hoped that it would signal that it might crack like a thin wineglass, at which point I would put my shoe through it and run like hell, but it was evident that the thick glass was more solid than a wall.

They'd left me my piece, but at the moment a gun would do me no good. I had no idea what material my clear tube prison was made of, and firing point blank in a confined space could set up a hilarious all-night ricochet, at

the end of which the distillery cafeteria staff could use whatever was left of me to strain spaghetti.

Somebody had heard me tap on the inside of my tank. A speaker crackled to life directly above my head. A little red light of a camera winked on.

"Ah, Attorney Shyster. I'm glad you're awake. First off, I must tell you that I'm very, very sorry about all this. I mean that sincerely."

The son of a bitch actually did sound sincere. I could hear the determined, sad-but-simultaneously-smiling frown in his tinny voice, and I knew at once that I was being addressed by the kindly, moon-faced bastard who'd been in conversation with an as-yet unidentified SOB ghost while I was being rudely jabbed in the neck outside his lab.

"I'm equally sorry," I replied. "Everybody who knows me knows that I'm the most happy-go-lucky bastard in town, so apparently this situation is contributing to the sorrow of both of us. To ameliorate our respective sorrows, why don't we both agree to let me go? I don't know about you, but I'm pretty sure that would at least begin to make one of us deliriously happy."

I hadn't seen a seam in the outer white cocoon that encircled my glass prison, but the seemingly solid exterior wall parted and rolled back in on itself, revealing as it slowly split apart a sinister, cinderblock laboratory. The separating white wall folded only in half, whirring to a semicircle stop that continued to block my view right and left.

Directly in front of me — holding the remote control that had opened the outer wall, and wearing the most genuinely sorrowful face of anybody who'd ever shoved me inside a gigantic beaker — was the son of a bitch scientist with the cherubic face. His chubby neck was probably

too fat for me to get my hands fully around it, in order that I might strangle the sadly grinning bastard to death, but I hoped to at least get the opportunity to try, fail, and try again as many times as proved necessary.

The name "Dr. Lance Boyle" was stitched in blue script on his lab coat, and I would have found it much funnier if I wasn't sure he was about to kill me.

He put away the remote control and took a microphone with an old-fashioned trailing cord from his pocket. The waddling SOB looked like Jerry Lewis at the Labor Day Telethon before the year he became a zombie and forewent his usual "You'll Never Walk Alone" shtick and, in lieu of singing, ate John Byner, Charo, and cohost Ed McMahon live on the air for pledges equal to $50,000 in human brains.

"Did you know, Attorney Shyster, that the United States is home to seventy percent of all the lawyers on the planet?" asked Dr. Lance Boyle, whose name, I had to admit, was hilarious after all, despite the fact that he was going to murder me. "Every other nation combined doesn't come close to having as many lawyers as we do."

"We can ship them some of ours," I suggested. "We'll start up a collection. People can leave lawyers in bags for the USPS to pick up once a year like they do with cans of soup. We can put dumpsters in mall parking lots for people to toss used lawyers in. As far as I'm concerned, poverty-stricken areas of Africa don't already have a shit enough existence with malaria, starvation, and drought. What they need is a massive influx of lawyers to sue the hell out of the mosquitoes, hunger, and sky."

"If only," Dr. Boyle said wistfully. "If only," he repeated, just as wistfully as time #1, since apparently he, like so many assholes, thought his life was a goddamn movie, every scripted line of which required the stink of Meryl Streep smoked ham. "It's an illness, you know. Being a

lawyer. Do you know what the right supramarginal gyrus is?"

It was a *Jeopardy!* question I never expected to be asked again for the rest of my life, but since my life would be ending shortly I figured it might be cramming in as many worthless repeats as possible, like a *Gilligan's Island* marathon during the Apocalypse.

"It's the area of the brain where empathy is born," I replied, like the smug, cheating bastard that I am. "It's located at the junction of the frontal, temporal, and another lobe I can't successfully haul out of my ass at the moment."

Dr. Lance Boyle was genuinely surprised, which he was justified in being since he thought I was a lawyer and so to him I was, therefore, an asshole ignoramus.

"You're the first lawyer we've tested on who's known," he said, impressed. "The others all *said* they knew, of course. Lawyers are incapable of thinking they don't know something. It's hardwired in their brains. Sadly, that's why you're here."

"I'm here because I wandered away from my tour group, and somebody jabbed me with a needle while I was looking for the shitter. Why do *you* think I'm here?"

"You are here, Attorney Shyster," he replied, "to help me find the cure. The cure this country needs more than all others. The cure for the disease of being a lawyer."

The asshole seemed to be waiting for a dramatic chord of music to underscore his portentous statement, but apparently John Williams was busy with the latest shit *Star Wars* movie since this was goddamn real life.

"I always thought the cure for being a lawyer was to deprive them of nourishing booze, which is the mother's milk of their drunken breed," I said, interrupting the film score that was playing inside Lance Boyle's dumb bald cranium. "However, you people here at My Grain Distillery

have gone the opposite route, and are supplying them with spiked punch. Yes, I know that you're slipping some kind of poison that only works on lawyers into your bottles of hooch, then shipping free samples all over town."

"All over town only *for now*," Dr. Boyle said. "It was a test of the efficacy of my doomsday formula. I want you to know that, as far as I'm concerned, that is only our option of last resort. I still want more than anything to develop a cure. But if I can't make a breakthrough soon, Attorney Shyster, free My Grain bottles will be shipped all around the state, then all over the country. I'm afraid that this eventuality is becoming an inevitability, and it is coming much sooner than I hoped. My partner is, shall we say, impatient."

"Is that the ghost you were powwowing with?"

The loose-lipped SOB would have told me. He was more chatty than a Tarantino movie, and apparently a million times more nuts. But his bean-spilling was interrupted by a younger bastard with a clipboard, two black eyes, and an *H* of white tape strips that was preventing his nose from fleeing his bruised face and running like hell the minute his nostrils laid eyes on me.

The nerd who would regret sticking me with a needle every time he picked his honker for the rest of his hopefully short life, shot me a murderous glare as he handed the clipboard over to the decreasingly humorously named Dr. Lance Boyle.

"I'm afraid, Attorney Shyster, that we're ready for you now," the good maniac doctor said, nodding an apology that I was not of a generous mind to goddamn accept. "We are ready for *all* of you."

He unplugged his microphone and, clipboard in hand, hustled off stage right and out of sight.

I leaned as far into the glass as I could in order to see

more of my surroundings, but the white wall that formed the semicircle around my P.I.-size beaker prevented me from seeing anything more than a narrow forward view of the lab. As far as panoramic views went, the job of the guy who makes postcards of seagulls standing on shit-smeared rocks or donkeys soaring majestically over the Grand Canyon was secure.

One floor up was a viewing station behind plate glass windows, like a surgery theater with me as autopsy-in-waiting. Boyle and his assistant with the busted conk appeared behind the glass, joining several other bastards in white coats who were already deeply involved in the boring, clinical minutia of arranging my homicide.

Somewhere a button was pressed, and the white semicircle wall at my sides slid back, then sank through the floor, vanishing entirely from sight.

With the obstruction gone, I was finally able to see my entire prison.

As it turned out, I would not be dying alone, although lamentably I didn't see anybody from the laundry list of bastards — Wasserbaum the dentist, Vincetti the fishmonger, Zombie Cher — I hoped to take with me when my number was up.

Stretching out to my right were seven more solid glass tubes identical to the one in which I was being held captive. Each cell was occupied, one per customer. All but one of my fellow prisoners was a fat guy in a rumpled business suit.

There was evidently plenty of air getting into each glass cage, because it was clear that their confinement was not suffocating their insufferable arrogance. Frankly, it was surprising that the ever-expanding universes of their asshole egos hadn't already flooded the tanks and busted them out. The thickness of the glass walls prevented me from hearing

what the trapped men were saying, but it was easy enough to guess from their furious, beet-red faces and their fat, stabbing fingers that they were all threatening the glass with a lawsuit if it didn't immediately transform back into sand.

The only member of our ass menagerie not arguing with a sheet of glass was my immediate next-door neighbor, who was second in from the end of the line.

Attorney Sue Yu of the law firm of Crook, Shaft & Fleece, whose delicate foot was last seen turning my convex head concave, was currently using the heel of her hoof to kick the hell out of the wall of her cell. It made not a sound to my ears, but the thick glass wall appeared to shimmer slightly as it sloughed off the vibrations.

There wasn't room for me to kick anything except, perhaps, myself in the goddamn ass for coming to My Grain Distillery in the first place. The dame, on the other hand, was small enough that she had no problem winding up and lashing out again. Again, the wall of her prison shook slightly, then quickly stopped shivering.

She'd apparently been going at it for some time. Her face was glistening with sweat, which I had to admit even under the less-than-ideal circumstance of my imminent death was not without some romantic appeal of the south-of-the-border variety.

The dame saw me, but rudely pretended that she didn't, even after I reminded her of our past friendship by flipping her the double-bird, lest the pair of us die without her appreciating the full extent of my loathing. She couldn't reciprocate as she was apparently too busy imagining a spot on the glass was my head and her foot was Windex.

"Prepping Subject One for vapor test," a voice shouted down from the speaker over my head.

There were only two of us on either end of the line of

eight tanks, so — assuming they were going in first come, first kill order — there was a fifty-fifty chance I was the Subject One in question. I snaked my hand under my trench coat and felt the cold steel of my gat. Attempting to blast my way out might be a one-way ticket on the undertaker express, but asparagus in lunar modules were Pine-Sol to Tony Danza's napkin dispenser.

Goddamn, whatever hippie horseshit the bastard with the busted-nose had injected me with had a kick like Francis the mule and repeated like a scratched LP on a warped turntable. I shook off the Woodstock flashback.

Another switch was flipped from above and, one by one, speakers were switched on in all the tanks. The overlapping voices of my fellow captives were suddenly all hollering down at me all at once.

"…*lawsuit*…"

"…*sue you personally*…"

"…*will sue My Grain*…"

Sue, sue, goddamn sue-dio.

If I absolutely had to use my gun, the first thing I'd shoot out was the speaker over my head. If it continued to work, next up was my brains. Hopefully my marksmanship was up to snuff, as I'd never before been required to hit such a miniscule target.

The repetitive *clunk, clunk, clunk* that I could now hear coming from Sue Yu's foot as it rapped the wall of the adjoining tank was a pleasant distraction from all the pompous pettifoggers who were continuing to wag their furious fingers at the glass and threaten lawsuits against their own reflections.

"Are you yelling at me?" one lawyer halfway up the line screamed at his screaming reflection. "You *are* yelling at me!" he yelled at his yelling self in disbelief. "Stop yelling at me!" he yelled, so maniacally absorbed in his

screaming match with himself that he launched some froth-ing spit on the glass. "You just spit at me!" he howled at himself. "That's assault! I have witnesses." He pointed at the reflections of the lawyers in the tanks on either side. "They saw it all. I'll sue you!"

Ninety-nine percent of lawyers give the rest a bad name. If that's a joke, it's on all the rest of the population who aren't goddamn lawyers.

My next-door neighbor, lovely young Attorney Sue Yu, was not allowing the morons shouting down from over her head to distract her. Sweat ran down her face as she continued to repeatedly *clunk* her foot against the wall of her tank.

I'd kept a careful eye on her, not least because the sweating little Asian dynamo might be the last vision from this life that I'd be taking into the next, and she beat all to hell fat-faced asshole Dr. Lance Boyle or a bunch of hol-lering lawyers.

The dame attorney gave her tank one final particularly vicious kick, but to no avail. She collapsed to her ass, exhausted. Only when Sue Yu dropped back to the floor did I finally see a possible opportunity for escape. Of course, it was too goddamn late.

"*Release valve on test Subject One!*" a voice from overhead yelled.

I had my hand on the butt of my gat and was about to whip it from my holster when I heard a distant whoosh and splatter of liquid.

A quick check of the nozzles which were attached to the hoses that snaked up to my tank revealed that no liquid was splashing in around my utterly dry Florsheims.

It quickly became apparent that I was not Subject One. The whoosh was coming from the speaker above my head, and when I glanced down to the tank at the far end of the

curved line I saw that the most distant glass prison was rapidly filling with liquid.

"What is the meaning of this?" Subject One pompously demanded. He glared at his feet, which were thoroughly submerged. His pant cuffs bobbed momentarily on the rising tide before joining his shoes at the bottom of the sea. "I will have you know that I am a senior partner at the very prestigious law firm of Haggard, Hooker, Swallows & Spitz," Subject One insisted to his reflection (God, lawyers are morons), "and as a very important and super-smart lawyer with a very high I.Q., I demand—"

Subject One stopped dead.

The swirling liquid had risen as high as his knees, and was still climbing.

He sniffed.

The churning brown liquid was up to his waist and continued to rise.

Subject One didn't wait for the booze to reach his mouth. It wasn't even to the midpoint of his chest before he was dropping desperately down below the water line. His necktie floated like a single strand of kelp in front of his face, and he batted it crazily out of the way of his mouth as he gulped down as much liquor as was humanly possible.

Then he gulped down more liquor than was humanly possible, which was, frankly, taking work away from me.

Then his lungs sucked in more liquor than was advisable, even for a practicing attorney. His alveoli quickly exceeded maximum occupancy. He gulped a few feeble times, a string of thin bubbles escaped from between his lips, and the poor bastard from Haggard, Hooker, Swallows & Spitz drowned with a delighted smile plastered across his fatally plastered face commensurate with his larger-than-life lawyer ego.

"Initial vapor test successful!" Dr. Lance Boyle's cheery voice announced over the speakers. "Well done, everyone! You're all just swell as all heck at your jobs."

A cheer went up from the assembled mob of murdering scientists. Through the window, I could see them popping tabs on vending machine soft drinks and tapping the cans together like aluminum champagne glasses. It was an approximation of human jubilation that only comes from assholes who wouldn't know "fun" if it fell over a piece of phony plastic dog shit right in front of them, shattering its pelvis and breaking its leg in three places, which ultimately required installation of hilarious pins and rods and subsequent thigh-slapping months of intensely humorous physical therapy.

The congratulatory Mountain Dew soiree broke up as quickly as it started.

"Clearing tank number one!" a cheerful voice on the speaker announced.

The sucking coming from the end of the line rivaled that of a Will Ferrell film.

The liquid rapidly drained from the first tank, quickly lowering the bobbing cork-of-a-lawyer down to the floor. Subject One was dripping wet and dead, but, judging from the look on his face, deliriously happy.

In the gallery window, looking down on his first test subject below, Dr. Lance Boyle's eyebrows arched in deep and creepily sincere sympathy. He put his Fresca can on the sill and nodded to his men to carry on.

"Prepping vapor test for Subject Two!"

After the death of Subject One, Attorney Sue Yu had renewed her desperate and futile assault on her tank. Her pigheaded determination to shatter the shatterproof glass proved to be the perfect distraction, as the bastards above were used by now to her calisthenics and were thus com-

pletely ignoring our end of the line. Consequently, Lance Boyle, et al, weren't witness to my unbelievable and, frankly, utterly ingenious escape, which I accomplished with impressive dexterity and relative ease, especially for a wheezing, middle-aged wreck.

Free from my tank, I raced over to Sue Yu, who was in the process of winding up another massive kick. Her eyes nearly popped from her head when she saw me standing free as a Lynyrd Skynyrd song on the other side of the glass.

"*Banyon!*" she yelled, shocked.

Luckily her voice was absorbed into the chorus of shouts that blared down from wall-mounted speakers all around the room, and so the dingbat's moronic, full-throated shout of my name wasn't picked up by Dr. Lance Boyle or the rest of his team of assholes leering down from their observation room windows.

After my great, improbable, and miraculous escape, I kept from marching out into the open. Once I'd hopped the distance separating our two glass prisons, I'd made the genius move of hugging the back of Sue Yu's see-through tank, which pretty much made me a mannequin hiding out in Macy's front window.

When Sue Yu yelled my name, I pressed my finger to my lips in the universal sign of "shut up, you moron." I calculated a better than fifty percent chance that she wouldn't get it, and would shout her mystification regarding my pantomime at the top of her lungs, and so I was pleasantly surprised when the dame immediately buttoned her lip.

I rapidly searched the area for a switch or lever that would open her tank.

"Release valve on test Subject Two!"

Both my bloodshot eyes and Sue Yu's frightened

peepers snapped in the same direction.

The second lawyer in line, having just witnessed the drowning death of his fellow leech on society, managed an impressive gymnastic leap off the floor of his prison. The corpulent slob pressed the back of his off-the-rack suit against one side of the tank and the soles of his shoes against the other. For a moment he managed to remain glued in place in defiance of fat-ass mass squared, times McDonald's, minus, apparently, gravity.

Nozzles yawned open beneath his dangling ass, and a high-pressure storm of delicious murder swirled furiously into the tube.

It quickly became clear that the vapor from the booze with which Dr. Lance Boyle was flooding his tanks was too much for any of his lawyer test subjects to withstand.

Subject Two blinked a few times as the same look of wonder and disbelief that had afflicted the bastard from Haggard, Hooker, Swallows & Spitz slowly descended on his ruddy face. It was the expression of a kid on Christmas morning, rubbing his disbelieving eyes with the backs of his hands over the ten-speed Schwinn parked under the tree. (Which image is the Norman Rockwell ideal of what happens in normal households, while in the sepia-hued Banyon chalet of my idealized childhood the only thing rolled in under the tree on December 25th was my old man with an empty bottle in each hand and, on that last Joyeux Noel, a petition for divorce taped to his forehead with a cheap Woolworth's bow.)

The liquor rose rapidly, but the son of a bitch didn't wait for it to reach his ass. Subject Two yanked his feet from the wall of the tank and did a massive cannonball into the surging swirl of distilled bliss. Through the murky liquid I could see him gulping for all he was worth, which

in a matter of seconds was less funeral expenses.

The jubilation from above was less pronounced than it had been after the first murder, but there was still more backslapping and high-fives than was usually expressed on the back end of a double homicide. Apart from his underlings, Dr. Lance Boyle offered a sincere apologetic nod to the latest body.

"Clearing tank number two!" a voice from the speaker called.

The booze in the second tank quickly drained down, leaving a second sopping wet officer of the court for My Grain's overworked, underpaid janitorial staff to mop up.

I had found nothing at the rear of Attorney Sue Yu's tank that would free her, and so I slipped around the side towards the front, keeping my back plastered against the curving glass at all times. I immediately spied a panel recessed in the floor a couple of feet out, which was hidden from view by a raised steel bar.

I weighed the risk of running out into the wide open — being caught — against the benefit — freeing a dame who'd kicked me in the head. I didn't have a hell of a lot of time to put my great intellect to the task of finding an upside.

Apparently, Sue Yu hadn't quite gotten the message after all when I'd pressed my index finger to my lips a few moments earlier. It was possible that she'd misinterpreted it as a clumsy sexual advance, in which case it was likely that I'd be on the receiving end of a sexual harassment lawsuit were we to escape. If so, it was lucky for me that Sue Yu virtually sealed the deal on us not getting out of the room alive by selecting that moment to begin pounding on the tank on the side opposite the back of my head.

"*Banyon!*" she demanded at the top of her goddamn lungs in order to be heard over all the cross-talk coming

from the scientists above and the four remaining lawyers still trapped — now panicking — in their as-yet dry tanks. *"I asked you how did you escape? Can you hear me out there, Banyon! Hey, Banyon!"*

The sudden, horrible silence that descended on the room was the same hideous hush that strangles laughter in the throats of sensible moviegoers when the aforementioned Will Ferrell commits comedy.

The infinitesimally brief pause before all hell inevitably erupted permitted me just enough time to glance up at the observation window and straight into the shocked face of Dr. Lance Boyle. Everybody in the observation room raced forward to crowd the windows around their boss. The entire slack-jawed gaggle of murderous bastards was staring straight down at me in disbelief.

"Okay, maybe I'm no longer successfully hiding behind a sheet of glass," I hollered up to them. "And while, yes, I do feel pretty stupid right now, I feel compelled to point out that up until this dingbat opened her fat yap, I *was* doing a pretty spectacularly successful job of hiding from all of you behind a sheet of glass. So let's admit that there's plenty of stupid to go around, you give me a couple of crates of booze that hasn't been poisoned, and I'll get out of your hair and let you get back to your important work of killing lawyers which, frankly, I can't really work up all that much indignation against anyway."

I had a sliver of hope that sheer hubris, a knowing wink, and a confident tone might carry the day, and that I'd be in a My Grain Distillery company car loaded down with sloshing crates and halfway to Brazil before they realized their error.

Boyle was first to regain his senses. He offered me the most sincere of apologetic shrugs, then hollered so loud into a microphone which was suddenly clutched in his

white-knuckled hand that he nearly brought the ceiling down on all our heads.

"*Kill him!*" screamed the demented doctor.

His bastard team on the other side of the window erupted in crazed activity.

The asshole whose nose bone had very briefly been connected to my elbow bone slammed his palm down on an unseen button on an unseen panel and immediately an electronic voice began howling from every corner of the distillery.

"*Red alert! Red alert! Red alert!*"

The house lights dimmed. Flashing red lights abruptly erupted all around the vast room, turning the joint into a commie disco with me cast as Comrade Travoltov dancing a sissy solo in the goddamn strobe spotlight.

A klaxon blared to life, because all the screaming from the speakers might be insufficient to deafen everybody who lived in a three-mile radius.

I decided that a little more noise couldn't hurt anybody's eardrums any more so than the current cacophony, so I yanked my gat from its holster and blasted a couple of well-aimed slugs in the direction of the second-floor windows. The middle two panes of glass in the observation room shattered into a million pieces, dropping glistening shards to the metal plated floor below.

Terrified men inside the observation room ducked and covered and otherwise dropped the hell out of sight.

I wheeled back around to find myself confronted by yet another headache.

Apparently as part of some doomsday failsafe, the geniuses currently sprawled on their cowardly bellies upstairs had wired mass-murder directly into their alert system.

All five remaining tanks — including that of the lovely,

young, suddenly terrified Sue Yu — had begun to rapidly flood.

Lab rats in the same circumstances would have been desperately treading water while searching for an exit. Unlike their smaller rodent counterparts, the remaining four rat male lawyers had become pearl divers, swimming with all their might against a rising, swirling tide as they delightedly dived to the murky bottoms of their respective tanks.

The only exception was charming Attorney Sue Yu, who was dog-paddling around the surface for all she was worth. The dame was fighting a losing battle, and the booze line quickly rose past her head. She rose right along with it as best she could, jamming her face into the last pocket of vanishing air at the top of the tank.

As Sue Yu fought for her last gulp of air, I flew out from beside her tank to the panel in the floor and slammed my fist on an unlabeled button that I guessed was a release switch and hoped wasn't the knob that activated the spin cycle.

The glass tube instantly detached from its stationary lid and began to recede into the floor. The cascade of liquor over the sides of the tank that I'd expected never materialized. Instead, there was barely a splash over the edge, accompanied by a huge sucking sound as the bulk of the liquor was drawn into a manhole-sized drain — which, in a pinch, served as a perfect P.I. escape hatch — that yawned open in the floor of the tank.

Sue Yu avoided being sucked down along with the booze, and once the empty tank had fully descended, she flopped out on all fours onto the metal grate that formed the platform on which all eight glass cages rested.

I left her gasping for air as I turned away and heroically raced off to save more drowning lawyers for a reason unclear to me at the moment, and which I'd likely have rejected

had I taken more than two seconds to think it through.

I punched the next release switch and didn't wait to see what dropped out as I ran to the next, then the next.

I ran from one end of the clanking metal floor to the other, hitting every switch along the way until I reached the tank in which I'd last seen Subject Three performing the same diving routine as the other four lawyers who'd been alive when the alarm went off. I didn't bother with the final two tanks, in which the corpses of Subjects One and Two floated in the happy oblivion of their final, greatest binge.

Only when I got to third tank from the end did I spin back around. The remaining four tanks had sunk into the floor, sucking down the booze brine and releasing the bobbing bastards who'd been bottled up inside.

Of the five lawyers who'd been alive mere seconds before, only Sue Yu was kneeling on the floor and coughing like mad to clear her lungs. The other four mouthpieces were lying damp and immobile on the floor.

I raced back, clearing lawyer corpses like an Olympic hurdler in the second most fun track and field event after the ex-wife javelin catch, and hastily helped the spluttering dame to her feet.

"Shouldn't we—"

She coughed, gagged, then tried again.

"Shouldn't we give them mouth-to-mouth?" Sue Yu asked, displaying incredibly unlawyer-like empathy for a fellow human being.

"No offense, lady, but I'd suck on a tailpipe to revive a dead Chrysler before I Frenched a lawyer. If you fail to save one in quite the precise way they envisioned being saved, the inevitable lawsuit would bankrupt even Bill Gates. Besides, they've gone to lawyer heaven. Which the rest of us generally refer to as 'Hell.' Let's go."

As if I needed help punctuating the direness of our

situation, the sharp report of a single gunshot suddenly blasted in my ears.

A bullet zinged over my ducking head and slammed the rear wall of the room, chipping a divot in the cinder-block wall.

I noted a single, deeply worrisome spark at the point of impact even as I grabbed the dame by the arm and began racing for the door.

Thrilling gunfire erupted all around us. Bullets whizzed crazily past our fleeing asses as the two of us dashed like mad across the floor.

As I ran, I took vague, terrified note of several uni-formed security guards who'd heeded the summons of the klaxon and had joined Dr. Lance Boyle in the observation booth. Luckily, they were distillery guards who were appar-ently paid in booze, and so the wasted bastards were suc-cessful only in shooting the hell out of everything in the room that wasn't Sue Yu or me. They used their weaving handguns to boozily blast merrily away at walls, lights, dead lawyer bodies, and — as I feared — the floor.

It didn't occur to the inebriated marksmen as they attempted to draw a bead on our fleeing feet that the product produced by the company for which they worked was basically delicious gasoline.

It took only a single spark on the metal floor on which pooled one of the small puddles that had spilled out when the tanks receded.

I heard the FOOM! and felt a wave of sudden heat at my back just as we reached the door. I flung the door open, bravely hurled Sue Yu into the hallway, and had just enough time as I was slamming the door shut to see that the fire had already raced across nearly every square inch of the floor, and was beginning to rage up onto the platform where five of eight tanks had sunk into the floor. The base of each

tank and the dead lawyers thereon were so thoroughly soaked in booze that each performed its own Olympic torch lighting ceremony as the fire roared across the platform.

Up above, panicked scientists were grabbing papers into their arms and fleeing the observation room. Dr. Lance Boyle stood frozen in shock, flanked on either side by drunken guards who were blinking confusion at the spreading conflagration below.

"Oh. Okay. Um," one guard could be heard saying over the crackling, dying speaker system. "So do you want us to shoot the *fire* now, or…?"

A confused hiccup was the last sound I heard out of Boyle or his stooges before the nearest melting speaker burst into flames and dropped from the wall.

I slammed the door just as the fire reached the two sealed tanks in which Subject One and Subject Two were still blissfully dead.

The ensuing explosion blew one of the flaming SOBs straight through the door with a legal zoom, blasting it off its hinges and flinging burning shards of door and lawyer across the hallway. An instant before the explosion, I'd yanked Sue Yu by the arm. The two of us were already halfway down the hallway, running like mad, straight through the double security doors, and racing like maniacs for the nearest emergency exit.

We burst into the great outdoors and I did the best impersonation of a gazelle that rank cowardice could inspire as we loped majestically across the Serengeti parking lot to the accompanying strains of goddamn Judgment Day.

Explosions came as fast and furious as a lousy movie franchise as the fire spreading throughout the complex rapidly sought out tanks, barrels, bottles and anything else in which was stored a product that — while admittedly fatally injurious to lawyers — was truly beloved by dis-

cerning winos everywhere who, come evening, would be slurring stirring eulogies to imaginary rabbits in alleys all over the tri-city area.

The ground heaved beneath our feet as we ran, fissures split the parking lot as if from an earthquake, the air grew thick with smoke, and the heat of a thousand goddamn suns seared our fleeing backs. Chunks of busted metal, glass, and brick were blown out of the My Grain Distillery complex by a succession of increasingly shit-inducing blasts, and our path became a minefield of flaming debris dropping from the sky.

Up ahead, the group of coots whose tour group I had ingeniously infiltrated hours before were calmly shuffling back onto their bus as if the world wasn't coming to an end. The last codger had just managed to haul the tennis balls on the feet of his walker up the steps. One ancient hag remained outside, standing impatiently at the open door.

The withered old prune nearly popped out her cataracts, so hard was she squinting at me and Sue Yu as we ran past the bus.

"*You*," the angry old bag scolded, stopping me dead in my tracks. "You wandered off the tour, you naughty, naughty boy. Hurry up, now. On you go."

She clutched a clipboard in her arthritis on which fluttered a sheet of paper that I was manifestly not on. I am not, however, one to look a gift horse in the busted dentures, and so I escorted Attorney Sue Yu up onto the second-from-last mode of transportation everybody on board would ever ride prior to hearse.

By this point, the entire My Grain Distillery complex was a fairly spectacularly raging inferno. Thick black smoke curled into the sky, punctuated by dramatic spouts of flame, like alcohol-fueled solar flares shooting from the roof, to the accompaniment of fresh explosions. Employees fled

every exit, and though I didn't see amusingly-named Dr. Lance Boyle, his pal with the even more amusing busted nose, the drunken guards, or any of the other murderous asshole scientists who'd tried to marinate me alive, there was no way of knowing if they were all still inside or if they'd escaped.

Two seconds later, at the precise moment the entire burning main building caved in on itself, I heard the fire alarm inside finally kick on, and I found great encouragement in the fact that there was a greater deathtrap in town than O'Hale's Bar. Since I'd escaped this far worse fire hazard, I now had the experience necessary to save my ass when Jaublowski inevitably accidentally turned his dump tavern into an inferno when he made the mistake of turning the lights on in the storeroom or flushing the toilet.

The geezer express on which Attorney Sue Yu and I had somehow inconspicuously parked our asses passed through the front gates and pulled into the street.

Sue Yu was panting like mad from running, certainly. From panic, probably. From smoke inhalation, possibly. And almost absolutely from being completely and hopelessly turned on by the incredible heroics I'd displayed in the previous five minutes. The dame was staring at the back of the headrest in front of her as if in shock, which was obviously an attempt to mask unbridled lust.

I would have expected at least a word of thanks from the lady lawyer. I could have left her to drown in her tank since, after all, she'd put her foot through my head at our last encounter when I'd walked in on her ransacking my goddamn office.

"After you've caught your breath," I said, "you can thank me."

She didn't take the hint. She continued to stare numbly ahead.

"Being a lawyer, you might not know what thanking someone is," I said. "I'll get you started with one from me. Thanks for not kicking me in the head again, as it would likely have impeded me while I was rescuing your ass."

"Shush!" snapped the decrepit dame with the clipboard from her Gestapo perch at the front of the bus. Her tongue was picking around the many gaps in her busted dentures as she kept an eagle eye out to make certain nobody slipped up and enjoyed themselves.

"They're all dead," Sue Yu managed to say, so softly even the old bag with her hearing aid cranked up to eleven didn't hear.

The two dozen ancient buzzards jostling silently in their seats were decked out in all manner of crap from the My Grain Distillery gift shop. There were My Grain hats, My Grain T-shirts, and My Grain pendants. Also My Grain mugs, My Grain buttons, and My Grain bumper stickers for the cars their kids had stolen from them and turned over to their grandkids when the old folks had gotten old-folksy enough to be betrayed and abandoned.

Since the place was currently burning to the ground a block back, everything the tour group had blown their Social Security checks on was suddenly a rare collectable. The fact that the snoozing codger with the busted jack-o-lantern dentures in the seat across from mine could make a fortune hawking his hugely expensive My Grain baseball jacket on eBay made me feel entitled to swipe the brand-new silver My Grain hip flask that was sticking out of his priceless My Grain duffel bag.

The flask was, to my delight, loaded, which I sincerely hoped I would soon be. I tugged off the gift shop price tag and, after sampling the merchandise, passed it off to Attorney Sue Yu, who had demonstrated immunity to whatever the hell demented Dr. Lance Boyle had laced the distillery's

product with.

The dame not only accepted the flask, she made a distressingly rude attempt to suck my hard-earned stolen container dry. When I was finally able to wrestle the flask from between her lips, a boozy focus had overtaken her glassy-eyed stare.

"They're all dead," she repeated.

"Yes, I was there," I reminded her. "You may recall I was the one saving your ass. Although, since you're a lawyer, you've likely already rewritten the events of the past fifteen minutes to make yourself the hero. As for the current moment, would you please keep your voice down? I'm trying to enjoy getting drunk, and I can't do that if I'm worrying that the withered prune whose massively broken dentures are eyeballing us from the front of the bus is going to throw us off for the crime of not being as miserable as she's trying to make us."

"Not at My Grain," Sue Yu insisted. "At Crook, Shaft & Fleece." She looked at me, eyes pleading. "Every lawyer but me at my law firm is dead."

I considered for a moment what an entire practice full of dead lawyers might mean to the functioning of the American legal system. I held my brand-new flask aloft.

"I'll drink to that," I said. "Also, given the shit nature of the past twenty-four hours, to anything else. But dead lawyers especially, obviously."

"Quiet!" the bitter old crow with the clipboard hollered.

I wondered if it might not be worth the effort to hijack the bus and see if there was a nearby distillery fire into which I might drive us all straight into the goddamn heart of.

13

The tour bus was — I soon realized due to only a faint stink of piss — brand new, and was the recently purchased property of Antediluvian Acres, a charming pre-cemetery facility where, when they weren't touring booze factories, the lonely residents spent the dismal hours between bingo games thinking about the adult kids who'd stuck them there. As for their kids, all they spent was their parents' dough. It was the goddamn circle of life, and I only hoped that when the bastard son I never knew I had came out of the woodwork to ship me off to the Old P.I. Home and claim ownership of my bank account, that I had two bullets left in the chamber — one for him, as well as a second one for him just to make sure the greedy little son a bitch was really dead.

The one good thing about a joint like Antediluvian Acres was that they served supper by three in the afternoon, and so I was able to grab a quick bite with the fossils before Attorney Sue Yu and I ingeniously knotted a couple of Depends together and made our daring escape by walking out the front door.

There was a legitimate bus stop at the corner, and we sat on the legitimate bench to await the arrival of a legitimate city bus which would, like the one from the old folks'

home, also almost certainly stink like piss.

"So," I asked, "how'd a sexy plate of chicken chow mein like you end up bobbing for egg rolls in a distillery tank?" (I'm not flattering myself when I admit that I am as smooth as Billy Dee Williams and as culturally sensitive as a sociology professor with a model U.N. Building jammed up her woke ass.)

Sue Yu's instinct was to button her lip. But then she remembered that everybody she worked with was currently floating around in limbo in search of a court from which to sue Heaven for its discriminatory practice of barring utter assholes from entry.

"Someone has it in for lawyers," she said.

"Everyone has it in for lawyers," I replied. "No one, in fact, has it out for lawyers, unless you count wallets and middle fingers. Now, what happened at your office?"

"We had a breakfast meeting at Crook, Shaft & Fleece this morning," Sue Yu explained. "The senior partners were bringing in someone from Madison Insurance Equities to discuss why the families of several of the junior partners who have died in the past three weeks wouldn't be getting their life insurance."

"Robert Sherman Planck," I said.

She was evidently surprised, which she really had no cause to be as by now she had been sufficiently exposed to my unparalleled genius.

"How did you know?"

I didn't find it necessary to let her know Planck, through his cheapskate insurance agency, was footing the bill for my current client, the snot-nosed little brat whose entire life would be ruined if a total stranger didn't shove thirty bucks under his pillow.

"Planck's the big gun that Madison HQ sends out when they're screwing only the most important people," I

explained. "For little shit screwings like basement flood-ings or fender benders, you don't see somebody of Planck's stature. In most cases, they screw you at a much more intimate and folksy local level through your worthless local agent."

The dame nodded, then picked up where she'd left off.

"This morning's meeting was also going to cover how the senior partners had gambled away the firm's pension fund — legally, of course — and how the paperwork all of us signed when we joined the firm made them the beneficiaries of all our estates, just in case any more of us dropped dead. We started the meeting as all law firms do, with a prayer to Satan. Then the senior partners broke out the eight-thirty a.m. liquor, just like any other day. We did the usual roundtable bragging about how we successfully abused the law in order to steal — *legally* steal — bank accounts, jewelry, real estate, etcetera, for ourselves and our clients. Then everyone just dropped dead."

"And I take it that this delightful capper deviates from a typical finale at a law practice meeting," I said.

Our bus had just appeared up the street, and immedi-ately got bogged down in traffic.

"Everyone but *me* dropped dead," she said, clearly not cheered for some baffling reason by the memory of a roomful of dead lawyers. "At first I thought they might have passed out, which lawyers do all the time, but they were definitely dead. Everybody had just had a drink, so I guessed that the liquor had been tampered with somehow. But I'd had half a bottle — which is the usual lawyer amount — and it didn't kill me. I checked outside the boardroom, and the rest of the non-lawyer staff was unaf-fected. I figured the case of liquor had come from a rival law firm we'd pilfered clients from, like Gross, Butz &

Toole or Roach, Leach & D'Louse, but Attorney Fleece's
secretary said it had come free from My Grain Distillery,
with their compliments. After the medical examiner's
office finished throwing the bodies out the window into a
garbage truck, I went straight to My Grain to meet with
someone in charge to tell them that there might be a con-
tamination problem, and that I planned to sue the hell out
of them one way or another. They set up a meeting for me
with Dr. Boyle, but I never met him. I remember going to
his office, but I must have blacked out. I woke up in that
tank."

Attorney Sue Yu had given a valuable answer to one
question. The bottles that the distillery had initially sent
around the city evidently only worked on lawyers in the
midst of bragging about how they'd manipulated the law
and turned the simple act of living into agonizing torture
for nonmembers of their clique. I'd seen it happen firsthand
to the fat-ass bore who'd swiped my stool at O'Hale's, I
was sure it was the case with the dead booze-bag on my
ghost neighbor's welcome mat, and Sue Yu had just
described the scene that had taken out the entirety of
Crook, Shaft & Fleece, save the delightful Miss Attorney
herself. I had to give Dr. Lance Boyle credit for being a
diabolical genius (in addition to the extra credit that should
obviously be tossed his way for killing lawyers). Since
attorneys were chronic alcoholics who self-aggrandized
like the rest of us transform oxygen into carbon dioxide,
it was a simple enough matter for them to activate the
dormant agent specific to lawyers Boyle had hidden in
the golden depths of a My Grain bottle. And now the
smiling little mass-murdering lunatic had developed a
next wave poison for which not a spoken bragging word
or so much as a single boasting thought was necessary.

The lawyers in their tanks needed only to be exposed

to the vapor and were instantly and eagerly willing to drown themselves in booze on the spot, as opposed to waiting the four or five decades it usually took.

"Were any of the dead lawyers at your firm named Boyle, or do you know any lawyers around town by that name?" I asked.

She clearly didn't get the brilliance of the question.

"Not that I know of, why?"

"In those precious few seconds when he wasn't trying to murder us, Dr. Lance Boyle said he was looking for a cure for lawyers being lawyers. He didn't strike me as the philanthropic type, especially when he started slaughtering everybody. It's possible that he started all this because he's looking to cure one lawyer in particular. A sibling, son, spouse. You sure you don't know any Attorneys Boyle around town?"

"No. I mean, there *could* be, but I don't know any."

There had to be a legal reason for Boyle's involvement. I was willing to bet that if I shook Dr. Lance Boyle's family tree, a rotten apple attorney would drop out.

"I'll have my assistant check into it," I said.

The traffic unsnarled and my stalled bus began inching down the block at a pace significantly slower than I would have been able to walk to the goddamn moon.

The dame was uninterested that our carriage was closing in and, assuming a solid tailwind, would be quickly arriving shortly after the turn of the millennium. She was back visiting the memory of the Crook, Shaft & Fleece boardroom.

"I don't understand why it didn't kill me," she said, shaking her head. "I drank from the same case as everyone else."

Clogged traffic stalled our goddamn bus again. It was close enough now that I could see the driver's frustrated

face through the encrusted remains of a lunch that had evidently missed the mark one hundred percent of the time. The starving bus driver with the mustard mustache revved his engine like a weekend drag racer, repeatedly glancing furiously down at the cars that were blocking him in.

"Well, we know now that your immunity, whatever the reason, isn't limited to whatever they put in the bottles," I said to Attorney Sue Yu.

Apparently "we" didn't know any such thing, if the frown of confusion the dame offered me was any indication.

"Except," I amended, "it's now evident to me from that baffled look you just wrapped halfway around your head that you didn't notice that you were swimming for your life in that tank while every other lawyer went for the bottom faster than a San Francisco hairdresser. You were clearly immune to Boyle's vapor test, as well. You are evidently much different from other lawyers."

She proved once more just how different an attorney she was when she didn't immediately puff out her chest and start *vive*-ing all *la differences* between herself and the entire rest of the mortal realm. Instead, she chewed the inside of her cheek and shook her head.

"I don't know what it could be," she said. "I did do well in law school. Mr. Shaft's assistant headhunted me, but that's nothing special."

"See, there's your problem right there again. *All* five trillion lawyers in this country are special, and they'll go hoarse telling you why. And a lawyer doesn't 'do well' in law school. You all graduate at the top of your class. What's more, even if you went to the seventh or thirteenth shittiest law school in the country, you all claim that you really got into Harvard but opted not to go there for some fill-

in-the-blank bullshit reason. And somebody's crummy little assistant didn't track you down, the senior partner himself drove his limo onto the stage the instant you snatched your diploma from the King of Saturn and whisked you off to the biggest law firm in the solar system. I don't know how you are at the actual job of lawyering, lady, but I've never met a lawyer as lousy as you are at *being* a lawyer."

She attempted an angry lawyer face. "That's slander, Mr. Banyon. I could sue you for…" She instantly deflated. "Oh, what the hell. You're right."

"And a lawyer never, ever, not in a billion centuries, ever admits that somebody else is right," I said. "Case, you'll pardon the expression, closed."

The bus driver had finally had enough waiting and decided to break the traffic logjam by very carefully driving through the cars that were blocking his path. Horns honked and angry fists raised out car windows as he very slowly negotiated straight up the middle of the road, cleaving traffic in twain like waves on the prow of a ship. Amid the sparks and grinding metal, I could see the spirited fellow's mustard-smeared mouth laughing like an absolute lunatic behind his big steering wheel, and if I didn't have to wait another whole fifteen minutes for the next bus to appear I might have considered not placing my life in his maniac hands. On the other hand, a certifiably nuts bus driver couldn't do a worse job as caretaker of my existence than I had thus far.

"We can continue this discussion at my office," I said, standing.

"I don't know what the hell is even going on," Sue Yu muttered in frustration. "On top of everything else, I might be out of work. I don't know what's going to happen with Crook, Shaft & Fleece."

"It's an unbelievable coincidence that three people with those surnames would go to law school, find one another, and then partner up in a law firm," I said. "Since it's improbable that three other lawyers with those exact names will ever come along and form another partnership of the same name, I'll concede that in that very narrow sense the death of your firm is a slightly less hilarious tragedy."

"Oh, all of them have sons who are currently in law school," Sue Yu offered. "I imagine the sons will eventually take on the name."

"Do you know what day trash pickup is in this part of town?" I asked. "I don't want to be sitting here for a whole week after I shoot myself in the goddamn head."

The arrival of our battered city bus interrupted my suicide.

14

Vincetti the downstairs fishmonger was scraping the sidewalk with a broom so ancient that what little worn-out straw remained at the end ran the risk of bursting into flames every time he drew the giant matchstick across the cement.

"Get outta here, you!" the old bastard snarled as Attorney Sue Yu and I cut across the front of the building to the side entrance.

The fishmonger's wearily shouted command was nearly as toothless as the decaying black-and-yellow city skyline that he called a mouth, and if that feeble bellow was the best he could muster at the sight of me I was worried about the health of the horrible, choleric, fascist SOB.

It turned out Vincetti hadn't even seen me.

"Go! Yeah, you. You go. You getta outta here now! Shoo!"

He held his broom up like a spear and waved it menacingly back and forth at what appeared at first glance to be the vacant air in front of his store.

The nasty old son of a bitch had been flirting with senility for years, and I briefly had very high hopes that he'd finally stopped flirting and had at long last gotten

dementia back on the sofa at his place and managed to get its bra off.

Then I saw that which had the old bastard so exorcised, which, in light of what had Vincetti up in arms, was what the whole goddamn building needed to be.

Vincetti's For the Halibut Fish Bazaar had a threadbare awning that cast a weak shadow over the sidewalk, and in that shadow beneath it I could just barely make out the floating outline of the building's resident custodian ghost.

"Get outta there! Youse a-chasin' away alla the customer!"

Vincetti might have had a chance of dispersing the ghost if there had been an actual brush on the end of his broom. Instead, he was merely swiping a stick through the waist of the incandescent figure. The janitor ghost was undeterred as his two halves separated and quickly mended in between Vincetti's attacks.

"I have to repair the *doooorbell!*" the ghost howled.

In his hand, the forlorn spirit clutched a solid screwdriver which he tapped fruitlessly against the rusted screws of Vincetti's doorbell which — like the fresh fish inside Vincetti's shop, as well as the old fishmonger himself — hadn't been touched by a living human hand in over two decades.

It was rare to see the ghostly janitor twice in a month, let alone in less than twenty-four hours. However, I was grateful that he had roused himself from his boiler room exile a second time if only to give the fishmonger something other than my recently bruised cranium at which to swing his warped broom handle.

I bundled up sexy Asian Attorney Sue Yu in the crook of one arm and had nearly hustled her to the side door when we were spotted at the last minute.

"You!"

It was not, lamentably, Vincetti's pidgin English that howled after us.

"Youuuuuuuu!" the janitor ghost repeated, dragging the word into a mournful cry, because goddamn ghosts just can't help themselves.

The spectral custodian dropped his screwdriver and started floating after us, an accusing finger extended before him. When he passed from shadow into sunlight, he nearly completely vanished, but I had a good enough bead on his trajectory to track his dotted outline coming straight for us.

Rather than express gratitude for drawing the ghost away from the front of his shop, Vincetti demonstrated his contempt for the lot of us by vaguely waving his naked broom handle in our direction. He then turned his makeshift wooden sword on the mailman, a passing stray dog, a couple of pigeons, and a discarded Moxie can before heading off into the depths of his market to berate his dead inventory.

For my part, I hurried Sue Yu through the door and led her rapidly past the wall of mailboxes and onto the elevator. The doors had not yet fully closed when the janitor's ghost came floating between them. He took up a frowning sentry position before us.

"Youuuuu!" he moaned angrily.

I reached through him and pressed the button for the third floor. I hoped that he'd remain planted on the ground floor and the car would pass up through him, but the dead bastard had prepared himself for the ride. The car jumped, and he rose right along with it.

"Look, I'm not fond of ghosts," I said. "In fact, no offense, but I hate you people. Go back to pestering Vincetti and leave me the hell alone."

"Not you, Banyon," the ghost said contemptuously. "My, you have a very big *eeeeeeego!*" He aimed his glowing finger at my companion. "*Youuuuuu!* Sue *Yuuuuuu!* You were our attorney. You're the reason my daughter still hasn't gotten a single penny for my death."

The diminutive lawyer made a show of thinking hard, but came up empty.

"You don't even recognize me," the janitor ghost said, appalled.

The elevator doors opened, and I started to step off. Sue Yu remained behind, offering a non-lawyer-like apologetic shrug.

"A lot of clients come through our offices," she said. "Maybe you can refresh me on the details of your case."

"Goddammit," I said, reaching straight through the ghost once more, this time to grab the lawyer dame by the arm and drag her out into the hallway.

The janitor ghost busted apart and vanished as she passed through him.

We'd only gotten a few steps up the hall when the bastard materialized beside us, dogging us as we hustled down to my office.

"I was buffed to death," the ghost said. "*Buuuuuuffed.* My daughter went to Crook, Shaft & Fleece right after I died, and I wafted along to keep you fellas honest. You and one of them senior partners over there promised her a ten million buck settlement. Then you spent two years not doing anything but talkin' every couple of months to the lawyers at Black & Decker and charging my poor little Lulu a arm and a leg for all them conversations. When the lawsuit fell through 'cause poor Lulu didn't have the money to keep payin' you forever, I told her at least there was the insurance money. But Madison Insurance Equities refused to pay. You said you'd look into

it, but there were fees. Endless, endless *feeeeeees*. Even if a settlement ever does come in, there'll be nothing left. It'll all go to Crook, Shaft & *Fleeeeeeece!*"

We had reached my office door, which thanks to some ghostly manipulation of time and space had taken longer to reach than normal. The old shit-stain couldn't figure out how to screw in a light bulb, but he had managed that ghost trick where hallways seem a mile longer than they really are. He had doubled the normal distance from the elevator to my office, which was like doubling the delightful amount of time it takes for a plane to crash or a guillotine blade to exit the other side of your goddamn neck.

When we entered my offices, the janitor ghost floated straight through the wall beside the door and took up petulant residence in my outer office.

I welcomed him into the warm embrace of the Banyon Investigations, Inc. family by flipping on the switch to the ceiling fan.

"*Bastaaaar….*" was the best he could manage before he broke apart like a weak fog and vanished from our midst.

My trusty elf assistant had been cleaning the mess Sue Yu had made in my inner office, and came hustling out at the commotion. He found me shedding my coat and fedora and relocating them to the rack in the corner.

"Oh, hello, Mr. Crag," Mannix said.

Mannix had taken off his adorable little suit jacket and hung it over the back of his cute little chair. His shirt sleeves were rolled up to his elbows.

My personal little miracle worker would have given Annie Sullivan a run for her money, and I had no doubt that given enough time Mannix could have helped my filing cabinets grasp the concept of water and taught the

water cooler Braille. As it was, he'd managed to re-file everything that burgling Attorney Sue Yu had dumped all over the room in those halcyon minutes before I'd walked in on her and she had decided to defy physics by occupying the space of my skull with her foot at the same goddamn time.

Mannix smiled at my diminutive Asian companion. Sue Yu had changed from her liquor-soaked clothes into a T-shirt and sweatpants purchased at the sporting goods shop down the block, and in her new gym attire was unlike the usual floozies I brought home, whose only exercise consisted of bending elbows and lifting wallets.

"Hello, Miss..?" Mannix said, offering his tiny little hand.

"There's no need to be nice to her, Mannix," I said. "She's a lawyer. This is Attorney Sue Yu, the second-story artist who trashed the joint last night. Yes, I realize that this is the third floor. Just go with it, as I'm in no mood to split hairs. I've had a hellish twenty-four hours, which most recently included barely escaping a distillery explosion with my life, yet somehow without a bottle of their product clutched in each hand. I could manage without my life, but the thing that'll give me nightmares is not grabbing some free hooch on my way out the door."

Mannix's oversized eyeballs widened, and he hustled over to his little desk, on which lay the afternoon edition of the *Gazette*. He held it up for me to see the headline. While he clutched the paper, Kilroy-like in both hands, his tennis ball eyes peered worriedly over the tops of the huge letters.

BLAST CALL!

I had to admit it was one of the better glaring, ten-foot tall headlines the *Gazette* regularly deployed in a vain attempt to thrill the masses into buying their worth-

less kennel carpet. I snatched the paper from the elf and perused the story.

"Are you all right, Mr. Crag?" Mannix asked worriedly.

"I'm still here, so no," I replied, as I scanned the front page story. "I'll have to make do until Attorney Sue Yu manages to kick my brain through my ear hole."

Mannix fixed a scolding gaze on my lawyer companion.

"It was very naughty of you to kick Mr. Crag in the head," he admonished.

"I know," she admitted, in defiance of all legal precedent.

"It was also very naughty of you to mess up his office," reproached the elf.

"I'm sorry," said Sue Yu, who clearly had no idea that being an attorney meant never having to say you're sorry, wrong, fat, stupid, adulterous, or sober.

"There's nothing here about Dr. Lance Boyle being killed," I said. "It says the fire department is sifting through the smoldering wreckage looking for bodies, so we can still cling to the hope that they'll find a bald bastard brisket, along with the rest of the assholes who tried to murder us. At least they left me out of it." I tossed the paper back to Mannix's desk. "I hate that I'm even partly responsible for the murder of a distillery, even an evil one. It's like an imam accidentally blowing up a mosque with a bomb that he was intending to use to blow up anything other than a mosque."

Mannix and Sue Yu trailed me into my inner sanctum.

My able elf assistant must have been finishing cleaning up when we came in, for the room was so spotless in its usual horrible and depressing manner that I nearly continued straight past my desk, out onto the fire escape

and out into open air. But with my luck gravity had taken the afternoon off, and I couldn't think of anything worse than being suspended in air reading my peeling name off the window while Mannix attempted to drag me back inside with a mop.

My weary ass located my chair and successfully docked on the first attempt.

"Mannix, I need you to work some of that tedious magic of yours. I'm looking for a lawyer, possibly here in town, by the name of Boyle. I have no first name, and I have no idea about age or sex. As an aside unrelated to our current case, my ex-wife and a thousand one-night stands can confirm the latter. If it helps your search, this mystery Boyle will have a demented relative with the mildly amusing name — which is actually becoming increasingly tiresome with repetition — Dr. Lance Boyle. The crazy doctor could be an uncle, father, cousin, husband, or any other relation — conventional or twisted — you can dream up. Let me know as soon as you've got something."

"Yes, sir!" my elf assistant said, beaming.

He spun on the heel of his tiny little shoe and darted from the room.

I had no doubt that the search for the missing-link Boyle was in capable, albeit tiny and adorable little hands. Mannix's many varied skills included an unparalleled ability to plow through the kind of mind-numbing scut work that always left me longing to suck on a thirty-eight caliber lollipop two seconds in.

"Now," I said, addressing Sue Yu. "Why were you searching for the Tooth Fairy?"

She very clearly had a lower opinion of me than even I did, since it was evident by the surprised look on her mush that she thought I'd never get around to asking her

the most germane question in the solar system. Apparently she assumed I hadn't noticed that the missing molar king was the reason the two of us had been repeatedly brought into each other's orbit.

There was the hesitance she'd displayed at the bus stop, followed by the realization yet again that her law firm was — at least until the law school graduations of the oily progeny of its deceased founding triumvirate — defunct.

"The senior partners have been worried the past few weeks," she said with a sigh. "They were having all kinds of closed-door meetings. I eventually found out that all the junior partners were being snuck in for secret meetings as well. Every lawyer in the office was being briefed. Everybody except me. I started eavesdropping on their conversations, and I found out that for some reason everyone was worried about the Tooth Fairy going missing. I had no idea why. He wasn't a client. And it wasn't just Crook, Shaft & Fleece. I found out that the senior partners were having meetings with Willy, Cocksure & Seaman, which is one of our biggest rivals. Also Schnoz, Fleming & Hocker, and the Chinese firm of Wing, Wang & Wong. All the biggest firms, from all over town. *Everyone* was scared that the Tooth Fairy was missing."

"Do you know what precisely worried these bastards, whose law firms all have improbable and comical names, about his disappearance?"

"Not really. All I did hear a few times was them talking about some legal loophole. They were panicked that they weren't able to exploit it any longer."

I nodded sagely to give the impression that I had some clue what the hell was going on, which I absolutely did not.

"What can you tell me about the queen?" I asked.

The last time I'd asked her that question, she'd launched the heel of one of her clodhoppers through my temple. I hadn't been prepared the first time around, but this time I was reasonably certain I was safe. For one thing, we were both sitting down. And this time, a desk separated us. Also, if she made any sudden moves I was pretty sure my reflexes were sharp enough that I'd be able to hide under my desk and shoot at every ankle that came in eyeshot while Mannix phoned the National Guard.

"You asked me that last night, Mr. Banyon. I don't know what you're talking about. I don't know any queen."

I wanted to catch her in a lie, but my big-mouthed gut was informing me that the dame was telling me the truth.

"So why the hell did you kick me in the head when I asked about her?"

She shrugged her narrow shoulders. "You'd just caught me red-handed breaking and entering and rummaging through your office. Wouldn't you have panicked and kicked somebody in the head under those circumstances?"

"As a general rule, no," I said. "I'm usually the one who gets clobbered over the head and wakes up either in a jail cell or in some elaborate, Rube Goldberg-esque contrivance from which I have to rescue myself and some dame du jour. Mostly it's just jail, as the construction costs for complex traps are prohibitively expensive, especially when weighed against their effectiveness, which is ultimately virtually nil."

There was one more important question to ask the hot little bowl of wonton soup.

Mannix had tidied away my great discovery of the

hidden messages related to the mysterious queen that apparently appeared in every legal document in the goddamn world. When my assistant was in a tidying mood, he always stored away in my main desk drawer items he guessed were related to a current case. I opened it and, indeed, found piled up the sheets of paper I'd salvaged from the sidewalk after my post-midnight battle with the gang of lawyers from Swindle, Steele & Robb.

Another item unrelated to that law firm sat atop the stack.

"God — if Thou art listening — dammit," I said.

I picked the item up. It was a postcard-sized piece of white cardboard. Goddamn glitter rained down on my desk, hands, trousers, chair, shoes, floor, and, I assumed, into every hidden crevice throughout the entire multiverse.

Glitter and cockroaches are the only two things that will survive nuclear Armageddon. The giant, mutated cucarachas of the future that scuttle out from under their radioactive refrigerators into the hellscape of Man's folly will sparkle like goddamn diamonds while they're feasting on moldy Ding Dongs.

"Mannix, what the hell is with this glitter card?" I hollered.

My assistant came hustling back into the room, a phonebook clutched in his little hands. I held up the card for him to explain himself, which succeeded in forcing show-and-tell glitter everywhere it hadn't already gotten, including my right eye.

"I went to your apartment to do your laundry," the elf explained. He frowned, momentarily distracted from the card in my hand. "The ghost in your building's laundry room isn't a very nice man, Mr. Crag," he said.

"No," I agreed. "He's a dead Confederate veteran

asshole who changes the settings on the machines when you leave for two minutes to see if the janitor has anything good to drink on his solvents shelf, then tells you he's claimed the rinse cycle for Robert goddamn E. Lee. The *card*, Mannix."

"Oh. I found it under your pillow when I was changing your sheets. I thought it might be important."

As usual, Mannix's instincts were correct, although he might have at least sealed the thing in a Glad bag. It was like one of those Christmas cards that people send out as acts of revenge to their worst enemies on their Yuletide list. The card might look fancy as hell, but they explode like a can of hilarious compressed spring snakes and leave a sparkling mess that you're still sweeping up on Labor Day.

With my one good eye I read the card once more.

BACK OFF, OR ELSE.

I'm generally the ideal target audience for threats, since I am, by both nature and choice, an out and proud coward. But it's difficult to get all that terrified when the letters on a threatening note have been written with Elmer's glue in ornate, effeminate cursive, and then dusted with a pound of silver glitter.

"Hold it a minute, Banyon," Attorney Sue Yu commanded.

When I looked up with my only remaining functioning eyeball, the dame had hauled her damp clothes out of the shopping bag in which she'd been schlepping them around, and was rummaging excitedly around in the pocket of her sensible lady business suit. Also, Mannix had apparently fled the room, although now that I was half-blind I conceded it was possible he was hiding somewhere on the half of the room that had vanished on the other side of my squinted-shut right eyelid.

"Here!" Sue Yu announced in triumph.

She held aloft a stack of cards similar to my own, which she had sensibly stored inside a Ziploc bag. As she passed the bag over to me, Mannix hustled back into the room toting a vacuum cleaner and, yet again proving his great value, a bottle of Visine.

"I've found them under my pillow every morning this week," the dame lawyer explained. "I couldn't ask outright at work or people would know what I was up to, but I hinted around about it. I don't think anyone but me was getting them."

As I washed off my eyeball, Mannix vacuumed up the sparkling mess the note from my apartment had made. The elf stood at the ready as I very carefully removed Sue Yu's notes from the plastic bag.

LEAVE ME ALONE
STOP POKING AROUND
THIS HAS NOTHING TO DO WITH YOU
I'M NEVER, NEVER COMING BACK

"Let's all note the fact that he's nicer to you than he is to me," I said. "This from the same bastard who, when I lost my two front teeth in first grade, shoved a pink plastic hair roller and a dog track betting form under my pillow."

I replaced the dame's notes in the bag, and for good measure slipped in with them the note Mannix had retrieved from my apartment. Once they were all carefully packed away where they could do no harm, I tossed the bag in the trash.

"Shouldn't we save those for evidence?" Sue Yu shouted over the sound of Mannix's vacuum cleaner.

"Evidence of what?" I asked. "He threatened me, not you, and, in case you didn't know, worrying ages one prematurely. If I wasted all my time worrying about all

the threats I get in this job I wouldn't be able to continue to pass for a boyish twenty-nine while actually being in an advanced stage of decrepitude."

Mannix had finished vacuuming, and hustled over to yank the plug from the socket. Vacuum in hand, he hurried from the room.

I retrieved the Swindle, Steele & Robb documents from my drawer and promptly spilled another fifty pounds of goddamn glitter all over the room.

"I would set fire to this dump," I said, "if I thought this shit would burn."

I shook off the residual glitter into the trash as best I could, then laid out the documents on the surface of my desk.

"Care to explain?" I asked the dame lawyer.

Sue Yu got up and picked up the paper nearest her. She scanned the document from the top with the bored eye of somebody used to reading boring legalistic bullshit day in and day out. She had opened her mouth to speak, presumably on the horseshit content of the legal document, when she came across the first letter I'd circled. Her eye traced the phrase down to the bottom of the sheet of paper.

We live for the queen.

She picked up the next paper and went immediately for the circled phrase. She began snatching up scraps of paper two at a time, glancing from hand to hand.

"What does this mean?" she asked once she was through.

"I was hoping you could enlighten me," I replied.

"I told you, Banyon, I don't know anything about any queen." She waved her hand at the letterhead on the nearest document. "These are all from Swindle, Steele & Robb. Maybe they know something."

"I found the same hidden phrases in legal documents from Shyster, Pilfer & Fraud, the ambulance chasers in residence one floor down," I informed her. "Also…"

I reached into my desk and took out one of the files I'd pulled before I'd headed to the morgue earlier that day. It was a threatened lawsuit from a client who had retained my services several years earlier, and who subsequently didn't have the dough to pay me for finding her missing husband, but whose MIA old man — once found — had the wherewithal to hire a law firm to threaten me with a lawsuit if I continued to have the nerve to expect to get paid by his wife for services rendered.

Attorney Sue Yu gave a long, careful, stunned perusal of the cease and desist order from her own law firm — now happily deceased — of Crook, Shaft & Fleece. On each page of the three-page document I had circled a reference to the entire goddamn legal system's revered and thus far invisible queen.

"I had no idea, Banyon. You must believe me."

"Since you're a lawyer, my instinct is not to," I said. "But you're a lawyer unlike every other one I've ever met. Not to mention if I call you a liar to your face, you might kick my head out the window into traffic, and I'm in the middle of using it right now."

Sue Yu hurried to keep up as I got up and marched into my outer office.

Mannix was hard at work at his desk, surrounded by open phonebooks and with a comically oversized phone propped up between his little shoulder and pointed ear.

"Mannix, keep looking for Attorney Boyle, wherever and whoever he or she is," I commanded as I retrieved my hat and coat from the corner rack where they'd spent enough time goofing off. "In the meantime, if you need me I'll be at my apartment."

"Yes, sir, Mr. Crag," the elf said, nodding.

I headed into the hall, hoping like hell the janitor ghost wasn't waiting to leap out at us from the ether and start boring the shit out of us again.

"Wait, you're going home?" Attorney Sue Yu asked, dogging me on my ghost-less way to the elevator. "What about our case?"

"Lady, we have no case. You haven't hired me, and even if you wanted to I'm irritated enough with my current client without ladling you on top. Having said that, I do have a Tooth Fairy to catch. I am therefore going to bed. Care to join me?"

15

A half-hour after leaving my office, I crawled into bed accompanied only by an ego whose accustomed bruises were no match for the physical battering to which my middle-aged husk had been victim the previous twenty-four hours.

I was undeserving of an assistant who looked after my welfare as much as did Mannix. If it was not for the work he did above and beyond the regular call of duty, my dirty sheets would have long ago rebelled and, with the help of the resident Dr. Jack Kevorkian bedbugs, scurried off my mattress to find the nearest clothesline from which to hang themselves.

As it was, the clean pillowcase under my head and the equally clean sheets under the rest of my occasionally and always regrettably ambulatory disaster zone offered very nearly comfort enough to help me nod off two seconds after I'd dropped onto them. I fought like hell the urge to sleep even as, to the outside observer, I gave an Academy Award worthy imitation of the kind of blissful slumber impossible to achieve without booze or a hammer.

I wasn't sure how long I remained supine. Counting the seconds would have effectively dressed every number

up in a mohair vest and set them loose to jump hurdles on mutton legs. I would not then have been awake to feel the very slight pressure under my head of a hand sliding under my pillow.

My own hand shot out blind in the dark and snapped shut around a narrow wrist, and I hastily swung my legs around until I was in a sitting position.

"Got him," I announced.

The nightstand lights abruptly switched on and I found myself face-to-startled-face with the Tooth Fairy in all his swishy glory.

He batted his long, artificial lashes and fluttered his wings in confusion.

"What? *How?"* he demanded.

Before he could complete his journalism degree with "when, where, and goddamn who," his head snapped around to locate the source of a noise over by the door.

Across the room, Attorney Sue Yu's hand fled the light switch.

"We did it, Banyon!" the dame enthused, her face flushed crimson. Apparently in the thrill of the moment this had become a team effort, even though it had been entirely my idea, and her function in it could have been assumed by a twenty buck Kmart Clapper.

Although I really couldn't complain about Sue Yu. Unlike every other lawyer in the universe, when I'd explained my simple plan to her, the last surviving attorney from the late, unlamented firm of Crook, Shaft & Fleece had not insisted that she had an even better idea, only to suggest something utterly moronic and convoluted and completely unworkable. Her role in the scheme was to hide behind the dresser and turn on the lights, which hopefully wouldn't cost me five hundred bucks an hour, plus goddamn paralegal fees.

I reached under my pillow and pulled out the card the Tooth Fairy had slipped under it when he thought I was asleep. It left a trail of glitter across my clean sheets and dumped about twenty goddamn pounds of the shiny shit to the floor.

I KNOW WHERE YOU LIVE

"Why was it even necessary to write that?" I asked, tossing the glitter bomb onto my nightstand. "You already left one of these calling cards last night, so clearly I'd be aware that you know where I live. And while we're on the subject, would it kill you to invest in a felt-tipped pen? There is no one on the planet who doesn't hate this shit."

My prisoner, like pretty much everyone else in my life, completely ignored me.

"Unhand me, you vicious brute!" the Tooth Fairy snapped.

His wings flapped madly and his pink ballet slippers rose from the floor. The little four-foot SOB weighed about sixty pounds soaking wet, so the best he managed after liftoff was to lock in parallel to the floor. He realized when I didn't let go that there was no way he was reaching escape velocity, so he quickly lowered back to the floor.

He began desperately twirling his hand in the air, and instantly a tiny vortex through which he hoped to make his escape yawned open two feet above his fingertips. All the quarter-sized hole in the air managed to suck in before I slapped his hand aside was most of the glitter that had splashed across my bed and floor. The sucking vortex collapsed in on itself, and the glimmering silver glitter that had failed to be vacuumed up inside it remained suspended in midair for a moment before scattering everywhere I wouldn't find it until it was too late, such

as in my tube of toothpaste, the half a tuna sandwich in the fridge, and my underwear drawer.

The regular means by which he entered and exited kids' bedrooms closed to him for now, the Tooth Fairy redoubled his more conventional efforts.

"I said let go, you monster!"

With his free hand he punched ferociously at my wrist, which would have been more comical in its total ineffectualness were his mouth not a perforated garden hose and had his shouting not sprayed a bucket of spit all over the room.

"That's one option," I conceded. "Let me suggest another."

I picked up the phone from my nightstand and attempted to dial a number which, after years of doing business with the bastard I was attempting to contact, I should have known by heart. In my defense, I generally wasn't holding a squirming Tooth Fairy as I tried to dial one-handed. After two wrong numbers to the same Eskimo takeout joint, plus one to an Antarctic weather station on the goddamn Ross Ice Shelf, I gave up and dialed *O*.

"Robert Sherman Planck, vice president at Madison Insurance Equities," I told the operator. "No, operator, I am not able to write the number down, since the SOB I'm holding hostage was already wriggling like a maniac before I mentioned Planck's name, but has now gone completely and utterly insane. Also, the three pencils that were on my nightstand an hour ago have somehow mysteriously vanished. Please connect me."

"Don't turn me over to him!" the Tooth Fairy begged.

"You're turning him over to Planck?" Sue Yu demanded.

"No!" the Tooth Fairy insisted.

"Possibly," I said. "Probably. Let's split the difference and call it definitely."

"You didn't tell me you were looking for him for Madison Insurance," the sizzling plate of sukiyaki said.

"I'm not. Not technically, although they're footing the bill for my client, the kid whose file I noticed you searched when you busted into my office. Madison wasn't mentioned in it, since the Thompson brat is officially paying the check. Not that any of this is any of your business. It's just that I'm distracted because I'm on hold right now and enduring the unendurable banality of Barry Manilow blaring in my ear on one hand, and on the other hand there's a Tooth Fairy who is currently attempting to pry my index finger off his wrist with a pink plastic magic wand that looks like he got it in the party supplies aisle at Big Lots."

"Let me go, you horrid, horrid beast!" the Tooth Fairy cried, with such stereotyped hysterics I was sure some league or group or association would soon be forcing me into an insincere Facebook apology and a year of indoctrination therapy just for letting him talk in my goddamn apartment.

"Hold that spittle," I told the little fairy, since the bastard I was calling had just come on the line. "Planck? Banyon. I've got him. No, at my place. Look, I can't stay on the phone. He's fighting like a bastard right now. Just get the address off my policy, since I'm stupid enough to insure through you thieves."

I jabbed my finger on the cradle, severing the connection.

"I'm not sure you should turn him over to Madison Insurance," Sue Yu said.

"Well, *I'm* sure, sweetie," the Tooth Fairy insisted, violently swatting me with his wand which, thank Allah,

was still the plastic store-bought one.

"Why are all the law firms in town scared that you went missing?" the dame demanded, before her head snapped back to me. "What about that queen, Banyon?" she said. To the Tooth Fairy, she asked, "Who's the queen who was sending all those threatening letters to your office, and what does she have to do with lawyers?"

"Talk to the wand, missy."

He held out the same, as if he were offering a lick off his lollipop.

It was disturbing no end to realize that this was not the most miserable I had ever been with company in my bedroom.

What Sue Yu, Attorney-at-Law, didn't get was that there would be plenty of time to question the Tooth Fairy while we were waiting for his ride to arrive, and so I ignored the two of them and dialed *O* again, offering my bedroom companions my side of my conversation with the unpleasant Ma Bell employee on the other end of a line with which I would have strangled her were both my hands free.

"Operator, get me the main police station. Aren't you the same surly dame who gave me a hard time two minutes ago? I still don't have a pencil with which to write, and I've still got a fairy trying to yank my arm out of its socket, so I haven't any hands with which to write even if I had a goddamn pencil. You people have every telephone number on earth at your fingertips, and all the hardware and software you need to connect the King of Siam to his long-distance girlfriend in the Horsehead Nebula. Why is it that whenever anybody asks you to connect them to somebody on the other side of town, you act like a.) we've just harassed you in the middle of making a chocolate soufflé, and b.) it's not your goddamn job?"

I was not sure if our call was being monitored to ensure quality service, but if it was I only hoped that the dame wasn't fired for her impressive foul-mouthed diatribe before she connected me to the cop shop.

I had the police switchboard connect me to my least favorite cop on the force, who generally ran homicide but who was so lousy at his job that it was depressingly possible that he forgot. Besides, I didn't know anybody in missing persons, and I didn't feel like going through the song and dance of making a brand-new enemy when I had a familiar asshole that was more broken in than Gomer Pyle on date night.

"Jenkins, it's Banyon. Yes, and I loathe you, as well, only at depths so much greater than yours that the fish of my loathing are hereditarily blind and require trained dogs in bathyspheres to help them locate plankton. Now that we've got that out of the way, I've found the Tooth Fairy everybody's been looking for. How? Because I've been on the case for one day, while you boys in blue have only had three weeks to not track him down. No, at my apartment. Look, Jenkins, this guy's hotter than Racquel Welch in a fur bikini, so you'd better hurry up and collect him before somebody else beats you to it."

I hung up the phone and, now that the cops and Planck were out of the way, next had to deal with the two confused faces at my bedside.

The Tooth Fairy had briefly stopped fruitlessly attempting to break free. Beside him, Attorney Sue Yu shook her head.

"Why did you call the cops, too?"

"Because, like anybody who has ever had to deal with insurance company assholes, I would paddle across the Atlantic in a lifeboat made of Swiss cheese cinderblocks before I trusted them. Finding him—" I nodded

to the Tooth Fairy, who was once more attempting to create a vortex with his swirling hand, "—is a police matter." (I swatted my detainee's hand and the nascent vortex collapsed in on itself.) "I don't care who hires me, I'm not getting my license pulled for failing to inform the cops I caught the little SOB. If they get here first, I turn him over to them. If Planck and that detestable Thompson family who hired me get here first, I give him to them, make them sign for him, and let the cops know who has custody of him when they show up."

It was a perfectly brilliant plan that instantly began to unravel with the crashing sound that suddenly erupted in my living room. From the sound of shattering, scattering glass, something huge had just busted through one of the windows.

The first crash was followed a split-second later by another crash of the second living room window, which was simultaneously accompanied by yet another goddamn crash coming from what could only be the bathroom window.

I didn't have to wonder very long about the nature of my apparent multiple unwanted guests, since the instant after the crash from the bathroom, the bedroom window above my bureau suddenly — and by now not entirely unexpectedly — exploded inward with category five hurricane force.

When Sue Yu and I had entered the apartment a couple of hours before, I'd drawn the blinds on the dying sun. It was now fully night, and only the ambient light of the post-dusk city illuminated the outline of the thing that was at first amusingly caught in a tangle of blinds, then comically rolling over my bureau with its many limbs jutting humorously through the slats of the blinds that it had ripped from the window, then finally dropping to the

floor onto its six horrifying furry legs with a shit-inducing thud.

The thing opened its mouth, baring twin rows of spiked and glistening white teeth. A deep, wet growl rose up from its thorax and rolled from the tip of its drooling, darting tongue, and I was reasonably certain that I would soon — if it was not already the case — desperately require a change of underwear. Unfortunately for me, the multi-legged bastard was blocking my path to the drawer containing my spare drawers, and so in the name of personal hygiene, the moment it began to charge across the room to murder the three of us, I had no choice but to yank my gat from its holster and blast the terrifying thing between one of its three sets of freakishly blinking eyes.

It stopped dead and roared again, rearing up on its most distant set of legs. I noted before I fired another round — this one a fatal blast into its exposed chest — that each thick leg appeared to end in a polished pair of Bruno Magli shoes.

The scream from the creature appeared at first to echo throughout my apartment, but I quickly realized that what I was actually hearing was at least six more of the things I'd just killed replying from the recesses of my ratty residence to the dying cry of their companion.

The rearing whatever-it-was crashed to the threadbare carpet, and a final gush of air fled its lungs.

I had only a brief second to get a glancing look at the freaky bastard.

It was, for lack of a better description, and with apologies to goddamn Franz Kafka, a five-foot long, hundred-and-fifty-pound cockroach topped with something very much like, but not quite beyond the uncanny valley, a human head.

I only had time for a glance since I could hear an army of what I assumed were identical creatures scurrying up the hallway toward my closed bedroom door.

"Hold him!" I hollered at Attorney Sue Yu, passing off the Tooth Fairy like a relay baton as I leaped for the door.

I slammed my shoulder into the bookcase beside it, and knocked the five-story hunk of furniture across the doorway at an angle just as the mob attacked.

Something bounced hard against the door. The combined weight of me jamming my back against the bookcase, as well as the bookcase itself filled with first edition John D. MacDonald hardcovers wasn't enough to hold them back. The door popped open a few inches; just wide enough for a half dozen legs to jam through the crack.

"*Banyon!*" Sue Yu shouted.

A few years before, I'd taken a case to track down a missing bird. A Polish scientist who'd taught his parrot the secret formula for making ice had been murdered, and the bird stolen. Nobody else in the country had the recipe, so they needed somebody to find the parrot before they were forced to suffer through a summer of warm drinks and a winter of melted hockey rinks. The other, frankly, degrading details aren't important; only that it wound up that ninjas were involved, and when I recovered the bird from Dow Chemical, the emperor of Japan presented me with a samurai sword, which Attorney Sue Yu had just discovered leaning in the corner with my spare dress shirt airing out over it.

The dame had clearly seen far too many movies and thought that she could heave a wickedly sharp sword across the room and that I'd snatch it spectacularly from the air and suddenly turn into goddamn Errol Flynn, hacking off limbs and buckling swash all over the asses

of our attackers.

Since I didn't feel like getting harpooned in the heart, head, or several other far more hilarious body parts (which was a reasonably likely result of standing like a moron in the path of a hurled sword), or severing all my fingers by accidentally grabbing the blade if I was stupid enough to try to catch something that was nearly entirely razor-sharp, I did the most sensible thing money could buy and jumped like a goddamn sissy girl out of the path of the flying sword. I preserved a very small portion of my dignity by not screaming like same.

Lucky for me and for the rest of the quivering cock-roach buffet cowering in my bedroom, my cowardly leap flung me back like a fired cannonball onto the tipped-over bookcase and against the door. The shoved door crushed limbs that had heretofore been grabbing for me. Several screams issued from the hallway, and the multitude of legs rapidly withdrew, allowing me time to slam the door firmly shut and to get a better angle on propping the bookcase up under the doorknob.

The subsequent pounding on the door was so violent that the rattling wall knocked to the floor a lamp — which smashed to bits — an ashtray; and a box of golf tees from a small table. I was only vaguely aware that I owned the table, but I had absolutely no idea what the hell I was doing with an ashtray or the busted-open box of golf tees, since I don't smoke and since golf was more boring than *Moby Dick* and was invented so that Scotch perverts had an excuse to look up each others' skirts while fishing balls out of small holes.

While at least two of the creatures remained to kick and punch their Bruno Magli's against my bedroom door, I heard several of the screeching steroidal cockroaches pounding down the hall, their stomping feet fading across

my living room. I was certain they would circle around and soon be using as a way in the same bedroom window through which their late companion had made his dramatic entrance. Unfortunately, I had only four rounds left to cover a multitude, and my spare ammunition was inconveniently stored in a locked case at the gun store, since I'd forgotten to pick some up for the past eight goddamn months.

I grabbed for the sword, but naturally Excalibur had harpooned the floor and was jammed in so hard that I couldn't pull it loose without a Gold's Gym membership and six months of protein shakes.

The frame around the bedroom door suddenly cracked and I was nearly decapitated by the transverse architrave, which popped loose and swung down from where it had been content to do its part framing the doorway for a hundred years. When the board cracked, the creatures in the hall smelled success in the air, presumably over the stink of terror that was the contribution of my armpits to the festivities. The giant roaches redoubled their efforts, screeching encouragement to one another.

"*Portal!*" I hollered as I yanked at the unbudging sword stuck fast in the floor. "*Now would be an exceptionally good time to make a goddamn portal!*"

Across the room, cowering behind Sue Yu's metaphorical skirts, the Tooth Fairy apparently had forgotten in his abject terror that he had the means to flee the room. He had to blink a few times to get the fog to lift, but the instant his eyes cleared he began rapidly swirling his limp-wristed hand in the air.

"Make him make it big enough for all three of us!" I hollered at Sue Yu.

The dame nodded understanding. She held the little bastard by the neck of his sequined shirt and, as he

worked, she gave an extra hard twist to keep him honest.

I heard the squeals of several giant cockroaches approaching outside the window. Simultaneously, the side of the doorframe abruptly cracked. A three foot length of wood splintered and popped loose. The door sprang open several inches, shoving the bookcase hard into my toes. The furry, grabbing limbs appeared once more. The shoes had been kicked off some of them, and I saw rudimentary opposable thumbs reaching out for me as the furry foot-and-hand-like appendages snatched crazily at the air.

I was lucky Anton Chekhov was dead, because he'd be all pissy in a commie accent that great sword stuck in glorious floor was goddamn Red herring.

I gave up on the recalcitrant blade and instead grabbed the hunk of doorframe that had flipped to the worn carpet. I abandoned my post at the door and ran like a maniac to where the Tooth Fairy was swirling his hand, palm out, like mad.

Rather than open a portal in the air, the little bastard — under the watchful and terrified eye of Attorney Sue Yu — had created one in the floor, so that those of us not magic-capable, and therefore unable to shrink ourselves down for typical otherworldly vortex travel, could simply allow gravity to do the job for us.

Apparently in order to accommodate the size of normal mortals who couldn't shrink down as small as a pea before leaping into it, some alterations to the nature of the portal were necessary. For one thing, unlike the previous ones he'd attempted to open up, this one created a typhoon-like deafening wind that rattled the walls of my bedroom.

The vortex was the size of a manhole, and Sue Yu was first to leap into the sewer that had yawned open in

the floor of my bedroom. I thought the gushing wind might be powerful enough to launch her straight back out and splatter her against my ceiling, but the lawyer dame dropped neatly from sight.

Behind me, the door burst open. I barely heard it over the howl of wind roaring out of the vortex in my floor.

My bookcase barricade spiraled across the room just in time to trip the first of the creatures that had just scurried at a hundred miles an hour through the busted window. It tumbled end-over-end and slammed comically upside-down against my bed, jolting the box spring into the nightstand and knocking yet another lamp to the floor, shattering the glass base and popping the bulb.

With the only two lamps in the room out of commission, the bedroom was instantly plunged into near total darkness, which made the approaching shadows of the running, snarling giant cockroaches all the more goddamn comforting.

"Jump, you awful man!" the Tooth Fairy yelled.

I wasn't about to leave the SOB to make his own escape now that I'd caught him. With at least one of the massive creatures snapping at my heels, I took a flying leap for the hole, grabbing the Tooth Fairy by the arm on my way through.

We plunged through the hole and into open air.

Beings like the Tooth Fairy have limited magical gifts, but that didn't make the ones at his disposal any less spectacular. Every night, the fairy needed to be in a million bedrooms, so like Santa Claus he was able to bend time and space to make sure he could cover his entire route so that kids didn't die of old age while waiting to collect a quarter for their first lost tooth. He also had the ability to access any bedroom on the planet, which the powers that be were wise to bestow on him and not

me, since I'd have used it to poke around Michelle Pfeiffer's underwear drawer when she wasn't home.

The Tooth Fairy and I bounced off an unbelievably conveniently positioned mattress trampoline, were flung off the bed, and did a tumble impressive for its utter gracelessness into a wall which, frankly, could have been a lot goddamn softer.

It turned out that the only soft part of the hard wall was Sue Yu, who had apparently followed the same flight path as ours during her freefall.

"Get off me," the diminutive attorney-at-law demanded, swatting at the pair of us.

The little SOB Tooth Fairy got his bearings before me, and I barely prevented him from creating another portal through which he could make his escape.

I climbed to my feet, which at my age should have been a three on a ten-point difficulty scale, but registered at roughly eighty-seven billion on my creaking knees. I kept a firm grip on the slippery Tooth Fairy's arm as I surveyed the area, assuming we'd landed in the master bedroom of either a Mongolian yurt or a grass hut in the Sudan.

With the incredible gift to transport us anywhere in the world literally at the tips of his fingers, it came as a pretty substantial disappointment that the bedroom to which the Tooth Fairy had supernaturally evacuated us was clearly not in Buckingham Palace or even shithole Detroit. The layout of the room, the peeling gray paint that made the joint look like a particularly depressing prison, the delicious cracked plaster for the kids to eat, and a view nearly identical to the one from the window of the bedroom we'd just fled combined for the easiest guess in the history of Trivial Pursuit.

"This is the same goddamn building," I snapped, as

quietly as humanly possible. "*My* same goddamn pile-of-shit building. With the entire planet to choose from, you dropped us through a hole in my goddamn floor?"

The Tooth Fairy didn't have time to defend his lack of imagination.

"Banyon?" an angry, quavering voice from across the room demanded. "Crag Banyon? What the hell are you doing in my bedroom?"

The voice belonged to a familiar wrinkled prune who stood in the open bedroom door wearing a shocked expression.

Fortunately, her expression wasn't all she was wearing or I would have used the doorframe board that I still clutched in my hands to beat my eyes to death. Massive pink plastic curlers weighed down the old dame's few remaining strands of gray hair, and were color-coordinated to match her threadbare pink nightgown and ratty pink slippers.

Mrs. Flora Willhausen was clutching her poodle Bruno in the sagging flesh of her forearms, which nearly tied the human-faced cockroaches in my bedroom as the most disquieting thing I'd seen all day, since the mangy mutt had died five years before when Mrs. Flora Willhausen, dingbat extraordinaire, had attempted to dry it off in her toaster oven and nearly burned the whole building down.

The cut-rate taxidermist who'd preserved Bruno for the ages had done his best to fill in the missing patches of burned fur by gluing on tufts of nylon pillow stuffing, which might have worked had the dead mongrel been left up on the mantle instead of being schlepped around the house like a four-legged handbag.

I turned to the Tooth Fairy.

"*One* story downstairs?" I whispered. "You didn't

even drop us two or three stories down? You have the ability to transport us to any bedroom on the surface of the entire goddamn planet, and you select the one immediately downstairs from the giant, ravenous mutant insects that want to eat us alive?"

The Tooth Fairy shrugged his wings.

"I panicked, sweetie," he explained. "I can do another one."

The howling racket that the large portal had made in my bedroom was loud enough that it would have brought the things crashing down on us. It was best to hunker down and remain silent until the risk of being eaten alive by giant bugs had passed, which was a scenario most people don't have to worry about in their jobs, but which I'd dealt with a discomforting number of times in my ten-year career as a P.I. Our accompanying attorney — who I still hoped wasn't billing me by the minute — had the same thought.

"Be quiet," Sue Yu commanded with an urgent hiss.

The lawyer dame held her finger to her lips as she looked up at the ceiling. She was hunching slightly, apparently under the impression that a fraction of an inch would take herself significantly farther away from death than the rest of us.

I could hear the giant cockroaches stomping furiously and aimlessly around all four corners of my bedroom. With nobody left to consume, and apparently no clue we were holding our collective breath only one floor down, they were circling without purpose and would likely soon give up, which was a historically accurate reenactment of the behavior of most guests to visit le boudoir de Banyon.

"Banyon!" Mrs. Flora Willhausen snarled, in a tone that explained why her husband, the late Horace Will-

hausen, had chosen to eat himself into a fatal heart attack at sixty-three rather than spend another three decades with audio ice-picks in each ear.

"I'll explain everything in a minute, Mrs. Willhausen, you old bat," I whispered, attempting to force a smile to calm the ugly ancient dame whose bedroom we'd invaded. "Assuming, that is, we don't all get killed in the next sixty seconds. In the meantime, if it will give you something to do to help keep that exploding dynamite you call a voice from continuing to go off, why don't you stick a roller skate under Bruno's stuffed ass and take him for a walk around the coffee table?"

It was, frankly, not only the nicest thing I'd ever said to the nasty old biddy, but was practically a Shakespearean sonnet compared to the screaming serenades the hag and her dead husband used to coo loud enough at each other that the entire building had courtside seats as they carved one another up with their machete tongues.

For some bizarre reason, the hideous old bag took offense at my all-out charm offensive.

"*I said what the hell are you doing in my bedroom, Crag Banyon!*" the hag with the dead dog nestled in her arms screeched at top volume from across the room.

The stomping upstairs immediately ceased. Every stamping foot above us made an instant beeline in the direction of my bedroom window.

I was surprised that the next screaming woman's voice wasn't my own but was, rather, once more that of my previously irate, now terrified, neighbor.

"What the hell is that!" Mrs. Flora Willhausen abruptly shrieked.

I would have expected her to be pointing at her window, which I anticipated would be hosting a cockroach invasion any second now. Instead, she was aiming

a crooked finger in my direction and squeezing Bruno so hard that one of the mutt's glass eyes popped out and rolled under her battered hope chest.

A hideous, spitting snarl suddenly rose up next to Mrs. Flora Willhausen's bed, which I prayed to every god in the heavens, on the earth, and under the sea wasn't the reanimated corpse of a heretofore taxidermied, now awake and amorous, Mr. Horace goddamn Willhausen.

Apparently when the Tooth Fairy and I had jumped into the portal in the floor of my apartment, we hadn't noticed in the dark that the giant cockroach that had been snapping at my fleeing heels had followed us through. It had evidently not duplicated our impressive trampoline act, and had instead hit the floor and rolled under the bed.

If it had been stunned in the fall, its wits were now fully regained. It came charging at us on a half dozen legs.

You want to have a clear head when you're about to go into hopeless battle with a gigantic stampeding cockroach with a human-like head possessed of razor-sharp, flesh-tearing fangs. It's certainly not the ideal time to be having any rogue epiphanies. Unfortunately, in the moment the drooling thing came charging for us, as I heard the last of its compatriots stomping out of my upstairs window, as I heard the growling, snapping approach of the army that was charging down the side of the building in the direction of my downstairs hag neighbor's wide-open bedroom window, as I shoved a stunned and immobile Sue Yu from the path of our immediate insect attacker, as I considered how this one furry-legged bastard had accidentally joined us in the apartment of Mrs. Willhausen, the best course of action open to those of us who didn't want to be tomorrow's cockroach

shit sprang unbidden into my genius brain.

"If you can throw one of those vortices up anywhere—" I yelled at the Tooth Fairy.

I paused in mid-thought to take a mighty swing with the chunk of doorframe that was somehow miraculously still in my hands. The cockroach was suddenly Ginger Rogers, elegantly dancing backwards, away from my Fred Astaire swing.

"—I would highly recommend," I continued to the fairy, as the cockroach and I circled one another like prizefighters, "that you open the largest one you can possibly open directly under that open bedroom window. Also, make the other end of it a bedroom not one floor down in this same goddamn building, if it's not too much trouble."

To his credit, the Tooth Fairy not only didn't question my suggestion, the spark of understanding that sprang into his eyes meant he clearly got the message.

The little bastard began swirling both hands in the air, aiming them for the other side of the room like a demented orchestra conductor. As I swung my doorframe at my opponent once more, I caught from the corner of my eye a tiny portal yawning open in the floor. It opened and closed in on itself several times, like a sleepy eye, before suddenly rocketing outward in every direction until it had consumed nearly half the bedroom floor.

We were suddenly caught in a wind tunnel. Worn curtains were torn from bending rods. Threadbare pillows rocketed from the bed and into the abyss. Photos of the Mr. and Mrs. Horace Willhausens at various stages of their miserable life together — from ugly and miserable wedding couple to uglier and even more miserable silver anniversary — flew off walls and tables and disappeared into the Wile E. Coyote black hole.

"What the hell is that?" Mrs. Flora Willhausen bellowed from the bedroom doorway, seemingly more concerned about the disappearance into the vortex of her worthless knickknacks and ancient magazines than she was with the giant cockroach that was about to murder her upstairs neighbor. "Is that one of them interdimensional doohickeys? My Hummels! That's it! If you people aren't all out of here in the next thirty seconds, I'm calling the landlord!"

She had scarcely time to spit out her furious threat.

The portal had yawned open in the floor seconds before the first of the huge cockroaches began scurrying through the window and into the apartment. Mrs. Willhausen shrieked and flung Bruno at the first skittering bug, and both stuffed dog and insect plunged through the swirling hole and disappeared from sight.

On her screaming retreat from the room, the old bag lost a ratty pink slipper, which was sucked into the vortex along with the next giant cockroach.

Despite their multi-eyed, human-like heads, it was evident that the giant cockroaches weren't the brightest bug bastards on the block. The vortex made short work of the insect army as, one-by-one, they climbed in through the window and, one-by-one, were sucked into oblivion. A dozen of them checked in, and all of them checked out.

When it was clear the last invading bug had fallen into the vortex, the Tooth Fairy made a tugging motion in the air. The black whirlpool in the carpet began to close.

"*GRSHNRRRVVRBLRGH!*"

Evidently the pugilistic bug against whose head I'd scored a couple of pretty good wallops with my chunk of doorframe was displeased to lose his backup.

It wasn't the worst thing that could happen to him that evening, which I took as my duty to remind him when I suddenly remembered that I had a gun and that I no longer needed to preserve ammunition. Strictly as a "glass is half-full" lesson, I took out my gat and shot the bug bastard in the head, then shoved his twitching remains into the rapidly collapsing vortex.

There were so many holes in the ratty old carpet of Mrs. Flora Willhausen that I couldn't make out the one into which the swirling black whirlpool vanished.

Exhausted from my incredible heroics of the previous ten minutes, I decided it was worth the risk to my ass to collapse onto my old bat neighbor's filthy, unmade bed.

Being the first to discover a new species of animal isn't the wide-eyed wonder thrill that those PBS nature documentaries make it out to be, especially when it's a murderous human-insect hybrid big enough to drive a moped and with enough limbs that it could signal for four turns at once while picking its nose and playing with the radio.

"What…" I panted.

"…the hell…" I resumed.

"…were those things?" I concluded.

"Shit," I offered as an addendum when I realized my hand was resting on a weird, dry stain that looked like W.C. Fields in profile and which was one of many old-time celebrity silhouette blotches that decorated Mrs. Flora Willhausen's decrepit mattress.

"Those 'things,' dearie," the Tooth Fairy replied portentously, his voice disturbingly small and very far away, "are *lawyers*."

I wheeled around. In doing so, my hand landed on a long-dry Clara Bow stain on the grubby mattress.

"Shit," I repeated, hoping to hell it wasn't.

Unseen by me in the aftermath of battle, the Tooth Fairy had opened up another vortex, this one miniscule. He had already shrunk himself down to the size of a goddamn peanut. Too late to stop him, I could only watch him slip back into the hole and vanish.

Before the vortex disappeared, another voice echoed up from the depths of the tiny, swirling hole.

"*I-5!*" somebody in the far-off distance announced.

And the little vortex collapsed in on itself and disappeared.

"Dammit, Sue Yu, you were supposed to watch him."

I glanced around the room.

"I see now that you're not here, and were presumably sucked into the giant vortex with Mrs. Flora Willhausen's disgusting bedding and the slightly less disgusting massive killer cockroaches, so maybe I'll let you off the hook this one time."

In the quiet following the mêlée, a voice was screaming down the hall.

"Yeah, it's that Banyon and a whole bunch of his friends," the angry voice of my aforementioned downstairs neighbor was hollering into the phone in her living room. "How do I know? Some kind of party. I don't know what kind, I'm a decent woman."

In addition to being a poor housekeeper and a rotten neighbor with a creepy fetish for stuffed dogs, Mrs. Flora Willhausen was apparently also a bald-faced liar.

The bad thing about vortices is that the guy you've been hired to find can escape through one. The good thing is that when they trash an apartment, they take the evidence with them. The old bag could claim the worst, and I'd deny it all. Feigning ignorance is a breeze when one spends as much of one's life as do I marinating in the genuine article.

I snatched up the busted length of doorframe — the only evidence that I was ever in the joint — and climbed out the bedroom window.

Unfortunately, there was a fire escape outside it, so I was still on the goddamn job.

16

My first stop was my apartment, although I didn't even attempt to drag one foot over my bedroom windowsill.

I stopped at the busted bedroom window when I heard yelling coming from far away, from the other side of my closed and locked front door. The bellowing was accompanied by the angry pounding of a balled fist.

"Banyon!" the familiar voice of the worst cop in the history of cheap tin badges hollered. "Banyon, are you in there? This isn't funny, Banyon!"

In point of fact, anything that got Detective Daniel Jenkins as furious as he clearly was had an excellent chance of being the funniest thing since the discovery of banana peels and asses.

I'd imagined disposing of the bug I'd shot would present a problem for my bad back as well as create a permanent obstruction in the garbage chute in the hall, but apparently the motto of the insect SOBs was "no roach left behind." They'd taken most of the dead bastard with them, albeit apparently tucked safely away inside the sloshing digestive juices of their cockroach stomachs. At best, they'd had two minutes to devour their pal. The smear of fur and bug guts that remained on the carpet of my bedroom was an unpleasant notification of exactly

how capable the things were of reducing me to a similar stain in about the same amount of time it takes to microwave a bag of goddamn popcorn.

I very gently placed my cockroach bat to the carpet, on which the remains of my shattered windowpanes created a glistening mosaic of padded expenses on little Timmy Thompson's eventual whopper of a bill. All the parts of the room were at least near where they belonged, and if anything came of Mrs. Flora Willhausen's outrageous claims to the boys in blue of invasions of her apartment and vanishing stuffed dogs, all I'd cop to was me being a shitty housekeeper and she being an imaginative drunk.

As it was, Jenkins had only tenuous cause to enter my apartment, and I doubted even he would bust down the door on what might have been a crank call.

As for my part, I no longer had a Tooth Fairy to deliver to the flatfoot, and I didn't feel like spending the night in the tank for calling in a false report. I had been far too sober for far too long, and one night in the joint wasn't long enough to ferment a toilet-full of really high quality jailhouse gin.

"You're in a world of trouble for this! I hope you realize that, Banyon!" Jenkins was shouting at the floating dust in my empty apartment as I swiped my coat and fedora from where they'd miraculously and conveniently blown over to just below the window. I tiptoed as far away from home as the rusted fire escape would take me.

As it was, the landing took me as far as the window of my deceased neighbor two apartments down, who — although deader than the gnat-like lifespan of my ex-wife's vow of marital fidelity — still refused to evacuate his apartment.

I had planned to interview Archibald Jessup after I'd ditched Attorney Sue Yu. She already knew far too much of my business, which was none of goddamn hers. But since the dame attorney was likely busy at present being chased around a headboard by a dozen pissed-off giant cockroaches in a bedroom somewhere in the Hindu Kush, now seemed like an ideal opportunity to bust into my dead neighbor's place.

The window latch was an easy number to jimmy with a credit card, which I didn't have owing to several ancient disputes with every major provider of said cards re payment: i.e. credit card companies expect it, the bastards.

My expired library card proved an adequate pinch-hitter for those miserly SOBs at MasterCard, and after nearly breaking my hand prying the window away from years of paint, I found myself in the bedroom of the late Mr. Archibald Jessup.

The condition of the apartment came as one of the bigger shocks in a day that had included so many murder attempts I was on the verge of believing that my life might have some value after all, since so many people wanted to take it from me.

Then I remembered that mobs loot dollar stores in hurricanes. If people will risk a felony rap for a box of wax crayons or a stack of cheap cupcake liners, they'll take any little shit thing of no value if given half a chance.

Even though my faith in my own worthlessness was quickly reaffirmed, that didn't diminish the startling fact that Archibald Jessup, when he'd been alive, had been living in the lap of luxury.

The oak bedroom set was far too expensive for a crummy neighborhood like mine. It was antique, hand-carved, and was almost certainly valued at a lot more

than the combined worth of all the mismatched Salvation Army and curbside junk furnishings I'd assembled in my feng shui nightmare over the years.

It wasn't that the joint was Versailles, but neither was Versailles all it was cracked up to be, since the gilded palace of Louis XVI, was nothing more than a corner pimp aesthete given an unlimited budget to bling the hell out of his million-room froggy hizzle.

The hardwood floor still gleamed despite a veneer of dust, the tasteful drapes weren't hanging from cheap thrift store rods, and the rug was so Persian it practically screamed "death to America" at my every IED-conscious step.

Even though it had been hours since he'd fled the scene at the morgue, I wasn't sure Jessup's ghost had made it back home yet. I was buoyed in my unwarranted optimism that the dead moron wasn't still standing on a sidewalk across town futilely waving a translucent hand at every cab that would never stop for a ghost when I heard the muted sound of voices coming from down the hallway.

The living room was as well-appointed as the bedroom, loaded up with just the right amount of tasteful furniture, and with nary a mangy stuffed dog in sight.

A grandfather clock that was clearly worth more than I grossed last year (which, as far as the IRS was concerned, was just shy of a buck fifty) was holding up the wall near the front door. The clock had stopped at 11:33 which, assuming the thing had been working when its owner was alive a month ago, was most likely the exact time Archibald Jessup had been hilariously struck in the mouth by lightning, since timepieces often stop working when their owners die. (So do, for some inexplicable reason, toasters and bidets, but nobody gives a shit about

those unless they're serving Eggo frozen waffles at the wake and need to wash their mouths out with something less disgusting.)

The voices I'd heard from the bedroom came from a television that had presumably been left on since its owner's death three weeks before, since Jessup's ghost was shit for manipulating corporeal objects, a fact the spirit of the old codger was unwittingly demonstrating for me at that very moment as it repeatedly attempted to get the recliner it was sitting in to stretch out to its full length.

Jessup's glowing blue ghost hand tried both yanking and shoving the handle on the side of the leather recliner, but every attempt ended with his hand passing straight through the bar and the chair remaining in the upright and locked position.

He finally gave up on the chair's handle, sighed one of those creepy ghostly moans his kind are forever unleashing on us mortals at three in the goddamn morning when we're already having trouble aiming for the toilet, and reached for an apple on the table next to his chair. He'd set the piece of fruit there just before he died, and it was now rotting and covered in fruit flies. The ghost's hand passed through the shriveled apple and emerged from the other side clutching a perfectly healthy-looking ghost version of what the late, lamented piece of fruit had looked like in life.

Jessup tried to take a bite from the apple, but his ghostly choppers bit only the air in which the ghostly apple-rition was floating. He seemed to remember that he was dead, and he unhappily placed the ghost apple back inside its rotting deceased self.

"You are the sorriest excuse for a specter I've ever scarcely seen," I announced.

The ghost jumped in his Barcalounger and spun his head 180 degrees in my direction. Until he'd put his head on backwards, I hadn't realized how much he already looked like an owl, what with the pointed beak, giant glasses, and peaks of demented old man hair that spiked up over each sagging ear.

"Banyon!" Jessup said, grabbing his intangible chest. (His hand, naturally, went straight through. Asshole.) "You almost gave me a heart attack. What are you doing here? Did those lawyers send you? I'm not leaving."

I didn't much want to think about assholes-at-law at that moment. I was still encouraging my brain to ignore what the vanishing Tooth Fairy had portentously yelled about the gang of giant, murderous cockroaches with human faces somehow actually being lawyers. I had no idea how one got from A.) a huge, ravenous cockroach with viciously sharp teeth to B.) the bloated piece of human shit who'd been hogging my stool at O'Hale's Bar bragging about how big of an asshole he was right up until his engine stalled and he crash-landed like a Uruguayan soccer team on Jaublowski's sticky floor. The Tooth Fairy's claim was as cryptic as shit, and I strongly suspected I would soon be getting to the bottom of it, whether I wanted to or not. But although I didn't want to even hear the word "lawyers," I suspected my luck in that regard was about on par with everything else in my miserable life.

"Goddamn lawyers," the ghost of Archibald Jessup moaned, because it was necessary for the universe to punch me in the throat at every opportunity.

Ghosts are flighty as hell and, like a cat chasing a red laser pointer dot, they tend to get fixated on one thing to the exclusion of all else. That's why most of them haunt only the same hallways, basements, and attics their

whole afterlife. Jessup was clearly tethered to his apartment, so it was unusual for a ghost like him to have wandered so far uptown. And he wasn't the only one, according to Doc Minto. There was something about the bodies of all the lawyers stacked up at the morgue that was drawing a shitload of ghosts from their usual haunts.

Jessup had lost interest in me, and was once more futilely pursuing a horizontal position with a hand that stubbornly refused to grasp the handle on the side of his chair.

"Why were you at the morgue?" I asked.

He glanced up, startled. Ghosts always had one foot in their own goddamn ghost world, flitting around the edges of reality without taking firm root in it. They were like flighty, absent-minded scientists, without the benefit to mankind of a single atom bomb.

"Oh, you're still here? Push this down for me, Banyon," he demanded.

I did as he requested, hoping it would hasten things along. Once he was settled back in the chair that he'd been unable to budge for the three weeks since he'd died, he immediately grabbed for the remote control next to his rotten apple. His hand passed straight through the clicker as well as the table on which it sat.

"Damn," he groused.

"The morgue," I said.

"I heard you, I heard you," Jessup's ghost snapped.

He had given up trying to grab the remote, something he had no doubt attempted a billion times in the recent past. He leaned his face close to the little table and tried to nudge up the volume button with a single ghostly index finger.

My own TV back in my apartment was a barely-working cathode ray dinosaur that I'd found on a sidewalk

with a "free" sign taped to the screen. The late Archibald Jessup's was a state-of-the-art, wall-mounted flat screen, because even dead bastards apparently deserve better than me.

Jessup concentrated the hell out of his fingertip, and by focusing all his ghostly power succeeded in summoning the volume indicator on the big TV screen. The soft voice emanating from the speakers hidden around the room grew louder.

"…high pressure system moving down from Canada…"

Goddamn boring old SOB and his boring goddamn weather obsession.

I snapped up the remote and toggled the sound down to zero.

"The next stop for this is out the window," I said, waving the remote control under his nose. "I'd toss you out after it if you weren't buried across town, and if the only shovel I own wasn't locked in the trunk of my car which is currently misplaced. I have, however, sudden motivation to track down my errant Pontiac and the shovel therein, if only to see the look on your face as I shove your casket through this living room — which is far nicer than a dead bastard like you deserves — and shake the contents out into traffic. Now why the hell are you and every other ghost in town so interested in that pile of dead lawyers when nobody else is?"

"*Lawyers.*"

The old man ghost spit the word like a curse, which pronunciation was the first thing the see-through bastard had ever said in life or death that I could really get behind.

"You want to know what I did for a living, Banyon?" he asked.

"No," I said. "I want to know where I can buy a shovel."

"It's relevant. God, life is wasted on the living. I was a professional suer. Well, first I was a tollbooth collector for twenty years. Then I got into suing. I'd walk in front of cars, choke in restaurants, eat toothpicks and sue the toothpick company for not having warnings that you're not supposed to eat toothpicks. That sort of thing. Made more in a year as a suer than I did my whole working life in that damnable tollbooth. Then I got greedy. Made my big mistake. Sued Disney for not having any ham in their hamburgers or cotton in their cotton candy. False advertising, you see. Slam dunk win, according to my lawyers over at Hitler, Hitler & Rosenberg. Well, that damned rat turned right around and sued me *and* my lawyers. Been dragging through the courts for ten years." He paused and tipped his head. "I died, didn't I? I'm dead right now?"

"Yes, Jessup," I informed him, "you are as dead as my interest in this goddamn soliloquy."

"It's hard to remember. Funny thing about being a ghost. When you're dead, you're not really all here anymore."

"If it's any comfort, Jessup, a significant chunk of you had checked out long before you shit the eternal bed. By which I mean, in case it's not clear to your addled ghost brain, you were a stupid asshole four weeks ago, too, before the hilarious lightning strike to the mouth that I wish I had on tape to watch over and over like goddamn Norma Desmond. What about the lawsuit?"

"They were suing me for all I was worth, those Disney son of a bitches. Had me tied up in legal knots right up until the day I died. I don't got any heirs. Somebody'll wind up liquidating my assets and turning it all over to them bastard Disney lawyers. Over my dead body that's gonna happen."

I assumed he didn't mean the legal documents would be signed at his headstone, since the dumb bastard had clearly forgotten yet again that he was a stiff.

"You died with a legal matter still pending," I mused to myself.

My brain was doing some genius deducing. I sat back and allowed it to do its job, since it so rarely comes out of hibernation and is a wonder to behold when it does.

The goddamn ghost derailed my brilliant thoughts aborning.

"Ain't you been listening?" Jessup asked, replying to what was clearly a rhetorical comment, but which, since he was a moron dead or alive, he wouldn't have caught even when he was still breathing. "That's exactly what I said. They was suing the pants offa me. Then I heard something from that Confederate Civil War ghost down in the laundry room. Colonel Beauregard Q. Honeysuckle. He said somebody had come up with a plan to help all we ghosts who got unresolved issues keeping us here. Naturally, in my case that'd mean killing the goddamn lawyers who won't let me rest in peace."

My brain, which was clearly smarter than me, had already raced back to the building that housed my offices and to our resident janitor ghost who generally was rarely seen but who was suddenly like a mosquito that gets into your bedroom at night and keeps dive-bombing your ear whenever you're on the verge of passing out.

The dead janitor's ghost was still obsessed with his death at the hands of a runaway floor buffer, and the legal fallout from said amusing custodial fatality. He'd been angry with Attorney Sue Yu and her entire law firm of Crook, Shaft & Fleece, although I was unclear on the precise details as I hadn't given enough of a shit to switch my ears on while the SOB was droning incessantly about

his problems.

I thought of all the dead lawyers at the city morgue, but this time when I brought up the memory my brain wasn't singing the "Hallelujah Chorus" at full volume. I considered all the electric fans Doc Minto had set up to dispel a sudden invasion of ghosts interested in identifying the corpses. Corpses of dead lawyers.

Hallelujah! Hallelujah! Hallelujah! Hallelujah! Hallelujah!

I told my singing brain to shut the hell up.

"Do you know who this ghost savior is?" I queried, as I struggled to get a handle on Handel.

"I asked Colonel Honeysuckle that, but he didn't know. The ghost what told him said he only knew the guy who was saving us by 'R,' and that he worked at Bandito-Pharmaceutical. I remember that, on account of I get all my corn chips and heart medication from them. They got you comin' and goin', Banyon. I wonder if all them chips I ate in life were what gave me the problem with my heart."

"You can abstain from everything fun in life and at some point someone will still eventually, inevitably be hiding around a corner and drop a safe on your head. Besides, you didn't have a heart attack, Jessup, you got struck in the mouth by lightning. Which reminds me. When this is all over, if I don't have a safe parked on my fedora, I'll definitely have to see if there is any security camera footage of your death, because it sounds absolutely hilarious."

I asked the dead old man a few more simple questions, but I'd picked everything of value from a brain that was even more insubstantial than it had been when he was alive and pestering everybody about the remarkable fact that there existed weather, and that terrible

variations of naturally occurring phenomena would impact the world in ways that sometimes required deploying sunglasses or an umbrella.

I toggled the volume up low on his weather station, and returned the remote control to the little table next to the rotting apple.

I knew the ghost in the laundry room. Colonel Beauregard Honeysuckle, deceased, wasn't a chatty bastard. He rarely manifested, but when he did he was the more traditional kind of ghost who'd move your box of Tide an inch to the left or come charging out of the wall on a ghost horse, sword drawn, when you were sorting your socks and underwear. I doubted he was much more loquacious even around other ghosts, so I figured Jessup had supplied me with everything the colonel knew.

"I'm using your phone, Jessup," I said.

I got a pinched look of impatience from the late bastard, who was leaning forward in his recliner, desperate to hear what el Niño might be plotting six months hence.

"In the kitchen," he said, waving me off. "More rain for the West Coast, maybe?" he questioned the TV. "That mean more severe winter weather for the East?"

Jessup was an asshole, even unto death.

Before making my call, I took a quick peek out the front door.

Detective Daniel Jenkins had given up banging on my door. The lousiest of lousy coppers was on his way back to the elevators, and at that precise moment was walking only a few inches from Jessup's front door. I closed the door quickly and quietly and gave Jenkins a moment to prove he was as bad at his job as I knew he was.

When I eased the door back open it came as no sur-

prise that Jenkins, whose powers of observation had apparently been in the shop for repairs for the past four decades, wasn't standing on the other side swinging a pair of handcuffs from one finger.

I very carefully stuck my head out the door. The clueless flatfoot was fuming down by the elevators.

My own observational skills were at least sharp enough to notice that there was no one else in sight, which was exceedingly curious since Jenkins was not only not the only call I'd made, he wasn't even the first. Yet here was the cop, and no one else.

When the car came and Jenkins stepped on, nobody stepped off.

As the elevator doors were sliding shut, I very gently closed Jessup's door.

The old ghost was enthralled with the television. As he stared at the screen, he faded from sight. I knew he was still present on some level, still transfixed by weather that he, as a goddamn ghost, would never experience for the rest of eternity.

I headed for the kitchen and the phone therein.

The plate and silverware from Archibald Jessup's last meal were sitting dry in the kitchen sink, which was actually a little more strangely poignant than I'd have imagined, since I couldn't stand the weather-obsessed old bastard. A glass containing an inch of what might have once been milk had partially dissolved to orange-tinged, cobwebbed cream. The hookers down the block would be delighted to know that the half-loaf of bread on the countertop was well on its way to penicillin.

The phone on the wall still worked. Jessup hadn't been dead long enough for the phone company to cut off service. He probably wouldn't lose it for months, which was great for the kind of ghosts who liked to call rela-

tives and, even though they said nothing at all, whose family members knew for absolute certain that it was dead Aunt Agnes calling from the Great Beyond and not an automated crossed line from a Punjabi call center.

I wasn't sure Mannix would still be in the office at so late an hour, but due to the extra time required to clean up after Sue Yu's mess, I figured my diligent little pal might have stuck around to catch up on his normal duties, whatever the hell they were. As long as my eponymous corporation ran smoothly enough that I didn't have to involve myself in anything whatsoever to do with its inner workings, Mannix had carte goddamn blanche.

"Banyon Investigations, how can I help you!" the enthusiastic voice of my elf assistant announced after only one ring.

"Hey, Mannix. You're working far too late. You should be home avoiding that dump like the plague that it is. However, since you're there, did you hear anything from Robert Sherman Planck, or for that matter anybody from Madison Insurance in the past half-hour?"

"No, sir, Mr. Crag," Mannix replied. "The only person to call the office since you left is Dr. Harry. Did you expect to hear from Mr. Robert?"

"I expected to see him in person at my place," I said. "Instead, of the two phone calls I made about catching the Tooth Fairy, only Dan Jenkins showed up."

"You caught him!" the little guy enthused. "Do you want me to call the Thompsons to tell them the wonderful news?"

"It was more a catch-and-release situation," I said. "He's gone, Mannix. On the plus side, that lawyer dame who tried to kick my block off is gone, too. Make a note, Mannix. If Attorney Sue Yu calls for airfare from wherever in the world the Tooth Fairy sent her, charge her

eight hundred bucks for the phone call. That's five hundred for me, and three hundred for you assisting me by picking up the phone. Lawyers are the only bastards who bill you individually for what each staff member does. If I call a plumber about a leaky pipe, I don't get an itemized bill later on that includes a hundred bucks for talking to his wife because she happened to answer the phone and hollered for him to pick up. I say we turn the paralegal scam back on the lawyer."

I had a little more adrenaline flowing from the previous half-hour than I'd imagined. When I got done panting, I got a moment's hesitation from my assistant.

"I can't charge Miss Attorney Sue just for answering the telephone," Mannix said. "That would be wrong."

"Of course it's wrong. And you can't do it because you're a better human being than most humans, and especially lawyers," I said. "Anyway, forget it. Sue Yu is likely the latest lawyer to bite the dust, albeit the others weren't chewed apart by massive cockroaches, possibly sent by Robert Sherman Planck to murder us all."

"Mr. Robert tried to *kill* you?"

Mannix was a little more surprised by the suggestion than he should have been, since he was pretty much the only person I'd encountered in the past day who hadn't.

"The jury is out," I admitted. "However, a very large number of very large cockroaches did suspiciously descend on my apartment almost immediately after I called Planck, and Planck himself has yet to show his face. Let's set aside that treacherous asshole for the moment. You said Doc Minto called. What did he have to say?"

"Dr. Harry thanked you for the bottle you sent to him," Mannix said. "He thought I was you. I told him several times that I was me, but I don't think he

understood."

"Doc Minto's brain is on its last legs," I informed my assistant. "He is still, however, a genius medical examiner, with or without the requisite number of marbles. Did he tell you — or me, as it were — if he tested the booze?"

"Yes, sir." I could hear the rattle of a scrap of paper. "He said he's 'isolated the compound in the liquor,'" Mannix said, carefully reading his own note. "He said it is definitely what is 'activating empathy in the brains of the dead lawyers' and that he's let the police and the FBI know. He also asked you to get him some nice wool socks because his feet are cold and he thinks he lost all his own socks somewhere, but he isn't sure where. He thinks he may have put them on some swans at the park."

This was excellent news. (Not, granted, for any swans who might be slapping around the lakeside bike path in my mental M.E. friend's lost argyles.) The authorities had been hitherto uninterested in the deaths of thousands of lawyers, but a report from Doc Minto's department held sufficient weight to force a slugabed constabulary to act.

"I also think I found the lawyer you asked me to look for," Mannix said. "I found him searching obituaries."

"You had your work cut out for you, what with so many lawyers croaking in the past few weeks. You must have needed stilts to wade through all that ticker tape."

"Oh, no, Mr. Crag," my elf pal said. "He didn't die lately. The only Boyle I could find who was a lawyer was a Mr. Pierce Boyle who died in 1821. I searched relatives, and the Dr. Lance Boyle you mentioned is his great-great-great-great-grandson."

"I've met Dr. Lance Boyle, and he is definitely not great-great-great. If anything, he is shit-shit-shit, with a

couple dozen assholes thrown in for good measure. So, what are the particulars on the long late Attorney Pierce Boyle?" I asked. "Beyond the obvious: that his name is as mildly amusing as that of his shit-shit-shit-shit-grandson."

"Mr. Pierce wasn't a very good lawyer," Mannix said, clearly uncomfortable to be speaking accurately of the dead. "He overcharged his clients for work he didn't do. He showed up for court drunk. He was…*friendly* with ladies who were married to his clients. He stole inheritance money from his brothers. One time when he'd been drinking he drove his horse up onto someone's front lawn, then hid in a greenhouse all night, and in the morning he said he hit his head on the saddle and didn't remember what happened."

"So he was a drunk thief liar who ripped off his clients," I said. "I'm not seeing what differentiates this Paleolithic era attorney from its modern descendents."

"There isn't anything that I could see, Mr. Crag," Mannix admitted. "That was nearly it for his obituary. It does say how he died, if that's helpful. It says that he upset his last client, and that the man killed him."

"Okay, another dead lawyer. I don't see how this ancient one connects to the current non-crisis that is decimating the ranks of the descendant assholes of his profession. On the other hand, I must admit that I never tire of hearing their fatal stories. What was his?"

"According to a newspaper account from that time, Mr. Attorney Pierce was hung by his ankles from a yardarm with fish in his pockets for the seagulls to poke. Then he had to walk a plank with seagulls in his pockets for the sharks to poke. Then what was left of his body was stuffed in a cannon and shot at a French ship. The French ship surrendered. It says here that when France

found out, the whole country surrendered, too, just in case."

It was possible that Attorney Pierce Boyle had an unresolved legal issue, as did Archibald Jessup and my office's nuisance janitor. Maybe he was haunting his great-great-great-great-asshole-times-infinity-grandson, Dr. Lance Boyle. But the good doctor finding a cure for the lack of empathy in attorneys would only help the living, and would by no means cure a lawyer who'd been dead for two centuries.

There was, however, the very specific maritime-themed demise of Pierce Boyle — not lost on my brilliant ears — that might hold some significance.

"Give me Boyle's last case and client," I said.

"His clients were some very naughty pirates," Mannix said. "It says that their ship, the *Jolly Rogerer*, was stopped by the Navy for having a tail lantern out. They found some opium in the glove compartment and fifty thousand dollars worth of stolen whale blubber in the hold. When they hired Mr. Attorney Pierce to defend them, he charged them six chests of doubloons, then didn't show up for court until the trial was almost over. He told the judge he'd locked himself out of his horse in the parking lot of the Slurping Barrister Tavern, and that he had to hire a lock-smith, which it says here was a blacksmith who specialized in locks, to help."

"This is an amazingly detailed summary for a story that's two hundred years old," I interrupted. "I assume something equally very nearly amusing had been going on in court in his absence."

"Oh, no, it sounds terrible, sir," Mannix said, since he was a far better human being than me. "By the time he got there, half the crew had already been found guilty and sentenced to English cooking, which they say is why

they left England and became scary pirates. Just after Attorney Mister Pierce arrived, the captain of the *Jolly Rogerer* stole a cutlass and some pistols from the evidence table during recess and escaped with the rest of the crew, along with the poor lawyer. That's when they fed him to the seagulls and the sharks, then shot his body out of a cannon at the French ship. It's a very sad story."

"It absolutely is, Mannix, with the proviso that you substitute 'hilarious' for 'sad.' What happened to the captain?"

"He was caught again. The Navy sank his ship, and the whole rest of the crew died. The captain was put back on trial, and this time he didn't have a lawyer at all. He got a hundred million years for all kinds of naughty pirate things he did for many years, plus resisting arrest, and impersonating a porpoise."

"Name?" I asked, suspecting — because my brain is a more magnificent organ than the one housed in the sanctuary at Washington National Cathedral — that I might already know the answer.

"Captain Peter Barnacle," my assistant said.

"Bingo," I said.

I blinked at a sudden, unexpected flash of insight that had nothing to do with the fate of the ancient *Jolly Rogerer* or the captain thereof.

"Holy shit," I said. "In fact, the holiest of shit. This is the shit of the greatest and holiest of saints, preserved in a reliquary in the secret holy shit catacombs beneath Notre Dame Cathedral. The shit I'm talking about, Mannix, is just that goddamn holy."

"Mr. Crag," Mannix said, in his soft, scolding tone.

"I apologize profusely for the overuse of the word, Mannix, but in my defense this happens to be extremely holy shit we're talking about."

"What is it?"

"Nothing to concern us for the moment," I said. "I just cracked the most major aspect of this case. But we'll have to set it aside right now, because I can't afford to have it go spectacularly wrong again. As for the initial brilliant deduction that led immediately to the second, Captain Peter Barnacle, late of the *Jolly Rogerer*, is none other than Pirate Pete, the mascot of Pirate Pete's Fish 'n' Chips."

17

Before leaving the late Archibald Jessup's apartment, I first ticked off the most important item on the agenda. I instructed Mannix to order Doc Minto some replacement socks, just in case I didn't make it out of this one alive.

When I passed back into the living room, I noted that the TV was still muttering quietly at the seemingly empty room.

I assumed that Jessup's ghost was still sitting in his Barcalounger and enthralled by reportage of unsettled weather that was currently plaguing the Great Lakes region and which would bring precipitation to the East Coast by the weekend. However, since his chair appeared to be empty I couldn't be sure if the boring, dead old bastard was there or if he was on his way back to the morgue to see if the Disney lawyers who were keeping him forever bound to this plain had purchased the eternal farm.

Out in the empty hallway, Robert Sherman Planck of Madison Insurance Equities persisted in his complete absence.

I bypassed the elevators and headed for the back stairs on the off chance that Dan Jenkins had decided to play cop and stake out my building.

It was a reasonably safe bet by this point that AWOL

Planck, the bastard, had dispatched the army of giant human-like cockroaches to lay waste to my bachelor pad and any succulent P.I.'s cowering therein, a fact that would be addressed in the whopper of a bill that Madison would be receiving from the accounts payable department of Banyon Investigations.

I currently had bigger fish to fry than Robert Sherman Planck, and my shame at the inevitable deployment of the cliché was mitigated by the fact that the fish I intended to fry was, in point of fact, goddamn *this* big.

The ghost savior of both Jessup and the dead janitor at my building, as well as all the ghosts who were pestering poor old sockless Doc Minto, was known as "R," according to the Civil War ghost in my haunted laundry room. Colonel Beauregard Honeysuckle, via Archibald Jessup, had it wrong. It wasn't "R." It was "yarrrrr," which was the pirate lingo version of "you know what I'm saying?" in olde tyme lingua franca.

If my creaking knees weren't shit for the kind of acrobatics necessary to perform so delicate a self-flagellating maneuver, I'd be kicking the hell out of myself, since it so happened that I'd seen the pirate bastard myself, at least partially.

Back at My Grain Distillery, I had not been able to get a good look at the ghost that had been talking to Dr. Lance Boyle, since he'd been conveniently positioned behind a pillar. I did, however, glimpse a flamboyantly puffy phosphorescent sleeve. I'd even heard the asshole just before I'd been jabbed in the back of the neck by a syringe-wielding lab assistant lunatic. I'd thought the protracted "yaaarrrrgh" was actual language muffled by the window through which I'd been attempting to eavesdrop, but the seemingly inarticulate mumbling was evidently crystal clear piratespeak.

"Yaaarrgh" was, in fact, "R."

Pirate Pete's seafood restaurant chain was part of the Bandito-Pharmaceutical conglomerate, which also owned My Grain. Dr. Lance Boyle, whose drunken lawyer ancestor had overcharged Pirate Pete Barnacle then blown up the *Jolly Rogerer* captain's trial, worked for Bandito-Pharma. The corporate merger that had brought those two maniacs together now threatened to kill every lawyer in the country.

I stopped dead in the stairwell and tried to remember why, precisely, I was giving two healthy shits about stopping them. Although I drew a blank, I continued to the exit door anyway, assuming the reason would come to me eventually.

It was approaching midnight by the time I hit the street, and there was nothing I could do at so late an hour to drive a stake through this pain in the ass case. My own bed was currently off limits and, with Detective Dan Jenkins potentially on the warpath, so too was my office. I set aside a few bucks from my wallet for the suicidal scheme that I planned to foolhardily enact come morning, and so I had barely enough cash left on me to scrape together the one-night cost of a dilapidated mattress rental in a fleabag motel.

The night passed without incident in my room. The same, however, could not be said of the hallway Infidelity 500 that kept me awake until dawn, with altogether different definitions of air jacks, bottoming out, burning rubber, and Jiffy Lube. The endless door slamming that accompanied the all-night French farce ended at dawn, and so I was able to enjoy a couple miserable hours of unconsciousness before I embarked on what would, in all probability, be the last day of my life, and good riddance to it.

I had two quick stops to make before I found myself reluctantly stepping down from the city bus that deposited me on the sidewalk in front of the nearest Pirate Pete's seafood restaurant.

I carried a shipping box under my arm as I marched through the front doors.

In an incredibly convenient and highly improbable instance of magnificent timing, I arrived when the greasy dump was experiencing a customer-free lull. I strode across the empty lobby of the empty restaurant and up to the counter.

A young dame with a big smile plastered the appropriate distance below her paper hat was waiting to pounce on the cash register as I placed my cardboard box on the counter.

"Welcome to Pirate Pete's!" she enthused, in a delightfully perky and utterly insincere south-of-the-border accent. "How may I serve you?"

In an establishment that dealt in fish, I had, as it so happened, been fishing in my pocket on my way to the stainless steel counter. I yanked out my catch of the day.

I held my wallet high above my head, allowing it to flop dramatically open.

"ICE," I announced loud enough for the boys in the backroom to hear.

The young dame's smile vanished nearly as fast as she did, face-first out the drive-through window.

The rest of the Pirate Pete's team suddenly remembered that they might have left the gas on in Tijuana. I would have said they evacuated the restaurant as fast as greased lightning, but I was afraid the Thought Police might have the switch turned on, and I'd already bagged my twenty-four-hour limit on hate speech.

The entire Pirate Pete's staff departed as fast as very

fast lightning, and within ten seconds of my announcement I was standing alone in the lobby waving over my fedora what was turning out to be the most useful expired library card in existence.

I stuffed my wallet back in my pocket and picked up the box from the counter. I left the lid next to the cash register and quickly carted the box around the room, lightly scattering the contents on the red tile floor so that when I was finished there was not a square inch — from the dirty beverage refill dispensers near the counter, to the sticky plastic seats at the front window — that had not received a careful dusting.

Whichever corporate jester had decided to deploy the stale fish restaurant gag of placing "buoys" and "gulls" signs on the restroom doors deserved to have the carp beaten out of him, but I was on the clock and so had to leave it to the universe to beat his bass.

I happened to identify as a buoy that day, besides which no self-respecting gull would have anything to do with me, and so I bypassed the first door and shoved open the second.

The john was relatively clean by fast food standards. There were two stalls, two urinals, and no apparent customers according to the senses I'd elected to leave running.

I scattered the remaining contents of the box on the men's room floor, stuffed the box in the corner trash barrel, and went over to the pair of sinks where a long mirror reflected my weary mug with horrifying accuracy.

I stared deep into the heart of the mirror.

"Pirate Pete, Pirate Pete, Pirate Pete," I said.

It is a well-known fact that repeating the name of certain ghosts three times in a mirror is sufficient to summon these troubled spirits from their eternal golf game. I'd read once on a Pete's paper placemat that customer

complaints could be registered by summoning the chain's specter owner thusly, although the placemat cautioned not to do so for frivolous reasons such as not getting enough ketchup packets in your meal since the boss had been known to "run ye through yer gizzard, ye scurvy knave."

The instant the dead pirate's name had passed my lips the final time, the mirror contorted, twisting the reflected image of the bathroom and briefly spiraling me down into a tight knot, like water racing down a bathtub drain that works much better than the one in my shitty apartment. As quickly as the reflection of the room collapsed, it expanded back to normal.

The reconfigured mirror revealed that I was no longer alone.

Standing in reflection behind me was the gleaming blue ghost of Pirate Pete.

"What cowardly landlubber dares summon the spirit of Pirate Pete!" the ghost howled. "This had best not be about limiting the size of yer coleslaw again. Most of ye mangy curs was throwing it out. Pirate Pete was losing his shirt."

The Pirate Pete that was the cartoon mascot of the unlamented captain's chain of reasonably priced aquatic-harvested shit food was a smiling rascal who offered half-priced meals on Thursdays and special party discounts for parents who wanted to give Junior high blood pressure and elevated cholesterol for his sixth birthday.

The real version of the cartoon pirate was a decidedly more traditional image of a nineteenth century buccaneer.

Pete's pirate Halloween costume was a more miserable ensemble than the cast of *Saturday Night Live*. His cloth boots sagged, his pantaloons were torn rags on spindly legs, and his shirt looked like it had been tailored for a

brigand twice his size. Pirating might have been a high seas party, but it clearly hadn't put much gruel on the table.

While many men may have heeded the call of a thrilling life of adventure at sea, evidently there wasn't a dentist among them.

Clearly no one in life had advised Pirate Pete to put down the rum and yo-ho-ho himself up a bottle of goddamn Crest fluoride rinse. His mouth looked like a map of the Galapagos where half the islands had fallen out and the rest were rotting out to sea. The Atlantic Ocean of his gums had the worst case of gingivitis in all the seven seas.

It's usually a huge effort for ghosts to produce even a faint aroma, which is why you only get a hint of grandma's favorite perfume in the hallway, and why that tiny whiff is gone when you take a step back. To say Pirate Pete was an atypical case when it came to ghostly odor was an understatement of epic olfactory proportions.

In a restaurant that stunk so badly of grease that in less than two minutes it felt like my clothes had been batter-dipped and deep fried, Pirate Pete's B.O. was enough to not only blow the man down, but to take out everybody in said unfortunate ground-zero man's immediate vicinity.

Pirate Pete glanced around the bathroom, trying to figure out where he was, since the trip for him to the john from wherever he'd been lurking had been instantaneous.

The ghost gave me a good naval gazing.

His eyes went wide. Or, rather, at least one eye went wide. His other wandering eye had apparently wandered right out of its socket. Pete had sacrificed depth perception for pirate chic, and was sporting a stereotypical eye patch over the spot where a right eye should go. He wasn't satisfied being half-blind, and was doing his best to pop out

his left eye, what with all the surprised comic bugging it was doing in yours truly's direction.

"Sink me, if ye ain't the landlubber what was at the distillery what makes the finest of Bandito-Pharmaceutical spirits!" Pirate Pete cried.

"So, is this an act for the tourists, or did you just not have time to learn to talk normally in the two hundred years you've been dead?" I asked.

"Why ere ye summonin' me here, yer rusted scalawag!" the ghost howled.

"It would seem to be the real deal. God, how I hate ghosts. Although apparently not as much as you hate lawyers, since I've never hatched a scheme to kill all of you."

His face fell. Had he been a zombie, he'd be on his hands and knees trying to scoop it back up again, but since he was a ghost it only meant that his wide-open mouth afforded me a better view of the paper towel dispenser through the back of his transparent head.

My bombshell delivered, I turned and marched out of the bathroom.

Once I was back in the restaurant proper, I positioned myself in the middle of the dining area floor and turned around to face the crapper door.

A moment after I'd exited the shitter, Pirate Pete rapidly drifted through the buoy's restroom door. The prior look of shock on his glowing face had been replaced with an expression of cold malevolence that gave a pretty solid idea of the terror on the high seas Pirate Pete Barnacle had been before he'd died and become a cartoon face on the sides of onion ring bags and 24-ounce cups of Royal Crown Cola.

The ghost set his lone evil eye on me, and the solitary peeper expressed the tiniest flicker of surprise to find that

I wasn't running out of the joint. A thin smile cracked the oasis of mouth that existed between gnarled ghost mustache and matted ghost beard.

"What does ye think ye knows?" Pirate Pete demanded.

"You and Dr. Lance Boyle, madman scientist for Bandito-Pharmaceutical, are the ones who poisoned the booze at My Grain Distillery. Boyle is the shit-shit-shit-shit-grandson of the lawyer who screwed you and your crew at your trial. You have it in for lawyers. The only thing I don't know is Boyle's angle. He's nuts, so there's that, but I don't think that's reason enough to help you kill every lawyer in the U.S."

"Yer as clever as a crow, me laddie," Pirate Pete said.

As he spoke, the ghost floated past me and circled around my back. I turned right along with him, at all times keeping two eyes on him for every one he kept on me.

"Do ye know why ghosts walk the earth?" the reeking pirate spirit asked.

"I've never really given much of a — or indeed, any — shit," I honestly replied.

"Did ye never wonder why most ghosts only be from the past few hundred years? Tis true! Yer not be having yer caveman ghosts, nor any of yer Bronze Age ghosts floatin' 'round yer attics or bell towers or yer spooky bemusement parks. Does yer wants to know why, matey? Pirate Pete will tell ye. They was able to pass on in peace on account of there be so few lawyers in their times to forever tie them to this here mortal plain, with their befouled endless motions to delay and heresies of continuance requests."

I didn't take ghost cases. I'd arranged my professional life so that I had very little contact with the spectral deceased. But I had to admit that what Pirate Pete was moaning as he slowly floated his glowing ass around my

lackluster posterior made perfect sense, and jibed with what I'd learned from questioning my annoying ghost neighbor.

Late Great Aunt Penelope wasn't haunting the parlor of the house she'd lived in for eighty years out of morbid sentimentality that extended beyond the grave. She was more than likely sitting in that same dilapidated easy chair knitting invisible scarves for all eternity because some asshole had gotten a lawyer to put a lien on the dump. Leave it to lawyers to find a way to ruin our lives even after we're goddamn dead.

"So what's crazy Dr. Lance Boyle get out of this?" I asked.

"Hah! I be roundin' up all the spirits who still haunt the mortal plain who'd hired his accursed ancestor for lawyerin' chores," Pirate Pete said. "At me bidding, a hundred ghosts been hauntin' the good doctor for more'n a year's time now. Arrr. We drove the villain mad, then I got him to mix up the potion that'll send every last lawyer in the country to Davey Jones' Locker. When the lawyers be gone, we ghosts'll be free of what binds us here. We will all be able to move on. It'll be like a huge season finale of *Ghost Whisperer*, but without that saucy lass with the big yarrrs."

It was heartwarming to know between the haunting and the french fries and the schemes of mass murder that Pirate Pete found time to watch really shitty TV.

"For some reason, Pirate Pete, I am opposed to killing all lawyers," I informed the circling apparition. "I'm not precisely sure why. Frankly, it's an initiative I really should be endorsing. I suppose it's some kind of moral thing, although I can't fathom how my conscience is contorting morality to put me on the opposing side of something so inherently magnificent."

"Yer'll be havin' no choice but to climb aboard me plan, ye scalawag," the ghost of the pirate captain informed me.

His multiple circuits around yours truly had brought him back around to the side windows of the dining area.

As was the case in all Pirate Pete's seafood franchises, the dump was overloaded with nautically-themed knick-knacks. Harpoons and fishing nets hung on all the walls. You couldn't wave to a health department official about the filth on the underside of a table without getting your hand caught in a goddamn ornamental lobster trap.

The tacky maritime décor extended even to the window blinds, which were held in place by rods that were fashioned in the shape of cutlasses.

Only when Pirate Pete reached up and wrenched the nearest curtain rod by the handle did I realize that my observational skills might not be entirely up to snuff, a fact that I attributed to my admittedly limited brain having spent the past day being drugged, kicked, and — worst of all — forced to give the tiniest shit about saving the life of every lawyer in America.

The blind tumbled from the rod, bouncing off the table and orchestrating a perfect Slinky-like walk to the sticky floor.

Pirate Pete held aloft what I could now clearly see was a viciously sharp sword, relatives of which he must have stashed in full view in over 1,200 locations around the country for just such an improbable scenario, which seemed pretty goddamned unlikely to me, but since I was currently staring cross-eyed at the gleaming tip of a curtain-rod cutlass I was in no position to point out the implausibility of my current predicament.

"Join yer captain, me damnéd hearties!" the dead pirate captain shouted, his single eye spinning wildly. If ghosts

had been capable of producing spit, the buccaneer bastard would have been foaming like one of his reasonably priced cups of Hires root beer. "We'll be deep-fryin' this brigand's cullions before we hoist his scurvy skeleton up the flagpole in yon courtyard, between the picnic tables and the recycling barrel! Yarrrr!"

The temperature in the restaurant abruptly dropped thirty degrees.

Out of the ether, one after another, appeared the ragged remnants of the long-dead crew of the *Jolly Rogerer*. I was quickly surrounded by a sea of peg legs, patched eyes, and terrifying dental neglect.

Unlike dead asshole Archibald Jessup, my worthless weather watching neighbor, Pirate Pete's crew had centuries of experience in the ghost trade, and were thus able to levitate objects, a skill that they eagerly demonstrated by tearing down the remaining curtain-rod swords that hung around the dining room. There weren't enough blades to go around, but the remaining ghosts weren't content to go into battle empty-handed. Gnarled, spectral hands tore down decorative nets and stretched them out to me, eager to wrap me up like a flounder as a present for their gleeful nutbar captain. Others grabbed harpoons that were clearly so ridiculously sharp that somebody in some city inspector's office somewhere should have picked up on the obvious safety hazard, and whatever lax bureaucrat was responsible for the oversight in my town would be receiving a stern letter of complaint, assuming my tongue remained attached that I might dictate my intense displeasure at the failure of local government to my office elf stenographer.

"*Yarg!*
"*Yarg!*"
"*Ahoy!*"

"You be havin' a purty mouth!"

(Goddamn sailors.)

To cap off a scene which, as far as my cullions and I were concerned, was already crammed with a large enough cast of characters, a ghostly parrot flew out of the straw dispenser and began circling the ceiling around the unmoving paddle fan, which the army of navy ghosts had failed to take notice of, but which I had at least been perceptive enough to espy when I'd earlier scattered around the floor the contents of the box I'd carted into the reeking dump.

I had also — score one for my sluggish brain — taken care not only to find the wall switch that turned the fan on, but had made certain that I was positioned within arm's length of it just in case everything, as was usually the case, turned to shit.

I reached out and snapped the fan on.

I suddenly remembered that I hadn't been bright enough to test to make sure the thing wasn't busted, so I was immediately forced to take away the single point I had just awarded a brain that was, frankly, sleeping far too much on the goddamn job lately.

Luckily, whoever inspected Pirate Pete's seafood shithouse hadn't been entirely asleep at the wheel. Although the speed at which the goddamn thing flew on could have launched the restaurant from the deck of an aircraft carrier without need of a catapult, so any kudos to city hall were wiped away by the fan's lethal, decapitation-level efficiency.

Nearly every ghost in the dining area was instantly blown apart. Solid weapons slipped from spectral fingers and clattered to the sticky floor.

Pirate Pete himself was spared complete disintegration by floating quickly backwards and plastering his back against the door of the gull's room.

"Arrrg! The mangy dandy be hoistin' anchor!" Pirate Pete bellowed as I set sail on fleet feet for the front door. "Turn off yon switch to that infernal spinning contraption!"

I was leaping a Parris Island obstacle course of seaside yar sale shit and closing in on the front doors when behind me I heard the desperately rotating fan whir to a stop. Pirate Pete's ghost crew must have been quick to rematerialize, for I heard the sounds of weapons being dragged from the tacky floor. A harpoon whizzed past my ear and sank into the great white trash barrel next to the door, knocking the bin over and spilling cardboard trays and half-melted ice cubes across the floor.

My heel caught a dripping ice cube and I made the door in a half-slipping gallop, laying into the glass with my shoulder and stampeding out onto the front sidewalk.

I raced into the sunlight, glancing back just in time to see the doors burst open in the most dramatic fashion that neither Madison Insurance Equities nor any other insurer would ever pay out on, since no policy in its right mind covered acts of ghost.

Both doors blew apart as if from a cannon blast. Glass shards formed deadly hail, and I had to yank my trench coat up around my head to avoid getting my pulchritudinous puss rearranged into a Pablo Picasso plastic surgery hash with two mouths on one cheek and a postnasal forehead. Chunks of glass pelted my coat and fell to the sidewalk, busting into smaller shards and scattering like hail around my Florsheims.

It was over in seconds, and when I came up for air I found Pirate Pete glaring confusion from the wide-open doors of his fish-themed shit shack.

The metal of both doors was twisted in either direc-

tion, as if some asshole driver had taken the drive-thru sign too literally and had, subsequent to his first embarrassing error, correctly interpreted the meaning while misconstruing utterly the spirit of the main EXIT sign at a hundred goddamn miles an hour.

Pirate Pete's cutlass was extended out into the sunlight, but his hand had not crossed the threshold. The ghost restaurateur's floating body remained stuck in the doorway, like a fly in amber, or at the very least like a fly fused to the sticky underside of a disgusting table in one of his million convenient locations in North America, Europe, and those parts of Asia that had embraced the discovery of fire and could stomach cooking the parasites out of their fish.

"What be this devilry?" the trapped ghost captain shouted.

I could hear similar expressions of angry bafflement emanating from his crew in the depths of the restaurant.

Pirate Pete strained like mad to exit the dump in order to kill me in his front yard, but he was unable to free himself from the doorway. The effort was so great that he lost his concentration on his sword. The cutlass curtain rod slipped straight through his hand and clanked to the sunny sidewalk.

"I would suggest that you send out a corporate memo directing your employees to actually clean your floors, rather than slop the same filthy mop across them once every other century, but you're unlikely to be around to dictate it. Maybe your corporate bosses at Bandito-Pharmaceutical will draft it after you're gone."

The ghost clearly didn't grasp that he was in the presence of genius.

"Goddammit," I groused. "It takes half the brilliance and all the fun out of it if I have to explain it. Clearly,

Einstein, I took the ingenious precaution of spreading sacred dirt from St. Regent's Drive-Thru Cathedral's graveyard all over the floor before I summoned you."

Evidently the dead captain hadn't dedicated two seconds of his two centuries as a ghost to learning a single goddamn thing about the nature of his afterlife.

"Yar?" Pirate Pete asked.

"Look, this isn't a tutorial. Blessed earth traps ghosts for later, permanent disposal. It's that simple. I can't help it if you didn't do the homework. You can look it up on your own. I was afraid for a minute that if I had to turn on the fan it might blow the dirt away, but your floors are in worse shape than the carpet in Harvey Weinstein's hotel room."

I turned to go. I'd taken only two steps when the ghost cried out behind me.

"Wait, me hearty! This! Take it!"

I glanced back to find that the trapped pirate ghost was waving a cheap paper placemat above his head. His tiny cartoon doppelganger was grinning at the opening of a simple little maze, in the center of which was drawn an open treasure chest spilling over with gold and jewels.

"Tis a map to me buried treasure!" Pirate Pete desperately explained. "Every map ye have ever seen in seafood restaurants and on cereal boxes be a map to real buried gold! We pirate mascots been hidin' our spoils under your mortal noses all your lives! Cap'n Crunch be richer than Sandy Duncan, the bowlegged barnacle! Me treasure be yours if ye but release me! Yer'll be rich, me salty pretzel! Rich as the kingdoms of Poseidon and Mrs. Paul combined! Yarr, etcetera!"

"No thanks," I replied. "It's not just that I don't trust you, which I definitely don't. And it's not that I'm pretty much one hundred percent certain you'd run me through

with that sword the first second you got a chance. It's that I am deeply concerned about the health of my bartender if he were to learn that I had suddenly come into millions of dollars in buried treasure. He'd have a heart attack when he found out I was rich and still wasn't paying my bar tab, which I definitely wouldn't, and I have enough to worry about without having Ed Jaublowski's death on my conscience."

I left the ghost bastard and his crew to angrily shiver their impotent timbers, unable to depart the four grimy walls of the fast-food fish restaurant, and headed off to locate either a phone or a drink, whichever was first to arrive on the scene.

18

As it was, I was able to satisfy both my inebriate and telephonic needs simultaneously, since in my attempt to frisk my coat for a quarter for the latter, I exhumed the brand new My Grain Distillery flask that I'd forgotten I'd stolen.

As I took a swig from the flask that I'd lifted from the buzzard with the busted choppers on the old folks' home tour bus, I reminded myself that I'd been hired because the Tooth Fairy owed some little pissant punk thirty measly bucks, and that so far the only good to come out of the entire affair was in my hand. Still, the flask represented a link to the final piece of the puzzle that I'd been retained to assemble, but which I could do nothing with until I sorted out the rest of the mess I found myself embroiled in.

Evidently, the local indigents had mistaken the phone booth on the corner near the bus stop for a lavatory. I would have strangled my nose to death with the phone cord, but I needed to stretch it to its maximum length in order to place my call so far outside the box that I looked like a water skier being pulled by Ma Bell's entry in a far less mind-numbingly dull speedboat version of the America's Cup.

"Federal Bureau of Investigation, an FBI agent speaking," announced a voice on the line whose bored tone, bordering on surly, my tax dollars were paying for.

"My apologies if I interrupted anything grotesquely unconstitutional with which you might be occupied," I said. "I just assumed you'd like to know I captured the primary bastard responsible for killing all those lawyers, which is something I don't support for some reason."

"The Federal Bureau of Investigation won't confirm or deny that there is, was, or ever will be an investigation into that matter."

"That's fine with me. Aren't a lot of you guys lawyers? So are your politician bosses. Again, I can't really see why I'm against this. However, I seem to be, in spite of long-standing, deep-seated, utterly justified contempt, so if you want him, he's yours."

I gave the G-man a quick rundown of Pirate Pete Barnacle's current whereabouts and the sea captain's revenge scheme against all lawyers for the inadequate representation he'd received from his attorney, which, if bad lawyering were an actual capital crime, would have meant lines of lawyers stretching from the town square to Neptune, as well as swapping out worn-out guillotine blades like Gillette disposables every half-hour. I mentioned Attorney Pierce Boyle, the legal eagle ancestor of Dr. Lance Boyle, as well as the maniac doctor himself, who may or may not have combusted in the distillery where he conducted experiments on lawyer guinea pigs. I gave the federal agent pretty much the whole shooting match, laid out in easy-to-read steps and tied up with a big presentation bow.

When I was finished my monologue, the G-man had only one question.

"You realize, sir," he announced sternly, "that the

term 'guinea pig' is prosecutable under a dozen federal hate crimes statutes?"

I'd dealt with moron cops enough these past two days.

"And you realize that by calling me 'sir' you assumed my gender?"

The FBI agent sucked up such a massive shocked gulp of air at his own inadvertent hate criming, that I suspected he'd inhaled his phone and that I would be conducting the rest of our conversation with his esophagus. How the hell these bastards ever got their own TV show, I had no idea.

"Bring a box of blessed dirt with you," I informed the Fed. "I used all mine up. I'll send J. Edgar the bill."

I hung up the phone.

The holy dirt I'd spread around the floor was enough to keep the ghosts locked in the seafood restaurant, but another box would be necessary to get them out for disposal. Ghosts couldn't fight the pull of blessed dirt, and were drawn to it like rats to politics. If the Feds set a box of sanctified earth down by the Pirate Pete's soft drink dispensers, the litter box would be loaded with buccaneer spirits before tomorrow's lunch rush.

Having finished doing the goddamn Feds' job for them, I turned my bleary sights to the next item that was likely to get me killed on my ridiculously complicated agenda.

The ten-minute bus ride to the law offices of Swindle, Steele & Robb wasn't anywhere near enough time to work all the kinks out of a devious plan that would see my ass safely through the next hour, at the end of which my aforementioned end would be deposited in one cleft piece on a stool at O'Hale's Bar. It did, however, afford me the time necessary to firm up an utterly suicidal

stratagem, the first step of which I executed upon descending to the sidewalk from my city bus carriage.

Although it broke my heart to do so — and pissed the hell out of my appalled liver — I unscrewed the cap from my stolen flask and poured a small quantity of the precious liquid within onto my collar and necktie.

I was sniffing my tie to ascertain if it bore a stink sufficient to pass for that of a sloppy inebriate when a voice chimed in behind me, snarling a word that was in the top seven of my most despised English language words, jostling for first place amongst alimony, marriage, wife, husband, lawyer, and sobriety.

"*Banyon!*"

No, it was still a distant # 7. Still, my name wasn't something I had hoped to hear hollered in public at that moment, standing as I was on the sidewalk in front of a law firm which had dispatched a half-dozen of its best legal minds to assault the hell out of, then subsequently kidnap, my gorgeous ass two nights before.

I had the option to pretend I'd gone deaf, but when the human foghorn began blaring my name a second time, I was left with no other choice.

"*Ban-*" the dame's voice began anew.

I wheeled around and clapped a hand over Attorney Sue Yu's wide-open talk hole.

My mitt clamped firmly in place, I helpfully guided the lawyer dame around the corner to an alley where, in a reluctant concession to outdated Judeo-Christian tradition, I didn't murder her on the spot.

"It would appear that the Tooth Fairy's portal didn't drop you into the master bedroom of a headhunter's hut in the Amazon," I whispered.

"Mghg gridnt bahr frume ba brrlah!" Sue Yu replied.

It was the smartest thing I'd ever heard any lawyer

say, and was only due to the fact that my hand was still pressed firmly over her yak box.

"I'm going to let your mouth go," I informed her. "Before I do, please inform it that the building we're currently standing next to is infested with lawyers that very likely want me dead, and won't give two shits if you're caught in the crossfire."

I closed my eyes and carefully released my grip on her face. Instead of the air raid shriek I expected to let loose on the unsuspecting vermin of the alley, Sue Yu managed to crank her volume control down to a furious hiss.

"I didn't fall through the portal," the lady lawyer informed me, which, I realized, was what she'd been attempting to tell me a moment before as she'd been licking my palm in the least sexy interaction we'd had since our first meeting in the Tooth Fairy's offices, save that one time she'd kicked me in the goddamn head.

She angrily shoved away from me and smoothed out her short black skirt.

"I hid under the bed," she snapped. "I had to be down there a half-hour with my hands clamped over my ears before I realized you were gone. You know, Banyon, those things could have eaten me alive if I'd fallen through that hole with them. You didn't even look for me. You just left me there in that old lady's apartment."

"I'm not in the habit of looking under random beds," I informed her. "Too much of my professional and private lives are spent hiding out under them. At my age, there's a limited number of times that my knees will get me down and back up again, so I'm saving bending them for when it's absolutely worth it. At this point, that pretty much limits it to when I'm the one who has to do the

hiding, plus one deathbed conversion."

"Yeah, well," she growled, "I had no idea you'd even left. I barely got out on the fire escape before the cops arrived. What's with you and some detective named Jenkins? I didn't hear much before I got out of there, but he really hates your guts."

"My entrails aren't writing sonnets to his viscera either," I said.

When I'd fled my old bag downstairs neighbor's apartment after going nine rounds with an army of giant cockroach men, the hag Mrs. Flora Willhausen had been on the phone with our landlord. Whichever one of the pair of assholes had summoned the police, Detective Daniel Jenkins had apparently been fast to arrive on the scene.

His ace detective instincts had incorrectly determined that my call to him about capturing the Tooth Fairy had been a false alarm. My guess that he'd staked out my building out of spite was probably right. Jenkins — who had problems thinking in one dimension, let alone three — had most likely been sitting out front as I slipped out back, and got summoned to the Willhausen manor over the radio.

The local cops were a dead end as far as assistance went. If I called them again, I'd be in lockup within the hour, at which point I'd be a delicious goat staked out in a clearing for a gaggle of ravenous, giant cockroaches. (Robert Sherman Planck — vice president for Madison Insurance Equities, and the sugar daddy of my current client, little Timmy Thompson — had still earned a knuckle concerto to the kisser for siccing those multi-legged bastards on me, and said fisticuffian retribution remained high on my list of incentives for getting through this caper alive.)

I'd set the Feds on the right path with my courageous capture of Pirate Pete and his murderous ghost crew, but who knew how deep the G-men would dig? I gave them their suspect, as well as his motive for wiping out America's entire lawyer class. The FBI could close the case that afternoon, and might never tie in the Tooth Fairy's disappearance or the mysterious lawyer queen, obeisance to whom by members of the legal profession cryptically appeared in every legal document in the country.

Even the pirate ghost captain might not have a clue about that which was unfolding concurrent to his diabolical mass-murder plot, the evil nature of which was mitigated substantially by the fact that he was killing goddamn lawyers. Although, it would seem, I was, at least for the moment, stuck with one still-breathing barrister who was currently fuming at me in the alley beside the law firm of Swindle, Steele & Robb.

"I'm still pissed at you, Banyon," Attorney Sue Yu informed me, wrongly determining that the murderous glare currently occupying her little Asian mush was insufficiently expressing her feelings on the all-important subject of me.

"And yet apparently I'm meant to have gotten over the concussion your foot gave me," I said. "Not to mention, since you haven't, the thank-you I have yet to receive for saving your life. Take your thumb off the scales, lady, because they clearly tip fairly goddamn heavily in my direction. Now, setting all that aside, can I convince you to get the hell out of here and let me figure out on my own how to finish this?"

She vehemently shook her head, something which I still dared not do, thanks in large part to the unprovoked stomping the dame had given my delicate cranium.

"Fine," I said. "If you're going to tag along, we have

to make you look more like a lawyer, because in your case law school was woefully inadequate for the task."

I uncapped my stolen flask and, over her objection — which I overruled — dumped the last of my precious hooch out onto her hair and blouse, the latter offering not even one cheap thrill on the way to my funeral, since goddamn Aunt Jemima makes a bustier product.

19

As it turned out, impersonating a member of the bar was pretty much as easy as falling off the wagon, an experience unfamiliar to members of the legal profession since they would have to climb onto something — their secretary, to select the most obvious for-instance when it came to lawyers — before they could tumble off.

The guard in the lobby of the Swindle, Steele & Robb Building sniffed my damp tie and Sue Yu's soggy hair and, satisfied we bore the identifying stench of the lawyer species, permitted us to pass over to the elevators.

The lobby directory informed us that the Records Department was on the top floor, a choice that instantly sent up a crimson flag. Records departments are traditionally squirreled away in dank, windowless basements. In point of fact, I had been in the Swindle, Steele & Robb Building two times in the past, and both times Records had been located below street level. I had last been there only two months before, which meant the disappearance of the Tooth Fairy three weeks ago fell neatly into that same time period during which the basement Records Department had been relocated.

The monumental undertaking of moving the Records Department to the opposite vertical end of the building

suggested that not only had something bigger than Records displaced it, but that whatever it was that had forced the move was something important enough to the firm to leave whatever it was off the lobby directory.

I took note that the basement — and whatever the hell was down there — had been scrubbed free from a directory that now began on the ground floor.

Sue Yu was oblivious to whatever sinister might be going on beneath the polished marble under our feet. The attorney dame was more annoyed at the booze on her blouse, which she sniffed with unlawyerly distaste as she trailed me onto the elevator.

"What are we doing here, Banyon?" Sue Yu said once we were sealed alone in our upright coffin and had started our ascent.

"Getting caught and probably killed, if you keep yelling my name," I replied. "Although they likely won't murder me right away. First, they'll still want to know what I might have learned about the Tooth Fairy's whereabouts in the course of my investigation. You, on the other hand, they'll probably immediately toss out the nearest window, then sue your estate for the cracks you make in the sidewalk."

She offered a derisive snort, folding her arms over her absence of a chest.

"I'll tell them you found him then let him go," she said, staring at the floor lights blinking one-after-another over the doors as our elevator continued to climb. "If I'm going out a window, you're going out right after me."

I let her arrogant lawyer assumption slide and addressed her initial question.

"We are trying to uncover any information we can about the queen, whoever the hell she is. In fact, 'whoever the hell she is' is at the top of the list of information we're

looking to uncover. A bunch of thugs from Swindle, Steele & Robb tried to kidnap me, and they didn't just send paralegals. They were supervised by Senior Partner Montague Swindle himself. It stands to reason that if they were working in the interests of this queen — whoever she is — that they were working under the direction of said queen. Consequently, if anyone in town knows who the hell the queen is, and her interest in the Tooth Fairy, it would be the law firm of Swindle, Steele & Robb."

"Well, we better find out what's going on soon," she said. "My ass is on the line, Banyon. I don't want to wind up like all those others."

It occurred to me that she hadn't a clue about Pirate Pete's diabolical scheme, or the solving by yours truly of the ghost's plot to murder every lawyer under the sun. I would have told her that I'd cracked that case, not to mention remind her that she was clearly a unique specimen of attorney who was evidently immune to the allure of the My Grain product that had wiped out so many of her legal colleagues. However, I was disinclined to kick an ounce of benevolence in her direction given her persistent, oblivious, dimwitted insistence on using my goddamn name every three seconds.

On our way to the fortieth floor, the elevator doors opened on a few random floors and a couple of lawyers scuttled on and off the car on six-hundred-buck-an-hour legs, which came to an outrageous three hundred simoleons per patella. Each time the doors parted, I noted the vast, empty, gilded corridors on each floor.

Ordinarily, the hallways of Swindle, Steele & Robb, LLC would have been crawling with attorneys, but Pirate Pete Barnacle and Dr. Lance Boyle had thinned the local herd dramatically enough to put lawyers on the endangered species list. The sweeping, empty vistas of each floor at

which we stopped only worked to amplify the manifest unfairness of a society in which every corner of a forty-story office building had, until the past few days, been infested with highly paid law school parasites while out in the real world strippers, junkies, muggers and equally far more valuable members of society went to court broke.

As I had been attacked by representatives of Swindle, Steele & Robb — led by bastard Senior Partner Montague Swindle — I was concerned that I might bump into one of my late-night assailants on our way to the top floor. As it stood, I'd only spotted two of my would-be kidnappers piled up downtown at the morgue. That left four — plus the driver of the getaway car, whose face I had not seen — unaccounted for. Luckily, none of the mugs that got on and off the elevator seemed to recognize me, nor I them.

By the time we reached floor number forty, the car had shed all other occupants.

This hallway was even more dead than the others. One lone male clerk manned a brilliantly white, space-age semicircle desk beneath a silver "RECORDS" plaque.

Only one lonely lawyer stood before the desk. The baggy-eyed SOB glanced at Sue Yu and me, then headed for the elevators, clutching a manila folder in his manicured digits. With a ding, the doors closed on the only other face on the otherwise empty floor.

If a tumbleweed could have figured out how to manipulate the buttons on the elevator, it would likely have selected that moment to bounce past for dramatic effect.

"Can I help you?" the kid at the desk asked us. "Oh, I'm sorry. You don't have a pass. That's okay. You can just run downstairs and get one."

The clerk was in his early twenties, and possessed the glow and confidence of youth that you just want to punch.

In addition to having the gall to be younger than me in front of a hot Asian babe, the kid was insolently fitter, impertinently better looking, and presumably wanted to be a lawyer when he grew up, which were all reasons enough for any decent middle-aged failure to hate him on sight.

"You mean 'may' you help me," I corrected. "I'm a lawyer, so I know everything about every subject in excruciating detail. Rather than run down and get a goddamn pass, which will waste my important lawyer time, I'll instead use the time saved to stand here all day correcting your grammar. Also, do you want to know precisely how your desk was constructed and who invented the coffee mug?"

I waved a hand at the items in question.

The fresh-faced young bastard waived our passes and hastily waved us down the hall.

Swindle, Steele & Robb had been tirelessly fleecing clients and gumming up the gears of the judicial system for decades. There was at least one room dedicated to every letter of the alphabet, and when an A, B, or C room had been filled to capacity, A1, B1, and C1 annexes were added, with appropriate alphanumeric identification from the Home Depot mailbox department nailed to the doors. "Q" was still flying solo, across the hall from a door marked "M16."

Sue Yu and I entered the home of the loneliest letter of the alphabet and I quickly shut the door behind us.

Once we were alone, I flipped the switch inside the door. Rows of weak florescent lights reluctantly twitched to life, buzzing like swarms of amorous hornets, illuminating row upon row of gunmetal gray filing cabinets.

I had the very strong inclination to condemn at length a practice, not to mention the larger profession Swindle,

Steele & Robb represented, that had been able to pile up so many cases related to the goddamn orphan letter of the alphabet. Unfortunately, at that moment I didn't have the time to rip the bastard barristers an additional crap cavity.

I steered Sue Yu straight for the cabinet marked "QUEEN."

There was a disheartening glut of "queen" files arranged in a dozen separate drawers. Most were related to individual surnames. Two involved members of the famous musical combo. There was one Dairy Queen, one *Queen for a Day*, one "Queens, NY v. Kevin James (re: fat and unfunny)." Apparently, and unknown to the newspapers, the Queen of England had once sued the Queen of Albion for identity theft.

My attorney accomplice shook her head as I dumped half the teetering pile of queen files in her arms.

"We can't possibly go through all of these, Banyon," the dame said.

"There is that disturbing lack of hubris again," I replied. "Are you sure you're really a lawyer? Maybe you actually went to medical school and just got confused when you couldn't read the shit penmanship on your diploma."

She didn't reply with a pathetic, unfunny jab, which further underscored a personality remarkably unlike that of the typical law school graduate.

Sue Yu's eyes were suddenly propped open wide, and she was wordlessly aiming her excited chin at the topmost file in the manila garbage dump in her arms.

I hadn't read the labels on the files I'd yanked out of the top drawer and piled onto her forearms. The tab on the top file read: "LAWYER QUEEN." "SHH!" "TOP SECRET." "NOT TO LEAVE THIS BUILDING." "HAIL, MOST MAGNIFICENT, GRACIOUS, ENCHANTING AND TERRIFYING ONE, RULER FOR ALL ETERNITY

OF ALL ATTORNEYS-AT-LAW."

Evidently whoever filled out the file tabs at Swindle, Steele & Robb was one of those Guinness World Records assholes who, in his spare time, wrote the entire King James Version on the heads of pins.

I scarcely had time to snatch the file away and slap it down on top of a cabinet, there to hastily peruse the top page, when a voice that belonged neither to Sue Yu nor my internal monologue chimed in from somewhere near the previously closed *Q* door.

"We'll be having that discussion about the Tooth Fairy now, Mr. Banyon," sang the smug bastard whose voice I instantly recognized.

I took a second longer to turn around than was prudent, and my hesitation cost me my .38, which another bastard I hadn't even heard sneak up behind me snatched from my hand before I could fully fumble it from my holster. The looming goon pressed my gat to my succulent ribs and, with a glare, dared me to start the barbecue.

The hinges in the Swindle, Steele & Robb Building were, like the attorneys employed therein, exceptionally well oiled.

Framed in the file room door that neither Sue Yu nor I had heard open was rotund blob of suet, Attorney Montague Swindle. His sweeping wave of dyed-orange circus clown hair offered a Bob's Big Boy middle finger to the humming florescent lights.

Standing next to the man who put the "Swindle" in Swindle, Steele & Robb was the baggy-eyed bastard lawyer who'd been standing at the record clerk's desk down the hall when Sue Yu and I had arrived, and who had wordlessly scuttled into the elevator.

"Let me deduce," I said to Swindle. "Your driver."

Montague Swindle's face split into an open-mouthed

Pac-Man smile with capped teeth and a victorious tongue that hung out so far it looked like his owner had forgotten to fill his water dish with Jack Daniels.

To the younger lawyer, I announced, "You hit everything in the street during your getaway, including something that may have been my beloved misplaced Pontiac. Expect to be hearing from my lawyer about the damages, assuming there are any lawyers left in town when I get home."

"Oh, there are still plenty of us," Swindle said. "And once you give us the location of the Tooth Fairy, we'll being filling our diminished ranks back up *tout suite*."

I didn't correct the rotund bastard's bastardized French, as I likely only had a few minutes of life left on the mortal plain and I didn't want to squander any of my precious final seconds giving so much as the slightest of shits about the goddamn French.

"Take them to—" Attorney-at-Large Montague Swindle paused for dramatic effect. "—*the conference room,*" he announced with a twisted grin.

His attempt at a cackling laugh as he waddled from the room echoed with what he hoped was gleeful supervillain evilness, but merely sounded like a wheezing fat lawyer who needed a mouthful of Flintstone chewable statins just to make it to the elevator without having a fatal heart attack.

Swindle's SOB driver joined the mook who still had the barrel of my own gun pressed in the neighborhood of my ninth and tenth ribs. Together the pair of assholes ushered me, along with a very worried Attorney Sue Yu — whose complete inability to slap on a poker face had probably gotten fifty of her clients the chair — from the *Q* records room.

20

The thirty-ninth floor conference room in the Swindle, Steele & Robb Building offered a magnificent view of a city that had been made significantly more shitty thanks to decades of bastards who'd planted their ample lawyer asses in the two dozen lush leather seats that were parked at attention around a conference table so polished that the sunlight reflecting off it threatened to ignite the equally glossy ancient oak walls.

Sue Yu and I were shoved into the conference room by Swindle's goons. The double doors locked behind us with a fatal Schlage click.

The chairs around the table were empty of lawyers, as was the rest of the room, save for the frightened lady attorney to whom I had been lately manacled.

The instant we were alone, Sue Yu immediately spun around and began fruitlessly rattling the doorknob. Apparently lost entirely on the panicking dame was the trio of facts that 1) we had both clearly heard said door being locked, 2) that there was at least one armed gorilla stationed outside it, and 3) that the entire building had by now been alerted to our presence, thus severely incommoding any escape attempt.

I, on the other hand, took advantage of this fully antici-

pated postponement of our murders to hastily reconnoiter our temporary prison.

A single scrap of white paper had been placed on the conference table before each chair. I perused the contents of the closest one, but found only boring agenda items that mostly had to do with soaking wealthy clients. Somewhere beyond the locked door, a secretary was currently typing an addendum to the scheduled items to alert the firm's partners to the impending double homicide that would cap that morning's meeting.

A crystal glass was set within delirium tremens reach of each chair. Eight thick crystal decanters were carefully positioned up the center of the table, filled with intoxicating brown libation. It was entirely likely that the collection of decanters and glasses cost more than my annual salary, which added an unnecessary physical twist on my already crystal clear opinion that I'd chosen the wrong goddamn profession.

At the door, Sue Yu gave up her titanic battle with the rattling doorknob.

"Why would he just lock us in here and leave us?" she demanded.

"As a lawyer, you don't know one hell of a lot about *being* a lawyer," I said, turning from the conference table and casting an eye around the rest of the room. "Right now Swindle is on the crapper, or yapping on the phone with his mistress, or otherwise killing time. The invoice for billable hours will later claim that he used this time preparing for our murders. If we want to dispute it, we'd have to hire yet another lawyer to sue him for the obvious fraud. That lawyer, in turn, would do the same goddamn crooked thing, resulting in the need to hire yet another lawyer to sue the second thieving lawyer, thus perpetuating a cycle that will continue until the sun explodes."

There was a small kitchenette off the conference room. I noted a cardboard case stamped with a familiar logo parked just inside the open door, and made a beeline for it.

The unopened box was one of the complimentary cases that had been sent all over town by My Grain Distillery. A handwritten note from an SS&R employee had been Scotch-taped to the top of the sealed box: "FBI WARNING! DO NOT DRINK!"

The rest of the little room was more amply stocked with booze than the trunk of Nick Nolte's car. It was clear that the law firm's partners hadn't yet worked their way around to the My Grain case before the G-men warning had been issued, courtesy Doc Minto and yours-goddamn-truly.

For the next twenty minutes, I had to endure Sue Yu yapping endlessly in my ear like a Japanese Chihuahua, to the point where it was a relief when the lock on our prison finally clicked and the twin conference room doors swung open like a gallows trapdoor.

Attorney Montague Swindle was first through the doors, a drunken ringmaster in a horribly dyed orange fright wig leading a circus parade of degenerate barrister clowns up Main Street, USA.

Hot on the heels of Swindle came Anthony Steele and Haverbrook Robb, fellow marquee senior partners whose mugs had graced billboards around town since long before all the capillaries in their rum-soaked faces had burst and their noses had lit up like ruddy road flares. The rest of the procession consisted of shysters who had climbed to every high rung of the Swindle, Steele & Robb ladder, and whose heel marks were no doubt imprinted on the foreheads of all the other lawyers in the building who were clawing zombie-style to reach the crème-de-la-crètin

level of this exalted pack of assholes.

The partners stumbled to their seats and, because it was early still, most of them managed to settle ass to leather on the first try.

A couple of aides hustled around the table, passing out fresh paperwork and filling glasses from the crystal decanters.

The assistants didn't speak, at least not in any language vertebrates would be able to comprehend. The young helpers clicked their tongues and bugged their eyes, and two of them rubbed their legs together in a communication dance that was incomprehensible to everybody in the room who wasn't on the Swindle, Steele & Robb payroll.

Montague Swindle clicked his tongue right back at his subordinate crew, and when he rubbed the backs of his wrists together, the handful of junior lawyers scurried from the conference room.

Before the door closed once more, the goon guard leaned in and flashed my gat as a friendly warning that he'd relocate my forehead to the carpet if given half a chance.

The door closed again, but this time it distinctly did not lock.

"Good morning, good morning," Senior Partner Montague Swindle announced from the head of the long table. "Before we get started with the regular agenda — prayer to the Prince of Lies, rolling around in the cash we've bilked from our clients, etcetera — we've got a most important item to deal with. I have, at great personal risk, successfully captured Mr. Crag Banyon, the private investigator who was retained by our friends at Madison Insurance Equities to find that missing malefactor, the Tooth Fairy."

A meadow's worth of clicks and chirps accompanied

many excitedly nodding lawyer heads. Swindle raised his hand to silence the bughouse symphony.

"Please. In English, in deference to our guests. Or, rather, at least to one of our guests. This lovely young lady is herself an attorney," the bloated bastard said, waving a hand so vaguely in the almost-direction of Sue Yu that it was evident he'd either started the celebrating early or had mistaken a small silver trash can five feet to her left for the hot Asian dame. "MacAbee, Hallstead," he said nodding to a pair of lawyers at the end of the conference table nearest Sue Yu and me.

Attorneys MacAbee and Hallstead — male and female, respectively — hopped to their polished Guccis and scuttled over to us.

Sue Yu grabbed my arm and shrank up against me as the pair of attorneys slowly circled us. They held their hands up to their foreheads and extended their index fingers in the air. They twitched their makeshift antennae, clicked their tongues, and otherwise freaked the shit out of the terrified lawyer chick — who was squeezing my bicep as if trying to get the last mouthful of Crest out of the tube — as they continued around us.

Suddenly, Ms. Hallstead, the dame lawyer, dropped her sniffing fingers to her sides and straightened up. "She's not one of us," she concluded, darkly.

MacAbee's fingers concurred.

The pair of them scurried back to their chairs.

"I suspected as much," Swindle announced. "She had the stink of one of the one percent, but these old fingers don't smell as good as they once did. In any event, our beloved queen is immensely pleased with the capture of Mr. Banyon. She has ordered us to extract any information he may have gathered about the missing Tooth Fairy."

Senior Partner Haverbrook Robb, who was seated at

Montague Swindle's left at the head of the conference table, released a series of low clicks while giving me the stink eye. Swindle nodded as he listened carefully to the incomprehensible mouth noise.

"Now, now," Swindle said when his partner was through. "I was informed personally by Robert Sherman Planck — a fellow attorney, I might add — over at Madison Insurance that Mr. Banyon here is very thorough, and has been an asset to Madison many times in the past. First, we'll find out what he knows, and then, yes, when he's finished we'll eat his head."

This announcement clearly cheered the lawyer crowd no end, and the lot of them gathered up their glasses to toast the imminent consumption of my delicious noggin.

"Excuse me," I interjected.

The two dozen lawyers froze, their crystal tumblers still raised in military salud in the air. All four dozen beady little legal eyes turned my way.

"First, I have to point out that you missed out on the chance to make some kind of hilarious reference to 'picking my brain before you pick my brain.' Not that, obviously. Something like that, but funny. I'm under considerable stress right now, so I can't be expected to bring my A material. But I find the fact that you didn't do so to be pretty monumentally inexcusable, as it is so utterly goddamn obvious a joke to make. However, setting the lawyer lack of any sense of humor aside, I want to make something absolutely clear. For the record, I can't convince any of you to not kill me and eat my brains, or to spare the lovely Miss Attorney Sue Yu, Esquire, the same gruesome fate?"

I was met with a furious chirping so resoundingly committed to dining on my cranium and the contents therein, that I waved both hands in surrender.

"It was essential that I make absolutely certain," I announced.

Two dozen delighted attorneys raised crystal glasses to exultant lawyer lips.

The entire celebrated board of Swindle, Steele & Robb slugged down the contents of said glasses.

There was a momentary pause after they'd put down their thick tumblers during which preprandial pause they may have been contemplating the banquet between my ears.

They may have, on the other hand, already been dead.

With Swan Lake precision, nearly two dozen heads simultaneously flopped forward. Almost two dozen foreheads clunked with thunderous finality on the gleaming surface of the SS&R conference room table.

A momentary silence flooded the room, into which seconds-long gulp of stillness flooded a single, very confused chirp.

The only breathing bastard left in the room besides Attorney Sue Yu and myself was one lonely, baffled SOB lawyer with a horrible orange dye-job, who at that moment was blinking utter incomprehension at the head of the table.

When the junior staff had swept through the room prior to the commencement of the meeting, Senior Partner Montague Swindle had declined the booze that had been offered from the decanters lined up in the middle of the table. Swindle had opted instead to slug down half a bottle of his own private port, cut with a carefully measured teaspoon of orange juice to remove the curse of antemeridian inebriation.

The last remaining Swindle, Steele & Robb partner — senior or otherwise — was holding his nearly empty glass of breakfast in his bloated fingers and wearing a look

of perplexed horror on his rum-blossomed mug as he stared at the bald patches on every dead head around the mahogany conference table.

As shocked as he was by the surprising turn of events, Swindle's recovery of his senses was remarkably swift.

"Wilson!" the fat bastard roared. "Get in here!"

The goon with my gun — who was apparently named after a goddamn tennis ball — was quick to respond. I, however, had taken the Boy Scout motto to heart and was prepared for the behemoth's stampeding entry.

When the door burst open, I was waiting on the other side.

The door flew forward only a few inches before I reversed its course and sent it flying back at the moron who'd flung it open. The door panel met the forehead of my wannabe killer with a crack solid enough to split the veneer.

I helped the dazed goon tip forward into the room, and when I closed the door behind him I slammed the back of his head on the reverse side for the sheer fun of it.

The unconscious bastard hadn't hit the floor before I'd scooped up my stolen gat and whirled on the utterly shocked and extremely fat Montague Swindle.

"One word out of that gaping halitosis factory and you'll be full of more holes than a JJ Abrams plot," I warned the bewildered barrister. "Which reminds me."

I reached in my pocket and removed a handful of bullets, which I proceeded to load into my hitherto empty gat.

Beside me, Sue Yu blinked astonishment.

"There weren't any bullets in it?" the dame asked.

"Of course not," I replied. "Why the hell would I give a loaded gun to somebody who wanted to kill me?"

Just because the lady lawyer had decided to tag along didn't mean that I had to share with her every tiny little aspect of my ingenious plan. Like, for instance, the fact that I'd calculated on the bus ride over that there was a near one hundred percent chance that I'd be caught. Since I'd be dealing with lawyers, I couldn't rely on my theoretical captors being smart enough to frisk me. I'd have to see to it that my piece was liberated from me, which I had done in the records room. Naturally, they wouldn't check to make sure the goddamn gun was loaded, since their natural lawyer arrogance wouldn't allow them to conceive of a scenario in which they weren't in total genius control. Said arrogance — now armed and thus even more overconfident — would carry them straight through to the point where I'd find it convenient to retrieve my roscoe, which was five seconds before Sue Yu asked a second annoying question.

"And I suppose you knew you'd get taken before all the firm's partners?" the lady lawyer demanded with more skepticism and impertinence than, frankly, she should have of somebody holding a very recently loaded .38.

"It was a possibility," I replied. "Although I admit I didn't imagine so many of them would still be alive. I hadn't anticipated that only the lower orders had gotten around to drinking the tainted My Grain booze. Fortunately, the fat dope with the bright orange dye-job who is currently gulping in confusion at the far end of the conference table left us alone long enough for me to switch out the good hooch in the carafes."

I waved my gun at Montague Swindle in both thanks, and to advise the tubby bastard to get to his feet, which he managed to do after several attempts to get his shaking hands and boozy eyes to figure out which of the table edges he was seeing was the real deal.

"I assume there's a private elevator for you SOB bigwigs," I said.

Swindle nodded. "Just down the hall," he replied.

"Does it require a key?"

From the collar of his dress shirt he rescued a thin chain that had been suffering the nightmare fate of being secreted in the sweaty corridor of his fat-guy décolletage. From the end of the chain dangled a silver key.

Before we left the room, I ducked back into the kitchenette for a quick second, my thoughts briefly devoted to Robert Sherman Planck — insurance executive benefactor of my short-pants brat client — who Swindle had surprisingly unmasked as a lawyer, a fact previously unknown to me. Once my gat and I returned to Sue Yu's side, I permitted the tubby drunk senior partner to lead us out of the conference room with the proviso that he'd be joining the rest of the upper echelon of his firm if he hollered for help.

Fortunately, there was a paucity of peepers in the corridor owing to the fact that most of the firm of Swindle, Steele & Robb had by now likely joined most every other lawyer in town on a slab downtown at Doc Minto's standing-room-only morgue.

A private door marked "PRIVATE" led to a private hallway, at the end of which was the private partner elevator which was, because lawyers can't help their asshole selves, also marked "PRIVATE." Senior Partner Montague Swindle unlocked the panel and summoned the car which arrived in excruciatingly languid due course, and onto which the three of us piled our respective asses.

"I can't believe you killed the entire board of Swindle, Steele & Robb," Sue Yu hissed once the door was closed and we were zipping down to the lobby.

"First off, it was self-defense. You've apparently for-

gotten that they were unanimous and unwavering in their support of our murders, as well as the posthumous consumption of my head, which would have been particularly succulent thanks to the fact that you recently tenderized it with your foot. Second, apparently you haven't noticed that one of them is still very much alive and is currently staring anxiously at the lighted floor numbers. And third — because clearly you haven't figured this part of it out yet — they weren't human. I used to think it was hilarious to say that about lawyers, but I find it to be slightly less amusing now that I've found out that that particular joke, like every other allegedly humorous goddamn thing, has been on me all my life."

"I don't understand," Sue Yu said.

"If you haven't figured it out, I'm not going to explain it to you," I said. "I will only say that I began to have something of a theory quite a little while ago, which has been largely confirmed in the past half-hour. You've been present for enough of it that you have essentially all the same information I have. If you can't figure it out for yourself, I'd tell you that you can read all about it in the newspapers. That is, if I wasn't suddenly unsure that we'd be getting out of here alive after all."

The elevator was suddenly descending at an alarming rate. We weren't yet going fast enough that I could characterize it as plummeting, but the car was most definitely flying down at a pre-plummet pace. If this was the creeping edge of the Civil War, we were firmly at the very end of the anteplummet period, with a Fort Sumter plunge and subsequent body-mangling crash beginning to peek ominously over the horizon.

I stabbed the eighteenth floor button, which would have been the next stop, assuming the elevator decided to cease dropping at a hundred miles an hour and resume its

job of responding to digital commands.

Nothing.

We continued to speed down at a rate that was increasing with every passed floor, and which building velocity did not leave me any time whatsoever to ponder the absolute appropriateness that life's final act against me would be to literally give me the shaft.

I pissed my pants (probably) and repeatedly stabbed the emergency stop button.

Still nothing.

I wheeled on the blubbery, orange-capped mass in the corner of the car.

"*Stop the elevator, Swindle*," I commanded.

Montague Swindle shook his thinning strands of ridiculously dyed hair.

"I can't," insisted the last of the Swindle, Steele & Robb partners. "She knows all. She sees all. She sends for us. Rejoice and fear, human, for you have been summoned by the Queen."

I wasn't really doing all that much rejoicing in our falling elevator, but I most definitely had the fear covered, strictly in the "scared utterly shitless" sense.

"Banyon, what do we do!" Attorney Sue Yu cried.

As we continued to accelerate, the dame lawyer was clinging to the silver railing that was bolted to the wall and was trying to keep her feet planted on the floor.

"'Defy gravity' would be good," I hollered back. "If you can master it in the next two seconds, by my estimation you should have a whole other second to teach me."

I stabbed a dozen separate floor buttons like a crazed, two-finger typist.

Each floor light flashed briefly, as if the car were considering my various suggestions, but they each immediately winked out.

Montague Swindle seemed disturbingly calm, the reason for which I didn't much want to contemplate. However, given all that I had deduced, a bloody crash might be the more attractive alternative.

The three of us in the plummeting elevator car were fighter pilots fighting G-forces that flung Swindle's flabby chins up to form a hammock for his greasy chin, and which very nearly awarded Sue Yu the chest that she — or at least I — always dreamed of.

My shoes were suddenly filled with helium and, as the air whooshed around the sides of the plunging car, I felt myself begin to float off the floor. My stomach clawed its way up my throat to displace my brain as my body's dominant organ, which pissed off my liver no end because it thought it was in command all this time.

The numbers above the door flashed by at lightning speed.

Eighth floor. Seventh floor. Fifth floor.

My stomach, which was doing a better job thinking than my brain ever did, felt there should be some department to which I could complain about the fact that we were now picking up so much speed that we were skipping whole goddamn floors.

Third floor.

No time to register a formal complaint at the lack of a fourth floor, as we'd just blinked and missed the second.

First floor.

If we were lucky, the end would come in a mercifully fast pulverizing and fusing of metal and bloody flesh. But lucky isn't a dame that ever deigns to dance with a palooka like me, and so I pushed all my chips on double-zero certainly that the preordained roulette outcome would be resoundingly goddamn unlucky.

Of course, with my shit luck, our rapid descent was

abruptly arrested.

We didn't slam on the brakes in any way that could be reconciled with accepted Newtonian custom. If such a rapid stop had taken place within the normal physical world, it would have resulted in our bodies being flung to the ceiling of the car, pureeing our bones just before the entire car accordioned around us. That was the best case scenario. Instead of a traditionally cataclysmic interruption of our descent, the world appeared to slip into a weird, swimming slow motion.

My worst fear was realized as we found ourselves suddenly passing through what felt like a band of molasses. The world warped around us, and we were looking at the interior of the car through a kaleidoscope that was being twisted and wrung out like a soggy washcloth. The air was suffused in a bluish glow, through which we could view the shimmering waves of molasses that muted all sound and distorted our vision.

As quickly as we passed into the freaky hippie mind-altering strip of unreality, we were through the other side. The three of us were deposited on our feet as if the previous twenty seconds of hundred-mile-an-hour freefalling had been a typical elevator ride to the Swindle, Steele & Robb Building's basement.

The bell dinged, the doors parted.

And we came face-to-hideous-face with a goddamn bug-eyed monster so enormous that even diehard fans of Rosie O'Donnell might have been motivated to search the sofa cushions with pudgy fingers for a remote control lost amongst the scattered Cheetos and crushed Ben & Jerry's containers to see if there was something slightly less horrifying on another channel.

Chapter 21

Unfortunately, real life doesn't give one the option of choosing between realities, and so, for instance, switching over to a Gene Hackman or Robert Duvall rerun of *The Naked City*, however alluring, was not a practical option. I was, I realized with a sinking feeling in the pit of my brain, stuck with staring into the many eyes of a creature uglier than a marriage license with my signature on it.

It was technically an insect, in the same way a dinosaur is technically a bird. No shoe made by man could have squashed this hissing, oozing nightmare, and no refrigerator was big enough for it to scurry under when the lights switched on.

It towered over the three of us, casting into the elevator car a misshapen shadow trimmed at the far edges with a penumbra of trembling, fuzzy legs. Great, bent, hairy feelers twitched high atop an enormous light bulb head.

The thing had a round mouth that breathed an open-sewer stench, which I would have recoiled from had I not already been shrinking bravely away from the giant pincers that stuck out from either side of its face like a pair of aggressively snapping parentheses.

A couple of absurdly large eyes were subdivided by crisscrossing grids that gave the thing so many littler

peepers within the larger pair that Moe Howard would have worn his fingers to nubs trying to poke them all out.

The thing's dozen bent, black legs, all of them as tall as me, supported a body divided into three segments that stretched nearly the length of a city bus, and would have been only slightly less disgusting to ride to the dog track inside of.

"All hail the Lawyer Queen!" Attorney Montague Swindle cried, sinking in terrified reverence before the otherworldly monster.

The Rust-Oleum-capped legal eagle shouted the words in English purely for our benefit. An instant later he had his hands slapped to his forehead — index fingers extended — and was clicking up a storm at the huge bug.

The big bug clicked back a few terse commands, after which it released the elevator button which it had been holding firmly with the razor-sharp tip of one leg. It retreated a few yards from the mouth of the elevator in order that we might disembark.

Left behind on the floor after the insect's short retreat was a pile of a dozen spherical objects. A few more had dropped loose as it scuttled back over the basement floor. Even as it squatted, rubbing its forelegs together, a seemingly limitless supply of the things continued to drop out of the ass segment of the gigantic bug, since just looking at it standing there apparently wasn't disgusting enough for human eyes, so it had to continue to endlessly shit for our benefit.

The objects it was secreting were slightly smaller than bowling balls, and were covered in viscous goo. The things were translucent, and glowed a soft amber. Amorphous black shapes swirled ominously within the glowing globes.

"You will never guess what these are, Banyon," Montague Swindle announced smugly, gesturing to the near

pile of shimmering amber balls.

"Let's get this over with," I replied. "They're lawyers. They are, as we are continuing to bear disgusting witness to, the offspring of this massive, other-dimensional roach. At some point a bunch of decades ago, this inexhaustibly fruitful bedbug made some kind of deal with the Tooth Fairy. I assume cash. His business model of paying kids for their teeth was unsustainable from the start. For the payola, he would deliver these embryonic lawyers to the unsuspecting uteruses of dames in our dimension. The Tooth Fairy has the ability to sneak into any bedroom in the world, which is something your queen here can't do, since she'd have to knock out the wall to get into most bedrooms, and people would notice an enormous, reeking bug scuttling around the armoire. You called the portals he created to deliver the eggs your 'legal loophole,' since, being lawyers, your thought it was clever. It isn't. The Tooth Fairy became your queen's delivery system, bringing her offspring into our dimension. The Tooth Fairy sneaks into a house to bring a quarter for a lost incisor. While there, he leaves one more unsuspected present. Nine months later, little Johnny has a little brother. Except nobody knows the new arrival is really one of these things that has hijacked the DNA of its host."

I could see by the deflated look on the front of Swindle's blubbery head that I was batting a thousand.

I glanced at Sue Yu to see if she was as turned on at my deductive prowess as I was. The dame lawyer was more bothered than hot. It was evident that she was as shocked by my monologue as Swindle was disheartened.

"If you're worried that you're actually descended from a bug, don't be," I assured the lady lawyer. "These things are lawyers before they're even born. That's all they were

ever destined to be, and it's why the United States has more lawyers than the entire rest of the world combined. Our lawyer population seems to multiply like bugs because they are, in fact, bugs. However, there will always be a small percentage of the normal human population that, for whatever unfathomable reason, will elect to become lawyers. According to asshole Swindle himself, you're one of the one percent of actual human lawyers, which is a higher percentage of human lawyers than I'd have thought existed even before all this."

Swindle had regained his composure.

"How can you possibly know all this, Banyon?" the fat lawyer demanded.

"Because I had to become, at the very least, adequate at my job," I replied. "I couldn't attach myself like a tick on the dog of a system designed by and for lawyers to suck the life out of the rest of us and then, with my fat suckling lips firmly attached to the rest of the world's wallet, slurpingly lecture everybody about my indispensability."

I had taken the time while dazzling them to scope out our location.

It was still the basement of the Swindle, Steele & Robb Building. However, it was one of those deals where dimensions have been forced to overlap, so that the cellar existed in a sort of pocket dimension between the Lawyer Queen's world and ours.

The good news was that it appeared to conform to our rules of reality. It's a pain in the ass when you're sucked into a dimension where time isn't linear, women are allowed to be sportscasters, and where they've forgotten the "it" in gravity so that every time you fall down you float up into a puddle of gravy.

The bad news was that I'd noticed a hundred large,

dark shapes scurrying around the cavernous basement. Judging by their dimensions and general creepy-crawly-ness, I determined they were the same human-headed cockroaches that had arrived back at my apartment, unin-vited and without a polite visitors' bottle of booze in their mitts. This suspicion was confirmed when a pair of the hissing creatures rolled out of the shadows, sharing a furious embrace, into the brightly lighted area where the Lawyer Queen was engaged in the dual responsibilities of menacing me and dropping out disgusting fresh attorney eggs.

The queen hissed and stomped a couple of feet at the interlopers, and the pair ceased fighting. She clicked angrily at them and the two combatants withdrew from the light, their many eyes creepily directed at me as they slunk back into the shadows.

"As long as I'm dazzling you with my brilliant deduc-tions," I said, "let me make one more. I'm assuming those giant cockroach things are what lawyers actually look like if allowed to grow into their natural form in your dimen-sion. Wait, here's one more bonus guess that just came to me. These ones crawling around the basement are drones that take care of the eggs for the queen until the Tooth Fairy delivers them to their human hosts."

The peeved look on Swindle's face was enough to let me know that I'd guessed correctly about the natural appearance of the lawyer species. My second guess about the duties of the drones was so obvious that I imagined even Sue Yu had figured it out by now.

I glanced at the dame. The saucy little bowl of beef-and-broccoli was still blinking in shock and horror at the towering monster in our midst. Clearly I had once again given the lady lawyer too much credit. Although in the unlikely event that she had time to calm down before the

Lawyer Queen snipped our heads off with her mighty pincers, she probably would have gotten there in the end, too.

The entire basement had been hollowed out and turned over to the use of the queen. There were no walls, only the occasional concrete pillar supporting the ground floor above. In the weeks that the Tooth Fairy had been MIA, the Lawyer Queen had apparently not set her biological clock back so much as one hour for Daylight Savings.

Mountains of eggs were mounded in V-shaped piles all around the vast floor. The corners were crammed full to the rafters. Those areas of the floor not turned over to piles of eggs were merely corridors between the mounds through which the occasional shadowy figure of a full-grown lawyer cockroach could be seen scurrying. Even the lanes between mounds were beginning to get clogged by eggs, since it was apparent that the exceptionally fertile insect queen didn't have a uterine off switch.

The Lawyer Queen exhaustedly dropped out a few more eggs, wiped her fuzzy forehead with one furry forearm, and began clicking up a storm to Swindle.

The fat lawyer nodded through the barrage of clicks, then turned to me.

"The queen demands you tell her everything you've learned about the Tooth Fairy," Montague Swindle insisted.

"Well, she's unreasonably impatient and absurdly demanding," I said. "So she's definitely a dame. That's just in case the fact that she's a female wasn't driven home to me approximately every ten seconds when she immodestly persists in giving goddamn birth right in front of me. I should point out that even my ex-wife would have, unlike your queen, given me at least twenty-four hours on the job before she sent you to kidnap me. But while most detectives wouldn't have laced up their shoes in the amount

of time she gave me, as it so happens I've had all the time I need. In point of fact, I know precisely where the Tooth Fairy currently is."

For some reason, this revelation received a surprised reaction from Attorney Sue Yu, who you'd think would have known by this point that she was standing in the presence of the greatest goddamn private eye in recorded human history.

The Lawyer Queen apparently understood English, for she began clicking like an excited teletype at her obese lackey, asshole Attorney Montague Swindle.

The giant bug was so excited that said exhilaration caused the goddamn miracle of birth to be induced four more revolting times. A quartet of glowing eggs dropped from her ass segment in disgusting rapid succession. Rolling around inside their goo-soaked prisons, four swirling black shadows bouncing into the walls of the translucent membranes. The nascent lawyers were lost spirits looking for an unsuspecting womb to invade, which described pretty much every one of my Saturday nights.

"*Where is he?*" Swindle demanded. "*Where is the Tooth Fairy?*"

Behind the lawyer with the terrible, orange Marks-A-Lot dye-job, the Lawyer Queen bugged her bug's eyes in eager anticipation.

There was no way in hell I was telling the location of the Tooth Fairy to the fat pantload attorney or his disgusting, oozing queen. (Taking into account, naturally, the standard torture disclaimer wherein I would have sung like a privet hedge crammed to the rooftop with nightingales at the first sight of a bamboo shoot, especially if it was part of some unholy Polynesian drink concoction.)

As it turned out I needn't have been concerned about the possibility of torture, since the fire alarm that started

blaring through the building chose that instant to more-or-less go off right on schedule.

Emergency lights flashed red in the ceiling, agitating the swirling black clouds of amorphous lawyer embryos within their mounds of goo-smeared eggs. The honking blast of the fire alarm startled the Lawyer Queen, causing her to shit out another half-dozen future incompetent real estate attorneys. Along with the swirling lights and echoing siren, sprinklers that were scattered around the basement ceiling erupted to life, spraying a drenching downpour on the giant bug queen, her army of attendant cockroaches, and piles and piles of eggs that were awaiting delivery to unsuspecting surrogate human hosts.

The only one of our group who was unsurprised by the sudden activation of the building's fire alarm and suppression system was me, owing entirely to the fact that I was the one who'd set the damn thing off, and so — being thus prepared — had responded to the completely predictable downpour by grabbing Attorney Sue Yu by the wrist and running like hell for the nearby stairwell door.

A horrible, furious shriek accompanied our exit, and I glanced back to see the Lawyer Queen rearing up on a couple of rows of her hind legs. She was screaming bloody murder, which might not have been the best idea, since one of the pincers next to her wide-open yap snagged a pipe that ran along the ceiling.

The Lawyer Queen yanked her head, and the pincer sliced straight through the pipe like a warm knife through cheap margarine. She ignored the audible hiss that erupted from the severed pipe as she dropped back down on all her many feet and launched herself for the open door.

I managed to pull the door shut just in time, and was rewarded by a clang of insect head on metal that dented the door massively inward and nearly ripped the hinges

from their cinderblock moorings.

"What's happening?" a breathless Sue Yu demanded as I wheeled from the still-rattling door and propelled her toward the stairs.

"You really are terrific in a crisis," I replied. "If I'm ever on trial for something that could get me placed in front of a firing squad, I'll be sure to hire you. You can sit at the defendant's table looking mystified from opening arguments straight through to when the state inevitably shoots an apple out of my mouth. *Go*."

Her shoes clattered on the stairs as she began her ascent. In the meantime, I fished around in the pockets of my trench coat for a couple of items I'd picked up at the hardware store before I'd headed over to the Swindle, Steele & Robb Building.

I pulled the tabs on two cans of roach fogger, tossing them to the floor of the stairwell before turning on my heel and racing up after Sue Yu.

The foggers quickly flooded the bottom of the stairwell, so that when the scratching at the handle ceased and the damaged door flung open, the first of the cockroach drones who scurried into the stairwell promptly grabbed their throats, flipped onto their backs, and died with their amusingly out-of-place leather shoes sticking in the air, parked at the ends of their hilariously twitching legs.

I hadn't time to gloat over my remarkable resourcefulness, as Sue Yu and I had just encountered the shimmering barrier between dimensions.

I hate traversing mystical barriers. Passing through one makes you feel like a piece of pineapple suspending in the middle of a mound of quivering Jell-O. We hadn't been able to see this one from the basement, as it existed between floors, but I knew that the only way out would be to punch our way through the space between

dimensions.

It was clearly visible in the stairwell. The same bluish molasses barrier that we had passed through on our elevator descent hung shimmering in the air above us like low cloud cover over an airport. We had no choice but to run straight up through it, and were rewarded by our frantic 78 RPM ascent abruptly playing at a terrifyingly relaxed 33 1/3.

The area wasn't wide — only a few feet thick — and the vise-like crush of swirling bluish silence into which I'd stuck my head quickly popped like a balloon and was replaced with the normal buzzing white florescent light of an ordinary, ugly stairwell.

The rest of my body was in no great hurry to pass through. My slow-motion torso eventually emerged, and I kept my arms raised lest they drop back down into the leaden air between the law firm's basement and the real world.

Sue Yu had escaped before me, and was standing on the next landing and waving at me to hurry up, as if an army of human-sized cockroaches and their city-bus queen wasn't incentive enough to get my sluggish legs up out of the swirling blue soup.

"Give me your hand, Banyon!" insisted the lawyer dame, who'd evidently seen far too many plucky, empowered broads save the hero in the thrilling third acts of films.

"Clearly they don't teach physics in law school," I suggested as I struggled to yank my right foot up out of the ethereal muck. "You weigh about ninety pounds, whereas my doctor's broken, lying scale insists I'm pushing two hundred. You're standing above me in a stairwell, with nothing to hold onto. I would appreciate your offer more if there wasn't a nearly one hundred percent certainty that me relying on you to pull me out would result in the

two of us falling back down this flight of stairs and into the snapping forelimbs of one royally pissed off Lawyer Queen."

In the amount of time it took me to politely decline her generous murder/suicide offer, I had nearly pulled my left foot free.

The most pressing of my immediate concerns in the instant before I brought my second Florsheim up to join its impatiently waiting mate was that something horrible would latch onto my ankle in the split-second before I pulled it from the barrier, which, naturally, it goddamn did.

Unfortunately for my would-be assailant, my intimate acquaintance with being given the shit end of the stick had ensured that I was fully prepared for this eventuality. When the unseen human-cockroach snatched onto my leg, I simply pulled the tab on another bug fogger, which I'd wrestled from my pocket during the journey up from the basement, and let it loose.

The fogger slapped the top of the barrier and stuck there for a moment, clinging to its home dimension as if this one wasn't as shit as the next one. Then, like a man's hope for a goddamn peaceful marriage where he's not getting hollered at for not having more ambition every second of the day, the hissing can was sucked through the outer edge of shimmering muck and was gone.

The blue barrier instantly turned utterly black. The death grip with which the unseen bug had been crushing my ankle immediately sprang loose, and I yanked my final appendage up to freedom where it, in concert with its panicked counterpart, ran me the hell up the rest of the flight of stairs.

Sue Yu and I exploded through the exit door and onto the first floor.

It was monsoon season in the lobby of the Swindle, Steele & Robb Building. Water sprayed crazily from sprinkler heads as we ran for the front doors.

"How did you manage this?" the dame asked, waving at the water, the flashing lights, and the blaring alarm as we slipped through the puddles that were soaking the expensive marble floor that a million victims of legal misery had built.

"For liability purposes, I won't say who wadded up some aluminum foil and newspaper in the conference room kitchenette microwave," I told her. "I am only grateful to whatever genius had the foresight to do so."

As we approached the lobby elevator, the door suddenly dinged open.

I was concerned that a stampeding herd of five-foot cockroaches might come exploding out of the car to impede our egress, an eventuality for which I was prepared in the form of the fully loaded roscoe clutched in my hand. I found that I was able to save on the cost of replacement bullets when the parting doors revealed four of the bastards lying motionless on the floor of the car, their human tongues lolling from bug mouths.

The barrier through which the bastards had to pass was apparently sufficiently poisoned by the can of bug spray to prevent them from traversing the single floor that separated our respective dimensions.

I holstered my piece and hustled Sue Yu out the front door, even as I heard the doors on the elevator ding shut behind us.

The fire alarm had emptied the building. There already hadn't been much left to the staff of Swindle, Steele & Robb in the wake of the great lawyer die-off. What remained of the law firm's drenched skeleton crew was shivering on the sidewalk across the street. All eyes were

directed at the thirty-ninth floor from which flames were pouring from the busted-out windows of a conference room for a mysterious reason I would swear on a stack of nondenominational bibles I knew nothing about.

We had exited the building at the precise time the fire department and cops were descending on the joint. It was my goddamn luck that the first flatfoot to step from an unmarked cruiser was the biggest asshole on the force, Detective Daniel Jenkins.

"Banyon," the copper snarled, nearly tripping over several fire hoses in his haste to hustle across the street to hassle me. "I should have known. Wherever there's trouble, you're in the thick of it. I'm looking forward to this."

The bastard already had his handcuffs in hand and was reaching for my wrist. Unlike usual, however, this time before he could slap the bracelets on, something short, damp, and royally pissed off leaped between us.

"Excuse me, officer, what is my client being charged with?"

Sue Yu's angry eyes were doing battle with her dripping black bangs as she shot daggers up at the flatfoot.

"Get out of my way, lady," Jenkins ordered.

He attempted to nudge the lawyer dame to one side.

"You just placed your hands on me in front of all these witnesses," Sue Yu snapped, gesturing wildly to the crowd of SS&R employees, as well as to the firemen who were uncoiling hoses, none of whom could have given less of a shit. "That's assault. As for my client, you still haven't told me what you're charging Mr. Banyon with. You can't just slap handcuffs on people for no cause. This isn't Nazi Germany."

Poor Dan Jenkins looked utterly baffled and was actually glancing at me — his best enemy in the whole world — to save him from the little kamikaze in size three heels.

"It isn't," I informed him, since he seemed suddenly unsure of everything. "You can tell it's not, Jenkins, because, while Nazi Germany endowed every creep loser under the sun with mountains of power that they could criminally abuse, even evil, creepy pervert Nazis would have drawn the line at giving any kind of authority to you."

Jenkins' scowl returned.

"He filed a false police report for one thing," the cop insisted to Sue Yu, puffing himself up and trying to regain control of a situation that had somehow rapidly gone bafflingly out of control.

Sue Yu shook her head, flipping water from the ends of her slapping bangs.

"It wasn't false. I was there. My client did find the Tooth Fairy. It is not Mr. Banyon's fault that the Fairy managed to escape. Mr. Banyon does, however, know the Tooth Fairy's current whereabouts. He's prepared to let you know, but he will be understandably reluctant to share whatever information he may or may not have if you persist in harassing him."

Jenkins was clearly lost. The crummy cop's usual harassment of yours truly always followed the same pattern, wherein I was tossed in a cell for no good reason until such time as he remembered I was rotting away — usually after several days — at which point he'd let me go with a warning not to be innocent of the same false charges in the future. This time, however, he was being forced to think, which for Jenkins was like dropping a mackerel in the middle of the Mojave and telling it it'll be fine if it just takes some deep breaths. Luckily for Jenkins, the terrible burden of exhausting, impossible thought was taken out of his hands.

"Did I hear correctly, Jenkins?" a gruff voice announced

behind the flatfoot. "Does this man know the whereabouts of the Tooth Fairy?"

Unseen by Jenkins, we had been joined by a uniformed captain who'd just hustled through the maze of rescue personnel to join us in front of the building.

"Yes, it's true," Attorney Sue Yu said, stepping in for gulping Jenkins.

I tugged at the back of the dame's blouse to get her to ratchet it back a notch. While I was reasonably certain I did, in fact, know the whereabouts of the missing Tooth Fairy, there was a one percent chance I was one hundred percent wrong. But there was no off switch to her sudden faith in me, as well as her feisty underdog lawyer posture.

"Good," the captain said. "My grandson has a pile of teeth under his pillow from this past month. I'm glad *somebody's* on the case." He shot an accusing glare at Jenkins. "What are you doing with those cuffs, detective?"

If Jenkins was anything like me, he was preoccupied wondering why nobody was alarmed that every kid in town had apparently lost a mouthful of teeth in the past thirty days. Rather than question the level of flouride the city was (or wasn't) dumping in the water supply, the flatfoot reluctantly stowed his handcuffs back in his pocket.

"As long as I have a receptive audience," I announced. "In the course of my investigation into the Tooth Fairy's disappearance, I have uncovered a scheme by the firm of Swindle, Steele & Robb, along with dozens of other law firms throughout the country, to facilitate the takeover of our dimension by an army of hostile bugs. This plot goes back over a century, and has already successfully devastated the United States."

I'd had enough of the surprise exhibited by Sue Yu at every revelation, and despite her newly minted confidence

in my investigatory abilities, I imagined the shock of this latest bombshell had dislocated her jaw. I didn't even glance at the dame as I reached into my trench coat and pulled out the stack of papers I'd swiped from a now empty — possibly currently burning — manila folder in the fortieth floor *Q* records room.

"Everything this world needs to know about the Lawyer Queen, her takeover scheme, her evil egg offspring — many of whom have debased themselves even further by becoming politicians — and the complicity in her demented conspiracy of nearly every lawyer in the country is contained in these pages."

"Which is the privileged property of the law offices of Swindle, Steele & Robb!" an obese voice rang out behind me.

Apparently Black Flag, while devastating to human-sized cockroaches, wasn't toxic to tubby lawyers who could hold their breath for one short elevator ride.

Attorney Montague Swindle chose that dramatic moment to burst through the front door of his law firm, puffing and red-faced enough to be sued by the Sioux for the hate crime of cultural appropriation, or whatever the hell the thin-skinned asshole gatekeepers of the shifting sands of virtue had invented to ensnare us today.

He had run through the lobby waterfall in his haste to obstruct justice. The orange dye in which the last surviving Swindle, Steele & Robb partner marinated his dwindling strands of hair had washed from his thinning follicles and had formed dark, Just for Men racing stripes down the busted capillary roadmap of his pasty, puffy face.

I didn't have time to hold the papers high in the air and revel at the sight of the corpulent SOB hopping around like a tormented schoolchild trying to retrieve his *L.A. Law* lunchbox from the neighborhood bully.

There came a terrible, muffled shriek from the lobby of the Swindle, Steele & Robb Building that, for a change, had nothing to do with a client reacting to an outrageous bill. The gathered crowd scarcely had time to collectively shit itself and turn around before the front door and half the lobby windows exploded out into the street, scattering glass and twisted metal frames across the pavement.

A huge, dark figure loomed within the lobby. Water gushed from busted ceiling pipes, forming a staggeringly out of place rainbow crown around the creature's head.

The ground shook as the Lawyer Queen stepped out in the wake of the busted glass. Her endlessly feeling antennae were the first to be warmed by rays of sunlight of the new world she had conquered solely by screwing up an entire goddamn legal system.

She was too tall even for the high lobby ceiling, and she had to duck to get the first third of her segmented body outside. She raised her head to let loose a gloating scream, which wound up pretty short-lived.

I couldn't take all the credit for everything that happened next.

I could definitely take credit for the flaming blinds that had until recently been part of the spectacular blaze on the thirty-ninth floor, since they were a result of a fire in a microwave so worthless you couldn't cook a roll of Reynold's Wrap and two copies of the morning paper in it for twenty minutes without it burning the house down. The Lawyer Queen shook the building enough with her dramatic exit that the shockwaves rattled all the way to the upper floors, so she was responsible for that. But when the burning blinds broke loose from high up in the building and plunged like a flaming arrow to the sidewalk, that was all me, with a partial assist from the good folks at Whirlpool.

What I could not take any credit for whatsoever was

the pipe that the Lawyer Queen had inadvertently severed with her pincer during the hissy fit she'd thrown over my brilliantly engineered basement escape.

It was possible that they didn't have natural gas lines in the Lawyer Queen's dimension, so even if she'd had time to register her last moments on earth — which came immediately subsequent to her first moments on Earth — she wouldn't have gotten the whole hilarious ironic twist that it was her own goddamn fault.

The massive gas explosion took out the entire first floor of the Swindle, Steele & Robb Building. Glass, steel, and bug guts rocketed out on plumes of smoke and fire.

I joined the army of terrified bystanders diving for cover behind cars, fire trucks, ambulances, fire hydrants, mailboxes, each other, and whatever else we could bravely launch our asses behind. I personally selected an idling FedEx truck for my cowering needs, which rapidly became superheated in the orange inferno that engulfed the entire city block over which the SS&R building towered.

My FedEx shield was rocked violently on its shocks, and for a moment I thought it might tip over and — since irony was in ascendance at the moment — squash me like a bug. The tires on the far side of the truck exploded, either due to intense heat or from building fragments launched from the ground floor blast.

The devastating detonation quickly reversed course.

When the initial smoke and flames parted, I discovered that I wasn't alone. I hadn't even noticed the pig-pile under which I was partially pinned. I struggled to pull my legs out from under the stack of survivors, which included Sue Yu, Jenkins, Jenkins' uniformed boss, Montague Swindle, and the driver of the FedEx truck whose hand was taking intimate advantage of our collective near-death experience.

Sue Yu didn't even give me time to extricate myself from the mound of sweating sexual harassment before she was pointing skyward and screaming as if some giant reptile du jour had just appeared over Tokyo.

"My God!" Sue Yu gasped. "The building's coming down!"

Indeed — and not surprisingly — it was.

I glanced up to find the Swindle, Steele & Robb Building doing a solo hula that none of the other surrounding wet blanket office buildings were joining in on.

The building swayed drunkenly — which briefly made it appear to be the most sensible thing in the whole neighborhood — and then it dropped.

The ground floor infrastructure collapsed, and suddenly the second story was at street level. A heavy, horrible groan ensued, and the entire building began to pancake in on itself, each floor dropping down on the one below it, shattering windows and launching a massive cloud of dust into the street.

Panicked chaos exploded all around me. Even my momentarily experimental FedEx paramour ran off as if I'd tried to stick a ring on his groping hand.

As the surrounding screams reached a crescendo, Sue Yu's face was suddenly an inch from mine. The dame grabbed me by the front of my trench coat and hollered in my face, which reminded me of marriage other than the fact my ex-wife would have been shoving me back into the collapsing building rather than attempting to rescue me from it.

"Banyon, why are you standing there? We've got to get out of here!"

As a general rule, my job is to twirl the drum majorette's baton at the head of the stampede during panicked mass exoduses. This time, however, there was no need

for me to don a dress and wig and make my way for the prow of the nearest lifeboat. In fact, if I smoked, this would have been the perfect opportunity to coolly light up a butt and impressively regard imminent death — as opposed to future emphysema and lung cancer — with the insouciance of a beret-wearing sophisticate Euro-sissy.

Lacking a tobacco prop, all I could do was peel Sue Yu's fingers from my coat and calmly shake my head.

"Wait for it," I said.

The it to which I was referring didn't make us wait long.

There was a loud pop, followed immediately by a weird, shimmering bubble that flew out around the entire city block. It passed through me, through Sue Yu, and through our FedEx truck shield. It passed through rescue vehicles, Dan Jenkins, firemen, and goddamn Montague Swindle, who was still alive for some reason.

For an instant the entire area was contained inside a lame Stephen King plot device.

As quickly as it came, there was a reverse pop — which, out of palindromic obligation, was also a pop — and the bubble was flying back in on itself.

All the glass, dust, paperwork, metal, fire, smoke, dead Lawyer Queen bug guts, and rubble of the past five minutes had suddenly reversed course and was flying back into the Swindle, Steele & Robb Building.

The bulk of the building itself had, in collapse, largely remained contained on the block on which it had been constructed. Half the building's height had been lost as the stories had crumpled in on themselves. The wobbling remnants of the half-demolished structure absorbed the returning material which raced in at warp speed.

The twenty-story mess didn't wait for everything to zoom back in. It continued to collapse, but it was suddenly

doing so from the bottom up. The ground floor debris rose up in the air like a Lego stuck to the sole of a bare foot, allowing a clear view straight through the vast area where the building had stood for decades.

As the bottom rose, the top continued to collapse, until the twenty remaining stories had been compressed to ten, then five, then eventually only a single wedge of building wavering eighty feet off the ground.

The invisible trash compacter that had crushed the building from top to bottom began to work its magic from all four sides, rapidly reducing the single super-floor that remained into a cube small enough to fit into it one of the many offices that no longer existed in the building, since the entire building no longer existed, including the cube, which promptly vanished in a tiny puff of smoke and a single white, quickly fading, dot.

All that remained of Swindle, Steele & Robb was a hollowed-out hole in the ground and a red-faced bastard with a sticking-up mass of horribly dyed orange hair.

"How?" Montague Swindle asked no one in particular as he dumbly stared at vacant air that had until moments ago been occupied by his asshole law firm.

"You allowed another dimension to overlap with ours," I explained. "Which, by the way, breaks about a million local, state, and federal laws. It was stable until your queen blew the joint up. The blast caused a rupture. Interdimensional rifts always seal themselves by sucking in the thing they're built in. I paid zero attention in high school and even I know that. What the hell do they teach you morons in law school anyway?"

Swindle's busted capillaries drew into a pinched scowl that made his mug look like the ugly handiwork of a drunk kid with a red pen and a Spirograph.

"Oh, you're *so* clever, aren't you, Banyon?" the fat

lawyer snarled. "Well, as long as I'm alive, so too is Swindle, Steele & Robb, and that paperwork you're holding is still our property."

He was correct that, despite all that had just occurred, I was still somehow miraculously clutching in my sweaty hand the top-secret Lawyer Queen file.

Swindle wheeled on Jenkins and the uniformed captain, who had both survived the excitement of a building collapsing in on itself like the last TV screen pixel, and were dusting themselves off while doing a magnificent impression of cops oblivious to what was going on under their own goddamn noses.

"You are *not* to take possession of that paperwork," Swindle warned the cops, "or you can kiss your pensions goodbye." He spun back to me. "Hand it over, Banyon, or I'll have you tied up in litigation for the rest of your life. I will ruin you, Crag Banyon."

It was impassioned. It was sincere. It was red-faced. It was saliva-launching. It wasn't possible, since I had already ruined myself.

It — being Montague Swindle — was also too distracted to notice the huge and ever-widening shadow that had appeared overheard and was rapidly closing in.

By the time Swindle heard the whistle of air breaking around the incoming object, I'd already taken a couple of steps back. With a yank on her arm, I encouraged Sue Yu to do the same.

A single, five-foot-long chunk of granite from just below the roof ledge was all that remained in this dimension of the Swindle, Steele & Robb Building. Attorney Montague Swindle looked up just in time to see it descending toward him at mach two.

I'd never in my life seen a lawyer crushed to tomato paste before my eyes, but it's an experience all Americans

should enjoy at least once in their lives, like Mount Rushmore or the Grand Canyon.

Once disgusting cosmic justice was finished dealing with the orange puddle that was the late Montague Swindle, Attorney-at-Law, I held the incriminating Swindle, Steele & Robb documents up for Jenkins' and his captain's shocked peepers.

"Now, about this lawyer scheme to crash and burn Western civilization."

It would have been a great dramatic moment on which to cap a pretty goddamn remarkable series of events, which is why the hell was annoyed out of me when the air around us suddenly plummeted to below freezing, the sun vanished behind a cloud, the street grew dark, and a figure robed in black with a skull head and a rusty scythe stepped out from the nothingness of eternity.

"Okay, where's the bod—"

The hooded figure of Death looked down at the crushed remains of Attorney Montague Swindle.

"Shit. *Very* funny, Barbara."

22

I am the first to admit that I'm the greatest hero in the country that the country has never heard of. Credit for discovering the location of the Tooth Fairy ultimately went to "Kurt Branson," a triumph of incompetence for the fact-checkers at the *Gazette*, since a quick finger-walk through the yellow pages turned up not one P.I. with a name remotely similar, including — as far as I was concerned — mine.

At least the local flatfoots permitted me, in their magnanimity, to sit outside Antediluvian Acres retirement home while they went in to retrieve their famous missing person.

The cop generosity of spirit knows no bounds, which is why they gave me a front row seat for the action. Said front row seat was technically the backseat of a squad car with the doors locked and the windows rolled up tight. Either they'd get their man, or I'd die trying, an obvious conclusion I had not shared with Attorney Sue Yu since it seemed like the only break I'd get from the dame was if I was unjustly locked away for a month.

Confident in her erroneous assumption that the police gave a shit about the law where it intersected with my innocent ass, and armed with a new self-assuredness in

her recent (likely temporary) blossoming skills as a legal mouthpiece, the dame had eagerly ditched me in order to figure out which of the many ambulances that had shown up on the scene of the imploding Swindle, Steele & Robb Building she was going to chase. With the local lawyer population at a dangerously reasonable level — at least for the time being — the last living billion lawyers in town were about to see an uptick in business, and Sue Yu was eager to get in on the frivolous ground floor.

I wasn't entirely sure that the Tooth Fairy would be at Antediluvian Acres. After all, there were a lot of old folks' warehouses in town.

When the Fairy had escaped through a portal at the apartment of my downstairs neighbor, nasty hag Mrs. Flora Willhausen, I'd heard a voice say "I-5."

There was something about that voice that was familiar, even though at the time I could barely hear it over the terrified snare drum that was my pounding heart. It took a little while for my lethargic brain to make the connection. It was only an inadvertent use of one word during a phone call to Mannix that sparked my synapses.

"I-5" could have been a reference to Interstate 5, a Horatian ode, a couple of jubilant Cockneys slapping hands, or a million other things. Or, as it turned out, it could have been somebody hollering out the letter and number on a goddamn bingo ball.

The instant I made the bingo connection, I realized the voice I'd heard rising up from the Tooth Fairy's portal in battle-axe neighbor Willhausen's apartment belonged to the pushy old crone on whose joyless Dickensian-workhouse tour bus Sue Yu and I had stowed away to make good our thrilling escape from My Grain Distillery. When I placed a prune-like face on that disembodied voice, the fact that so many of those old buzzards on that bus

had been missing chunks of bridgework — not to mention having disposable cash to blow on distillery tours and crap souvenirs — delivered me straight to one blaring conclusion that made immensely logical sense.

Although, from my prison perch in the rear of the squad car in the parking lot outside Antediluvian Acres, it seemed like the cops were taking more time than they should have to roust one measly Tooth Fairy, and for a moment it began to seem that my brilliant deduction streak may have gone off the rails.

My confidence in my infallibility was restored when Detective Daniel Jenkins emerged from the front door of the old folks' home, flanked by a pair of uniformed cops, and propelling the handcuffed and despondent little fairy before him.

"Banyon," the Tooth Fairy lifelessly grunted when his flatfoot escort sprang the rear door of the car and Jenkins allowed me to step back out into the light.

"Pirate Pete," I replied.

The Tooth Fairy's saucering eyes and guilty mug was all the proof I needed that the little winged SOB was tied in with the B-side of this pain-in-the-ass case.

"So what was it that finally made you betray the Lawyer Queen?" I asked. "You had a cozy deal. You could have kept it going forever, or at least until the glut of lawyers you helped create irreversibly crippled and ultimately destroyed the world. Which, by all scientific measurements, happened more than thirty years ago."

The Tooth Fairy shook his dainty head. Sparkling glitter dandruff fell to his shoulders and spilled down onto his pink tutu. His wings sagged with exhausted resignation.

"You can't imagine the guilt, Banyon," he replied. "At first I thought it would just be a few lawyers. I figured I'd

make a few extra dollars — quick, under the table — and it would be over. But that's never how it works out, is it? Before I knew it, it was a hundred lawyers, then a thousand. They multiplied exponentially, feeding on the lazy, get-rich-quick view to life that — get this — *her own offspring helped foster*. They transformed society, and still she was never satisfied. She kept laying lawyer eggs, year in and year out, and she kept forcing me to deliver them. Lawyers, lawyers, lawyers. I was in over my head. I couldn't take it any longer. Don't you get it? It's all my fault!"

"Yes, it is," I said. "Hey, don't give me that look. Find a priest if you want absolution. All I will give you is that if she hadn't roped you in, she would have found somebody else with the ability to slow time so that he could sneak into a million bedrooms every night. Santa Claus, Warren Beatty in his prime, Wilt Chamberlain before he became a zombie. As for Pirate Pete's scheme, what was your involvement?"

"Not much," the Tooth Fairy insisted. "A little techni-cal advice, a couple of bucks on the side when he was getting it started and wanted to keep it off Bandito-Phar-maceutical's books. Then it turned out after it started that nobody cared when all those lawyers started dying. It took a month and somebody hiring you to find me for anybody to even notice. Don't you see, Banyon? I had to try to undo the damage I'd caused. It used to be about the teeth. I needed it to get back to the teeth."

It was one of the most damning, uncoerced confessions I'd ever witnessed, and any one of the half-dozen uni-formed cops in the area with body cameras could have popped in the DVD and wrapped up the trial two minutes after opening arguments. Except Dan Jenkins was super-vising the scene, and had naturally wandered away for the previous two minutes and corralled every cop there well

away from the open back door of the squad car.

"What did I miss, Banyon?" the flatfoot snarled, choosing that precise tardy moment to arrogantly Barney Fife his way up beside me.

I shook my head. "Nothing but a pound of goddamn glitter spilling all over your back seat, detective," I replied.

Every right thinking person had pretty much instinctively known that lawyers were soulless bugs from another dimension, yet we'd all let it slide our whole lives. Who knew how the courts would handle this whole mess, if it ever even saw the inside of a courtroom? All I did know was that we were all as guilty as the Tooth Fairy. Except for me, of course, because I've always hated and mistrusted goddamn crooked asshole lawyers.

"Make sure you don't let him form a portal, Jenkins," I advised. "If he escapes down a rabbit hole, even my genius might not be great enough to track him down for you again. Although, granted, the little bastard doesn't make it all that hard."

The Tooth Fairy was clearly surprised that I hadn't ratted him out to the cops.

One of the uniforms climbed into the back of the black-and-white in order to keep an eye on the little fairy's magic hands.

"Senior residents say he's been popping into their rooms for the past month," Jenkins blandly stated, informing me of that which I'd already surmised. He couldn't bring himself to look me in the eye, and instead stared disdainfully at a spot over my left shoulder. "He'd pry teeth from their dentures and leave money under their pillows. When they'd run out of teeth, he'd give them back, then show up that night and pay the senior victims all over again for the same teeth. I don't get where he was getting the money to keep shelling out for the same teeth

over and over for a month."

"The same way, Jenkins, he'd gotten the dough to pay off kids for the past century. The lawyers that had been sent over to this dimension by their queen as embryos — embryos the Tooth Fairy delivered to bedrooms around the country — grew up and made sure, on orders from the Lawyer Queen, that the Tooth Fairy got the cash he needed to keep operating a business that was run worse than Tesla. Although for the past month he hadn't been paid dime one to make zygote lawyer deliveries, so he was running down whatever savings he'd managed to build up over the years. It's all in the pile of paperwork I gave your boss. I'd read it to you, Jenkins, but you'll never learn if you don't do it yourself. Just ask one of the older cops to help you sound out the big words."

When Dan Jenkins and the rest of the uniformed officers that had accompanied him to Antediluvian Acres piled into their various cars, I couldn't help but notice I was still standing out in the parking lot.

"I suppose this means you're not giving me a ride back," I said.

"Do I look like a taxi service?" Jenkins grinned out the window.

"A person can't look like a taxi service, Jenkins. A taxi service would include the personnel, vehicles, garages, etc. It's like asking if you look like an airline. What the hell would that even mean? Nothing. You *can* ask if you look like a cabbie or, I suppose, a cab, if you were yellow and blockish enough. But that would be a hate crime against fat Asian slobs, so somebody would probably sue you for asking that. Rather than a taxi service, which makes no sense, ask me if you look like an asshole. I can not only answer that question definitively, I can easily expound on it for the entire ride back into town."

At least Jenkins was no longer smirking as he peeled out of the parking lot.

Alone and abandoned, I glanced around.

The little bus that had driven around the old buzzards who'd hidden the Tooth Fairy for a month was parked at the rear of the lot. I thought of a truly terrific moral to impart upon the residents of Antediluvian Acres who had given succor to the MIA Tooth Fairy, as well as to the home's criminally oblivious staff, who obviously hadn't noticed the little fairy running from room to room every night for the past thirty days. That is, assuming somebody had left the keys in the ignition.

I am always eager to impart life lessons to those not as fortunate to be wonderful human beings like me, so I Good Samaritan-ed my ass across the parking lot to take a peek.

23

Two days later, I was back behind my desk at Banyon Investigations, Inc. enjoying the thundering bass beat of a well-earned hangover and wondering why I couldn't reach up and pinch out the sun between thumb and forefinger.

Every pin that dropped within a three-block radius was a tree falling in the forest and making the biggest goddamn sound imaginable, then getting carted off to a lumber mill, being cut into boards, shipped off to an expert woodworking craftsman, getting whittled down to a sharpened stake, which was ultimately delivered to my office on angel's wings and stabbed repeatedly through my head.

Every footfall in my outer office repeated the hilarious sequoia-to-wooden-ice pick-through-the-brain gag, yet I bravely soldiered on in my futile attempt to tune out the quiet stomping taking place on the other side of the wall. I gave up on the struggle to keep my brains from dribbling out my ears when Mannix came tiptoeing into my office on TNT shoes.

"I'm sorry, Mr. Crag," the elf gently whispered at the top of his lungs, "but the mail came. I thought you'd want to see it."

The envelopes thudded to my desk along with a news-

paper that snapped and crackled so loudly I was sure he'd dumped a gallon of milk on it before bringing it in.

On the top of the pile of mail was a business envelope with the return address:

Lawyer Sue Yu, Attorney-at-Law, Esquire.

With the fate of her former firm of Crook, Shaft & Fleece in limbo, the dame had apparently decided to hang out her own shingle. The news came as a bit of a surprise, since not every bug lawyer in town had been exterminated in the past month, and there were still plenty of law firms with hilarious names that were up and running and looking to fill their diminished ranks, such as Swagger, Bragg & Crowe, Weiner, Dickman & Cox and the highly successful lesbian law firm of Manhate, Lapp & Munch.

"There's also some good news you'll be happy to hear," Mannix promised me, before turning and hustling delightedly from the room.

He had clearly forgotten that I'd told him not ten minutes before that the only news I was looking forward to hearing today was a doctor calling my time of death.

I had a letter opener somewhere, but I'd rather stick my head in a wood chipper than subject it to the cannon blasts of rolling open my desk drawers looking for it. Naturally, all the pens and pencils that should have been on top of my desk weren't, which left me with a finger to rip open Attorney Sue Yu's letter.

As I sliced my way up the spine of the sealed envelope, wincing at the prolonged sonic boom of tearing paper, I could hear my eternally happy elf assistant fussing around the next room.

I prayed that Mannix's happy news wasn't that Doris was returning to work after her wedding dress-buying binge, which would have been a misapplication of the word "happy" so egregious that I would have insisted he

bring all of his dictionaries in to the office from home so that I could set straight any other lies Misters Merriam and Webster were telling him.

My erstwhile secretary had stopped in for a paycheck the previous day. I'd asked her whose she wanted, as I'd decided to pay the water cooler her former salary, since it was always on the job when it was needed and, except for an occasional burp, kept its fat yap shut. My previous day's hangover had suffered gravely for that extremely rewarding observation, and my dearest hope was that Doris was off somewhere today picking out grossly inappropriate white veils and wasn't waiting on my doorstep to go round two with the present pounding in my skull.

Mannix came trotting back into my office after a moment's absence with a small box in his little hands and a large smile on his wide face.

I held out the letter which, in his absence, I'd extracted from Sue Yu's envelope.

"A bill," I informed him. I attempted to keep from yelling the news, since I was pretty sure if I raised my voice my head would crack like the Liberty Bell. "The worthless dame, whose only contribution to the entire pain-in-the-ass affair was kicking me in the head, has sent me a goddamn bill."

Mannix took the bill for services not rendered by a lawyer that was useless even by lawyer standards, and allowed a moment to give it a frowning once-over. He clearly didn't find it to be as ludicrous as did I, since he scarcely gave it a serious nod before he lost complete interest. He set the bill aside and returned his full attention to the box he'd placed on my desk. His smile returned as he fished around inside it.

"Mr. Buck finished with them this morning," he announced as he began lining up my prodigal flasks, like

gleaming silver soldiers, on the edge of my desk.

They all looked brand new, even the oldest one which had been a confirmation gift from an uncle so fun even my terrible parents had banned him from spreading joy around most of my miserable childhood.

The last flask was not quite as shiny as the rest.

"I got this one from your coat," the elf said of the final flask. "Now that the rest are back, do you want to keep
i   t   ?   "
"You'd better give that one to me," I said, reaching for the odd-flask-out, which at one point I had completely emptied over Sue Yu's head to cleverly disguise her as a lawyer; a waste of good liquor that I now very much regretted.

I set the My Grain Distillery gift shop flask to one side and set about the vital task of refilling my newly refur-bished regulars from my desk drawer hooch supply. Mannix was distracted from helping out when some unwanted visitor selected that moment to open my outer office door, which would stop happening if he'd followed my repeated order and nailed the damn thing shut.

My best pal and ace office assistant hurried from the room, hopefully to inform whoever had intruded on my hangover that we were a bakery and I had a gun.

As I worked, I glanced at the copy of that day's *Gazette* that Mannix had thoughtfully left alongside the mail.

Apparently an unidentified juvenile delinquent had taken for a joyride a bus belonging to a local retirement home. It had been discovered submerged in a duck pond at Abe Vigoda Park, which just happened to be a stone's throw away from O'Hale's Bar. The police were asking for assistance tracking down the miscreant who'd dumped the bus in the lake. I would have loved to do my civic duty and help out the boys in blue, as it so happened that I had,

coincidentally, been in that park at the same time the bus was estimated to have been dumped in the lake. Unfortunately, I hadn't seen anybody in the vicinity who wasn't a fine, handsome, upstanding citizen.

By an amazing coincidence, every other front page story was in some way related to the events of the past several days, which saved wear and tear on my hungover fingers having to turn the noisy pages.

One article told of a bunch of six-foot long cockroaches that had entered the Pope's bedroom at the Vatican through a mysterious portal a few nights before. The giant bugs had chased his Holiness around St. Peter's Square for an hour before the Swiss Guard finally managed to trap them in the Popemobile and bug bomb them.

Another story alerted readers about a flood of lawyers that was making its tsunami-like way into town. Apparently, the abortive attempt by Pirate Pete to wipe out the indigenous population was as futile as spooning out the ocean. A California Gold Rush of ambulance pursuers was on, and experts were suggesting that we'd wind up with an even greater infestation of the things than we were afflicted with before the bastard pirate and Dr. Lance Boyle had started sending out free samples of their poisoned rotgut.

As for Pirate Pete Barnacle and his salty goddamn crew, the FBI had quietly buried a box of blessed earth in which they'd been trapped in an underpopulated corner of the graveyard at St. Regent's Drive-Thru Cathedral. Pirate Pete's shitty restaurant chain was mourning the loss of its spokes-scalawag by lowering the Jolly Roger out front to half-mast and offering fifty cents off every kid's meal, with coupon.

The outlook was bleak for the ghosts who'd hoped Pirate Pete would deliver them from a boring eternity of

squeaking floorboards and knocking pictures off walls. Their savior ghost's interment put an end to any hope of them getting out of here before all the rest of us had left the building. Since the legal ties that bound them to this plain still existed, the nation's ghost population was forever stuck in the upstairs hallway in the big Victorian at the end of the street or in the boiler room of the abandoned nuthouse across town. Still, it could be worse for ghosts like my dead, weather-obsessed neighbor Archibald Jessup. I had just learned that morning, and at the top of his dago voice, that Vincetti, the downstairs fishmonger, had cut a secret deal to sell his entire fetid inventory to Pirate Pete's Fish 'n' Chips — a deal that had now been torpedoed in part thanks to me. You may think you have it tough hiding behind a headstone for weeks on end until somebody walks by for you to jump out and yell "boo" at, but it's nowhere near the hell of getting chased every morning on your way to work while intensely hungover by a demented, broom-wielding fish-peddler in a dirty apron and a Mussolini uniform.

There was some controversy at St. Regent's, the *Gazette* noted. Attorney Montague Swindle was to have been buried in the churchyard once they finished ringing his remains out of the sponges that had been used to mop him up. The massive chunk of granite under which he'd met his amusing end had already been shipped to the cemetery and planted in Swindle's prepaid vacant plot. It happened that the only surviving chunk of the Swindle, Steele & Robb Building had broken off from the section into which the firm's name was chiseled. Although his name would be vertical and on the jagged slab of granite that had crushed him, it already had most of "Swindle" cut into it, and so had the benefit of saving a couple of bucks on a real headstone. However, many parishioners,

as well as a few of the churchyard ghosts, had registered complaints about being buried in the same boneyard as a bug that was only mimicking the characteristics of a human being.

The final newspaper article was titled "Body Identified," and was about a charred corpse that had been recovered from the ruins of the My Grain Distillery complex. Apparently, Dr. Lance Boyle hadn't made it out alive after all, which was terrific news for everybody against whom the demented asshole had attempted murder. The only downside to the grinning bastard's death that I could come up with was that his lawyer-murdering formula had likely perished in the conflagration with him, so whatever tainted bottles of hooch remained at large was all there would ever be of the marvelous elixir.

The first page was already pretty astoundingly packed with stories, and so there wasn't room enough to fit a humorous capper to Boyle's death article. It finished with a suggestion for readers to "turn to page eight for punch line," which was, frankly, just lazy writing, especially since the *Gazette* had managed to find room to cram an O'Drunkegan's Pub ad ("*Get Drunk Again, At O'Drunkegan's*") in the corner where the article could easily have been wrapped up.

I was lamenting the current state of journalism, which was pretty consistently shit with all the previous states of journalism, when Mannix reentered the room, a gaggle of unwanted company trailing in his tiny little wake. My elf assistant's instinctive good nature was already strained to the breaking point after spending only a minute with our repulsive guests, and he couldn't wait to abandon me and hightail it from the room.

It was less than a week since the first time Robert Sherman Planck of Madison Insurance Equities had

ushered the odious Thompson family into my offices.

Mater Thompson could still neuter a man at twenty paces, Pater Thompson was still cowering within her blast zone, and Little Timmy Thompson still should have been disciplined off the nearest high roof. The kid immediately climbed on my office sofa and began jumping up and down as if it were his mother's angry mug, which probably wasn't the brat's fondest wish but at the moment was definitely mine.

The only change for me was Robert Sherman Planck, who in the course of my investigation had been revealed to be a lawyer and, consequently, the adult larval offspring of a giant, murderous, world-conquering other-dimensional bug.

Planck attempted a businesslike nod in my direction, which I would have responded to with an equally professional finger if not for the fact that I was hungover as hell, and I figured old lady Thompson would have reprimanded me with both lungs if my hand said anything disapproved of by her perpetually furious peepers.

"I don't even know what we're doing here," the dame groused to Planck.

"No kiddin'," junior shouted from midair over my sofa. "I got my thirty dollars. *Finally.*" He shot me a scowl and stuck his tongue out at me to thank me for getting him his dough in under a week.

So the Tooth Fairy was back in business. I only hoped the Thompsons would invest the money wisely, in a muzzle and some goddamn horse tranquilizers.

"It's just a formality, Mrs. Thompson," Planck assured the brat's miserable mother. "Since Madison is paying Mr. Banyon's fee on your behalf, we need all parties to sign these final documents together." He produced said forms, which he laid out on my desk.

The mother of the brat hadn't even looked in my direction, and only dragged her pinched eyes with enormous reluctance to my desk once the documents were spread out. Only then did she see my flasks, funnel, and bottle, to which she reacted with the exact horror I imagined her relatives displayed when she accepted on behalf of the loathsome Thompson clan an insincere and obligatory Thanksgiving invitation.

"Are you putting alcohol in those *in front* of my child?" she demanded.

"I was," I replied. "Now that you've opened your screech hole, I find it necessary to put some in me."

I did, straight from the bottle.

"*Mr. Planck*," the dame snapped. "I mean *really*."

"Please sign the forms where noted, Mrs. Thompson," Planck said, "and we can get you out of here as quickly as possible."

The insurance lawyer produced a pen, which in old lady Thompson's claws created a Normandy invasion racket as it scratched across the paperwork.

The dame's castrated husband signed as well, after which Planck held out the pen to me.

I shook my head. It still felt as if my brain was trying to punch its way out of a lead straitjacket.

"Plus an extra thousand bucks to repair the sofa," I said.

Unobserved by his parents, the little bastard with the yellow cowlick had discovered a small hole in my couch which he had enlarged, and from which he had managed to yank most of the stuffing, which he was mounding up on the floor.

Planck was in the mood to finish this quickly. The bastard pulled out his checkbook.

"Cash," I said.

The checkbook went back into storage, and out came his wallet, from which he extracted ten hundreds, which he placed in my palm.

"I'm going trust you on this until I get the paperwork, Crag," Planck said.

"I don't know why you're paying him *anything*," Mrs. Thompson snarled. "According to the newspaper, it was a Kurt Branson who helped the police, not him."

"The terrific irony of the only Kurt Branson in town getting credit for my work," I said, as I stashed the dough in my pocket, "is that word is he's a recent law school graduate whose phone is now, presumably, ringing off the hook."

I stood up and began ushering the lot of them from the room.

"Now, if our business is finished, I'd appreciate it if you'd get your horrible little vandal the hell out of here. What you do with him once you're gone is your business. I recommend shipping him to a country with relaxed child labor laws or, if they won't take him, shoving him down an elevator shaft. Don't use ours, however, because the last thing I want is that little shit haunting the hell out of every hangover for the rest of my life."

Robert Sherman Planck was gathering up the paperwork, and mentioned that he had further business to discuss, and so it was the trio of Thompsons that I saw out to the hallway.

The lady of the house spun around as we parted and aimed a bony finger at my sternum.

"You are a *terrible* man," Mrs. Thompson accurately insisted.

"So, lady, are you," I even more accurately replied.

I slammed the door in two generations of horrible, aghast mugs.

"That wasn't very nice, Mr. Crag," Mannix cautioned from where he was working at his little desk.

"Good. Then I did it right."

On the way back to my inner office, I scooped up the scraps of paper Mister — in the most gender fluid use of the term — Thompson had dropped on the awful family's way out, unseen by his harridan wife or inevitable future lawyer offspring.

The desperate notes the nominal patriarch of the Thompson clan had scribbled this day were far more succinct than the one he'd left behind at our first meeting wherein he'd pleaded for assistance locating a divorce attorney.

HELP! begged every single one of the dozen scraps of paper.

With the indigenous divorce lawyer population at near-extinction level until the new lawyers flooding the zone could set up shop, poor trapped bastards like Thompson would need all the friends they could find. I felt my heart swell with pity, but quickly realized it was actually residual gastric unpleasantness resulting from half a burrito I'd discovered behind the empty ketchup bottle in my fridge.

I filed Thompson's notes in a wad in the trash and returned to my office in search of Alka-Seltzer to alleviate my false sympathy symptoms.

Upon my return, Robert Sherman Planck was just finishing drawing his finger across the top of a filing cabinet and was inspecting his treacherous whorls for dust. He glanced up at my entry, smiled a weaselly smile, and slapped imaginary dust from his palms.

"A lot has happened these past few days, Crag," Planck said. "I just wanted to make sure that we're good."

"You could be tried at The Hague for torturing the

definition of the word 'good' to get it to include you. You know, Planck, how people are always saying to just be yourself? That only has a shot at working if you aren't unremittingly horrible. My advice to you is to be someone else, and vigorously so."

"Remember when we started together, you and I, Crag?" Planck persisted. "I gave you one of your first cases. That bigamist from St. Ives, remember? That and the rest of the work I tossed your way kept you afloat those first years."

"I remember you sending a bunch of cockroaches to my apartment to murder me and take the Tooth Fairy back to your queen," I said. "I don't remember one whole hell of a lot prior to that."

The SOB flashed a tight grin.

"I'm an attorney first," Planck said, dismissing my attempted murder with a shrug. "I serve the Queen. But, hey, it worked out fine for you. My bosses at Madison are very impressed. We'll definitely hire you again. As for me, I'm surprised you survived."

"Nietzsche tells us that one should die proudly when it is no longer possible to live proudly. It's unlikely given my instinctive pusillanimity that I'll manage the former, and I've never accomplished the latter, so I am, in all likelihood, immortal. I only wish I'd understood when Death said at the very second dead attorney body I encountered that your kind don't have souls. I'd have wrapped it up even faster. However, I assumed at the time that he was speaking in the figurative sense and not in the literal sense that — as a result of you being the grown-up products of eggs laid by a giant insect from another dimension — lawyers do not, in fact, have human souls. I feel compelled to repeatedly point out that, in hindsight, it's one of those obvious things we all should have realized a long time ago."

"I just wanted you to know that I'm fine to continue our arrangement," Planck said.

The bastard was being inexplicably gracious for somebody who'd just lost the progenitor of his entire race, in addition to having his fruitful dead queen's plot of world domination exposed. Then there was the fact that the rights of lawyers as a species were suddenly now in question, to the point where enterprising sportsmen were arranging expensive hunting trips to the quads of fourth-tier law schools and setting up duck blinds on Wall Street with Rolex and Lagavulin bait.

I suspected Planck's affability was, in point of fact, explicable as hell.

I picked up the morning's *Gazette* and flipped around for his perusal a front page that was — honestly — incredibly coincidentally jam-packed with items directly related to the case I'd just cracked.

A photo taken outside a trendy downtown nightclub revealed a familiar figure stepping out of a limousine, a stacked babe hanging off each tiny arm. The little fairy's wings had been flapping so ecstatically when the paparazzo took his picture that they were blurs in motion.

He resembled his brother more than he had the day I'd questioned him at Fairyland bar, most likely because he had cleaned up his act in a major way. He was no longer a slovenly reprobate dressed in rags. Judging by his remarkable makeover, the Snot Fairy had recently come into a great deal of cash.

There was no story accompanying the photo, only the headline "**Mu-Kiss and Tell!**" and directions for the reader to flip to the lifestyle page.

"You already have a new queen," I said. "You just inadvertently revealed it yourself when you said you 'serve the queen.' Present tense. So after your Lawyer Queen

died, one of those slimy giant cockroach drones took over, which happens sometimes with bugs when their queen croaks. And clearly you have a new courier to deliver this new queen's eggs in this dimension. You might want to tell the Snot Fairy to not telegraph so loudly that he's taken over the gig from his brother."

The insurance lawyer bastard flashed an oily smile.

"I won't confirm or deny," he said, confirming every goddamn thing I'd just said. The lawyer bastard's grin widened. "I *will* say that there's no sense fighting it. We'll win. We've already won. Nearly every politician is a lawyer. They're meeting in statehouses and in Washington right now to extend all human privileges to us. Even if they weren't, you humans wouldn't be able to do without us. You're junkies, and we're pushers getting rich off your addiction to suing the hell out of each other. Have you or someone you love been injured in a car accident, by a medication gone wrong, used weed killer in your driveway, or had a doctor try to help save your life? If so, your kind is coming to us, Banyon, no matter how we were hatched. Try to undo a hundred years of us worming our way into every corner of your lives. It can't be done, because ultimately you don't *want* us gone."

Robert Sherman Planck exuded attorney arrogance, and for a change the smugness was justified since he was more than likely right.

"So do I tell my bosses at Madison that we can still kick work your way or not?" Planck asked with a smarmy lawyer grin.

My gleaming, newly renovated flasks were to my right on the top of my desk. One lone flask sat to my left.

I'd emptied the last drop of booze within it over Sue Yu before we'd infiltrated the Swindle, Steele & Robb Building — and were subsequently captured and impris-

oned, then unwisely left to our own devices in a conference room on the thirty-ninth floor — and I had not filled it minutes before when I loaded up the others. Yet when I picked the flask up from my desk, liquid sloshed around inside.

I uncapped the flask and held it out to Robert Sherman Planck. A greedy, glazed look descended on the asshole-insurance-lawyer-interdimensional-bug-bastard's face.

"Let us," I graciously suggested, "seal the deal with a drink."

A Note from Jim

If you enjoyed this book, please take a minute to post a review on Amazon. Every review helps, even if it's only a sentence or two. Believe me, the elf would appreciate it. I'll appreciate it even more. Thanks.

— *Jim Mullaney*

About the author

James Mullaney is a Shamus Award-nominated author of over 50 books, as well as comics, short stories, novellas, and screenplays. His work has been published by New American Library, Gold Eagle/Harlequin, Marvel Comics, Tor, Moonstone Books, and Bold Venture Press.

He was ghostwriter and later credited writer of 28 novels in *The Destroyer* series, and wrote the series companion guide *The Assassin's Handbook 2*. He is currently the author of *The Red Menace* action series as well as the comic-fantasy *Crag Banyon Mysteries* detective series.

He was born in Taxachusetts, and wishes he were an only child, save one.

Other books by Jim Mullaney

The Crag Banyon Mysteries series:

- One Horse Open Slay
- Devil May Care
- Royal Flush
- Sea No Evil
- Bum Luck
- Flying Blind
- Shoot the Moon
- The Butler Did I.T.
- X Is for Banyon
- Habeas a Nice Corpus
- Death Sentience
- Banyon Investigations: A Crag Banyon Anthology

The Red Menace series:

- #1 Red and Buried
- #2 Drowning in Red Ink
- #3 Red the Riot Act
- #4 A Red Letter Day
- #5 Red on the Menu
- #6 Red Devil
- #7 Ruses Are Red
- #8 The Sky Is Red

Watch for Crag Banyon's
newest mystery

DEATH SENTIENCE

Crag Banyon Mysteries #12

by James Mullaney

Watch for the newest adventure of

The Red Menace

THE SKY IS RED

The Red Menace #8

by James Mullaney